Tulips
Chips
&
Mayonnaise

Tulips
Chips
&
Mayonnaise

DAWN CAIRNS

POOLBEG

First Published 2000
by Poolbeg Press Ltd
123 Baldoyle Industrial Estate
Dublin 13, Ireland
E-mail: poolbeg@iol.ie
www.poolbeg.com

This edition published 2001

A catalogue record for this book is available from the British Library.

ISBN 1 85371 938 2 (UK) £5.99   1 84223 041 7 (Irl.) £6.99

Set by Pat Hope
Cover design by Slatter Anderson
Printed and bound by
Omnia Books Ltd, Glasgow

About the Author

Dawn Cairns is a twenty-six-year-old Estate Agent, who recently moved back to Belfast from Edinburgh where she lived for the past nine years. When she is not shopping, sitting in the pub chatting or selling houses she can be found in front of her computer frantically writing her second novel. *Tulips, Chips and Mayonnaise* is her first novel.

Acknowledgements

I would like to thank the following people for helping me write this book – without them the spelling would be much worse! First and foremost, I would like to thank Gaye Shortland, possibly the loveliest and most hardworking editor in the world – ever. I would also like to thank Dr Pamela Cairns for her medical advice and her entertaining late night phone calls. To Stuart, Lisa, Gail, Eric, Carlin, Claire, Jane, Jude, Jutta and George without whom my world would be a much less entertaining place. Finally I would like to thank Poolbeg for taking a chance on me. I hope it pays off!

*To my mum, who told me I could do it
and I believed her.*

Chapter One

"He's proposed!" Chloe screamed down the phone.

I held the phone away from my ear, before my eardrum was perforated.

"Oh God! Congratulations, I'm so pleased for you," I heard myself saying.

"Oh Sorrel, I want you to come over to look at the ring, it's beautiful, he picked it himself."

Call me picky but there's your first problem; not so much that yet another good friend, in fact my best friend, has got engaged and due to the sorry state of my social life, soon I'll be going out on Friday nights by myself – But he picked the ring himself? I'm sorry, but no man should be allowed to pick out an engagement ring on his own. I mean what if it was totally foul? How would you know how much it had cost? What if his mother had helped him? These questions were rushing round my brain and I felt the need to sit down, so I *did*. Chloe was still chatting away about her imminent wedding like an overexcited budgie, while I found it difficult to imagine liking someone enough to want to see them every day.

I love my best friend dearly, and David (the fiancé) is a very nice chap, but 'very nice' has never really been my thing. To tell you the truth I don't know what my *thing* is, having had very little experience in the meaningful-relationship department. So I'm probably the least qualified person to be giving my opinion. So for Chloe's sake I held my tongue and tried to imagine what it must be like to be really in love with someone, rather than in my usual last-a-week lust.

"So will you come then? Sorrel? Sorrel, are you still there?

"Sorry, pardon – will I go where?"

"To help me pick out my dress, *thicko,* are you listening to a word I'm saying? If you're watching Riki Lake while I'm telling you I'm getting married I'll come round and thump you, you cheeky cow!'

"Of course I'm not watching TV," I said, as I turned down the volume. "I'd love to come and help you pick out dresses. When do you want to go? This weekend?"

"No, I can't, we're spending the weekend with David's parents – we haven't told them about the engagement yet."

I took a large gulp of my coffee, which I promptly spat back into the cup – it was freezing – yuk. "What's the ring like?" I asked tentatively, wondering how good David's taste was – with apparently no input from his mother whatsoever.

"Oh Ellie, it's just what I would have picked!"

I waited for her to add "If I was a drug-crazed lunatic with a spare fifteen pounds" but she didn't. She was genuinely pleased – well, perhaps I had been too hasty with my damning judgements.

She was off again, chatting about no time to waste – bridesmaids' dresses – what colour was I thinking of?

"Maroon with an orange trim?" I helpfully suggested

"God, I'll have to book the church, the reception, there's so much to think about." She was clearly not listening to me, which was no bad thing since I didn't appear to have anything constructive to say.

I was wondering if I'd burst into flames when I entered God's House. It's been so long since I actually went to church. In fact the last time was Christmas two years ago when the vicar talked my father into doing a reading in one of the evening services. Dad thought it would be a piece of cake and didn't practise, telling my sister Lucy and me that there was nothing to public speaking – that "one just needed to project one's voice". Lucy and I went just for the laugh. Dad didn't let us down. The church was packed and he was so busy looking at the congregation to see if there was anyone he recognised that he lost his place, and rather than try and find it he made the rest up. The churchy ladies in the front row who follow all the reading with their own bibles got totally confused and asked Dad later on what version he was reading from. Lucy and I had to stuff our fists into our mouths to stop ourselves from sniggering – Mum just rolled her eyes.

Chloe persuaded me to go with her the following week to look at dresses and talk about what colour the bridesmaids should wear. Please God nothing floral, I offered up a prayer to the patron saint of taste, whoever she was. We chatted a bit more, deciding what shops to visit and wouldn't it be a scream to go to the Bridal Room in Jenners and give those snotty assistants hell? Jenners is Edinburgh's answer to Brown Thomas in Dublin, or Harvey Nichols in London, though on a less glamorous scale. While we talked it hit me that my bestest friend in the whole world was really going to get married and suddenly I wanted to cry, and hug her.

"Sorrel, are you OK?" Chloe suddenly realised that she was doing most of the chatting.

"Yes," I sniffed in reply, "I'm fine, sorry, just the thought of you getting married, it makes me feel, well . . . don't you remember how much we laughed when everyone else got engaged? I suppose I feel you've moved on and I didn't notice." An awful thought just hit me. "Have you told your mum yet?"

"Um . . . no, I'm kind of building up to that, you know what she'll be like, she'll have the fecking hotel booked before I'm off the phone. I want to get used to the idea myself first – you know, do sad things like sign my name Mrs Campbell on bits of paper and imagine what a small and intimate wedding party would be like, with just the people I want there."

Weddings in affluent County Down are like no others I've ever come across. In Edinburgh it is perfectly acceptable to have a small wedding in a registry office or church, with just a few close friends around you, if that's what the bride and groom want. However, at home in Northern Ireland we try to create 'wedding of the year', and get our picture's into the Ulster Tatler. The weddings are huge – as are the dresses – with several hundred people invited to the reception, and more to the evening, most of whom the bride and groom have never met. It is the perfect opportunity for the bride's parents, who usually pay, to show off. Bigger and better than any before – an attempt to not only keep up with the Joneses but to well and truly overtake them.

Chloe's family are very wealthy and have never been particularly shy in showing it, with perhaps the exception of her Dad, who is one of my most favourite men. While he is quiet and understated, his wife Margo is the other extreme: loud and obnoxious. So there was no doubt in my mind that Chloe's wedding, whether she liked it or not, would be huge. With half of Ireland on Chloe's side of the guest list (all hand-picked by her mother). I could see it now, Chloe being told not to be "so silly" when she suggested to her mum "Is it really necessary to invite three hundred people? Wouldn't thirty be much nicer?" She and David would have very little say in the whole thing. In my mind the best thing for them to do would be to hot-foot it to Las Vegas, get married by Elvis and stay in a hotel with a heart-shaped waterbed and leopard-print satin sheets. I smiled to myself as I imagined Margo having palpitations at the Vegas nuptials. David, bless him, handles Margo with outstanding brilliance, and though in Margo's estimation no one is really good enough for Chloe, David is the best of a bad bunch. She even blushes sometimes when he speaks to her – quite revolting. His saving grace is that he is a dentist with his own practice – someone she can boast about to her tennis friends.

* * *

My name (and don't laugh) is Sorrel Clarke, Ellie to some
family members and friends. My parents made the unwise
decision of naming me after a herb, but after twenty-six
years I have heard all the jokes and still haven't got round
to changing it by Deed Poll. I grew up just outside Belfast,
Northern Ireland. Chloe Williams is my best friend. We
have known each other since primary school. We know
pretty much everything about each other – we had
matching leg-warmers when we were going through our
Fame phase. As kids we spent weekends at each other's
houses talking non-stop about who we fancied, the pros
and cons of cinnamon lozenges versus floral gums, why
Keith Moran didn't think I was the greatest thing since the
sliced pan, teachers we wanted to poison, and if you
wrote to Jim'll Fix It, should you ask to be a ballet dancer
or Wonder Woman? We even moved from Belfast to
Edinburgh together. She sailed through University while I
struggled to find the lecture theatres. We lived together for
seven years until she moved in with David, leaving me
alone with a bumper pack of Doritos, and my West
Highland terrier Hector who comes a very close second to
Chloe, only his jokes aren't as funny. Chloe has a naturally
fantastic figure, which means that she can eat full-fat
products and as much toast as she wants without putting
on a pound. I keep telling her that once she hits thirty
she'll balloon; she just laughs and eats more toast. I on the
other hand am not naturally thin, or even close. I also eat
toast by the loaf, but it has rather adverse effects on me,
such as a pot belly and a flabby bum. "Just a bit of puppy
fat" is wearing a bit thin at my age.

It never really occurred to either of us to move back

home after we graduated from University. Most of our friends from home and University moved to London, something else that never really occurred to us, so there didn't seem much point in moving back to Belfast to sit by ourselves in the pub. Chloe had settled with David, I was happy with Hector, while considering looking for a new flat mate. We both had relatively good jobs – so why would we move? At least that's what I thought until Chloe announced that David had been offered a good promotion in a practice but it meant relocating to London. Chloe was very anxious at the thought of leaving Edinburgh and me behind. They were not going to move for another eight months but he wanted to get married before they moved. Personally I think he was scared that she'd change her mind and run off with someone who didn't insist she carry dental floss on her person at all times. So I wasn't entirely surprised that he had proposed to her in Prince's Street Gardens, in the rain that afternoon. But Prince's Street Gardens for pity's sake? Couldn't he have picked somewhere that wasn't bursting with American tourists? I feel it's a good thing to be dry and warm when making important decisions, preferably without the threat of kamikaze squirrels hiding in the trees, armed with acorns waiting to inflict head injuries on unwary passers-by. Chloe however was bowled over with this massive romantic gesture and immediately signed up.

At least I wouldn't have to give a speech – that could be left to Alex, David's ginger best friend (and therefore presumably best man). Though to be honest I'd beat him hands down on dishing the dirt – Chloe used to be a right old tart when we were at University.

The pair of us used to go out on the pull together, God help the boys in Edinburgh – but when we had the old beer goggles on, no one was safe. Many a morning we'd meet in the kitchen plotting how to get rid of the undesirables who were snoring in our beds.

Hungover and bleary-eyed we would compete for who pulled the bigger horror story.

It came as a surprise to both of us, with our unrivalled track records as yukky-guy magnets, when one Saturday night after our finals had finished, she met David at our local wine bar. We had arrived at Lainey's ready for the piss-up to end all piss-ups, and were waiting for Louisa and Clare to show up, (two friends who had not yet moved to London).

I was frantically waving at the ignorant Aussie barman when Chloe elbowed me in the ribs,

"Look, Sorrel, see that bloke over there?"

"Which one? The one with the orange shirt on?"

"No, you eejit, the one beside him with the blonde hair, and the lovely teeth. God, what a fab smile!"

The blonde with the teeth had noticed Chloe looking over and had smiled – a shy kind of smile, not a "hello darling, fancy a quick ride" kind of smile – it's amazing what you can tell from a smile.

She then caught the barman's attention and ordered two double gin and tonics. Chloe can always get the barman's attention, while I could die of thirst and he would barely notice. She hardly gave him time to set the drinks down before she had half of one down her throat – I was worried she might swallow the glass. I looked at her, knowing this speed consumption of gin usually meant she was nervous and fancied someone in the local proximity. True to form she was totally focused on "the teeth" in the corner. God, I was about to be ignored for the rest of the evening over some guy who was probably retarded, or foreign at the very least.

"Chloe!" I commanded, "Stop looking so pathetic, it's a well-known fact that men don't like 'needy' – try and look more aloof, and put your tongue back in your head."

"Bugger aloof, he's a complete ride – do you think he'll come over?"

"Not if you don't stop knocking back those gins." She was on her second double. "He'll be scared you'll throw up over his impressively ironed shirt." Indeed his shirt was very well ironed – I always notice these things as I am allergic to ironing, though I can't get my GP to admit it. Any man (assuming that he doesn't live with his mother) who irons for himself might not mind ironing for you, or your best friend. The thought of Chloe dating Mister Ever Press sent my mind racing in two directions: 1) It would be lovely having someone to do our laundry 2) She could end up snogging an anal-retentive, compulsively-neat type man which would result in endless misery for me, the girl who took pride in the fact she couldn't remember what colour her carpet was, for the piles of (unironed) clothes strewn over it.

Since Chloe was seemingly desperate to meet this man, the least a friend could do was to get them acquainted with each other, preferably before she rendered herself unconscious from the alcohol she was now swigging like water. Like the true pro I was, I walked over to the table where the gentleman in question was sitting, chatting to his friend in the disturbing orange shirt (why would a man with red hair feel the need to make matters worse by wearing orange?).

"Excuse me," I flashed my most attractive smile, aware that my teeth were not in the same league as Chloe's potential snog.

"Yes?" he replied, apparently not retarded or foreign.

"Um . . . me and my friend over there are dentists." Oh God, what am I saying? Stop now, stop, you moron! But I'd gone too far. "We couldn't help noticing your teeth and were wondering if you had – " (think of a dentistry term quick) " – caps?"

He looked slightly taken aback – oh shit, was that an insult?

"No, actually, I haven't – but I'm a dentist myself."

Shit. I smiled weakly, mentally kicking myself in the shins. I looked over at Chloe who was concentrating on an apparently interesting feature of the bar, unaware that I had just ruined her night. If not her life.

"Are you going to introduce your friend?" the teeth enquired.

Oh for God's sake, what are the chances of lying about your profession to probably the only guy in the bar who could catch us out – why hadn't I just said that we were lighthouse keepers? This could not get any worse, or so I thought. But before I had a chance to run for it, they both stood up.

"My name is Alex, pleased to meet you," the ginger-haired, orange-shirt-wearing sidekick grinned at me, displaying a much lower-calibre set of pearly whites to me.

"Oh right, I'm Sorrel, that's Chloe by the bar."

"I'm David," said Chloe's ex-potential snog "Please, bring your friend over – Alex was just going to get a round in, weren't you, Alex?"

"Yeah, what are you two girls drinking?" Alex asked.

"Gin and tonics, thanks," I heard myself saying – no, you tosser, leave while you still have your dignity! But it was too late, I had no dignity left and David motioned to Chloe to join us. It took her less than three seconds to reach the table, not exactly what I had in mind when I'd said 'aloof'. Not that it mattered now, I had managed to fuck up in less han five minutes, a new record.

"Hi there," Chloe was saying, grinning inanely at David.

"Sorrel was just telling us that you were admiring my teeth – you're a dentist? I'm a dentist too!"

Chloe shot me a look that would have soured milk

She plastered a smile on her face. "Are you really?" she said brightly.

As it turned out the night wasn't half bad. By the time Lousia and Clare showed up the four of us were fairly plastered. So the girls spent an hour playing catch-up with tequila and ended up more drunk than the rest of us. By eleven thirty Chloe had managed to get off with David the Dentist, while I had to explain to ginger Alex that we could only ever be friends. I then put Lousia and Clare in a taxi and made them promise the driver that they wouldn't throw up – and him promise that he woudn't throw them out when they did.

I waved them off to their cries of *"I looooove you, Ellieeeeeee"* fading into the distance.

Chapter Two

Amazingly David didn't seem to be at all surprised or put out by the fact that Chloe wasn't the dentist I had portrayed her to be. In fact, they got on so well Chloe took to shaving her legs on a regular basis and rediscovered eyelash curlers.

I on the other hand was left boyfriendless and with shins that could double up as human Brillo pads. My love life was so dead I felt I should have it cremated and keep it in an urn on top of the TV or scatter it over the Firth of Forth. So for lack of anything better to do I threw myself into my career and attempted to diet – all in the same week. A sort of soup diet, otherwise known as Miserable Bitch Week. The main ingredient was this special soup you have to make yourself which looks like runny ratatouille but with a lot less flavour. You are also allowed fruit and vegetables for most of the week, brown rice one day but absolutely no bread or potatoes. Potatoes are the one thing my body finds very hard to do without. I was all right for the first day. I ate my soup and vegetables and went to bed at seven thirty because

I was absolutely starving. The second day I ate a whole packet of freshly cooked baby beetroots from M & S which I actually really like, but by day three my pee was pink and, when I glanced into the toilet bowl, the deposit was a rather startling shade of purple. I was not entirely sure that that was healthy so avoided beetroot for the next two days. But by day five I was constantly fantasising about smoked salmon and cream cheese on bagels, my willpower was shot to shite, and at eight fifteen I ran out to the 24-hour garage and bought as much sugary, refined foods as my credit card would allow (£5.50 – I really must pay off the balance – Master Card make a fortune out of me, all for the love of lard).

I moved from my job covering sand-castle competitions and line-dancing grannies in the local newspaper to Caledonian Television as a researcher, working on a regional chat show. The programme itself was fairly naff, your basic Richard and Judy type of affair, only the male presenter wasn't half as irritating as Richard, so therefore not as effective. Still, the programme was very cheesy and never failed to cheer me up. There was nothing so funny as researching people like the child whose teachers had refused to teach her because she had tried to burn the school down – while it was still full of kids. That particular programme consisted of Jenny, the female presenter, making sympathetic noises and trying to understand where the child's aggression came from (seemed pretty clear it was sitting opposite her on the sofa, in the form of the parents). Other regulars were ageing pop stars staging comebacks; on the programme to perform their new single (while the make-up girls were having fits because there wasn't enough foundation in the world to cover over the wrinkles of years of alcohol and class A substance abuse). And then there were ex-glamour models attempting to kick-start their new legitimate careers, and not wanting to talk about the rich old men they had married who had just recently passed away and whose families were contesting the will. It was tough (but fun) finding suitable questions for Charles, the sympathetic male presenter, to ask that didn't mention the string of pornographic films or dubious photo sessions.

There was rarely a boring day and it was made even more hilarious by the fact that there were two of us researching, myself and a girl called Fiona, who was the most Scottish person I had ever met. She was from Aberdeen and was the only person I had met in five years in Edinburgh who actually wore tartan on a regular basis, loved haggis, ate shortbread on her tea-break and whose every second word was 'aye'. Fiona had worked for the programme for a couple of years. She looked like she should have had her own cookery programme, "Weel, hello, everybody oot there, welcome tae *A Taste o' Scotland",* with a wooden spoon under one arm and a plucked pheasant tucked under the other. Her accent was so strong I couldn't make out a word she said for most of the first day.

This was the kind of job I enjoyed, not to mention the three thousand pounds more than I was getting in my "guess the weight of the pig" reporting job. Fiona took it upon herself to show me around, with detailed information on important things like where the canteen was, office gossip, who was going out with who, and which of the male presenters used Grecian 2000.

At the end of my first week, Fiona took me to a bar where a lot of the staff drank. It was one of those theme bars, Irish ironically, so everyone was drinking stout or whiskey – I stuck out like a sore thumb with my Bacardi Breezer. Even in the most remote places in Ireland I have never come across shamrocks on the ceiling, and road signs stuck to the wall. These people clearly thought that the Irish employed the Ordnance Survey for any interior decoration needs. There was a band playing 'traditional' Irish music, so by nine thirty we were completely plastered, and I was attempting to teach my fellow workmates Riverdance. Considering I didn't know what I was doing the outcome was relatively successful.

In my inebriated state I decided to cut my losses and got off with a cameraman called Colin, who had a big nose but a lovely bum. He ran his hands through my hair as we embraced over the bar (don't you hate when drunken bollocks snog right at the bar?), muttering things in my ear, which only resulted in me dissolving into a fit of the giggles as I'm extremely ticklish. Colin took this as a personal affront, as if I were questioning his snogging techniques, and from then on avoided me at work.

A great start to a new job, alienating any good-looking cameramen.

Fiona was convinced that I didn't have nearly enough of a social life. She turned 'round to me about two weeks after I had started and said,

"Sorrel, I'm going to take you home to meet my flatmate, we'll go out for a night on the town."

This was not a question, rather a mission statement, so who was I to argue?

"That sounds great, cheers."

Apparently there was no time like the present, so that night after work we went back to her flat, but only after I made her promise not to cook me black pudding or anything disgusting like that. On arrival, her flatmate Tavy (short for Octavia), who I later came to believe to be certifiable, came bounding up to meet us as Fiona opened the front door, rather like a very glamorous Labrador. She was wearing a gold lamé boob-tube and a lot of hairspray, not entirely suitable I'm sure you'll agree, for her job as a veterinary nurse. She seemed a most unlikely candidate as an extra on Animal Hospital. The first thing she said was "Ooh God, look at the state of you, Fiona! Where did you get this creature?"

Before I had managed to say "Hello", I was left standing trying to decide whether to come back with a witty retort, or cry.

Then she burst out laughing. "You must think I'm a terrible bitch!" (Clearly not as Scottish as her flatmate, English as it turned out.) "I'm only taking the piss – you just looked completely knackered – that's what working with Fiona does for you, eh?"

"Och, you shut your gob, you. This is Sorrel, and I have decided to revamp her social life, care to lend a hand?"

"Oh, yes, please!" Tavy replied, with rather too much enthusiasm for my liking.

"Um, there really is nothing drastically wrong with my ability to make friends or enjoy an evening out, it's just that I've, um, been really busy." I tailed off at this point as I could tell that neither of them believed a word I was saying. So I shut up, and listened while they decided what hot spots we would hit that night, and tried not to be too nervous.

And so I was equipped with a rich and varied social life courtesy of Fiona and Tavy, not to mention an overdraft that Fergie would have been proud of.

17

Chapter Three

A couple of weeks before Chloe announced her engagement, I heard from Mum that Ben was going home to Ireland for the weekend and he was taking a friend.

Lucy and I have an elder brother, Ben, who is a successful stockbroker in the City in London, to the great pride of my parents who constantly hold him up as a shining example of how Lucy and I should live our lives. Personally I believe that just because you earn £50,000 per annum does not give you the right to be the favourite child – but this is a matter for discussion with Ben at a later date.

The weekend he went home Lucy and I went too (she lives in Dublin, with a cat called Victor). We hadn't seen Ben for ages, as he rarely went home and even more rarely invited us to visit him in London.

Our lack of invitations, he claimed, was because his flat was too small with both him and Sonia (snotty girlfriend, more on her later) living there. "Liar liar pants on fire" is all I have to say. Ben has two sofas the size of my living-room and more comfortable than my bed and Lucy gets so excited about anything that isn't covered in cat-hair (Victor is most definitely a moulter), she'd sleep on the carpet. Basically, Ben's apparent lack of desire to invite us to stay was because Sonia used to threaten to leave him every time we visited. Ben's friends were all so good-looking, Lucy and myself found ourselves incapable of holding back and, after several large glasses of red wine, inhibitions cast aside, we used to throw ourselves into engaging them with our sparkling wit and sex-siren good looks, not to mention exposing large amounts of cleavage. Sonia, without fail, looked on grim-faced and absolutely livid because Ben's drunken half-wit sisters had turned up once again and stolen all her limelight.

Let me fill you in on the love of Ben's life – apart from the fact she genuinely thought we were complete drop-kicks. Ben had been seeing her for two years; he met her at a drinks party while she was dating the host who was another wealthy city boy. My brother seems to have inherited all the charm and sexual magnetism in our family; after a couple of white wine and sodas he had her on her back in the bathroom and wealthy city boy number one was promptly binned. She moved in with Ben two months later complete with yoga videos, soya milk and quorn, and much to our horror the entire Mariah Carey back catalogue. She was a PA with an advertising firm, which meant she flounced around all day, tossing her hair, painting her nails and talking to her "it girl" friends about parties and clothes – at least that's what I told myself she did. The reality, that she was actually talented, would have been too much to bear.

Even my mother, who has been known to make Jehovah's Witnesses cry on her doorstep, was terrified of her. Even more terrified that Ben would marry her and have children with Home Counties accents who wouldn't be allowed to visit her as Sonia believed Northern Ireland akin to Bosnia with Guinness. Dad also used to slink away nervously when she visited, play an awful lot of golf and hide in the kitchen with Mum.

Sonia, however, was oblivious to the fear she aroused and used to order Mum around like a waitress. On one particularly memorable visit she asked Mum just to leave the breakfast tray outside her bedroom door. Mum nearly choked when she heard this. In our house there is no such thing as room service, unless a) it's your birthday b) it was previously negotiated by crossing my mother's palm with silver or c) you are genuinely ill and therefore bedridden, in no condition to fight off her offer of home-made broccoli and butter-bean soup (seriously gross).

The general picture was that Sonia was a right madam, not overly fond of her boyfriend's family. The feeling was entirely mutual, though Mum and Dad wouldn't admit it. When Lucy and I were at home we liked to get together and play 'Stick the Cellulite on Sonia's Thighs'. Mum always pretended to tell us off, but ended up joining in, and more often than not, winning. The rules were the same as Stick the Tail on the Donkey but instead of the donkey we used a photo of Sonia Lucy had nicked off

Ben, stuck to the fridge, and a cut-out of an obese pair of legs we found in a slimming magazine. This game gave us hours of innocent entertainment, roaring with laughter to see Sonia with a pair of fat legs stuck to her forehead. Dad had also been known to join in on occasion, especially after a visit from Her Ladyship. Chloe and I had a spin-off of the original in Edinburgh where I had sellotaped a photocopy to the back of our kitchen door, for Chloe to work off pent-up aggression after she had spoken to her mum (which requires the patience of a saint, a lot of tongue-biting and plenty of deep breaths). Chloe's mother, as you will have gathered, is the closest Northern Ireland will ever have to royalty. She is completely neurotic – she flaps so much she should have wings. She is also a compulsive curtain-twitcher – nothing happens on Oakdene Road that she doesn't know about. When she isn't peering out of the window glaring at every passer-by, she is gossip-mongering with her equally pass-remarkable friends over bridge, a game of tennis or a lunch for some charity or other.

But, to get back to Ben and Sonia, Lucy and I considered trying to break them up, but Ben was so in love with her we felt nothing short of her marrying someone else without telling him would put him off. Nevertheless, it didn't stop us from trying. We sent in an advert to the *London Evening Standard* on her behalf, to the 'lonely hearts' section. She was completely mystified as to why she was being winked at and propositioned all day from men in her office, who normally wouldn't have the nerve to even look in her direction, and why she was receiving armfuls of letters from guys who wanted to show her a good time. She only clicked when Ben showed her the advert – she was raging, he thought it was quite funny – though she could never prove it was us who had submitted the advert. From then on our relationship with Sonia went into a downward spiral. Sad really, when your big brother who used to hold you upside-down over the stairs till you gave him your packet of Wotsits, now wouldn't say boo to a goose, or boo to Sonia. Chloe and I even kept a vigil over the Evening Times to see if she would retaliate, but we didn't hear one peep from the humourless cow.

Anyway, to get back to that weekend.

When Mum told us that Ben was bringing a friend for the weekend it was of considerable interest to me, in my manless state. Hence my immediate arrival home. Mum was delighted to have us all minus Sonia and plus Ben's mate who none of us had met before.

I had talked to him – Jake was his name – on the phone. From his voice I imagined he was a rather portly chap – a kind, deepish voice – you know, the good-looking man's sidekick. We had a great laugh one night when I called Ben and Jake picked up the phone. Ben was cooking – he makes exotic things like Moroccan Rabbit, whereas I can just about manage Welsh Rarebit. So Jake entertained me while Ben finished the intricacies of raspberry millefeuille. Why Ben couldn't just order pizza, like normal brothers do, beats me. Jake said the only reason he was friends with Ben was because it saved him a fortune on takeaways. Anyway, my only contact with this bloke was one or two amusing conversations and, though I had my fingers crossed, it was electrifying to arrive home and find my mother chatting to unquestionably the most gorgeous man in the western world, while she set the table for dinner and he stirred the gravy.

My heart almost stopped, my grasp of the English language failed me and all I could manage to say was: "Oh, um, hi."

Luckily Mum appeared delighted to see me and the fact that I had turned into a moron was hidden in her enormous hug.

Jake smiled at me and extended a hand for shaking, then in true London style he kissed me on both cheeks, at which point my legs went from under me and I almost lost control of my bladder. Muttering that I must nip up the bathroom, I excused myself and rushed upstairs. I passed Lucy, managing a quick nod in my haste.

She followed me into the bathroom and sat on the edge of the bath. I only just avoided weeing on the carpet but once safely on the pot I was capable of communication once again.

"Isn't he totally yummy?" Lucy said with a grin on her face.

"Completely," I replied. You can't get less portly than that, I thought to myself.

"I'll bet by the end of the weekend you'll have fallen madly in love with him," she said in a distinctly amused fashion.

"I hardly think so – I'll bet he has millions of girlfriends in London."

"Yeah, probably, but that doesn't matter, eh Sorrel?"

She was referring to the one and only time I took someone else's boyfriend away. In my defence it was by accident and a totally regrettable experience. Steven Philips. I met him after I had just started University. I didn't particularly like him, but he seemed so keen that I thought going to the cinema would be OK, at least I would have someone to go out with on my first Saturday night in Edinburgh without Chloe, who wasn't coming over to Scotland until Sunday.

So Steven called round to my Hall of Residence, which wasn't very far considering he lived in the next building to mine. We went to see *When Harry met Sally,* which is now one of my all-time favourite films, but Steven kept trying snog me without so much as a bit of hand-holding or anything. I was totally revolted. What's more he had popcorn breath and sticky palms, not exactly a recipe for passion in my mind. I missed half the film while I was fighting him off. When it finished Steven wanted to take me out for a drink; I wanted to go back to my room alone and drink the rest of the bottle of gin I had stashed under my bed. I agreed to go for one, just to shut him up. I thought alcohol might take the edge off my revulsion and, to cut a long story short, I got totally hammered and ended up in bed with him, having unmemorable sex. At least it was for me. Thankfully the TV was on, so by angling my head I was able to watch *The Hitman and Her,* with Michaela Strachan and Peter Waterman, while Steven got carried away on top of me. He didn't appear to notice when I was reaching for the remote control to see if there were any late films on.

The next morning, with my brain bouncing round in my skull, I decided to put the night down to experience, not be such a slapper in future and avoid Steven for the next four years. Then I noticed that a note was slipped under my door. It was from Steven, he wrote that he was leaving his girlfriend (pardon?) for me, he thought he was in love with me and he would see me later when I was feeling better. What fecking girlfriend? There had been no mention of this the previous evening and how could he be in love with me, he didn't even know me. Oh bugger, now he was leaving her, who was this brave girl? How much shit was I in?

So, for a short while I became the focus of unwanted admiration from Steven, while Melanie, as the ex-girlfriend turned out to be called, came round to my rooms and tearfully announced that I had ruined her life. After I had explained to her what had happened she miraculously seemed to get over her broken heart, and informed me she was "off to break his bloody neck". I didn't hear that much from him after that – once his arm had healed, he wrote me a letter saying that perhaps he had been a bit hasty leaving Melanie, and wasn't in love with me after all. I believe they got married after they graduated.

Anyway I digress. A habit of mine.

Back to the bathroom.

"Oh shut up, Lucy, you know very well that was not my fault – I can't help it if I attract complete morons."

"Ah well, we all have our crosses to bear!" She could be a right evil little bitch when she wanted. "Yours happens to be undesirable men! I'm off to the kitchen to see if Jake needs any help with the gravy!"

It was only after she left I realised that I hadn't said hello to Ben or Dad. I went to my bedroom to tidy myself up, then remembered that I had dumped all my bags in the kitchen, so decided to raid Lucy's make-up instead. As I plastered bronzer across my pale face, I wondered why I was bothering; good-looking blokes always have girlfriends and are rarely interested in their mates' younger sisters. Still, a little lippie never did anyone any harm.

Once satisfied that I looked slightly less revolting, I headed downstairs to see Ben.

He was in the sitting-room chatting to Dad. As soon as they saw me, Ben got up and gave me a massive hug. "Ellie! Long time no see, how ya doin? You look great – been on a sunbed?"

"I'm good, no I haven't, you look well yourself." I was surprised at the amount of bronzer I must have piled on and with Ben's enthusiastic welcome – usually he gave me a dead arm.

"Hello sweetheart, you do look well, it's great to have you home!" Dad got up from his chair and gave me big hug. The one thing you could always count on in our family was the great hugs. Mum and Dad had brought us up to be affectionate, with lots of hugs, and lots of telling us we were great, especially when we were not.

"Hi ya, Dad, you're not looking so bad yourself!"

Dad was in good form; he had obviously been bonding with Ben and was clearly enjoying himself.

"Tea's ready!" Lucy bellowed from the kitchen.

I hastily flicked my hair into what was hopefully a casually desirable style, Ben looked at me sideways and then a smile spread over his face. He knew I was trying to impress Jake and he thought is was funny – git.

Jake had a tea towel wrapped round his head, and was making Mum and Lucy laugh pretending to be one of those TV chefs talking into the camera explaining what was on each plate.

"So only after the lamb is on the plate, can you then add the vegetables, and of course most importantly the gravy."

God, I'm in love – a man with a sense of humour, broad shoulders, dark hair, sea-green eyes, taller than me and a knack with Bisto – thank you, Ben, for knowing him. I had a quick look under the table to check if he had small feet, nope they looked at least a size 10 – Lucy said you could never trust a man with small hands and feet, can't remember why, but I always check just in case. Maybe it's because men with smaller feet are more agile and can run away faster, though knowing Lucy it's probably something to do with the size of their willies.

We all sat down and Dad filled up everyone's glasses. "Red OK for you, Jake?"

"Absolutely, Mr C, pour away," Jake replied and gave what I can only describe as a knicker-loosening grin.

This man was really something else. I held on to the edge of the table as for one moment I thought I was going to fall off my chair.

It was also clear that both Mum and Dad loved Jake. Of course, Ben can do no wrong (apart from Sonia) in their eyes so they were biased in his favour.

Dad never needs to ask the rest of the table if we want wine.

Mum thinks Lucy and I are complete lushes and always tells us that in her day people didn't drink to get drunk and she can't understand why we can't just have one glass – why does it have to be the whole bottle? Last visit, Lucy told her that she'd get beaten up by her friends in Dublin if she couldn't drink, the peer pressure is so great. Mum nodded agreement. "Yes, dear, the pressure must be awful," she said with a worried sigh. Me – well, if it's there I'll drink it. Unless of course it's vodka with chocolate sauce – I'd need to be really drunk to touch that! Ben's a bloke so Mum doesn't seem to mind how much he drinks, when he comes home, who he has been with, if he has fathered any illegitimate children, if he has a drug habit, she doesn't even get at him about his phone bill, like she does with Lucy and me. Mind you, we normally try to get Dad to pay it for us.

Thankfully, on this occasion, Mum was on her best behaviour and didn't start on at us – it would have been too embarrassing to live with.

It was bad enough that I was most unusually lost for words, completely mesmerised by Jake, who was thankfully unaware of the doe eyes I was making at him. Lucy had thrown a bit of roast potato at his head and he threw a couple of peas at her with his fork in retaliation. Lucy got carried away with this form of flirtation and threw more roast potato pieces – they were covered in gravy and slid all down his shirt. Everyone was laughing. Mum quite clearly fancied Jake too or she would have given off hell to Lucy for throwing her good roast potatoes around.

It had been so long since our family had all been round one table, let alone all speaking to each other; as my father would say *"the craic was ninety"*.

Dinner continued in the same vein, with much laughter and storytelling, everyone trying to outdo the other.

I began to relax and enjoy myself and in the end I couldn't help joining in. I told Jake about the time Ben tried to sell Lucy to a guy who had camels when we were on holiday in Lanzarote. She was only six at the time and Ben thought she would make a good slave, but Mum wouldn't let him – she told him we'd get questioned at the airport as it said on our air tickets that five of us were travelling.

Then Lucy told Jake how I used to tell her she was adopted from a family of pig farmers up the country called the Squitters, that we had only borrowed her for the weekend to play with but they didn't want her back, so we had to keep her. And the one when Ben told me that when I was little Mum and Dad hadn't really wanted me but I was the last baby on the shelf in Stewarts so they had to take me home.

Dad got up and opened another bottle of red wine, and filled up everyone's glass except Mum's who said if she drank any more we'd get apple crumble with gravy over it instead of custard. The threat of a ruined pudding was enough for Dad – he forced a glass of water on her before she served the apple crumble.

After the apple crumble Ben got up. "Right, who's for the pub?"

"I've never been to a pub in Ireland – I want some real Guinness," Jake replied with a grin.

"I'm in," Lucy piped up.

"Oh go on then, you've twisted my arm," I said, attempting to sound reluctant, but secretly delighted to get rid of Mum and Dad. Now how could I dispose of Ben and Lucy?

Dad offered us a lift down to the pub in his car. We all piled into the back of his Volvo and headed off down the road. The pub is about half a mile away from where we live, but that's half a mile too far when you have to listen to my father's taste in music on the way. I'm not fussy but I've never been a fan of the Shadows – Hank Marvin just never did it for me. Dad was tapping away on the steering wheel. I suppose I should have been grateful he wasn't doing his usual air-guitar impressions in front of Jake.

When we arrived at the pub Dad turned round to Jake in the back seat. "Now, I don't want to see any of my offspring inebriated, understand? You're in charge, watch them carefully."

"Not a problem, Mr C. I'll have the Diet Cokes lined up at the bar, beside my Guinness."

"Good man! Have a good night, I'm off home to make sure your mother hasn't broken all the crockery or isn't lying under the table. Cheerio!" With that he turned up the volume and sang his way back up the road.

We all traipsed into our local, The Deerstalker, one after the other. Ben went straight up to the bar and ordered a round of drinks. I love rich siblings. Lucy located a recently vacated table in the busy bar and we rushed to sit down before someone else grabbed it.

"Well, Jake, what do you think of the North of Ireland so far?" Lucy asked.

"Ah, sure 'tis a grand place," he replied in a mock brogue.

"Wrong end of the country for that accent I'm afraid," she reprimanded him. "Sure that's deepest Cork!"

God, I envied Lucy, who was so at ease with all good-looking males, which probably explained why she was rarely without some gorgeous and entirely unsuitable chap or other. She wasn't half bad at the accents either.

Though I thought Lucy was cracking a few too many jokes that night, a bit too funny for my liking, we all got on like the proverbial house on fire and Jake's sense of humour only pushed me further towards mild obsession. Many drinks were taken and several hours later it was four rather unsteady people who staggered into a taxi.

The rest of the weekend was great. Lucy would kick me under the table if she saw me drooling too much (my shins took weeks to recover). Sadly, just because you make someone laugh does not apparently make them want to shag you over the kitchen table in a fit of lust. Jake did not appear to return my sentiments. In fact, it turned out that he went through girlfriends quicker than I get through a bottle of Cabernet Sauvignon. He specialised in 'trophy' girlfriends (according to Ben, though *he* can *talk*) – you know, the ones that are attracted to wealthy young sex gods. Blonde, leggy, with a foreign accent and a budding career in modelling. The type that would probably drape themselves over a man. If I had attempted any such manoeuvre it would have almost certainly ended up with the man in question in traction for at least six months. Well, who wants to look like a travel rug anyway? I reasoned with myself. Though really wishing

I didn't like food quite so much. I firmly believed that any girl *that* good-looking could not possibly have anything to say for herself, apart from excusing herself from the table to go and throw up. Oh God, oh God, why was this man *soooo* good-looking? I really felt the need to see him naked. But other than knock on his bedroom door and offer him any sexual service his heart desired I was at a loss as to how to make him notice me – and he might think me a little forward.

But then why would an intelligent man whose attractiveness made Brad Pitt look like he had been beaten with the ugly stick, want to attach himself to a neurotic, weight-obsessed, decidedly 'untrophyish' younger sister of one of his best friends, unless of course he was severely concussed or had been paid a significantly large amount of cash? As far as I knew Dad had no slush fund hidden away for such emergency contingencies like daughters who men didn't find attractive. Just my buggering luck.

Chapter Four

The weekend came to an end. Ben and Jake flew back to London, Lucy headed back down to Dublin and I had to catch the boat over to Stranraer and drive back to Edinburgh with the car stereo of my trusty Fiat out of action and a radio which couldn't stay on one channel for more than two minutes. To pass the time I chainsmoked all the way (a three-hour drive) and arrived back jittery from the massive nicotine injection.

Hector, who had been staying with my neighbour, was utterly delighted to see me. It appeared that only dogs loved me. He joined me on the sofa while I fed him a packet of Tayto cheese-and-onion crisps I had brought back with me, and told him all about Jake. Hector did not appear wildly enthusiastic about this so I gave Chloe a ring. She wasn't in – probably having Sunday dinner with David's parents, who were over the moon since David told them he and Chloe were getting married. So I rang Louisa, no answer, rang Clare, no fecking answer. So in desperation I rang Fiona. Tavy picked up the phone, insisted that I come round that instant with Hector, who would need to be walked anyway, and fill them in on all the details of my sadly uneventful weekend.

Chloe told her parents over the phone about getting engaged and they were absolutely delighted. Her dad is a total sweetheart and I imagined he was dying with pride, as Chloe is their only child and her dad always liked David. As I had suspected and Chloe feared, her mum was highly excited, and was practically boarding the next flight to Edinburgh before she had hung up the phone. In fact I don't think she had been in such a good mood since she had a tummy tuck two years ago and all her friends' husbands commented on how good she was looking.

She didn't even run her finger along the skirting-boards of Chloe's living-room to check for dust when she arrived – as the old bitch had been known to do. She walked straight in the door as I opened it, did not even acknowledge my existence, gave Chloe a perfunctory hug (well, as close to a hug as you could expect from the Ice Queen – our nickname for her when we were little) and asked to see the ring.

"Um . . . I thought it might have been bigger. Don't dentists earn a lot of money?" She stared down at the glittering solitaire on her daughter's finger, determined to be unimpressed. I could not believe my ears. It was official: Margo did not have one nice bone in her body. Oh God, how I'd like to knock her teeth out.

"Well, we are saving for the deposit on a house, and I like it. What's wrong with it?"

I could see that Chloe was trying to hold herself together. Before she had time to retaliate Margo was off again.

"So, I was thinking of the wedding at the Church on the corner of the Circular Road, and – "

"But Mum, that's not our church!"

"Oh dear, no one worries about that anymore – the one on Circular Road is much more attractive, and the parking is better, you'll be able to get the Daimler right up to the front of the church and everyone will be able to see you walk up the path through the roses, as of course you'll get married in May. Right, now the reception. How about the Glencoe? Or would you prefer a marquee?"

The Glencoe is our local five-star hotel, where most well-to-do folk in the area held their receptions. I'm not sure if it is the best, but it is certainly the most expensive.

"Actually darling I think maybe a marquee would be better, the garden will be looking at its best, and we can get those lovely caterers in, that Nancy Thomson had but don't tell her I said that."

Jesus, was this woman going to stop for breath?! Chloe had gone slightly pale and I wanted to tell her it was OK, I'd push Margo off the top floor of Jenners.

"Right, darling, let's make some appointments with the Bridal Showrooms. Sorrel, are you coming too?"

Could she possibly have said that any less enthusiastically?

"Yes, of course I am, I wouldn't miss it for the world." I didn't add that I thought Chloe would probably need all the help she could get to stop Margo kitting her out in an enormous meringue, or some other hideous sugary confection posing as a dress. Chloe looked at me gratefully. How had she turned out to be so normal? Must be the influence of her Dad. Her mother was the most overbearing person I had ever met.

And so it became the worst two days in the history of either Chloe's or my life. Margo was a nightmare, or more accurately she was just her usual self. She insisted on dragging us both out for a very expensive dinner. Chloe is a vegetarian, and the restaurant in question did not really cater that well for non-meat eaters. In fact I believe Margo the Evil (another nickname of mine) had picked it for that very reason – well, that and the fact it was incredibly expensive.

"Oh for God's sake, Chloe," her mum admonished her, "why do you insist on being difficult?"

"Mum, I haven't eaten meat for seven years, and I'm not going to start now to keep you happy."

Chloe had become a vegetarian as soon as she had moved over to Edinburgh, as her mother hadn't allowed it at home.

The waiter approached, nose held high.

Oh here we go, I thought. Waiters with attitude were one of my favourites – I could feel myself going into difficult-customer mode before he was anywhere near the table. I am, in fact, probably the easiest person in the world to please when it comes to food, but for Chloe's sake I could be a nightmare. But before I could even get started Margo was already trying to embarrass Chloe.

"Would you mind terribly making my fussy daughter an omelette? I'm afraid she doesn't eat meat."

"Why, of course, madame, that is no problem. What

would you like with your omelette, mademoiselle?" He looked at Chloe with a remarkably warm expression, usually, I would have thought, reserved only for customers with Gold American Express cards – maybe he was a long-suffering vegetarian too. Or perhaps he instinctively knew that Margo Williams was "pain in the arse" personified. In any case, I was fairly sure my difficult-customer routine might no longer be required.

"Erm . . . I'm not sure, maybe . . ."

"Could I perhaps suggest spinach with pine nuts and mushrooms?"

"Oh yes, that sounds really lovely," Chloe smiled. "Thank you." She was left looking rather shell-shocked at the ease of the order and the general niceness of the waiter.

"For you, mademoiselle?" The waiter looked in my direction.

Ha ha, I'd been planning this since I picked up the menu – the "ordering the most expensive thing on the menu" game, which I usually reserve for crappy dates.

"Yes, I'd love the lobster, thank you." Knowing full well it cost eleven pounds more than Chloe's omelette.

"Very good, mademoiselle. And finally, madame, for you?"

"Could I have the poussin, *s'il vous plait?*" Margo gave a tinkly girlish laugh.

Both Chloe and I looked horrified. Not only was she ordering something that I had a sneaking suspicion was a tiny bird, but she was flirting. I felt sick. The waiter was ever the professional and smiled, as if he was flattered she spoke his language and he was unaware that this 'extra' from Dynasty was attempting to be coy.

"Very good, madame. Someone will come to take your wine order immediately." He gave a little bow and left the table.

"Well, I must visit the powder-room, please excuse me." Margo got up from the table.

Trust her to try and make going for a pee sound glamorous. But it gave me time to put the next stage of my plan into action: selecting outrageously expensive wine. Chloe was so hacked off with her mum at this point she joined in for once instead of telling me off. By the time Margo got back to the table we had ordered two bottles of a £60 wine, which neither of us had ever heard of. Margo evidently had as her jaw dropped every so slightly when she saw the labels, but she never said a word. Our wine waiter poured a little into my glass for me to try. I could have kissed him as Margo did not appreciate this and sat with her lips pursed like a cat's bum. I was starting to enjoy myself.

The meal progressed with Margo pulling out a notebook between courses and writing useful wedding information down so that she didn't forget. "Now, darling," she addressed Chloe, making it obvious that I was not to be included in this conversation, "I want you to talk to Jaques, my hairdresser – he might want you to grow it a little longer, for the day."

I nearly choked on my wine, as did Chloe.

"Mum, I think I'm old enough to decide that for myself, and it's a bit early to worry about hairstyles – I haven't even looked at dresses yet!"

"I'll discuss this with you later, oh and I've made an

appointment at Jenners tomorrow. Unfortunately, Sorrel, you will be at work."

"Actually, I'm off tomorrow, a day in lieu, from last month . . ." Sometimes I scared myself with how easily I could lie. I would have to remember to phone in sick the next morning.

"Ah, I see – I think maybe Chloe and I would like a little time to ourselves," she countered.

"Mum, I really want Ellie to be there," Chloe protested. "She has great taste and I trust her completely."

"And I don't have great taste? Is that it?" Margo looked a bit huffy.

"No, Mum, of course you've got great taste – I want you both there!"

God, what a diplomat – I'd have told her to just 'fuck off'.

Dessert arrived just in time to prevent Margo from any further complaining as she gave the crème bruleé her complete attention.

On the odd (and that's what made it so nice) occasion my mother visited me in Edinburgh she stayed in my flat. She loved Hector and even fitted in the vast amount of housework I left for her without complaint. We drank wine and got tiddly and she told me rude jokes that Dad does not approve of. We shopped, ate out and she filled me in on the gossip I'd missed from home. She usually gave me fifty pounds to buy myself something nice and then she got the train to Stranraer, then the boat and Dad picked her up at the other end – lovely. I used to end up wishing I saw more of her.

Things were sadly not the same for Chloe. Her mum stayed in a hotel and Chloe had to take time off work to see her, because Margo was so socially busy at the weekends she only ever visited during the week. Chloe used to panic for days before her mum came over. When she used to live with me we had to have a tidying frenzy, get rid of pizza boxes and hide takeaway menus (her mum does not approve) and practically lick the carpet clean. Margo had been known to inspect the insides of our oven and microwave when she thought we weren't looking. The oven was usually covered in burnt cheese from my Welsh Rarebit extravaganzas, and the microwave crusted with baked beans, yum.

After Chloe moved out she had to resort to having an intimate relationship with Mister Muscle the week before her mum came over. Even though Margo still stayed in a hotel she inspected Chloe and David's flat as if she were a prospective buyer.

I always tried to coach Chloe not to be such a weed in front of her mum, and used to tell her the next time Margo bitched about any imaginary dust, to lie back on the sofa, put her feet on the coffee table and say "dull women have immaculate homes". But she wouldn't, she said her mum would have a fit, which to be perfectly honest is the result I was hoping for.

This visit was no different. Margo was staying at the Balmoral, one of the top hotels in Edinburgh, and Chloe and I had to meet her at 8.30 am for breakfast, to go over her "game plan". God, I wanted to be sick. Who meets at 8.30 when they are skiving off work? More upsetting than that, Margo had already ordered us fresh fruit and muesli when we turned up five minutes late. I wanted a full cooked breakfast with extra fried bread. I was not happy as I sat down to pre-ordered sliced guava. Chloe seemed too nervous to care about food, strange girl. Margo was trying to look like Joan Collins, God knows why, but she was sitting there and I was amazed that she managed to remain upright with all that jewellery on, it must have weighed a ton.

"Now girls, we have Jenners at 9.15 am, then Emma Roy at 11 am, break for coffee, then the Brides to Be at 12.45 am. A quick bite of lunch, then on to Georgia's Wedding in Glasgow for 4.30 PM. We should be back around sevenish. I've booked us tickets for Cats tonight, Chloe. I did not think you would want to go, Sorrel."

I felt tired already.

"Will we really be able to fit that all in today?" Chloe asked. "I don't want to rush round, we'll only get tired and I'll miss something because I can't be bothered."

"Don't be silly, dear, I won't let you miss a thing, and anyway I'm only over for two days, so we have to fit in as much as possible."

Chloe looked like she was about to cry, and to be perfectly honest I didn't blame her.

Margo sucked out our will to live. She dragged the pair of us round every bridal showroom in Scotland, in a matter of two days. She was now convinced she and Chloe should go to London at a later stage (even though Chloe had seen several dresses that she really liked) and so did I.

As Margo got into a taxi for the airport I wanted to start cheering and high kicking. She gave us both a sedate, regal wave and the taxi sped off up the street. It was almost as palpable as the relief you feel when you've been holding in a fart during an exercise class or at the cinema with a new boyfriend: there is no feeling like it.

We decided that we deserved a drink, and put an embargo on any wedding chat, so we headed off to Lainey's for many glasses of red wine. Several bottles later we were completely plastered and I was waxing lyrical about my unrequited love for Jake and how I should write a song about it.

"You know, lotsh of people write songsh about lostsh love . . ."

"Yesh, but he never loved you, so that doeshn't count."

"He jusht doehsn't know me well enough, if he did he'd definitely love me."

"Well, thasht's true," was about all Chloe managed before she slipped off her chair onto the floor.

In my attempt to help her up, I fell on top of her, and we lay giggling as our fellow-drinkers eyed us with pity, no doubt thinking how sad it was when young ladies lost control of their legs. We eventually made it to standing and tripped out the door of the bar into the street where Chloe sat down on the kerb and rested her head in her hands while I ineffectually waved my arms about hoping to flag down a taxi – not much good when you're facing a chip shop. The owner, sensing my confusion, came out and pointed me in the correct direction – the road. Within seconds we were in the back of a black cab speeding towards my flat.

Hector looked distinctly pissed off at having been ignored all evening, only to be ignored again as we both collapsed onto the sofa, and I fell off.

In the morning I woke up to find myself on the floor, still in last night's clothes, with Chloe's foot hanging off the sofa and resting on my forehead. Ooh horrible spinny head!

I woke Chloe up and made for the kitchen, on a mission to boil the kettle. Once we had cups of tea in our hands we felt marginally better. I vaguely remembered telling most of the clientele at the bar about how much I loved Jake and how once he got to know me he would feel the same way too. Chloe also reminded me that I had planned to get rid of Sonia, then Ben would want Lucy, Chloe and me to visit all the time. Jake would realise that I was all he would ever want, fall deeply in love with me and never look at another six-foot, foreign blonde again. Red wine certainly had a lot to answer for. Chloe was getting the shakes, so I got up and fetched the paracetamol, and fed four to her. We got out of the last night's stinky clothes, into pyjamas and Chloe rang David to say she was fine and hadn't been attacked or abducted. She had to hold the phone away from her ear as he was quite cross, and that necessitated some shouting.

"David, I'm sorry, but you know how I get when Mum has been here. Ellie just took me out for a quiet drink and the whole thing got out of hand. Listen, go and play golf with Alex and I'll see you at home later on."

"Chloe, I can cancel my golf! It's not like I have been looking forward to it or anything!" I heard him bellow.

"Och David, just fuck off! I've got a hangover and stop your burning martyr routine – it's not fooling anyone!" And she hung up. I could be quite proud of my friend sometimes.

"Right, I'll get the Pringles, you put on the video."

"OK, do you want *Casablanca* or *An Affair to Remember?*"

"Um . . . *An Affair to Remember*, please."

I went into the kitchen to the Hangover Cupboard, which I kept full of exciting food, like crisps, chocolate, biscuits and anything else that was fattening and caught my eye at the supermarket.

Chloe put the video on.

"This is just like *Sleepless in Seattle,* you and I, best friends watching this together," she said.

We were sitting on my sofa with Hector in between us, a six-pack of Diet Coke and a tube of Pringles each.

"I suppose I get to be Rosie O'Donnell and you're Meg Ryan, but I don't recall them ever having bloody great hangovers."

"But Rosie O'Donnell is hilarious, she's got her own chat show in America and they take all that herbal bollock in Hollywood for hangovers, that's if they drink at all."

"Yes, but Meg gets to snog Tom Hanks. Actually, on second thoughts be Meg Ryan by all means. I don't want to snog Tom, he reminds me of that weird bloke at the swimming pool." The weird bloke used to swim after us in the pool and whenever we stopped for a breather he would try and start up a conversation. We stopped going swimming soon after that.

"You may be taking this a little too literally, Ellie."

"Ha, you don't want to snog him either – admit it – you'd rather have Harrison Ford."

The film started, so we both shut up and munched on our Pringles, Hector was doing his, I haven't been fed in days routine, which I was now totally immune to, but Chloe still fell for it every time and gave him the odd Pringle when she thought I wasn't looking.

"Chloe, the wee bugger is podgy enough without you giving him onion and sour cream breath and high cholesterol into the bargain. If you give him any more I'll make you take him out for a walk right now!"

"OK, OK, I'm sorry, but he is so cute."

"Cute but fat, just like his owner." Well, I'd heard that dogs can look like their owners, but I never imagined looking like a Westie.

"I'm not having this conversation with you, Ellie. You do not look like your dog, and you are not overweight. Since when has it been a crime not to fit into a Next size 14? Anyway, Hector has enough problems with his neurotic owner, without adding an identity crisis."

We watched the rest of the film in relative silence. Hector started to snore in the sad bit where Cary Grant's character realises that Deborah Kerr's character is still in love with him only she can't walk after she was hit by a car, and they have this enormous kiss, and I usually burst out crying. But Chloe was sniggering away watching Hector, and I usually can't stay cross with her for very long, even when she does call me neurotic, and I started to giggle too.

After the film I felt well enough to have a cigarette. I opened all the windows and apologised to Chloe for having the audacity to smoke in my own flat. It had been a bit of a bone of contention when we lived together, and she still couldn't resist being an annoying bitch and lecturing me every chance she got.

"Ellie, it's so bad for you, the flat will smell and Hector might get passive lung cancer."

"Not a chance – he goes and sits in the kitchen in his bed."

"Well, I had hoped you would seriously think about stopping now."

"Chloe, if you do not stop telling me that smoking is bad for me I'm going to put you out in the hallway in your pyjamas."

"All right, don't get so stroppy, I'll shut up."

Chapter Five

Several weeks later I was sitting on a window sill at work, looking out at yet another beautiful Edinburgh drizzly day – I was having one of those I-really-cannot-be-arsed-to-be-here days (I had about five a week) – when my phone rang.

Well, I nearly swallowed my own tongue when I picked up the phone and heard,

"Hello Sorrell? Hi, it's Jake here, how are you?"

In my own inimitable way I lost the power of speech immediately.

"Oh hi, I'm um . . . OK. And you?"

"Great. I'm great, glad to hear your voice. Listen, what are you doing tonight?"

I'm sorry I think you must have me confused with someone else, nice things rarely happen to me . . . oh well, here goes,

"Um . . . nothing as far as I'm aware, why?"

Cue hysterical laughter? Jake and Ben poking fun at me for being boring?

Instead I heard,

"It's just that I'm up in Edinburgh for work and I'd love to take you out for dinner, if that's all right?"

It did sound like he was on his own, and even though I was straining my ears I couldn't hear Ben in the background. Could it be possible that this was not a wind-up?

"Oh yes, that would be really nice, what time suits you?" What a great chat line, Ellie, maybe tonight you can discuss the shipping forecasts with him. Too much paranoia? Well, I suppose it helps to know what time you're expected.

"Eight o'clock OK with you?" he asked.

"Great. Where are we going?" Oh my God, oh my God, OH MY GOD, I'm going out for dinner with JAKE!

"Well, I don't know Edinburgh that well but one of the guys in the office told me that Calamare was worth a visit."

Gasp. Only the best and undoubtedly the most expensive restaurant in Edinburgh, the place to be seen and scrummy food into the bargain. I was impressed. Oh shit, what was I going to wear?

"Good choice – will I meet you there?" Please don't come to my flat! I was thinking of my ironing pile which was currently occupying the whole of the living-room and Hector had made a temporary bed in it.

"Well, whatever suits you. I could call round to pick you up – I've never seen your flat."

Oh shit. "Tell you what, I'll meet you at the Red Jacket – it's a pub on the corner of Dundas Street, near the restaurant, at say quarter to eight?" God, was that rude? But really I'd rather chew off my own arm than let Jake see my disgusting habitat, looking distinctly non-Habitat.

"Er, OK fine, I'll meet you in the Red Jacket between seven thirty and quarter to eight. See you then, Ellie. Oh and thanks."

"For what?" I sounded like a moron.

"Meeting me. I didn't want to have to spend a night on my own in a hotel room, you know how impersonal they are. Either that or have to fend off Joanne from Finance, who wanted to take me to see a Robert Redford film – I hardly know her and she's married. So I'll see you tonight!"

"Glad I could oblige, bye," I replied.

I put down the phone and promptly burst out crying

Oh super, so now I was the most attractive alternative to some nympho married woman or a night in with room service.

Well, seeing Jake was definitely more exciting than my night in with left-over lasagne and *Coronation Street,* whatever his reasons. I mopped up my tears.

Now what was I going to wear? If only I had stuck to that soup diet then I would be thin and glamorous instead of cuddly in a too-tight clothes kind of a way. It was too late to go shopping for anything and I didn't have the money anyway. Bugger, I'd better ask Fiona's advice.

Strangely, for someone attired in virtually top-to-toe tartan, she had amazingly good taste when picking flattering ensembles for other people, namely me.

I found her chatting up the man who runs the canteen, her theory being that she'll get free filled rolls if he thinks that she fancies him – I wasn't entirely sure this was a good idea. Bloke in question suffered badly from the ravages of acne, halitosis, and appeared to have had a severe beating with the ugly stick. But if cheap food was Fiona's idea of a good time then who was I to tell her any differently?

Out of breath after I had run round the building in search of my fashion advisor and unable to get the words out, I signalled at her.

Like something out of a Lassie film she put her head to one side and followed me asking, "What's the matter, Ellie? Do you want me to follow you?"

"Fiona!" I gasped. "I need your help! Jake! Jake has just phoned and he wants me to go out for dinner with him tonight! What the fuck am I going to wear?"

"But I thought you said you thought he fancied Lucy?"

"Oh shut up, he's only going out with me because he's stuck in Edinburgh on business and doesn't want to sit in with room service."

"Well, I like room service so I think that is quite flattering."

"He doesn't want to go out with Joanne from Finance either, so he had to make dinner plans with me to get out of it. I'm just the best of a bad bunch."

"So why exactly are you getting so upset over your friggin' outfit then?"

"He's taking me to Calamare and I don't want to look like some hick totally out of place."

"Ah, I see – so nothing to do with the fact you'd sell your kidneys to get into his pants then?"

"No, no nothing at all," I said grumpily. I suppose Fiona did have a point, but it still upset me that I wasn't Jake's first choice, oh shut up, shut up, positive thinking!

"OK, to be honest one choice of outfit springs instantly to mind, but you probably won't like it."

"What?" Trying to think: why would she pick it if she thinks I won't like it?

"Well, don't shout, but your orange shift dress with your knee boots looks fairly sensational."

"Oh God, not that! I don't want him to think I'm trying to do a fat impression of Twiggy – my knees are too flabby anyway. I haven't worn that dress in ages! It probably doesn't even zip up now!"

"I told you you wouldn't like it but, trust me, it really suits you. Go home and try it on. I bet it will still do up."

"All right, but I wanted something snazzier and not so orange. What about my gold lamé top with boot-cut trousers?"

"Fine, but you just said that you would be too fat to fit into your dress – your lamé top is very short and your tummy will be visible."

"Only if I reach up! If I keep my arms down I'd be grand."

"Whatever. You asked my advice and I gave it to you – don't blame me when you come in tomorrow weeping because your midriff was exposed by accident when you were putting on your coat."

I got changed into my outfit for the evening. I changed again and again and again. By the fifth change even Hector was starting to get annoyed with my indecision and was chewing my imitation Prada stilettos that I was too ashamed to admit I couldn't even walk round my bedroom in, let alone actually leave the flat. I gently encouraged Hector to continue his chewing by patting him gently on the head rather than launching into my usual bawling when he became too attached to an item of my high-fashion wardrobe. I phoned Chloe to beg her advice. Sadly she said the same as Fiona. It looked like it would have to be the orange dress.

"You know, Sorrel, this is only dinner. Don't panic – if you panic you'll look desperate and you know what you were always telling me about desperate women. Needy is not a good look."

"I know, I keep telling myself, but I don't seem to be listening."

"Well, just make yourself listen," Chloe said firmly.

Oh God, I didn't need a lecture. Right now I didn't want to be told firmly that Jake might not like me enough to propose on the first date even though technically it wasn't a date. I had more important things to worry about – like how to lose half a stone in an hour and fifteen minutes.

"Well, Chloe, you've been wonderful. Thank you for all your encouragement."

"I just don't want to see you getting hurt or disappointed, that's all."

"Thanks, Chloe! No really, cheers mate, here I am feeling like Horace the Heffalump asking for help to make me look less heffalumpy to go on a date with a man I have virtually worshipped for a whole two months and you already have the kettle on and the tissues out!"

"God, drama, drama! I was only pointing out the folly of building yourself up for a potential fall," Chloe reasoned.

"Now you sound like your bloody mother!"

Well, that shut her up.

"Chloe . . . ? Chloe . . . ? Are you still there?"

Silence.

"I'm sorry! I'm just totally wound up and you're not saying what I want to hear," I reasoned.

"Well, that's no reason to be downright insulting!" Chloe said, definitely huffy.

"Sorry," I said most humbly.

"If you really want my advice, and I suspect that you don't, I would wear the orange shift and be done with it. It's flattering and it always makes you look like you have a tan. Enough said."

I left Hector still chewing happily on my shoes and caught a taxi and arrived fifteen minutes late at the Red Jacket. Jake was leaning on the bar sipping a pint watching the door. He smiled as I walked in and my heart turned over. I reminded myself that it was a grateful 'saved from room service' smile.

He looked every inch the way I had remembered him – gut-wrenchingly gorgeous. As I walked towards him I had a smile fixed on my face and was trying to look unfazed but my legs were only just holding me up.

As my luck had it, my entrance was not as glamorous as I would have liked. I accidentally jolted a man's arm as I passed him and his pint went all over his shirt, and he dropped his cigarette on his girlfriend's foot and she happened to be wearing open-toed shoes and she shrieked and thumped him, spilling more of his pint. I skuttled past while their attention was diverted to the smouldering shoe.

When I reached the bar I clung to it for fear of falling over and looking like a prat. Not that I should have worried about that. Jake was already helpless with laughter.

"God, Ellie, can you not enter a room without everyone noticing? Though I am glad you could make it – I was wondering if I had the right pub."

"Oh yes, sorry, Hector was chewing my shoes and I had to um . . ." I could feel my cheeks getting hotter, and I knew I was turning an unattractive shade of crimson. And, oh fuck, I just realised that I had left my list of interesting conversation topics beside the sink in the bathroom.

"How about a gin and tonic?" Jake asked as he kissed my crimson burning cheek hello. He had dressed up for our dinner in a dark grey suit that screamed money, white shirt and a greeny-blue tie the same colour as his sea-green eyes. My cheeks burned more than ever as I took all this in. I should be wearing a slinky little number with spaghetti straps. Instead I was wearing an orange flag.

He was looking at me questioningly. "Gin and tonic?"

"Oh! Oh, that would be marvellous, thank you."

He turned to the bar and seemed to have the same knack as Chloe when ordering a drink – he immediately caught the barman's attention. I quickly fanned my face and wiped a couple of splatters of beer from the jostled pint-holder off my dress.

We found a table and sat down.

"So how have you been?" Jake asked.

"Oh just grand thanks," I replied. Oh no, stilted conversation hell.

"Good." He was looking amused again.

"We don't have long before dinner," I said, desperate to keep the conversation staggering on as inanely as possible.

"If you'd rather not go we don't have to," Jake shrugged.

Wow, a man so cool he would give up a highly coveted table in only the most desirable restaurant in town! But I wasn't about to. Nerves or no nerves I was going.

"No, really!" I said in some alarm. "I've been looking forward to it all day! Sorry about being late."

He smiled again as if he was enjoying my naive enthusiasm.

After a while I relaxed enough to begin to think up ways to get an invite back to his hotel room.

As I walked into Calamare, I knew why I had always wanted to visit. The tables and chairs were a very pale wood, the floor was a striking black granite. Stark prints adorned the walls. Minimalist was the word, very cool and understated, about as far removed from my flat as you could get. And I loved it.

The head waiter led us to our table and took our coats. This made me a bit nervous as my cellulite, which I was sure poking out from under my dress, was hidden by that coat and I felt very nervous as I partially exposed my thighs to the fashionable diners of Edinburgh.

All around us flowed the chatter of the other

customers; it was a nice atmosphere and I started to relax. Jake was the perfect dinner companion, not that I have had many. He seemed perfectly at home in the glamorous surroundings and didn't seem to be eyeing my cellulite. The restaurant was great, the food was delicious and even though I had immense trouble understanding the menu I ordered food that actually tasted how I imagined – perfect. I had a delicate little tart to start of goat's cheese and roasted peppers, then some glorious monkfish creation with giant prawns in a light and unfortunately (for breath reasons) garlic sauce. We laughed and chatted and got on very well, I dared to think.

I was beginning to think he was really enjoying himself, and while we talked my mind got to work on an imaginary post-meal conversation:

Jake to Ellie, "Would you like to come back to my hotel? It has a resident's bar open all night . . . or if you prefer I have a minibar in my room."

Ellie to Jake, smiling coyly, "Oh, your room, I think. I've always loved those cute miniature minibar bottles . . ."

I don't think so. He'd be anxious to get a night's sleep and, even if he did ask – say in a parallel universe – let's face it, I'm more your 'go puce-red and look at your feet' kind of girl.

We drank amazing wine. Normally I baulk at the thought of spending more than four pounds on a bottle of wine. But tonight it was perfect and I was not paying for it. I got quite pissed which I had promised myself I would not do. Being drunk with good friends is fine, funny and gives you all something to talk about the next day. Being drunk in front of the man you are desperately trying to impress is to potential romance what chips are to a diet – fatal.

In my case anyway.

I really had only myself to blame. Jake was being perfectly lovely, ordering more wine and laughing at my increasingly bad jokes. To the untrained eye he even looked like he was enjoying sitting with this loud, large orange woman. I had wanted Jake to try my dessert, blackberry and brandy ice-cream. I think, in the back of my sozzled mind, I was imitating trendy romantic heroines like Meg Ryan and the like, or maybe somebody from Friends. Waving away his protests that he was OK and didn't want to try any, I leant forward and poked the spoon at his lips, caught the spoon on his cheek and instead of spoon-feeding him with the food of lovers I managed to wipe it all over his face, missing his mouth completely. Jake sat there with a purple fragrant face, the ice cream dripping off his chin, smiling. I jolted back in my seat and in doing so managed to knock the very expensive bottle of wine onto the very expensive granite floor where it smashed into not so expensive pieces.

Everyone in the restaurant looked at our table.

I surveyed the scene: broken wine bottle, its contents everywhere, dream date with ice cream all over his face, appalled looks from other diners, waiters scurrying to the rescue. And I could feel that once again my face was clashing with my dress. Jake was looking at me. I could see his lips moving but I had no idea what he was saying.

Then I did an unforgivable thing.

Dawn Cairns

"Sorry, oh I'm so s-s-sorry!" I grabbed my bag and stumbled out of the most glamorous restaurant in Edinburgh leaving Jake looking like a stunned mullet to pay for the meal and deal with the debris I had left in my wake. I flung myself sobbing into the back of a nearby taxi. On the way home I realised I had left my coat in the restaurant, but it seemed like a fair trade-off.

I humiliate Jake publicly and he gets to keep my coat.

I paid the taxi driver with the five pound note I had accidentally mistaken for a tissue in my tearful haze. It was more than a little soggy but he took it anyway. He was probably afraid to object in case I started weeping again.

I pushed open the door of my flat and collapsed still sobbing into the nearest chair. There was a towel hanging over the back of it and I wiped my face with it. Hector cautiously padded his way towards me – if dogs could look concerned then he definitely did.

"Oh Hector!" I cried as I picked him up. "Your owner is a total and utter disaster!" I buried my face into his neck, and decided to bath him tomorrow.

"I just ruined a fantastic evening with a great guy who quite possibly could have liked me. Now he will never speak to me again, I'll probably get his dry cleaning bill on Monday, and Ben will laugh at me until the middle of next year – what am I saying, he'll laugh at me for the rest of my life! Oh God, why did I have to try and feed him? It was all going so well!" From that point onwards I started to rant a bit. Hector stoically took the tears in the neck without any complaint.

eps5
ftg

I had been sitting for what seemed like hours with Hector on my knee, telling him what an arse I had been, when the door-bell rang. Oh shit, not Jake, please not Jake! I had a vision of him sitting at the table while I sprinted out of the restaurant leaving him there to face any repercussions. I didn't think I could face any more humiliation in one evening. I looked out the window and saw Chloe's car outside, so I buzzed her in. She knocked on my door, I opened it and she came in with my coat over her arm.

"You left this behind, I believe?" She stopped, gaping at my tear-splotched face.

I gaped back, bewildered.

"Jake dropped it in just now," she said. "He thought you might have gone to bed – he said you were complaining of a headache. What happened? Did you have a row?"

"But how did he know where your flat is?" I snuffled at her through my blocked nose, amazed.

"He phoned me – he'd phoned Ben in London and got my number."

Oh God. Such lengths to avoid seeing me.

"Are you all right?" she asked."What happened? Was it awful?"

Her face was all concern. He hadn't told her. If she knew how I had behaved then she probably would have clobbered me over the head when she walked in the door.

"Really, Ellie, you look dreadful – are you ill? Can I get you some paracetamol?"

I must have still been drunk because I started sobbing again.

Chloe put her arms around me. "Was he a bastard to you?"

I tried to reply but all that came out was a series of violent deep breaths which should have said 'No no, he was wonderful, it was all my fault, oh God I hate this dress'. I tried again. "Oh Chloe, it was all my fault, he'll never want to see me again!"

"Why, what did you do? He told me you had a good time."

"He didn't mention anything about ice cream?"

"No, why?"

"Um . . . now don't be cross but . . ." I stopped.

"But what? Ellie, what did you do that has got you so upset?"

I proceeded to tell her the whole sorry tale. I was in fact brutally honest, and when I had finished I sat back and waited for the inevitable bollocking one fully deserves when one fucks up the first decent date one has had in over six months.

But Chloe only started to giggle. Apparently the idea of me leaving poor Jake covered in ice cream and surrounded by broken glass while I speedily made my exit was hilarious. She just kept saying, "Oh Ellie!" before dissolving into fits of giggles again

At first I got cross with her, and told her to shut up, but it just made her worse, so I ended up laughing about it too, though I really shouldn't have. When she had finished having hysterics she asked me to tell her again, and I did. She thought I should phone him.

"No! I really think I'll be the last person he'll want to see, or even hear from, ever again. Look at the lengths

he went to to avoid having to see me again! Phoning Ben
and you and all!"

"Oh, stop being so dramatic – he's a gentleman! He
didn't want to disturb you or embarrass you!"

Right enough I did find it rather odd that he hadn't
mentioned anything to Chloe. Well, he was probably still
cringing with embarrassment.

I couldn't quite believe that I had run out of the
restaurant and the very thought of it made me want to
curl up in shame. I asked her what he had been like
when he called round to her flat. She said that yes, he
had a funny mark on his shirt collar, and yes it was a
kind of blackberry colour.

"He said you had left the restaurant, which I found a
bit odd – I figured you'd had a quarrel or got sick – then
he said he realised you had left your coat behind, but
didn't think you were feeling very well so didn't want to
disturb you. What a bloody gentleman – and you treat
him like that! Is it any wonder you're single, you eejit!".

Don't you just love best friends, they really tell it how
it is. No feeling-sparing allowed.

Chapter Six

Chloe stayed the night to keep me company and the next day she tried to persuade me to phone and apologise to Jake, but to be honest I would rather have given up creme eggs than dial his number.

But she did have a point. I had been incredibly rude. Would a 'thank you/I'm deeply ashamed' letter do? Chloe thought better not. He'd be going back down to London today. I wondered if he would mention it to Ben. I was pretty sure he would – I mean it is the sort of thing you tell your best friend even if the topic of conversation is his sister.

Over the next couple of days I got a few telephone messages from Jake but I couldn't bear to call him back in case he was phoning to ask for half the dinner bill. But I rather thought not. Ben hadn't been on the phone laughing at me, no invoice from the dry cleaners had arrived – maybe just maybe, Jake hadn't told Ben and was just ringing to make me feel better. A born gentleman, as Chloe had said.

After the third day the phone stopped ringing.

About two weeks after it happened I was sitting on a pile of ironing in my living-room, trying to talk myself into dealing with some of it, when the door-bell rang.

Heck, that pizza was fast, I thought, as I buzzed the delivery guy in. It had only been ten minutes. In the gloom and doom mood which had persisted since the restaurant disaster I had decided on this rainy Friday evening to sit with Hector and watch loads of videos till my eyes hurt, as I was now officially a social leper.

But to my utter horror it was not the helmeted head of the delivery boy which appeared at the top of the stairs but Jake's. Oh shit, bugger, tits, and shit again.

"Hi Ellie," he said with a somewhat uncertain grin. "I hope you don't mind me just calling by – I know you weren't expecting me."

Well, how could I be expecting you? You live in London and you don't like me or at least you shouldn't. And you didn't tell me you were coming. I was wearing tracksuit bottoms covered in Terracotta One Coat from the time I had painted the living-room, my hair was greasy, I had spots, and I was not wearing a bra so my boobs were attractively pointing earthward. I could feel myself turning red.

"Oh no, not at all, please come in!" Why are you here? Why are you here?!

I ushered him into my living-room, which technically could be a fairly gorgeous room but, as I said, was currently serving as a second wardrobe. I had done quite a good paint job and despite Hector's best efforts my cream sofa was still relatively presentable or would have been if it hadn't been covered in ironing.

I cleared a small space and he sat on it. Then I sat on the ground facing him. "You're probably wondering what I'm doing up in Edinburgh again?" he said a bit awkwardly.

I wasn't making this easy for him. I decided to help him out. I owed him that.

I decided to be highly eloquent and repentant. "Well yes . . . and why you're visiting me. What I did to you last week can warrant the death penalty in some countries."

He promptly burst out laughing.

Now I was completely bewildered and embarrassed. Jake was supposed to go back down to London and tell everyone that Ben's sister was a practising alcoholic with quick getaways a speciality. That's what blokes do, not turn up a week later and want to laugh about it. I decided that he must be mentally unstable and probably six pints of lager and compulsory viewing of two Grandstand back to back would sort him out.

"Listen, Ellie," he said. "Forget about that. In fact, it was kind of funny."

This creature before me had one sick sense of humour. What had I let into my flat? Before I had time to ring Rentokil, he was off again.

"How about you come out for a drink – Diet Coke if you prefer? Or we could stay here if that suits you better? I really need to talk to you."

Oh, wow. I reminded myself that he was hardly about to propose.

I surveyed the scene. Devastation was the word that came to mind, and with all the determination of a dieter reaching for a bar of chocolate I got to my feet, picked up my jacket and followed the man of my dreams out the front door of my flat. This time I would not under any circumstances humiliate myself or him. Once, Jake might think me slightly eccentric; twice and he'd be ringing the psychiatric ward of the Royal Infirmary.

He took me to a little restaurant in Leith, the Docklands area of Edinburgh, after he had convinced me that I was looking thin (flattery really will get you everywhere). We ordered sea bass and mineral water and chatted while we waited for our drinks to arrive. I surprised myself by not sitting with a bright red face. I managed to chat like a grown-up and keep giggling to a minimum. After the drinks arrived Jake leant across the table and fixed his green eyes on me, his expression serious.

My heart gave a little skip and a thud.

"I've something I must tell you," he said.

My heart gave another sickening leap and my breath caught in my throat.

I stared at him – looking like a goldfish, I'm sure – or a sea bass.

"But you must solemnly promise not to tell your family."

Oh, not the proposal then.

I laughed so he wouldn't see disappointment plastered across my face. OK, OK, despite my leaping heart I knew he wasn't going to propose – I'm not that mad – but I had thought he might have been about to say he liked me.

"Sure," I said, laughing. "Whatever you want – what is it, are you a spy?"

Jake's expression did not break into the grin I had intended, and I stopped laughing. "OK, I'm sorry, what the hell is the matter?"

"It's about Ben."

My heart started its jolting again. "Oh God, what's happened? Is he alright? Jake what is it?"

My voice was rising and I realised that the rest of the diners were looking over to see who the soprano drama-queen in the corner was, but I really wasn't interested in what other people thought of me right now. My brother could be seriously injured in an accident, or worse, have gone ahead and married Sonia on a Caribbean island and not told any of us.

Jake had started to smile.

"Sorry, Ellie – I didn't mean to give you a fright. It's OK, nothing's happened to him. But he's done something rather out of character and I'm supposed to keep it a secret from the family till he rings your parents about it – maybe even tonight, in fact."

"Out of character and secretive? What's he done?" I was trying to keep panic out of my voice – oh Ben, what have you done?

"Well, it's all for a good cause really," Jake said, grinning, teasing me now.

"Will you stop having a bloody laugh and tell me what my fecking brother is up to!" I shrieked.

That sobered him. And all the other diners.

"He's gone to Nicaragua to build hospitals for the Red Cross, for a year, and he's persuaded Sonia to go with him."

My jaw dropped open. Ben is where? Building what? Ben hates hospitals, they make him feel sick. Persuaded

who to go with him? Sonia? How could she leave her
hairdresser and her soya milk behind? I was in total
shock, my brother the stockbroker, the sibling with the
largest disposable income, wearer of Saville Row suits,
diner in fine restaurants, partner to the most materialistic
bitch I had ever met, drinker of much lager and vino
collapso – what the feck was he doing in South America,
working for the Red Cross, had the ghost of Christmas
past come to visit him in the night?

"Why hasn't he told Mum and Dad? Surely he's not
gone already? What's he done with his flat in London?"

"No, he wanted to tell them once he got there – he
left three nights ago – and he's letting the flat in London
to a professional couple for twelve months."

"How long have you known?"

"He's been talking about it for a few months, but it
took a while for him to persuade Sonia. She wasn't that
keen to start off with."

"Yes, I can bloody imagine. For once I can see her
point of view. 'Darling, let's pack and head off to South
America, avoid kidnap by the mountain guerrillas and
spend twelve months living in a mud hut, in the arse-end
of hell, while we build hospitals for the underprivileged.
Nope, I don't see her going for it. How the hell did he
manage to talk her into it?" I was still in shock, I had no
idea that my brother had a social conscience. "I can't
imagine Sonia having to leave her woefully bad music
collection behind, and what about all those Chanel suits
she insists on wearing, are you telling me that she's left
them behind to wear shorts and a pair of hiking boots –
Jake, I think you must be taking the piss."

Jake had been listening to all of this with the usual expression of amusement I seemed to bring out in him but at this point he frowned and I thought he looked slightly annoyed. "Seriously," he said. "Ben reckons that they've had their priorities all wrong and it's time to give something back. Initially he wanted to drive Aid trucks to Eastern Europe but once he talked Sonia into going they wanted to do something they could do together. Sonia thinks it's a great opportunity to learn Spanish. Ben told her that it would look great on her CV – she could learn another language and learn a bit about charity work and what they do for all sorts of communities in the world."

"Jeez, Jake, you sound like you'll be on the next plane behind them!"

"Well, I have to say I totally admire them for going, even if Sonia has no idea what she has let herself in for. I think Ben omitted to tell her that they'll be living two hours from the nearest town and have no running water let alone electricity to plug in her hairdryer." He paused and gazed steadily at me. "I know what you think of her, but underneath it she really is a great girl, and she really does love your brother – he's lucky to have her."

All of a sudden the world turned upside-down. My brother was off helping the Red Cross on the other side of the world with his awful girlfriend who hated me, and had never even bought a single copy of the Big Issue; then the bloke I've been fantasising about for the last two months turns round and tells me I'm a bad judge of character and that the horrible girlfriend is really Mother Theresa's younger and much more attractive sister.

Sudden loss of appetite, sudden desire to go home, hug Hector and smoke large amounts of cigarettes until my throat hurt.

"Sorrel, are you OK?" Jake looked concerned.

I excused myself and went to the loo. When I looked in the mirror I saw a very pale face staring back. Why was I so shocked? I mean Ben was doing something good, so what was wrong with his slightly unorthodox approach? Then I realised that it was Sonia. She really did have her claws into my brother – sorry, gratuitously bitchy – she really loved my brother, and it looked like she was prepared to travel the globe to be with him. I should be pleased for them, they must be really happy, but all I wanted to do was run back into the restaurant and slap Jake in his smug pus and tell him what he could do with his sea bass and Saint Sonia routine. What annoyed me even more was that Jake wasn't even being smug – he meant it genuinely and that could mean only one thing: I was a bad judge of character and there was a slim possibility that Sonia had become a really nice person, even though she thought she was only going to Nicaragua to learn to speak fluent Spanish. Perhaps she really did want to help people – God, I hate it when people change the goal posts without anyone letting me know.

When I got back to the table the waitress was serving our sea bass, my appetite had somewhat diminished, but as I sat back down I resolved not to make a scene and embarrass Jake again. He was looking at me nervously, obviously waiting for me to do something erratic or behave in some odd fashion. I picked up my knife and fork and calmly began to cut into the fish on my plate, popped a forkful into my mouth and chewed calmly trying to smile.

"So how long will you be in Edinburgh this time?" I was determined to appear cool and in control even if it meant changing the subject, though I was dying to know why he was telling me before Ben had a chance to tell Mum and Dad.

"Well, I came up tonight to see you really, so I suppose I'll head back down south tomorrow."

"Oh . . . right, just to see me?"

"Well, Ben suggested I should – he thought it would be a good idea if you were prepared for the crisis before your parents find out – so you can help your mum deal with the shock, he said." He paused. "And I really wanted to see you again, just to let you know that the other night was OK and that you should forget about it. Oh yeah and to say that if you would like to come down to London for a weekend sometime soon you can stay with me – as you can't stay in Ben's any more." He grinned and added, "And it seems unfair if I have to do all the travelling."

"Why would you have to do any travelling? You only came up to tell me my brother has made a sharp exit from the country. Surely that's only a one-visit message, or do you intend to inundate me with interesting news on a weekly basis?" God, I sounded edgy. Bitchy even.

"Very funny. I, for some strange reason, thought that you might like to see more of me."

For the second time in the evening the world turned topsy-turvey. Jake, lover to attractive, statuesque and probably annoyingly talented women appeared to be asking me down to his place. FUCK. This was normally the point where I woke up with Hector's dog breath in my face. Nope, I'm still here, could it be true? Careful, Ellie, don't jump to conclusions, maybe he's just being nice again.

"So when exactly do you want me to come down to London?" I said, busying myself with my sea bass, playing it cool.

"Well, today is Friday so tomorrow is technically the weekend, so how about then?"

"What tomorrow? This tomorrow? I mean, this week? What about Hector?" I sounded flustered rather than cool.

"Hector can stay with Chloe or your friend from work."

"Fiona? Well, I'd need to ask her. Look, this is silly, why don't we leave it till next week? I can get away from work early, take the train down and meet you in time for a drink after work. By the time we get down tomorrow most of Saturday will have been spent on the train. I also have the uncanny knack of selecting a seat near the baby." Good. That sounded casual.

"Well, we'll just have to fly then, or travel first class on the sleeper tonight."

"Whoa, this is all moving a tad too fast for me!" I am unused to men actually wanting to be with me without excessive use of alcohol. Jake appeared to be only drinking mineral water, or was that a triple gin? If he wasn't drunk, he just had to be pulling my leg. "Let's just leave it for a couple of weeks and see how we go?" Did that come out right?

Jake didn't appear to be grinning quite so much now. Um . . . had I just shot myself in the foot? Could he possibly have meant it?

"OK, whatever you want. I mean, if you don't like me, don't feel you have to pretend – to save my feelings." And suddenly the bastard was grinning his head off again.

Oh God, this could only mean one thing: he knew how much I fancied him and he was making fun of me, big-brother fashion. Picked that up from Ben, I supposed.

As we proceeded with the meal my mind continued to race. What the hell had that conversation been all about? The only thing I was sure of was that I had blundered about and made an eejit of myself again.

Jake paid the bill while I hailed a taxi (this time facing the right direction). I suddenly wondered where he would be sleeping tonight. Should I ask him back to my flat? There was no room on the sofa – were my sheets clean? Oh God, I hadn't done this for so long, asked anyone back to my flat that is, not washed my sheets. If I got him back there under the pretext of offering him the sofa, who knows what would happen? My heart started heaving about again.

When he joined me in the taxi I asked him,

"Um . . . Jake, where are you staying tonight?"

"Well, I left my stuff round at Chloe and David's – they said I could crash on their sofa."

"Oh sure, yeah, of course." Damn, shit, bugger. "You'll be going back to London tomorrow then?"

"Yup, I think I probably will. Since I can't persuade you to come with me tonight and I've got some stuff that needs taking care of, I'd better get back. I'm taking my mum out for dinner tomorrow night."

"You don't strike me as someone who takes his mum out for dinner on a Saturday night – I would have put you in the turn-up-late-for-Sunday-lunch-with-a-large-bag-of-washing category."

"Well, as I've already told you this evening, you aren't that great a judge of character. I have, in fact, my own washing machine and tumble dryer and am proficient in working both. My mother is a dreadful cook and that is why I am more commonly found in the parental home cooking them both Sunday lunch. Dad is away on business this weekend, so I told Mum I would take her out to save her having to defrost anything from Marks & Spencer."

"Aha, a nineties man, I was wondering when I would meet one of those! I expect London is full of them since Cosmopolitan keeps writing about them and it would appear that there are none in Edinburgh, Belfast or Dublin – well, none that I have come across anyway."

"You can be a bit of a cynical cow sometimes, you know, madam. There are thousands of blokes who can take care of themselves in all areas of domesticity, in all areas of the country. You clearly go for the wrong type of bloke, which would explain your lack of interest in me."

At this point he slung his arm around my shoulders and pulled me close.

"If you lived in Edinburgh," I gabbled on pretending not to notice the arm and the closeness, "I think they would have you in an exhibition. Men like you don't really exist, you are a myth that some evil magazine editor thought up to upset every woman in the country and to lead to national dissatisfaction in the male species."

His face was very close. "Any more of that and I will have to insist that you come down to London and attend a dinner party where the male guests cook. Look at your brother, for God's sake. He's a superb cook – Sonia can't even heat a tin of beans."

"She wouldn't eat beans, you fool, she would eat tofu, and you don't need to heat that, just throw a few Rocket leaves and balsamic vinegar over it."

"I think you're missing the point. The point is that lots of men are not as useless as women like to believe them to be. You're just slow on picking that up."

What a strange conversation to be having with my brother's best friend, with his arm wrapped around me, while trying to think up ways to tempt him back to my tip of a flat – which he could probably tidy in five minutes. I decided to cut my losses and pretend to agree with Jake that nineties men may in fact exist, though of course my own personal experience of this was very limited.

"Well, in that case I'd better come down to London to put your claim to the test."

"Aha! I see you've fallen into my trap!" His eyes glinted close to mine. "You shall come down next weekend and I shall cook for you and take you out to see a show, basically dazzle you with my charms and then take advantage of you!"

God, that sounded good. And it sounds almost as if he means it. It's a difficult one, don't be too keen, but don't be too cold and totally put him off.

"Um . . . next weekend doesn't suit. Chloe and I are going for dress fittings – how about the following weekend?"

"I'm in Hong Kong the following weekend – we're giving the Hong Kong Bank a presentation. I'll be away for two weeks – can't you change your appointment?"

"I had better not. Margo doesn't even want to invite me to the bloody wedding let alone be a bridesmaid. I don't want to give her any opportunity to chuck me off the top table!"

"Surely Chloe could put her foot down?"

"You have not had the pleasure of meeting Mrs Williams, have you? Simple things like telling her it is her daughter's day and she can ask who she likes are just impossible, I'm afraid. She's the UN's secret weapon – if Iraq steps out of line, they send her over to scare everybody back into submission."

Somewhere along this conversation he had taken his arm away.

"Well, I don't want you to lose any teeth over this, so maybe it would be safer to postpone the visit till I come back from Hong Kong?"

"Yes, I think that would be better. You never know, by then you may have gone off the idea and never want to see me again."

"Oh I doubt that," and he smiled in a kind of sad way, or I thought that could just be me reading too much into smiles again.

The taxi dropped me home first and it took all my will-power not to drag Jake out of the taxi after me. If I did that he might end up bonking me – but it would all end after one bonk.

I paused before stepping out. "Will you ring me sometime this week, just for a chat?" I asked, hoping I was being encouraging but not too clingy.

"Sure I'll ring you! You can tell me what to pack for my trip."

"But I've never been to Hong Kong – I don't know what you'd wear."

"Somehow, Ellie, I think you would get it just right."

Oh yeah? Funny.

"Good night," he said. "I'll see you soon, but I will remember to phone and don't worry about Ben and Sonia – they'll be fine."

He leant towards me and kissed me on the lips but he didn't try to stick his tongue down my throat, leaving me wondering if that was a good thing or bad?

As the taxi pulled away he turned round and waved out of the back window. He waved until the taxi had turned the corner and was out of sight. I was left on the pavement, waving back at an empty street. I stood there until the sound of the taxi's engine faded away and then I shouted at myself for being so bloody stupid.

"For God's sake, Sorrell bloody Clarke! You are a liberated women and you can invite anyone you like back to your flat to do whatever you want, and no one will tell you off! Why did you just send the only good thing in your life in the past few months away in the back of a taxi never to be seen again, well not for the best part of a month anyway?"

I appeared to be making a habit of this. I toyed with

the idea of going round to Chloe's and apologising to him before ripping his clothes off, but I chickened out in case he was secretly relieved that I hadn't asked him in. Well, there is only so long you can talk to yourself on the street before people passing by start to stare at you and you start feeling cold, so I turned, and went inside my building.

Later, as I was making myself some hot chocolate, the phone rang. When I picked it up a barrage of insults assaulted my ears.

"You stupid arse, why is Jake sitting in my front room? Are you recovering from a frontal lobotomy you forgot to tell anyone about? Are you quite insane?"

Chloe was clearly unimpressed with my judgement too.

"Is he OK?" I asked.

"Of course he's OK, but I was just surprised to see him again tonight, I thought you fancied his pants?"

"I do," I said and my voice went up an octave – a very unattractive personality trait, squeaky voice when trying to talk my way out of embarassing situations. "I don't know why I did it, I wasn't sure what he wanted, I wanted to wait, I didn't want him to think I was easy – "

"Wait? Wait any longer and he'll have gone off with someone else. Sorrell, sometimes I really don't understand you."

"Did he tell you about Ben and Sonia?"

"Yes, how are you about that?"

"Och fine I suppose, what reason would I have to be annoyed? Only that the stupid bollocks didn't tell anyone, it came as a bit of a surprise."

"Well, yes, that and the fact he talked Sonia into going!"

"Apparently I have misjudged her for all these years. According to Jake she is a saint. God, men, they are so gullible!"

"I still can't believe you sent the sex god back to my house – you really are quite mad."

This conversation serving no purpose other than to reinforce the stupidity of my actions, I excused myself after promising Chloe I would go and bang my head off the nearest wall. After bruising my forehead, and pouring away the cold hot chocolate, I climbed into bed and was joined by Hector who, realising that now was not the time to chew my Winnie the Pooh's ears, curled up at the end of the bed and looked at me as he rested his chin on his paws.

I glared at him. "No doubt if you could speak you would hit me with a verbal assault too, so don't even begin with those big puppy eyes."

I lay back on the pillows and tried to think about something other than Jake and failed miserably. I was just picking up my copy of Wild Swans which I was valiantly trying to dig my way through (saved for occasions such as being in bed by 9.30 pm) when the phone rang again.

"Chloe, I've already told you I'm sorry – what do you want me to do?" I shouted at her before she could berate me again. "Come round to your flat in my jammies and apologise to him?"

"This isn't Chloe." An instantly recognisable man's voice. Ah no, not now! I can't be bothered!

"Hi Mark, how are you?"

Mark was my ex-boyfriend, ex of a year before, and

he still rang me up monthly to see if I had got over him. Since I finished with him because I had had enough, it seemed a simple enough concept that I should be fine, which I was. Mark, however, could not believe me.

"Hi honey, I was just ringing to see how you are – not too depressed, I hope?"

"Depressed about what?" Surely he couldn't know about Jake too?

"Well, I haven't phoned in a few weeks – I hope you weren't too lonely."

"No, actually, I've been fine, great in fact. The job is going really well, oh and I have met someone nice."

"Well, I think it's good for you to have friends."

"No, Mark, I've met a man, a new boyfriend." Time to lay on the lies, a touch of embellishment never hurt anyone. "He is gorgeous, a stockbroker, lives in London – I'm going down to see him next weekend."

There was a pause. Then,

"That's great, Sorrel, I think you're finally making progress."

What a patronising bastard! I was coming to the conclusion that Mark was totally off his head.

"Mark, I've been fine for ages. I really don't think you should call me anymore – "

"Ellie, I don't think you're ready yet – you'd be hurt if I just stopped calling. I think it would be too upsetting."

This was definitely getting a wee bit too creepy for me. Why did he insist on being part of my life? I was seriously beginning to dislike the direction this phone call was taking.

"Listen, Mark, I've got to go. I have people round and it's rude to be on the phone for too long."

"But I saw him leave you outside your flat. There isn't anyone there really now, is there?"

My skin was suddenly crawling, Mark didn't live anywhere near me, at least he didn't use to. Oh Jesus, had he been following me? I felt sick and a bit scared.

"OK, I've not got anyone round, but I have stuff to do, Hector needs feeding, I really must get on, thanks for calling, byeee." I hung up the phone. I sat staring at it, willing it not to ring again. I was worried that he would call me straight back. Nothing, silence. I breathed a sigh of relief and wriggled down the bed and pulled the duvet up round my ears.

Two minutes later I remembered that I hadn't treble-locked my front door, and visions of Mark walking into my bedroom at two in the morning made me leave the cosy duvet cave I had constructed to make sure I had the door deadbolted. After I had locked the door I went round checking to make sure all the windows were shut, and pulled all the curtains which is something I would never normally do but I got this weird feeling that Mark hadn't called me from his flat, more like a pay phone round the corner. I was fairly sure he hadn't taken up cat burglary as my flat is on the second floor but I was taking no chances.

"Hector, I don't want you taking treats from any strange men. I know you might recognise Mark but believe me he is becoming increasingly strange. I wouldn't be surprised if he tried to give you Bonios laced with arsenic."

I climbed back into bed and tried to bury down into my duvet cave which had collapsed but was still all lovely and warm. Hector curled up at my feet and almost instantly started to snore.

On impulse I picked up the phone and dialled 1471 and listened to the mechanical voice tell me that the caller had withheld their number, so wherever Mark was he didn't want me to be able to phone him back. *"Bugger!* Probably drunk or something, stupid arse that he is, with all his amateur psychology that really drove me nuts. He used to tell me that he would analyse our conversations when he was alone, I should have realised that he was a total fruit cake and run a mile." I was speaking to no one in particular and Hector was gently snoring on the end of the bed, so I turned off the light and shut my eyes tight, and thought about Ben and Sonia and hoped they got to Bogota, or whatever the capital of Nicaragua was, OK.

When sleep appeared to be evading me I found myself unwillingly thinking about Mark again. He had always had disturbing leanings towards healthiness – something I always found really irritating. Not that someone shouldn't be healthy, you understand, but when you are standing with your favourite packet of cheese and onion Tayto crisps (not to be confused with ordinary ones) you can do without disapproving glances and a comment along the lines of "Sorrel, think what you are putting into your body, preservatives, artificial flavouring and soooo much fat, sweetheart you would be so much better off with an apple". That sort of comment served only to send me running to the nearest corner shop for a litre of

Irn Bru to drink in front of him – what the Barr family didn't know about artificial flavouring and colouring I promise you is not worth knowing. Self-righteous bastard! Looking back I cannot quite remember why I went out with Mark. He annoyed me for a large proportion of the time we spent together, but he really was a great shag – sadly, once I was so shallow that this attribute made up for the fact he was a prick of gargantuan proportions. Even after we split up, when I thought about the lovely things he used to do to me in bed I got a shiver down my spine, though I loathed myself for it. I blame *Marie Claire* for raising women's expectations; nowhere do they say "Of course if the man is great in bed and pushes all the right buttons, then he is likely to be a total wanker and you will hate yourself for fancying him". Thankfully the combination of him spending a summer in an Israeli kibbutz and Louisa and Emma giving me a vibrator for my birthday meant that when he returned shaven-headed, tanned but full of The Good Life kind of ideas – you know, raise your own chickens and grow beans in central Edinburgh – I had no difficulty in telling him to fuck off.

Unfortunately Mark was currently demonstrating the other male trait that *Marie Claire* neglects to warn us of: the firm belief that 'no' means 'yes', and 'stop' means 'harder'.

Chapter Seven

In the morning my eyelids felt like someone had sellotaped them together. I dragged myself out of bed and into the shower. Feeling marginally better, I got dressed, fed Hector and ran out the door to catch the bus. As I got onto the bus I felt an odd sensation of being watched; feeling that this was perhaps my natural sense of drama kicking in again I paid the bus driver and climbed up the stairs to sit on the top deck.

"I notice that you don't wear aftershave for me anymore – I suppose she chose it for you?"

"Darling, I am not having an affair! Just because I buy myself a new aftershave does not mean that I have found some fancy woman, for God's sake!"

The woman in front of me had her arms crossed and was looking very angry and very unconvinced. Her husband (presumably) was desperately trying to convince her he loved her – God, I loved the bus to work, so many interesting things happening to other people.

"Leslie, in all the years I have known you I don't think I ever recall you going into Boots to buy yourself cologne – you don't even buy your own razors – and now you try to tell me this is all for my benefit! I hardly think so, bastard!" she really hissed the 'bastard' part.

Leslie now appeared close to tears. "Sandra, I would never cheat on you! I bought the stuff after reading one of your magazine articles on relationships – it said that, if couples stop making an effort round each other, familiarity breeds contempt and all that. Well, I thought I'd start making an effort again – that's is why I bought you the flowers on Saturday, not because I wanted to watch the football without pissing you off! I want to rekindle the flame of passion for us!"

I could hardly believe my ears. Could this be a fifty-something nineties man I was hearing?

There was a long pause while she gazed tearfully at him. He gazed back, eyes swimming. Then she said slowly: "So that's why you tried to take me out for dinner on Saturday night?"

"Yes, sweetheart, I thought we could try doing more things together – you know, like dinner, the cinema, that kind of thing."

The lady then burst into tears, the couple hugged and kissed, and I missed my stop.

"Oh fuck!" I ran down the stairs, leaving other people's dramas behind and tried to get off the bus as it was still moving.

"Damn, shit," I muttered as I attempted to sprint down the street, only managing a rather crap jog. I was going to be late for work, and I was supposed to be giving an

impromptu talk on TV researching. Fiona was doing it with me. Please, God, may she have done some preparation!

I burst through the doors and ran to our office. Fiona looked up at me as I collapsed wheezing into my chair, red and sweating.

"Big night last night?"

"No – missed – stop – on – bus." I was fighting to get air into my lungs. Jesus, I must start going to the gym.

"Did you fall asleep after a heavy night?"

"No, I had an OK evening," I gasped. "Discovered my brother has gone to South America with his bitch girlfriend who I have now been assured is actually quite nice, I sent Jake home, and I spent the rest of the evening having to fob off Chloe and bloody Mark on the phone."

"So, all in all, fairly eventful then?"

"Yes and I still haven't spoken to Mum or Dad so I don't know how they have taken it, about Ben I mean."

"What are they doing in South America? Why was Jake in your flat? Who is Mark? Is he that weirdie ex-boyfriend of yours? I need some information here."

"Building hospitals with the Red Cross, he took me out for dinner and I think Mark is turning into my own personal stalker – just in case I felt like my life was boring. Shit, I really need to phone Mum, I didn't even listen to my answer machine last night, I wonder how she is . . ."

I leant over the desk, picked up the phone and dialled home. Mum picked it up on the first ring – she must have been sitting on the bloody thing.

"Hi Mum, how are you?"

Fiona was mouthing "Stalker?" to me, I ignored her.

"Darling, it would appear that your brother has packed in his super job, let his super apartment and headed off to Nigeria to build hospitals with that spoilt bitch of a girlfriend of his. What did we do wrong, I thought we were good parents, why has he done this to us?"

"It's Nicaragua he has gone to, Mum." I could visualise her at the end of the phone with her head in her hands. "Mum, he's gone to do something useful, to help people, it's just a bit out of character that's all. Don't get upset, I'm sure you could go over to visit if you wanted to, but I'm not sure if they'll have running water. What exactly did Ben say to you when he phoned?"

"Well, he told us to sit down – your father didn't, so when Ben told us where he was your father fell down. Ben said that it was something he had really wanted to do for a while and living in London was turning him into a money-making machine. Mind you, I don't know what is so wrong with that, but anyhow he decided to give his head some peace and go and do some charity work with Sonia, whom I have to say and I know it's not very nice but I wouldn't have thought it would really have been her thing – she was always so, well . . . glamorous." Mum trying to be tactful.

"What you really want to say is that she is a complete bitch and you can't believe that she would actually pack in her good job, her oversize wardrobe and her lunches with her Sloany pals to trot after your son to build hospitals in a deprived country she has probably never heard of, am I right?"

"Well, darling, that's maybe a bit strong, but yes that

is the general gist of it. Anyway when your father got over the first shock he laughed and thought Ben was great. I have to say I know it's for a good cause – it's just I would have expected you or Lucy to do that sort of thing. But if it makes him happy then your father and I are happy too. Do you think he got all his injections before he left?"

"Mum I'm sure the Red Cross made him, or at least Sonia would have. Stop worrying – he's twenty-seven, he'll be grand, it really will do him the world of good. Then when he comes home he can build you that conservatory you've been after for so long."

There was a pause on the other end of the phone,

"Oh yes, I suppose he could . . . do you think they will understand him over there?"

"Yes, Mum, I'm sure the Red Cross speak English and anyway he and Sonia are going to learn Spanish – so no worries."

"I know you're right. They'll be fine. How are you?"

"I'm really good, Mum." I was pleasantly surprised at how well she was taking it all. "I'm about to give a presentation with Fiona to some undergraduates who are interested in getting into television researching, God knows why, but there we are. I had dinner with Jake last night, he was in good form. He's going off to Hong Kong for a few weeks with his job so it looks like I'm the only person not going anywhere! How is Lucy? I've not heard from her in ages – has she a new man?"

"How did you guess? She phoned last week, which was the last time that I spoke to her. She has taken up acting, apparently after watching a play with some man

Alan or something. Anyway she found him irresistible – now she's taking drama classes so that she can talk intelligently to him about his work. I think she goes too far sometimes."

"Mum, if he isn't highly unavailable or doesn't have an enticing, highly paid job she just isn't interested, you know Lucy. She sits at home in her flat with her flea-ridden moggie plotting how to get close to the elusive man, that's the thrill for her. Once they fall for her she runs several miles, before targeting the next poor absailing submarine captain or whatever. Lucy's love life is a constant source of amazement, so complicated no one can understand it, least of all Lucy herself. God, Mum, remember the time she fell for your man, you know . . . what did he do? He was a fruit-taster for Marks and Spencer – so Lucy went out and bought so much fruit she ended up on the loo for most of the week and actually missed her date."

"Oh God, yes, he was so annoyed. He thought she had stood him up and he wouldn't speak to her again – oh, that was funny, though Lucy had stomach pains for a while. She has never felt the same way about a Satsuma since!"

Mum had started to giggle, remembering Lucy's disastrous dates. Ever since she had been little she had tried to please the boys she liked and ignored the others as if they didn't exist. It was all or nothing for my sister – unfortunately, to date it seemed to be more 'nothing' than 'all'. Once she had them she didn't want to keep them – she had worked so hard that the reality was not as exciting as the intrigue. Quite how a fruit-taster for a supermarket could be exciting I was not exactly sure – Lucy said he travelled a lot.

By the end of our conversation Mum seemed to have got over her upset about Ben's disappearing act and she was laughing when Dad came home.

"Hi, Topper!" Dad had always called me 'Topper' since I was little and I still wanted to cause him grievous bodily harm every time he said it.

"Hi Dad, and less of the bloody 'Topper', OK?"

"I hear your brother has taken himself and that charming girlfriend of his off to do some good on the other side of the world – I mean, what some people will do for a tan." He was chuckling to himself as he passed the receiver back to Mum.

"Darling, I must go, it's our wine-tasting class tonight, and your father is insisting we take a taxi."

"Mum, it's only 9.30 in the morning. What time is the class?"

"Well, it's not till later on, but I have loads to do. Lucy still doesn't know about Ben so I must ring her. Incidentally, how did you know? Ben didn't phone you?"

"No, um . . . Jake told me at dinner last night."

"Oh I see." There was a pause. "Was he up on business?"

"I expect so – listen, Mum, I must go. I have that talk to give with Fiona in ten minutes and we haven't written any of it yet!"

"OK, change the subject, but I shall ring you later, and if you won't tell I'll try Chloe."

"You are an evil woman, Mrs Clarke, but I do love you – chat later, byeeee."

I put down the phone and turned to find Fiona surveying me.

"So I understand that Ben and the lovely Sonia have gone to Nicaragua to build hospitals for the Red Cross – well, that's no surprise."

Sometimes Fiona said the most ridiculous things.

"Fiona, that is probably the most suprising thing that Ben has ever done in his entire life – what the buggery are you talking about?"

"Ah come on, Sorrel, are you trying to tell me that you hadn't even suspected?"

"Fiona, I have no idea what the hell you are talking about and I don't have time to either, we have to think about this bloody talk – what are we going to tell them? You'll earn feck all until you decide to do the decent thing and move into advertising or marketing? How many are we expecting?"

"Around twenty, I think."

"Twenty! That's a lot – are you sure?"

"Pretty positive. Avril was just in here before you left and she had the numbers confirmed yesterday." Avril was the boss's secretary, so efficient it was frightening – well, it was for me.

"God, I wish she had mentioned it – then I could have phoned in sick today."

"And I would have kicked your arse from here to Inverness – you are a cheeky wee hen sometimes, you know that?"

"Fiona, less of the hen, I like it about as much as 'Topper'."

"S'cuse me, what?"

"Yeah, well – one of my dad's favourite nicknames but I don't have the time or the inclination to tell you about it now".

Just then Avril arrived to see how we were getting on – she really is shit scary. "Girls, Mr McWhin asked me to see how you were – all set? Do you need a projector or a slide machine?"

Fiona and I glanced nervously at each other. We didn't even have cue cards – not what you would call the greatest recruitment officers of the century.

"Och Avril, we're great – we don't want to scare them so we thought we would keep it informal, just keep it fairly short and to the point, I'm sure Mr McWhin would agree." Fiona knew no fear.

Avril looked seriously unimpressed. This was a woman who couldn't talk to her kids without a selection of pie-charts and graphs for back-up. God only knew what the conversation was 'round the dinner table – that was probably why she was so thin – she never picked up her fork as she was too busy pointing out the increases in the family expenditure for 1998 compared to that of 1997.

"Well, if you girls think you can handle it I shall not get involved. I shall let Mr McWhin know that you are all set."

She paused at the door of our office and sniffed her disapproval. As Fiona and I couldn't come up with any decent ideas for the talk – well, none in the next five minutes – we decided pure bullshit was the only way forward. We couldn't figure out why anyone (including ourselves) would like to spend their days being lorded over by presenters flouncing around in sweaters knitted by the viewers that would make Gyles Branrith blush.

As it turned out I don't think anything would have impressed our would-be media moguls. The front row of the students was made up of those terribly earnest and enthusiastic types that barely allowed you to get a sentence out before they bombarded you with questions. The rest were rather uninspired, looking like they had spent too long sniffing UHU – spotty youths, unwashed and uninterested, and not a bottle of Biactol between them, probably just killing time till the pubs opened at eleven thirty and they could go for their cheap pints – oh, those were the days. However, one of the girls in the front was taking copious notes, which was worrying as Fiona and I were talking complete shite and I was worried she might take us seriously. She wanted to know the relevant courses that would ensure her smooth entrance into the world of TV. We bluffed and waffled our way over that one. She didn't have to worry. I could see her working for the BBC as some war correspondent, a freckly Kate Adie type, very ambitious – she would overtake me within one year of graduating. For every question we managed to field and lob back to her, she came up with another one. Now she was asking us if we thought that the future of television was digital. How the hell should I know, was my first response. I looked to Fiona for help.

Fiona pointed at her watch like she was using sign language.

"Time up," I interpreted.

"Well, I thought that went quite well," Fiona said as the last of the great unwashed left the building.

"Hmmm."

"What do you fancy for lunch then?

"It's only eleven thirty, Fiona – have you got worms? Actually, I could murder a bacon roll – let's go get one."

Fiona winked at the canteen manager as she paid for our rolls. She was still trying to get discount but didn't appear to be getting very far.

"God loves a trier," I told her as we sat down.

"Ah fuck off – now what about your brother?"

"He has decided to save the world and has taken Sonia with him. Good luck, that's what I say."

"And the ex-boyfriend/stalker, when did he rear his ugly head?"

"Mark? He's got it into his head that I can't live without him. He's just a bit of a sad weirdo. I think I really messed up with Jake though. I have a feeling he came up to Edinburgh especially to tell me about Ben and Sonia before I heard it from my hysterical mother. He took me out to dinner and we were getting on really well after I had gotten over the news – well, I behaved like shit first – and then I let him go off in the taxi without inviting him back up to the flat."

"Oh, was he not that keen?" Well, that's what I think she said as she had half a bacon roll shoved in her gob at the time.

"Well, I think he was, but he didn't push so I chickened out. I feel like a bit of a berk really, I don't think he'll ring me again." I picked the rind of my bacon and squidged tomato sauce over the shrivelled rasher that sat sadly in my morning roll.

"Och shut up, if he had tried to strong-arm you into the flat you'd have freaked. He was being a gentleman –

he'll respect you for not shagging on the first night. I'll bet when you get home he has left a message on your machine – sounds like a top bloke to me." She had managed to finish her roll in three bites, pretty impressive.

"Yeah he is, that's the problem. He's been so bloody nice after the restaurant incident and all and I consistently seem to be a prize moron." For the second time in two days I lost my appetite.

Fiona helpfully took the unwanted roll off my hands.

"Ellie, he has a sense of humour. God, you are becoming seriously paranoid. Why don't we go to the pub under the guise of researching at the library? Just to ensure you're not losing what little self-esteem you have left." The two rolls gone she was standing up wiping flour and grease into her trousers.

I didn't take much persuading. We left with files and notes stuck under our arms and Avril sniffed at us again when we said we would be uncontactable for the rest of the day.

Twenty minutes later we were sitting in The Black Swan in the Grassmarket. We agreed it was sufficiently old-mannish not to have any of our work colleagues turning up over the lunch hour – most of them favoured more upmarket drinking-holes rather than ones that offered a lunch of battered haggis bites and chips to students for one pound fifty. We sat and chatted about nothing for the best part of the afternoon. Four pints of cider and a plate of haggis bites later we decided to go home. I was a little bit tiddly and after Fiona dramatically hugged me goodbye as if we would never see each other again, I swayed my way to the top of the

Grassmarket and squinted about to see if my bus was coming. My head was spinning so I sat down on a small wall which surrounds the site where the last hanging in Edinburgh took place – um, very cheerful.

"Don't suppose you've got a fag for an oul codger, eh?"

I turned round in surprise to see one of Edinburgh's homeless drunks – a tramp, who was in a far worse state than me, giving me his winning toothless smile with a can of McEwans Export in one hand and his other extended towards me in the hope I would have twenty Regal on my person and be only too glad to hand them over. I felt guilty so I routled about in my bag, pulled out my packet of Silk Cut and handed him one with a book of matches I had picked up in the pub.

"Fuck's sake, diet fags, keep it!" His expression changed to one of total disgust. He threw the cigarette back at me and got up and staggered back to his crowd of mates, who appeared to have Edinburgh's quota of nasty ale in blue plastic bags at their feet.

"Suit yourself, you fussy bollocks," I muttered at him, but he was already halfway across the road to see his pals and had forgotten about me.

I looked accusingly at my apparently inferior cigarette, turned down by a tramp. I lit a fag and sat on the wall feeling wobbly and wondering if I could phone Jake when I got home and apologise for being an arse – not a good idea.

He would know I was drunk and think I was talking shite, not a good way to try and rekindle an almost relationship with someone, when you are incoherent.

No, I'll wait till I have sobered up and then I'll call him. Like Fiona said, he's probably left a message on my machine and he didn't mind at all. Maybe he'll invite me down to London again – That cheered me up.

I was suddenly aware of raucous laughter coming from the direction of the crowd of export-drinking louts. Looking up I saw the toothless charmer I had offered a 'diet' cigarette to pointing at me.

"You're off your heed, wee mentaller – get yoursel some decent fags and then you can come back an sit oun our wall!"

"Aye and bring a bottle o'gin wi ya too!" They all exploded into hysterical laughter and coughing fits.

People were starting to look at me. I got up quickly, realising that I had been talking out loud, and walked away from the laughter. Forgetting I was trying to save money, I hailed a taxi and collapsed with relief into the back seat. I sat for a moment before I realised we weren't moving.

"Where to, love?" The taxi driver obviously thought I was upset rather than semi-plastered.

"Oh sorry, twenty nine Roger's Close please, just off The Shore."

The taxi driver nodded and I was relieved to discover he was not chatty and unlike some was not going to tell me how expensive petrol was for taxis these days, or how often he had to get his brake pads replaced.

When I got into my flat I was delighted to see the answerphone was flashing. I had turned the beep off as it seemed to really piss Hector off – this manifested itself by him eating the two predecessors to my current machine. I pressed play and took off my coat as I listened for Jake's voice to flood my living-room.

Instead it was that fucker Mark who invaded my private space. Even Hector managed to look aghast as he stalked into the living-room tail held high. His tail went down and he stood behind my legs as we both listened to Mark lecture me with his tinpot psychology.

"Hi sweetie, thought you'd be wondering where I've been. I've managed to get us a couple of tickets to see Oasis in Glasgow – I told you you would learn to love them!" He laughed at his own cleverness. " Anyway, they are on tomorrow night. I'll pick you up around seven thirty – ring me – my new number is -" The answer machine went dead – it appeared to have eaten Mark's number – shame. Was he really starting to lose the plot? Why was he trying to take me to see a band he knew I couldn't stand? I hadn't seen him in ages, what was he playing at?

The answer machine had also a message from Chloe, I know this as she rang half an hour later and gave out to me for not ringing her back. I eyed Hector suspiciously. Was this my terrier's penchant for answer machines or my fault for buying cheap goods?

Chapter Eight

The day of Mark's concert was Saturday. Unable to get hold of him to tell him to piss off on a permanent basis I decided to get my hair cut. I rang my usual hairdresser whom I love and who can do no wrong in my eyes. If she tells me I suit something then I believe her implicitly. Unfortunately, Jane was fully booked and even my threat of crying could not get me an appointment. I picked up the Yellow Pages and got back into bed to ring round all the good hairdressers she recommended, though she did point out that five more days without a haircut was unlikely to make me a public laughing-stock. Oh Jane, how I wish I had taken your advice!

Being a Saturday, all the hairdressers I tried were busy and I could not get an appointment anywhere – that is, until I phoned 'Kutz w'Klass'. The spelling should have told me all I needed to know.

"Kutz w'Klass, Donna speaking."

"I was wondering if you would have a space for a cut and blow-dry around eleven thirty this morning? I know it's short notice?" I had taken to apologising to each receptionist before she told me they had no appointments available and I would need to book at least three weeks in advance for a cut on a Saturday morning.

"Aye, that should be nay problem, hen. Eleven thirty. I'll see you then."

"Oh great, do you need a contact number?"

"Och no, I'll see you shortly." The woman on the other end of the phone hung up even as I realised I had not even given her my name. I sat back in bed and felt quite pleased with myself. If I was going to pluck up the courage to approach Jake again I wanted to look my best and since it was unlikely that I would be unable to lose two stone in a week, then a new haircut was the next best thing.

Now time for a shower. I hummed to myself as I plastered myself in more shower gel than was strictly necessary.

"La, la, dum de dum . . ." The smell of lemon made me feel great – that was until I got it into my eye, then it bloody stung.

"Oh shit, ouch!" I stuck my face directly under the showerhead in an attempt to get rid of the offending shower gel but only succeeded in having my eyelashes pushed into my eyeballs by the force of the water.

"Shiiiiit, bugger, tits!" I shouted, and had to have the rest of my shower with my eyes firmly closed and my face out of the direction of the spray. I groped round the bathroom to find my towel after discovering that if I opened my eyes it really hurt. Once dried and covered in talc, I washed my face in the basin hoping to remove the shower gel and retrieve my eyelashes. I managed

to remove my eyelashes but my eyes still stung like mad.

I squinted at my clock radio and saw that the time was eleven o'clock – hardly enough time to catch a bus up into town, which reminded me I must check in the Yellow Pages for the address of the hairdresser – I couldn't remember seeing them anywhere before.

"Twelve Rose Street Lane North, twelve Rose Street Lane North, twelve Rose Street Lane North," I repeated to myself as I stood waiting for my bus. My eyes were red and still hurt so I had to look at the floor of the bus when I paid the bus driver in case he though I was a maniac drug-user and wouldn't let me on (you also lose your rational when blinded by lemon shower gel). I sat on the first seat I came to, the ones that are reserved for elderly or infirm people, and tried to pretend that I didn't see the scowls from the two grannies on the seat opposite. When the bus got halfway along Prince's Street I got off as I couldn't remember which end Rose Street Lane North was. Rose street runs along behind Prince's Street, the main shopping street, and has lots of little lanes of similar names sprouting off it.

I arrived at Kutz w' Klass at quarter to twelve, sure I was going to be told that I was too late and had missed my appointment. It wasn't the easiest place to find. I pushed open the door, relieved to discover it was not very bright and maybe they wouldn't see my bloodshot eyes.

"Hi, I'm Ellie Clarke, sorry I'm late – I got a bit lost."

"You're fine, you're fine, I'm running late anyway. God, hangovers really knock me sideways."

Donna, it turned out, ran the salon with her sister Pat

and a junior called Shaz. She was a diminutive bleached blonde with a loud gravelly voice, as were Pat and Shaz, only Shaz didn't have a gravelly voice. Shaz took me off into the back to have my hair washed. It really was quite dark. I put my head back into the basin and relaxed as I awaited a scalp massage. I began to suspect that Shaz had not been a junior for long as she rather half-heartedly rubbed shampoo into my hair. I closed my eyes and reasoned with myself that not everyone is good at washing hair.

"Well, ma boyfriend he's in a band – they're called The Runaways, have ya heard of them?"

"Pardon? A band? Um no, I don't think so." I shut my eyes again praying she would shut up and just rinse my hair.

"They are totally brilliant, I can get you tickets for their next gig if you like?"

I winced as she rinsed shampoo into my eyes.

"Um . . . yeah, OK, where are they playing?" I had no intention of going to any gigs, whether the band were brilliant or not, but how do you tell a seventeen-year-old with a showerhead in her hand to go and get stuffed?

"They play every Thursday night at the Granary, you'll totally love them."

Thankfully she was on to the conditioner stage and I hoped to get away tangle-free before she wanted to swap addresses.

She wrapped a towel round my head and rubbed my wet hair. I kept my eyes shut, they were still stinging like mad and I wanted to thump her. She was still chatting away only I couldn't hear her as she rubbed the towel over my ears. I smiled, hoping this would suffice, as she lifted the towel away and led me back to the front of the salon where Donna was waiting, fag in hand.

"So, doll, how much do you want off?"

I was rapidly losing my nerve and the pink and brown decor was not instilling me with much confidence. Somehow salons that don't sell loads of over-priced hair products make me nervous. The only thing it looked like Kutz w'Klass sold were ashtrays and tickets for gigs of unknown bands.

"I think perhaps a couple of inches?"

She held up a piece of my hair and looked distinctly unimpressed.

"We may have to take a bit more off than that – it's very dry, you know."

This was said to me like I had deliberately been mistreating my hair. This is usually the point when the hairdresser insists that you buy something from their over-priced range of products, only I didn't see what she could sell me. I had plenty of ashtrays and had a contact for free gig tickets.

"OK, well, what about three inches?" I was now wondering how short my hair was going to end up. It really didn't look that bad to me – lots of people told me how glossy it looked.

"Yes, I think that would be more like it – do you want more layers?" She looked hopeful.

"Not really. I'm happy with the layers the way they are."

Her face fell.

She started combing my hair and I took the opportunity to look around the salon to see who else was subjecting themselves to Donna and Pat's dubious hair-styling talents.

Pat was liberally applying peroxide bleach to a young girl around eighteen who wanted to go platinum. Donna informed me that you can only bleach hair that doesn't have more than one dye in it or it will fall out! The young girl had assured them that she only had one dye (red) in her hair and she really wanted to bleach it.

Beside her was an elderly woman who was getting her weekly set and style, smoking Donna's fags and chatting away with her hair in tiny rollers.

"Last night me and the girls went to that night club, Walkers," said Donna. "What a fucking laugh!"

I was a bit taken aback with her language – not that I had a problem with swearing but I didn't expect it from a hairdresser, least of all one standing beside a seventy-year-old woman.

"Och hen, you and your fuckin' friends, it's a wonder ya dinne get arrested more often!" The elderly lady – Doris – threw back her head and almost laughed her false teeth out of her head.

Donna proceeded to tell me of last night's exploits of fifteen girls out on the pull – and she wasn't a day under thirty-five. "Well, ma kiddies are great, they help me up the stairs when they hear me come in. Some nights if they're sound out I lie at the bottom of the stairs till they get up tae watch the telly in the mornin'. Ach, they really are great kids!"

I tried to look like I wasn't shocked.

Doris passed me a cigarette while Donna dispatched Shaz into the back to get me a coffee.

"Did I tell you I had ma front teeth knocked out?"

"No, you hadn't mentioned that." I found myself grinning – though I didn't envy her kids.

"Me and the girls decided tae go for a night out in Glasgow, as the clubs in Edinburgh are not really up to much, ye know what a mean?"

I nodded as it seemed appropriate.

"We thought we might as well make a weekend out of it, so we went on the train, me and Shirley, that's ma best friend. Well, we had a whole bottle of Bacardi before we even got into Queen Street station. I tell you we were in some state by the time we got off the train. All the girls were totally pissed, I thought a was goin' tae wet ma knickers I was laughing so hard, a missed the platform and fell off the train and knocked ma soddin' teeth oot, right there in front of the conductor. All the girls were pissing themselves too, and the poor bloke didnae know where tae look as I had ma skirt up round ma waist and he had to help me back onto the platform. Shirley thought we were going tae get arrested, but nae bother! The bloke – Kevin – he had a sense of humour and left us to it! Well, I tell ye, so blocked, all of us, a think the blokes were a wee bit scared o'us when we hit the clubs that night – knee boots and wee dresses all round, know what a mean. Di ye like a drink yoursel? Judging by the state of your eyes, I'd say ye did."

I nodded agreement again, wondering how I could stub out the Regal Kingsize Doris had thrust into my hand without being rude. I had graphic images of Donna and friends out terrifying every bouncer in Glasgow, especially with that toothless grin. I was still nodding when she pulled out the photos of the aforementioned weekend. All I can say is I'm surprised Boots developed them – they needed an 18 certificate.

"So are you married then?" I hazarded a guess since she had mentioned she had kids.

"She is well out of that one." Doris grabbed my arm to make sure I understood how well out of it Donna was. "He was a cheating bastard who never deserved her! He ran off with the colourist six months ago. Well, when I say colourist she really was no bloody good. Donna is too nice for her own good."

Donna was nodding in agreement. I made shocked gasps and Donna smiled appreciatively at me, as if I knew what bastards men where.

"Aye, well, now I'm on ma own, just me and kids, but it suits us just fine."

She gossiped away to me, with Doris butting in every five minutes, as she cut off what seemed to me to be a bit more than three inches.

"Holy shit!" Pat screamed from the other side of the salon. She had just come in from the back and was staring at the eighteen-year-old, whose head appeared to have steam rising off it.

Donna dropped her scissors and she and Pat hauled the girl out of her seat and into the back.

"Shaz, get your arse back here now!" Pat yelled.

For the next ten minutes Doris and I sat with bated breath as we listened to the swearing going on in the shampoo area.

Doris shook her head. "Looks like that wee lassie lied about her hair, silly bitch."

"What? Sorry, what do you mean?"

Before Doris could answer a tearful Marri (as she turned out to be called) was led out by Pat. Her hair was pink but was no longer steaming.

Donna pushed her down into the chair, and inspected her scalp. Hair seemed to be falling out everywhere. I pushed my hair out of my eyes – yes, Marri seemed to be missing clumps of hair at the back.

"How many dyes did you have in your hair?" demanded Donna.

"Six," Marri sobbed.

"Och, bloody hell." Pat looked at Donna. Both of them stood there with their hands on their hips. Shaz was ringing the Wella hotline to see if they could give any advice.

Twenty minutes later, no joy from Wella, Donna and Pat had resorted to giving Marri a most unbecoming crew cut, a frosted pink one at that.

I had never had such an entertaining Saturday in a long time. Doris passed me another of her revolting cigarettes, I delved into my bag and produced a squashed packet of Silk Cut and offered her one of mine.

"I don't smoke those designer cigarettes, you'd have more fun trying to smoke a packet of Smarties."

We sat side by side smoking and drinking more coffee produced by Shaz and watching the snivelling Marri promise never to lie about her hair again. It wasn't that bad; a bit more had fallen out after Pat had blown it dry but they had done a pretty good job in covering up the bald patches. When Marri's tears had dried she was despatched out into downtown Edinburgh with a pink crop and a stern lecture on looking after your hair.

Donna resumed cutting my hair and seemed unfazed by the crisis or the fact that myself and doris had been sittting twiddling our cigarettes for what seemed like hours.

"Well, I don't think she'll be platinum for a while yet," she chuckled.

At long last I said goodbye to Kutz w'Klass and thanked them for an entertaining morning, Doris was still sitting in her rollers, on coffee number five and Pat and Donna where chain-smoking. Shaz promised to leave tickets for The Runaways for me beside the till and told me to come back on Monday to pick them up.

After all that, I wasn't very surprised to find that I had gone in with below-shoulder-length hair, and departed with a short bob, not sure how much this suited me. But it was different – well, it really was daringly short – very modern – cutting edge, really. Donna and the girls all told me it was terrific – maybe this was the new sexy me and men would now find me irresistible.

Like the second version of Gwenyth Palthrow in Sliding Doors – the one who goes on to have a great life and shag John Hannah.

I dandered round town as I had nowhere in particular to be. I was going to meet Chloe and Lousia at three and I had some time to kill. I headed for Waterstones on Prince's Street to have a flick through their new fiction section. I could have spent all day in there, surrounded by works of literature, none of which I would ever read, as I seemed to spend most of my time reading nothing more challenging than the latest Mills and Boon efforts.

Well, Mills and Boons made me laugh. All that Titian hair and heaving bosoms, and implied sexual encounters with throbbing manhoods. I once found a garage outside Comber in Ireland that sold Mills and Boons on tape and couldn't resist buying one. It was so funny I nearly drove into the car in front of me. I went back a couple of months later to get another one but they were all sold out.

As I made my way to the bookshop I passed Virgin and glancing in the window saw the advertisement for the Oasis concert in Glasgow that evening.

"Bugger," I said out loud and an old man in an anorak shot me a dirty look.

I had totally forgotten that Mark the Moron would be coming round this evening. Well, good luck to him as I was not going to be in.

A couple of hours later I was happily ensconced in Lainey's, the wine bar of choice, reading my latest glossy mag, educating myself how to have the ultimate orgasm – still no mention of the dropkick blokes who deliver such delights – the features editor has clearly never had sex with a Scottish amateur psychologist.

Lousia was next to arrive. She planted a big kiss on my cheek and stared at my hair. She must love it but doesn't want to embarrass me in public, I reckoned. Chloe turned up ten minutes later and her reaction was not quite as subtle.

"What in God's name have you done to your lovely hair?"

"I had it cut a bit shorter, do you like it?"

"No, I bloody don't, it's absolutely fecking awful. It makes your face look all chubby, *you total tit!* Did Jane do that to you?"

My heart took a dive to my boots. "No, I couldn't get an appointment, so I went somewhere else."

"Where did you go? Go and ask them to stick it back on!"

"Ah come on, Chloe, it isn't that bad, I quite like it." I was beginning to panic. Chloe never said anything she didn't mean.

"Have you had a good look at yourself?"

"Yes, of course I have – well, not exactly – but I liked it before I left, I doubt it has changed that much."

Chloe dragged me into the loos and shoved me in front of a mirror.

I looked like a footballer with a nasty step cut into the back of my head. And my face looked like the moon.

"She didn't show me the back!" I wailed.

"What a bloody awful mess!"

Lousia had a double gin and tonic sitting at my place when I finally had the guts to go back to the table, laughing her lovely blonde head off – bitch!

"Ellie, remember what you say! *Hair grows!*" She started to laugh again and this time Chloe joined in.

"Oh, piss off both of you, it will grow back, it just isn't the willy-magnet effect I was hoping for. I'll just have to put my Jake plan on hold for a while. Nothing is permanent. Hopefully it will be enough to put Mark off though."

I told them about the concert tickets. Chloe thought I should get my number changed and Lousia felt I should put the flat on the market and move to Aberdeen.

"Thanks, guys, always ready with practical advice."

Somehow it didn't seem so creepy when you told your girlfriends about it in the middle of the afternoon in a busy bar.

Chloe went on to tell us about her wedding plans. Her mum was currently not speaking to her – Chloe had told her she was to have nothing to do with picking the dress. Margo seemed to think it had everything to do with her.

Chloe had seen a dress that she really liked in a small non-designer shop and wanted our opinions on it. "It's just really plain, ivory satin with little pearls sewn onto the bodice. I think it's really flattering but I don't want to pick anything without you having a look."

She and David had decided to invite one hundred and sixty guests, eighty from each side; Margo didn't think that was enough as she had around two hundred people she thought should be invited. Chloe wanted a marquee in the garden and her dad was delighted; Margo wanted to hold it in a hotel. Chloe had a friend from home, Sally, a florist, who said she would be delighted to do the flowers for the church, the bouquets and the table decorations; Margo had an expensive London florist in mind. Chloe's aunt from her dad's side had offered to bake the cake and decorate it; Margo was spitting as she wanted to go where all the other brides' mothers got their daughters' cakes, Torte Estelle, a very expensive shop in Dublin.

God, this was a bit of an uphill struggle for Chloe and she looked exhausted. Thankfully she and David had taken a bit of a stand against Margo and told her in no uncertain terms that this was to be their day and their decision was final, or else they would go off to Las Vegas and get married by a Chinese Elvis (my original suggestion). Margo of course had had palpitations at this and was now refusing to speak to Chloe or David.

Chloe summed it up. "Mum is being a total pain in the arse."

We ordered some food from a passing waiter as all the wedding chat had made Chloe feel faint, Louisa had missed breakfast and lunch because she had been bonking Alfie all morning and I was still trying to get over a haircut that made the cast of Prisoner Cell Block H look well-groomed. The only downside to Lainey's was they only seemed to employ antipodean thickos so ordering anything always took twice as long, as they try to flog you garlic bread or side salads. Our waiter seemed very unimpressed that we only wanted chips – sorry, puffy wedges – posh chips. After several failed attempts to get us to order something more expensive he gave up and wandered away to the kitchen where we hoped he would eventually remember our order.

So we sat drinking red wine and eating puffy wedges with a side dollop of mayonnaise (the only way to eat chips in my opinion) until it got dark outside. Between us we had set the world to rights.

Louisa was having imaginary problems with Alfie her boyfriend. He was being so nice to her she was worried he was having an affair.

"Why does he need to be having an affair to be affectionate? Is that not standard behaviour?"

"God, Ellie, when was the last time you went out with anyone?"

"Ooh, excuse my naiveté, there was me thinking men went out with you when they found you attractive."

"Well, you know what he's like. I mean, I know that he loves me, he just has trouble showing it – you know, public displays of affection and all that. Do you remember the time I tried to kiss him outside his office? He was so embarrassed! We were in the car for fuck's sake, on the other side of the road! You'd think I had just stripped down to my g-string in the middle of the reception area!"

"God, yeah, I do remember you telling us about that," Chloe chipped in. "Mind, I think it's just Alfie dealing with commitment in his own way – he was single for a long time."

"God, Chloe, I didn't force him to do anything he didn't want to! He wanted me to move in!" Louisa's voice was rising and I thought she was about to cry.

"No, don't be an arse," I said. "Chloe didn't mean that at all – did you, Chloe?"

Chloe shook her head most violently, probably wondering what crap I was going to spout, I wasn't entirely sure myself.

"It's just men can find it difficult adapting to someone in their lives a lot of the time, especially a woman," I continued. "They have to get used to things. They don't in general like change – I know, I know – then just when they get things the way they like them, in walks a girl and knocks them sideways. Suddenly your knickers are drying beside his boxers, you borrow his razor to shave your legs and he can't watch 24-hour football, well not without a damn good fight."

Louisa started to giggle.

"I reckon he is just a little self-conscious," I went on,

"but he is now fully adapted and ready to plant the lips on you at any given opportunity. Only now you suspect him of cheating! Don't be daft – when would he get the time?"

Of course this made perfect sense coming from me, Ellie Clarke, whose grand total for long-term relationships currently stood at nil. I waited for Louisa to tell me it was all complete shit, and I would have entirely agreed with her, but instead she smiled, nodded her head and drank her wine.

Chloe stared at me and I stared at her. Could it be that I just said something that made sense?

"I suppose you're right, maybe it just took him a while to feel comfortable with me. Sorry, it was stupid of me to think he was seeing someone else. You know, our sex life has really improved – it's like he has been taking lessons."

Chloe and I looked at each other uneasily. Apparently Louisa had not read the same article we had, about men who pick up these new techniques from the blonde temp on the third floor behind the photocopier. Though surely not Alfie? He was devoted to Louisa – he demanded she move in with him two weeks after they met.

"Well, you know these men's magazines, they even have Barbie and Ken doing positions of the week! I'll bet he's been reading up!" Double points for quick thinking, I thank you.

"So Ellie, what about your life? Anyone special?" Louisa, happy now that I had put her mind at rest, was now going to torment me about not having had sex for six months – OK OK more like seven.

"Well, there's nothing really to tell, Jake was up a few days ago, he was really nice, took me out for dinner, got me a taxi home and paid for it, I came over like a nun and he stayed the night with Chloe and David. He went back down to London the next day and I have not heard from him since, nor do I expect to. I now am being stalked by my ex who thinks I have become an Oasis fan and want to go to concerts with him in Glasgow. Hector keeps eating my answerphones, so even if Jake phoned to declare his undying love to me I doubt I would get the message, so it looks like I'm destined to be ex-directory and celibate for the foreseeable future." I paused for breath. And continued. "You are having the best sex of your life, Chloe is in pre-marital bliss, Clare seems to have forgotten my phone number and, I am reliably informed, is shagging random blokes from bars without so much as a "what is your surname?". I'm about to be given my virginity back, I have seriously gross hair for which I paid ten perfectly decent pounds and I appear to be terminally unattractive to members of the opposite sex, especially the ones I fancy. I think I'll become a mail-order bride for rich gangster Russians and spend my days drinking vodka and eating blinis."

"Um . . . I thought it was *Russian* mail-order brides," said Louisa. "Have you ever been to Russia?"

"No but it doesn't matter, the women over there are all rotten so they will think I'm gorgeous no matter what my hair is doing."

"Ellie, how do you know all Russian women are rotten? Are there statistics?"

"God, Chloe, do you have to be so pedantic? You've

Tulips, Chips & Mayonnaise

read the magazines! They all wear tablecloths and their slippers and live in small Moscow flats, They have no money for make-up and they don't get their hair cut. It's true I read it in *Marie Claire*, or was it *Woman's Own?*"

"Sorrel, you are coming home with me tonight," said Chloe. "I think the whole Mark thing is going to your head. David can go round and fetch Hector and he can spend the night too."

"I don't think you should go to Moscow, Ellie," said Louisa, trying not to laugh. "We would really miss you and you wouldn't understand what anyone was saying to you."

"I know!" Chloe said suddenly. "Why don't we go on a girl's night out tonight? Like Donna and Pat!"

"That's fine with me," said Louisa. "I'm not doing anything and I think Clare will be free – we could see if Violet was free. And, Ellie, you could ring Fiona – she's always good for a laugh."

"OK, OK, I'll ring Fiona," I said. "Chlo, pass us your mobile."

"When are you going to get yourself one?" Chloe asked – she gets pissed off as half her bill is me borrowing the phone.

"Well, if you remember, I had one a couple of years ago but I lost it and by the time I found it again I had had myself disconnected, as I reckoned Lucy had nicked it and was making international calls from Dublin. Anyway it was more like a house-brick than a phone – I want one of those nifty chrome or tortoiseshell ones, very cool. Now pass us your phone, woman, this was your suggestion."

Chloe handed over her mobile and I rang Fiona.

115

"Greetings fae' Morningside, Fiona Macpherson speaking."

"Hi, Mo, just wanted to see if you fancied coming out tonight – the girls and I reckoned we might go out on the piss. Are you in?"

Twenty minutes later we were all set. We paid the bill. The waiter, it turned out, had a habitually unimpressed expression on his face, hired we thought to embarrass customers into spending more money, cunning marketing ploy from the owner. We had spent the whole afternoon watching him sneer at all the tables in the place – I don't think I've ever seen so many people eating garlic bread.

So that is why several hours later, after some clever backcombing from Clare, I found myself on the edge of the dance floor of a very new and trendy night-club. Fiona was dancing with a very tall man who had absolutely no rhythm in his bony frame, but then Fiona couldn't dance for peanuts either and they did look like they were really enjoying themselves. I turned my attention to Clare who was already snogging the tastiest bloke in the building. She had him pushed up against the wall beside the cloakroom – I gave them twenty more minutes before she dragged him back to her place and tied him up and/or covered him in chocolate sauce and grated cheese. Violet, who I don't think I have mentioned yet but she is terribly nice even if she has a slightly odd taste in clothes, was necking tequila slammers at the bar with Chloe. I could see one was left for me – perhaps if I was inconspicuous they would forget about me and drink it themselves. I was looking at Fiona and the tall man when someone tapped me on the shoulder. I looked round. Oh shit!

"Mark, what are you doing here?" God, I didn't even have time to hide under the table.

"Well, Ellie, I think I could ask you the same question considering you were supposed to be coming to a concert with me in Glasgow this evening!"

He looked really pissed off.

"I took the liberty of following you since you didn't even have the courtesy to return my call."

"But your number, my answer phone, you see Hector . . ."

"Yes, I've heard all these excuses before, Ellie, and I'm not prepared to accept them. Now get your coat, we're leaving."

I was quite drunk at this stage, but even if I was absolutely cross-eyed I wouldn't have walked to the end of the room with him let alone gone home with him.

"Mark," I said, in what I hoped was a firm voice, "I'm out with my friends, you gave me no warning about this concert, which I would not have gone to anyway. My answer machine cut off the end of your message which is why I could not phone you back – oh yes, you keep withholding your number on my 1471 call-back. You and I are finished and have been for some time so I think it's high time you stopped calling me under pretence of my still loving you, as I think we both know that just isn't true. Now I think you should go home and leave me alone."

Fairly impressive, I think you'll agree.

He looked shocked. "Now, Ellie, come on, you don't mean that surely?"

"Mark, leave me alone!" I shouted and lots of people looked round. A bouncer started to make his way over towards us.

Mark backed away. "I'm sorry you feel like this, Ellie – I'll be in touch."

Before I could tell him to sling his hook he had disappeared into the dry ice.

I felt quite shaken and upset afterwards and went over and joined Chloe and Violet who had missed the whole thing. Five tequilas later I was telling the girls how assertive I had been and how I would never be bothered by him again. I got a small drunken round of applause, then I fell over.

Chapter Nine

Chloe and I journeyed around Scotland calling into wedding-dress shops the length and breadth of the country, glamorous shops where all the dresses made Chloe look like a designer fairy, boutiques where we were patronised by the snotty assistants who thought we were winding them up, little tiny ones where I sat with the invariably tiny proprietress and drank tea while Chloe tried on dresses. After a couple of months of looking, Chloe had seen a couple that she liked but didn't want to commit to anything until she had exhausted her search. Basically Margo had made her so paranoid that she felt she had to visit all the shops in Britain in case she missed that perfect dress which was hanging in a shop in Croydon.

I, then, in a rare display of inspiration suggested a weekend in London where we could stay with friends and look in the big department stores – Selfridges, Peter Jones, Harrods, Harvey Nicols, Dickens & Jones, Fenwicks etc – and have a bloody good laugh in the process. I could do a bit of shopping too and save a fortune on hotel rooms by sleeping on an obliging sofa.

Chloe thought it was a great idea and we organised a weekend, keeping the whole thing fairly hush-hush so that Margo wouldn't come too, she of the expensive-store card fame. She likes to think that the assistants in the Escada department in Harrods remember her by name. Who is that 'sad'? I mean both for wearing Escada which you can only really get away with if you are Cilla Black and for wanting sales assistants to remember you.

Anyway, the weekend started as planned. Chloe and I caught the 8 am train from Edinburgh Waverley to King's Cross in London. We had decided, since it was a special occasion – it's not every day you go looking for wedding dresses – that we should travel first class and I surprised Chloe by producing two bottles of champagne and some plastic cups I had hidden in my bag.

"God, Ellie, I'll be steaming before we get to Newcastle."

"Och, shut up, when was the last time you got drunk for breakfast?"

"Graduation?"

"Well, that's far too long ago . . . here, drink up!"

I handed her a fizzing glass. We had a 'right on' family across the aisle who looked totally horrifed at us drinking so early in the morning – I raised my glass to them. *"Cheers!"*

They looked away and returned to trying to get their two unenthusiastic children to eat the muesli they had brought with them.

"But, Mummy, I want a glass of that stuff!"

The little girl (dressed like a French peasant) pointed at Chloe's glass, ignoring the spoon of straw her mother was trying to feed her. The mother, (interestingly also dressed like a French peasant) glared at Chloe.

"No, dear, you don't want be like those silly girls, now eat your homemade museli, it's *sooo* tasty – it will make you big and strong like Mummy."

Judging by Mummy's upper-lip problem, she should have added 'hairy' after big and strong.

To our amusement Swiss Family Robinson soon got up and, muttering about "bad influences" and "disgusting behaviour", dragged their little children after them into the next carriage.

We were going to stay with our friend Rachel who was living somewhere around Fulham Broadway underground station, with her flatmate Brian. Brian happened to be a great friend of my brother's and as he also knew Jake. I was hoping he would have let it slip that I was coming down for the weekend – that is, assuming Rachel remembered to tell him.

Brian had a massive crush on Rachel. They had met when Rachel was temping at his office – she was a receptionist for about two weeks when she first moved to London from Belfast. She was finishing college and had nowhere to stay and had just about outlived her welcome on a friend's floor. Batting her illegally long eyelashes at him, Rachel (with a little insider knowledge from Ben) told Brian about her accomodation problem. It took Brian about six seconds to offer her his spare room, conveniently forgetting that he had promised it to another friend, Harry. That was three years before and neither of them had shown any signs of moving out.

Rachel was now working for a promotion company and haring around London trying to organise dinners, exhibitons and fashion shows. About six months before she got incredibly drunk after a successful gala she had organised. When she got home she woke Brian up and announced to him that she had always had "a bit of a thing" for him and would he please take her now, before she changed her mind. Brian didn't need telling twice. Rachel couldn't remember a thing about it except that Brian kept telling her for the next week that she was magnificent. Ever since then, he kept trying to coax her back into his bedroom. Rachel pretended to be horrified by the whole thing but, secretly delighted that even when drunk she was terrific in bed, she just hoped he had told his workmates as she fancied about three of them.

Brian was working in the City selling things, though Rachel could never remember what, even though she worked there once. He made pots of cash, dressed in designer suits and had drop-dead gorgeous friends (another reason we wanted to stay with Rach). Brian could probably have had any woman he wanted but for some reason Chloe and I could not fathom, he was besotted with Rachel which was why he had stayed living with her in their tiny rented terraced house when he could have bought himself something slightly more salubrious. They were almost like a couple, except they had only had sex once (apparently not all that unusal). They went out together like a couple, he bought the drinks and dinner, they bought each other Christmas presents, went to the cinema, took long walks and even went clothes-shopping together. Rachel told him about her relationship nightmares, which must have been quite hard for the guy, but he always hugged her and helped pick up the pieces of her supposedly broken heart – but really more like her broken ego. Rachel has a burning desire to be attractive to all men and doesn't take rejection in any form well.

Rachel is one of those people who appear to effortlessly glide through life never realising the impact they make on other people. When we were little everyone wanted to be her friend, yet she seemed unaware and unimpressed by the whole thing. Her best friend was an enormous girl all the kids made fun of. They were inseparable, Rachel and Elizabeth. They went everywhere together and always seemed to be having a better time than everyone else. Boys used to call them names, really because they wanted Rachel to pay them more attention, but she didn't care and went on with her life regardless. When we were a little older Chloe and I became good friends with Rachel and Lizzie, and stayed good friends throughout the rest of our time at school. Lizzie died from leukaemia when we were sixteen. Rachel was devastated and moved away to London soon after the funeral. She had lost her best friend and thought the only way to get on with her life was to leave her old life behind.

I remember clearly the day she told us she was leaving. Rachel, pale-faced, staring out the window, telling

Chloe and me that she had decided to go to a college in London to finish her A levels and no one could talk her out of it. Her parents seemed to put up very little resistance to her leaving, they always seemed to understand what she was thinking, more than any other parents I have ever met including my own. We didn't see her again for three years; she sent birthday cards and Christmas cards but she never came home. After our A levels were finished, six of us had saved up enough money and flew from Belfast to Heathrow to spend a weekend with her in London as we couldn't convince her to visit us. She met us at the airport and took us back to her flat via the tube. None of us had ever been to London. It was so exciting and Rachel seemed so sophisticated; she didn't have a hair out of place as she pushed her way through the crowds of tourists, us desperately trying to keep up. She sailed through college and a marketing degree; her parents provided her with financial freedom and visited her often. To us she was the last word in cool.

We spent the weekend shopping, drinking and dancing, I don't think there was a single one of us that wanted to come home afterwards. After that weekend Rachel and I kept in close contact, she took to visiting me in Edinburgh every few weeks and I returned the favour and visited in London – my wardrobe and overdraft expanded at an alarming rate. Just before we graduated Rachel had to move out of her flat as the landlord had decided to sell. She was stuck for somewhere to live; that was when Ben told her there was a bloke he worked with who was looking for a flatmate and gave her Brian's number.

And so, after three years, they had developed their own brand of domestic bliss.

The rest of the train journey down to London was uneventful; we paid through the nose for some sandwiches which were really no nicer than the ones they sell in economy, and drank my champagne which made the sandwiches taste marginally nicer.

"You know, Ellie," Chloe had her mouth full of tomato and cheese sandwich, "we should try and see a show while we are down – I heard Sunset Boulevard is good. I wonder what Rachel has planned? Hey, she does remember we are coming down?"

"Yes, I rang her last night – she's really excited, and I'm not bothered what we do, I just want you to get a dress – it's not that long now, you know."

"It's still six months – don't worry!"

"Yeah, well, when are you going to pick my dress?"

"As soon as I have picked mine – I promise it will really be lovely."

When we got to Doncaster station a crowd of lads got on the train. Now experience tells you that should a crowd of drunken football supporters get on your train they will invariably sit in your carriage as close to you as they possibly can get with their cans of Tennents Super Lager in blue carrier bags swinging off their arms. Thankfully today they favoured the carriage behind us – we could still hear them quite clearly but it was a relief not to have to look at them. Chloe pulled out a *Brides* magazine and I pulled out my book and settled in for the last two hours of the journey as fields and towns whizzed by.

We had arranged to meet Rachel outside Piccadilly tube station. We planned to have lunch with her near her workplace in Soho and then Chloe and I would go shopping and meet her after work. After getting off the train Chloe and I dragged our bags down to the underground station and after some negiotation with a journey planner hopped on what we hoped was the Picadilly line. As we were on the escalators at Piccadilly it occurred to me that it was probably not the most sensible place for us to meet, considering the rest of London seemed to have the same idea. It seemed that hundreds of people had descended on Piccadilly Circus – very aptly named.

Miraculously Rachel spotted us immediately and cut through the crowd like a warm knife through butter. After all the hugging and 'I've missed you's' she helped us with our bags and led the way through the throng of people.

Ten minutes later we were in Soho, in a little Italian restaurant with very good looking but cheesy waiters. Five minutes after that we had large glasses of red in our hands and were toasting the weekend. Rachel never made it back to work: we got totally gibbered in the restaurant and lunch lasted four hours. By the time we left our waiter had my phone number – which Rachel had dutifully made up – we had spent thirty five pounds each on a lunch which had been three plates of pasta, some garlic bread and five bottles of wine.

As we fell back out onto the street we were all giggling maniacally. Then I realised I had left my suitcase in the restaurant and I had to go back to get it. Our waiter came rushing over to help me.

"Bella, let-a me 'elp you wit-a da baggage."

"No, really, I'm grand, I can manage." I manfully tried to lift my bag up, but the wine had somehow affected my balance and I almost fell into his arms.

He whisked the bag out of my hand and headed out the door.

Chloe and Rachel were in hysterics to see the waiter appear, grinning from ear to ear, carrying my bag with me following behind wittering away while he wasn't listening to a word.

"Thank you," Rachel said to him giggling.

"Prego!" He set my bag down with a flourish. Said *"Ciao, bella!"* to me, blew us all a kiss and disappeared back inside the restaurant.

The three of us wobbled off drunkenly to find a bus going in the general direction of Fulham.

An hour later, after we had got on the wrong bus twice, we arrived at Fulham Broadway and Rachel led the way to her house. We had been before, but to be honest my sense of direction – even sober – is crap and I would get lost in two minutes. When we got to the tiny terrace we dumped our bags in the front room where we would be sleeping.

"Brian is out at work at the moment," said Rachel, in fits of laughter.

"Where I should be too!" She burped and sat down on the sofa, quickly jumping back up again as she had sat down on a hairbrush. She grabbed the hairbrush, flung it away and it flipped over the back of the sofa. "He was

127

wondering – " She stood up on the sofa and reached her arm down the back to retrieve the brush, in the process she finding two pairs of her knickers (we didn't ask) and the TV remote control.

"Anyway," she continued, her head still down the back of the sofa and her bum in Chloe's face, "Brian was wondering if you would like to go out for dinner tonight with him, me of course and a couple of his friends from work?" She turned round triumphantly with a pearl earring in her hand, "I've been looking for that wee bugger for ages, hurrah! That saves me a fortune having to buy another one – Brian bought them for me last Christmas and I thought I was going to have to replace it before he noticed." She put the earring into the pocket of her trousers and looked at Chloe and me expectantly.

"What?" I asked.

"Dinner, yes or no?"

"Oh yes, please," said Chloe. "Well, that is if Ellie doesn't mind?"

"No, that sounds good. What friends are coming?"

"Oh, I don't know, I can never remember all their names. Don't you think men in suits all look the same?"

"Don't really know that many, to be perfectly honest," I replied, thinking that most of the men working in North Eastern Television wore pullovers in pastel shades, or lumberjack shirts – fashion was not an issue for them.

"So we go out for dinner then? Brian will be pleased – I should ring him, where did I put his number?" She disappeared down the back of the sofa again and appeared moments later minus the telephone number. "I think he put it on the pin-board in the kitchen, I'll get it in a minute, I'm knackered." She plopped down onto the sofa and picked up the TV control. "Oooh, I'm so glad to get this back! Do you want to watch a video?

I looked at my watch. It was five o'clock – not much point in going shopping now. "Sure, what do you have?"

We decided on *The Hunt for Red October* as we fancied looking at Sean Connery and listening to him doing his sexy Russian accent.

"Ellie was going to go and live in Moscow," Chloe told Rachel.

Rachel looked over at me. "Really?"

"Nah, not really, I'd just had my hair cut."

This seemed to be all the explanation she needed. She looked at my hair, nodded and turned her concentration back to the television.

Brian rang just as the film was ending. Rachel picked up the phone.

"Yes? Hi, yeah, they do want to go out for dinner . . . OK, we'll meet you there in an hour."

She put down the phone and stared at the credits rolling up the screen while we stared at her.

"Rach?"

"Yup?"

"Where are we going in an hour?"

"To a very nice restaurant, called um . . . 'Mirabelle' – some famous chef's place."

Chloe and I looked at each other.

"I think I saw a programme on that last week," said Chloe. "Are you sure?"

"God, I don't know. I haven't been, but Brian said dress up, it's very posh."

"Oh shit, Chlo," I said. "I don't think I brought anything amazing down with me, actually I don't think I own anything amazing."

"Is it Marco Pierre White's new restaurant by any chance?" Chloe was asking.

"Who's he?" Rachel and I both said together.

"Och you know, that stroppy chef who divorced his wife after five minutes because he didn't like her wedding dress. It was in *Hello* – you must have seen it."

"Oh yeah!" said Rach. "I think I remember him – doesn't brush his hair much?"

"Yup, that's the one. God, this should be very nice."

"Anyone want a shower?" said Rachel. "I think there should be enough hot water for you both."

Chloe and I raced into the bathroom armed with razors, hairspray and violent-blue nail varnish. Once we had removed all excess body hair, coiffed our hair into wildly fashionable styles and looked like we'd had our fingers caught in a car door, we were almost ready. Time to have a cigarette, a glass of wine and apply a large coating of make-up.

Twenty minutes later and we were finished. I, due to the lack of anything remotely stylish, had opted for black, black and a bit more black. Chloe looked lovely in a new steel-grey Karen Millen suit and Rachel, who could wear a plastic bag and still look good, was wearing an amazing leopard-print jacket with a very short matching skirt and a pair of heels you would have needed lessons to walk in.

"OK, so whose idea was it for you both to have fab outfits and pick an amazing restaurant, just so I could trail in behind you looking like the Grim Reaper?" I grumbled.

"Ah, shut your face, you look great."

"Taxi is here." Rachel was peering out the front window.

Making sure I had put my cigarettes back in my bag, I had a quick squirt of perfume and followed them out the front door.

"Did I mention that we're going to meet them in the pub first?"

We were sitting in the back of a black taxi and Chloe was applying more lipstick.

"No, you didn't. Eh . . . who's coming with Brian?" I was praying Jake wouldn't be there. I didn't think I could face him with my still crap hair and dressed like something from *Interview with a Vampire*.

"George and Harry, I think."

"So there will be six of us?"

Chloe had now moved on to yet another layer of mascara and had just poked herself in the eye with the mascara wand. "Bugger! It bloody stings." She now had a black smear on her nose.

When we arrived at the pub I paid for the taxi and we piled out and into the warmth of the pub. We spotted the guys and made our way over to them. I had met them all before through Ben but Chloe had never met Harry. Brian went off to the bar to get a round in before dinner and returned fairly quickly with a tray full of gin and tonics.

"I'm afraid there's been a change of plan," he said as he doled the drinks out.

"Oh!" we chorused, disappointed we weren't going to the stroppy famous chef's new restaurant (we'd been hoping there would be a fight in the kitchen).

"Instead, my dears, I'm taking you to The Condescension, Sven Svenenson's new place, supposed to be very dramatic, a glass bridge into the place and all that – food should be good too. It turns out Harry used to waiter for Marco Pierre White and he's been barred from all his restaurants for dropping a full ashtray on Princess Michael of Kent. So we felt it best to avoid any unpleasantness!"

"Oh well done, Harry, what did she say?" Chloe asked.

"Um . . . not much – she spluttered a bit. It was years ago but I think he would still remember me – I've a feeling I will be burned on his brain!"

Sven Svenenson was a Scandinavian, millionaire entrepreneur. He was famous for his trophy girlfriends and was constantly in *Hello*, pictured posing in his various Chelsea homes – rarely with the same girl twice.

Brian was surreptitiously looking at Rachel, pretending to read the menu board above her head. Never had I seen a man so clearly nuts about a woman. Maybe I should think about changing deodorant, or carrying Gold Spot in my bag on regular occasions (and using it). I wondered when they would get together. If Brian ever moved out I knew she would be knocked sideways; he was definitely her Prince Charming – only in an Audi instead of on a white steed.

The restaurant was the last word in pretension. We had to walk down a long glass walkway with lights shining underneath it, through huge glass doors into the restaurant itself. A charming hostess greeted us and took our jackets. then we were led upstairs. The dining area was like a gallery with an upmarket bar area downstairs. Conversation bounced off the walls and the place was buzzing with money.

We sat in armchair-type chairs in a *faux* mushroom suede and the napkins were so starched it was like unfolding cardboard. All the diners in the restaurant looked like they had just been for a photoshoot at *Vogue;* everyone was very glam, from understated elegance to very flashy, with diamonds on every light-reflective surface. I sat down quickly before any of these model lookalikes could scrutinise my clothing.

Rachel was looking like she came to these sorts of places all the time and the guys looked very relaxed. But then I suppose if you earn the sort of money that they do, you just fit in. I couldn't help thinking that if I had even half their salary I wouldn't be able to stop smiling!

The waiter handed us menus and the wine list, asked if we would like an apéritif and Brian ordered a round of Kir Royales.

Chloe was trying like mad to look calm – there were no prices on the menu and she was panicking. I delved into my bag feeling the need for a cigarette. Our drinks arrived very quickly and after a few sips of my gin and half a cigarette I felt brave enough to take in the surrounding tables. To the left of us there was a much older woman with a much younger man, must be a son or even a grandson. She looked about sixty-five and he looked about twenty-five; he was gorgeous and she was definitely not. Her clothes were absolutely fab though, Jil Sander I reckoned: beautifully cut trouser-suit, with sexy strappy mules and a face like an old leather bag. Then I noticed the young gorgeous man was holding her hand under the table. He leant forward and kissed her on the end of the nose in a distinctly un-granny fashion. He couldn't be her boyfriend, could he? Maybe he was an escort – I'd read about those.

Beside the odd couple were a foursome. I guessed they worked for a record company or some other working environment that necessitates no taste in clothing. The men looked like they had modelled themselves on the latest boy band to hit the charts: bleached cropped hair, sunglasses pushed up on their heads, tight T-shirts and combat trousers – wait for it . . . leather no less! They could have been twins. Unfortunately for them. they looked more Peter Stringfellow than Peter Andre. I was amazed the women could actually stand up – the weight of all that gold must have been fierce. Deep tans, the obligatory sunglasses on head and dresses which looked more like cunningly placed napkins, just covering enough of them so as not to be arrested. Really it could have put you off your food. I bet they had arrived in matching Ferraris.

From where I was sitting I couldn't see any other tables clearly so, turning to my right as if I was going to talk to Chloe, I gawked surreptitiously about and noticed a group of men who looked like they were having a business meeting. Seemed like a strange venue to choose, being so loud – it certainly didn't lend itself to the hushed tones of a business deal. The five men were all leaning into the centre of the table. looking very serious, drinking mineral water and eating salads. One chap was getting quite agitated, two were sitting back in their seats looking smug, the other two looked distinctly uncomfortable. The agitated guy was balding, red in the face and his paunch was pressed up against the side of the table. He picked up a piece of bread and shoved it into his mouth and chewed on it furiously. The jackets came off and went over the back of the chairs, two waiters materialised and whisked the jackets away, several ties were loosened and they all leant back into the centre of the table.

Beside them was a table of six girls – well, women if I'm being honest. They looked like they were on some sort of very posh hen night. I could tell this because one of the girls was wearing a tiara with a short veil attached, along with a rock on her left hand that could have caused damage to your retina if you looked directly into it. They all looked as though they had just walked off the designer floor at Harvey Nicols. Louis Vuitton and Hermes Kelly bags sat under their chairs, their Prada kitten heels were attached to very slender ankles which led to very slender legs which were crossed under very short Gucci skirts and Tiffany solitaire diamond necklaces were out in force. Their look screamed money, and it was probably all 'Daddy's'.

Oh Ellie, I thought, retract those claws. Jealousy will get you nowhere.

The Kir Royales arrived along with the wine and the waiter to take the order.

Just as he flipped up his little pad there was a small commotion behind him. I couldn't see what exactly was going on; then he moved out of the way. Standing behind him, looking slightly out of breath, was Jake.

My heart stopped and my hand automatically went up to my hair.

Shit, bugger and shit again.

I was totally unprepared for this. *Shit* – did I even have any lipstick left on? I pressed my lips together to see.

He still looked like the stuff seventeen-year-old (and my) fantasies are made of. Even the hen party had gone awfully quiet and were gazing appraisingly in the direction of our table.

"Sorry, guys, so sorry I'm late – we had a conference call with the States and you know what those guys are like, you can't just tell them to piss off you have to go out for dinner with three incredibly attractive women and three incredibly mediocre blokes!"

Everyone laughed while I thought I was going to throw up with nerves. What was wrong with me? We had gone out for dinner twice already (granted not very successfully), we were practically friends. So why was I acting like such an arse again?

"Hi, Rachel! Chloe, Ellie, how are you? Hope your journey down was OK? No leaves on the line or any of that crap?"

He leant over and kissed each of us in turn – he kissed me last.

"No, it was fine!" cried Chloe cheerfully. "Just some overpriced sandwiches courtesy of British Rail and champagne courtesy of Ellie. Then we had a very boozy lunch with Rachel and now I'm trying to fight off an impending hangover with more wine! How are you?" Chloe was amazingly coherent, I just managed to smile and nod.

"I didn't think you were coming," Rachel said smiling.

"You knew I was going to try and make it?" Jake looked puzzled.

I was going to throttle that cow when we got home. The bitch knew all along and never said a word. I was aware that a red flush was creeping up my neck. Brian was smiling at me in a horribly knowing fashion. Oh, what had that swine Rachel said to him?

"So what are you all having?" Jake asked as he unfolded his napkin. "Have you guys ordered already?"

"No, we were waiting for you!" Rachel beamed at him and then looked like she could bite her tongue. I had several violent thoughts towards her in quick succession.

The waiter was back with his notepad poised and we all ordered quickly except for Harry and George who hadn't even looked at the menu, they were so busy eying up the talent at the surrounding tables.

Jake had taken the seat opposite me which (why hadn't I noticed before?) had been left conveniently empty by the others. I could barely lift my eyes off my side plate, terrified I was going to blush again and knock my glass onto the floor which was granite and would have made a very impressive crashing noise.

"So, really, how are you?" Jake was looking directly at me and the others were caught up in conversations. So I guessed he must be talking to me.

"I'm fine thanks, you?"

"Yeah, I'm great, work is hectic, but I heard from Ben yesterday."

"Really? The toe-rag hasn't got in touch with me!"

"He's only just worked out how to use his Visa Card to make phone calls, I think he planned to phone home next and let your parents know he's still alive."

"Bloody right! It's been three months and just one postcard. Mum's convinced he and Sonia have been kidnapped by a drug cartel."

"No, they're absolutely fine! Sonia has actually started to enjoy herself – Ben said she was a bit of a nightmare to start off with."

"I'd say that was the understatement of the year!"

"Anyway," Jake ignored my comment, "they're both really well, involved in building a hospital outside a small town called, um . . . God, now I can't remember, but it's about a four-hour drive from the capital Managua, but the roads are totally crap, and it's a nightmare to get to a phone. The people that they are working with are really great. Ben says he has never been happier though he does miss us of course and Sonia is a bit homesick but proud of herself as she is learning to speak Spanish and picking it up very quickly."

Quelling bitchy responses about Sonia, I said, "I'm so glad they're OK. I was thinking about them today when we arrived – thinking of going round to their flat to see how everything is."

"I shouldn't worry about that – they managed to let it for a small fortune so it's paying their mortgage and then some, so they shouldn't be too much out of pocket when they get back."

"Jammy gits, why am I not surprised?"

"Well, that's Ben for you, always thinking practically. But he really is enjoying himself – they've met lots of locals and have totally immersed themselves into the local culture. He says they're bitten to bits by mosquitos and other such lovely winged insects and apparently malaria is a worry for people, but Ben and Sonia have been taking their tablets and so far so good. Though he does say it's terribly poor – but the people are lovely. I wouldn't be surprised if they apply to stay an extra year."

I couldn't retrain myself for another moment and keep my self-respect.

"What? Sonia without her home comforts for two whole years! Surely not?"

"Oh, Ellie, don't be a cow, I think it would do them the world of good. When you've had things easy for a long time it's good to have to work hard and remind yourself of some realities."

I knew I had gone an unsightly shade of puce on hearing him call me a cow. As an alternative to bursting into tears, I decided to do a big cover-up job. "Yeah, I know," I said heartily. "I'm proud of them, I really am! I just wish he would write or phone me – I miss him and oddly enough I miss Sonia too!"

Jake looked amused and I had the nasty feeling he could see right through me. I took an over-large gulp of my wine and ended up coughing helplessly, tears and mascara streaming from my eyes and splotching the pristine napkin.

It took me a while to get my usual poise back. Another couple of glasses of wine helped.

So there we sat in a fabulous restaurant in Chelsea, surrounded by the rich and possibly famous though to be honest I hadn't seen anyone that I recognised. But we could have been in a transport cafe on the M25 for all the notice I took after Jake arrived. I even went to the loo and didn't notice what they were like and that is normally a very big thing for me. We ate food that I was later told was delicious, drank wine and I chatted practically exclusively to Jake all night. He was attentive and kind. I began to think he had signed a pact with Ben to take care of me or something – not that Ben ever had, really, but maybe he had repented and reformed. We talked about Ben and Sonia a bit more, Chloe's wedding dress which we were going hunting for in the morning and the chances of Brian ever convincing Rachel to get back into bed with him. We chatted about our jobs, how his was amazing and that he was going to the States quite regularly, to Boston and New York. How mine was crap and not going anywhere and the how chances of me becoming the next Ulrika Jonnson were so minuscule I'd have more hope of becoming the next Al Jolson.

"Have you thought about a complete change?"

"Of what? Job?"

"Yeah, why not? You don't particularly like the one you have, you certainly don't get paid enough, you admit you're not going anywhere, so why not do something entirely different, what have you got to lose?"

"But what would I do?"

"Well, how about PR? Advertising, promotions, or publishing?"

"I'd like to get into publishing. I love books, though someone told me there isn't much money in it, but then I'm hardly in a position to retire at the moment. Or advertising – I could get into one of those big companies, change my name to something stupid like Bethsheba and earn pots of cash for thinking up amazing ways to sell Bovril!"

"There may be a bit more to it than that, but you should make an effort." Jake was taking this a bit *too* seriously. "I mean, you could even move down to London."

"I have another friend, Carol – she works for one of those massive agencies, so famous I can't remember the name. She has a right laugh with her products. But she does say sometimes when she watches the news, seeing the awful things that happen round the world, she has to question what she does."

"Yeah, I can imagine. The world of advertising is pretty fickle, agencies and people fall out of favour every day. But it would do you no harm to maybe move down south for a few years."

"Oh, now, I don't know about *that!* What about Hector?"

"There are dogs in London too, you know."

"Yeah but it's not the same – we live near the park at home."

"Like I said, we have parks here too. You should give London a chance."

He was pushing this so hard a little bud of hope was opening up in my mind. Why was he so keen to get me down to London? Could it be . . .

"Though saying that, I might be moving soon."

Wrong again, Ellie. "Where? Edinburgh?" I was ever hopeful.

"No, sadly not. I may have to move over to Boston for a couple of years. My company want me to be involved in the setting up of a new office. It will take at least two years to set up and get running smoothly – I'm kind of in the middle of negotiations with them at the moment."

"Oh." Oh God. My world was tumbling down. "What is 'kind of in the middle of negiotiations'?"

"Well, we're trying to work out a relocation settlement, and a salary, though I still haven't confirmed that I will go."

"But they want you to?"

"Yes, they do. I think they'll make it worth my while."

"Do you want to go?" I could feel the colour draining out of my face – God, I am so obvious, he's going to notice. I smiled madly, or showed my teeth anyway, trying to look excited on his behalf.

"I don't know. It would seriously push me up the corporate ladder. I mean I would be one of three guys in charge – that's a really good opportunity I don't know that I could pass up. Not to mention a fairly massive pay rise. But then I love my job at the moment, I like London and I'd miss my friends. But it wouldn't be forever."

"God, you must be really good at your job – I don't mean to sound like a moron, but wow it must feel great to be in demand." I really sounded like a moron. Way to go, Ellie.

"Yeah, it is, but then with that comes the added

responsibility. You have to deal with more, you're expected to increase your work load, work longer hours and all that."

I thought about my job. Sometimes I wondered if I didn't turn up would anyone notice – probably only Fiona. There was a definite lack of pressure in my current position. How could I ever win the respect of this man?

We chatted on, me trying to resist the urge to grab him by his lapels and scream: *'Don't go! I think, well, I'm sure that I'm in love with you!* If you go now then we may never have sex and that is more than I can bear!'

Of course I just sat there and tried to appear enthusiastic, mentally banging my head of the table. Chloe was looking at me; I think she realised something was wrong when she saw the ridiculous smile plastered on my face. The smile was stopping me from dissolving into a puddle of misery.

"You will of course promise that as soon as you think you might be picking up the old mid-Atlantic drawl you will phone me, because no one will ever take you seriously with that noncey accent."

Jake laughed and agreed.

Then I made him promise to ring me before any flight from abroad back to the UK so I could give him my duty-free order – that is, if they didn't do away with it, as they keep threatening to do.

But I just wanted to cry. Everyone else was getting blind drunk, though tonight I could have knocked back the Pinot Noir like it was water and it still would not have had any effect on me whatsoever.

The business men were leaving, every one of them smiling now – looked like they had sorted out their problem whatever it was. One of the women on the flashy table was so drunk she had started to summon the waiter by calling *"Wanker, oi, wanker, over 'ere I need more wine."* The other couple managed to look quite embarrassed but her husband was almost doubled up with laughing – in fact I feared his sunglasses might fall off. The odd couple had left long ago – they had held hands all through dinner and he had paid the bill – must have been her boyfriend. God, even old women could get decent boyfriends round there. The hen party were now all totally sozzled and I could see them trying to locate their bags from under their chairs to fish out their gold American Express cards before heading out to whatever club had been deemed trendy enough for them to attend.

George was just in the middle of telling a funny story when one of the hen party appeared between Jake and Brian. She was totally steaming, but annoyingly was still stunningly attractive, how come her make-up didn't slide off her face when she was drunk? Maybe that's what all the fuss is about expensive cosmetics. I had never really seen the point until now.

"I jusht wanted to shay that we – " (she gestured in the direction of her table) *"think you are lovely."*

She was looking at Jake – now I didn't say she was focused on him – but she was looking in his general direction.

"Would you like to come out *whish* us tonight? We are going to go *danshing*, and we want you to come *whish ush."* It was a statement rather than a request.

Other diners were looking over with exaggerated disapproving glances but Jake was trying not to laugh, "No thanks, kind offer but as you see I'm with some people."

She looked round the table squinting her eyes, and holding onto the back of Brian's chair.

"Well, what about you then?" She looked at Harry and George – Brian was staring into his wine glass.

Harry and George looked like all their Christmases had come at once.

"Cheers, love, we'll be right over."

She smiled, happy now, and headed back to her table to tell the others she had managed to secure at least two blokes.

"God, I love posh totty," said Harry. "Doesn't matter how drunk she is, as long as she sounds like she has got at least two plums in her mouth."

"And looks like she has got room for two more!" George interjected and they both fell about laughing at their own crap joke.

"Thanks lads," said Chloe. "I thought you were with us for the duration of the evening!"

"Sorry, you don't mind, do you? I mean how often do we get asked to accompany such fabulous creatures to a club?"

Brian shrugged his shoulders.

I looked across at Jake. "Don't you want to go?"

"Nah, I think I'll stay." He smiled into my eyes.

I was blushing again. I was going to buy some colour corrector first thing tomorrow. "Oh," was all I managed.

"Where are we going to head to?" Chloe asked.

"I don't mind," said Rachel, "We have booze back in our house, don't we, Brian?"

"Yes, that's true. I brought a bottle of vodka and a bottle of gin back from the States with me last week – they've hardly been touched – we could buy some orange juice and tonic on the way back to the house."

The guys paid the bill which had appeared like magic on the table. I didn't know how much it was and I was rather glad, as I think my Visa card would have fainted, not to mention my bank manager. Another waiter appeared at my elbow holding my jacket for me. Kissing us goodbye and telling us they would see us soon, Harry and George nearly fell over the flashy table in their haste to get to the lovely ladies of Knightsbridge and their night of potential debauchery.

Chapter Ten

We stood outside the restaurant and waited for a taxi. It was freezing cold, but then it November and that was not that unusual. Chloe, Rachel and I entertained ourselves by looking in the window of Joseph's at clothes none of us could afford (and I probably wouldn't have fitted anyway). While Brian flung himself in front of oncoming cabs, Jake tried ringing one on his mobile phone. He had more success than Brian who only succeeded in covering himself in mud from the side of the road. When our taxi finally appeared Jake asked the driver to stop at the nearest 24-hour garage so we could buy our mixers.

Back in Brian and Rachel's house, we congregated in their front room and shoved our bags out of the way. Rachel got the gas fire going and sitting in the front room beside a radiator with a vodka and orange in my hand I started to feel a bit happier. This happiness increased when Rachel produced a large bar of Galaxy from the fridge and passed it round – far more satisfying than any joint, in my opinion. We chatted for hours until Chloe was so tired that she went up and fell asleep in Rachel's bed. Rachel said she was happy enough to sleep on the sofa bed with me but twenty minutes later she was yawning, so Brian made her go and get into his large double bed. Very tipsy, she did as she was told without argument. A little while later we heard the toilet flush and Brian's door close. He jumped to his feet.

"God, I'm knackered – it's three forty in the morning, I'm supposed to go to rugby training tomorrow, I'd best be off to bed."

"But where are you going to sleep?" I asked him. "Rachel is in your bed."

"I know, I'll sleep on the floor – no sweat. Then I can make sure she's OK – during the night – what's left of it."

I raised my eyebrows but he ignored me. He shut the door quietly behind him, leaving Jake and me on our own.

"Do you want another drink?" Jake asked.

"Yes, please." God, no, it's the last thing I need! But I was desperate for him not to go.

Jake went over to the dresser and poured out the vodka from the now nearly empty bottle.

"Ellie, I think we need to talk."

My heart was in danger of stopping again.

"What about?"

"I think you know."

"About you leaving? Or the fact you are the only one my errant brother bothers to phone?"

I really didn't want to hear him say something like, 'I

know you have feelings for me but I don't have the same for you. I'm leaving to go to America so I think we should just be friends.'

"Stop messing around – I want to talk to you about you and me."

"Right." Please don't say it, please, please I really will cry. I was holding on to the arms of the sofa and my knuckles were white.

Jake sat down beside me and turned to face me.

"Ellie, I know you like me and I like you – but there are some obvious complications."

"Oh." This was clearly going to be another one of my fabulously coherent conversations.

"Yes, there are. Number one: I'm probably going to the States in a couple of months for two years or more. It would be stupid to start a relationship which is going to have to end in two months and stupid to try to keep it going long distance."

Oh, so he was going to be Mr Nice Guy, letting the poor girl – his best friend's sister, after all – down gently. I gulped back my tears. "But you live in London and I live in Edinburgh so it would have been long distance anyway," I said in a small voice. Pathetic, really.

"Yes, I know that, but the distance doesn't compare and I would have been up and down to our Edinburgh office fairly frequently – so I could have seen more of you, you know. Who knows, we're even looking into making it our main office in the North, instead of Glasgow or Newcastle. Perhaps I could have headed that up."

"That would have been nice," I said miserably.

"Ellie, listen to me!" He took my hands. "I've grown very fond of you."

So would it be appropriate for me to remove all my clothes, or should I perhaps shut the curtain first?

"That is why," he continued, "I am no longer in a position to begin anything with you."

"Oh?" I'm sorry – am I missing something here?

"It wouldn't be fair on either of us – the distance would be a killer. I know from experience it wouldn't work."

"I suppose you're right." What experience? He's had a long-distance relationship before? Anyway, if he fancied me he would make the effort.

"The timing has been appalling, I'm sorry. I didn't realise until tonight how you felt and that my leaving was going to be a problem for you."

I flashed him a look. How bloody arrogant could he get? That was so patronising of him! Well, I wasn't about to admit how I felt to him now. I hate men with consciences and this was becoming almost humiliating – as if he was doing the big brother thing again, being nice to little sister. I felt a stab of anger.

"Hey, don't worry about it," I said, cracking a grin. "We can still be long distance friends, can't we?" God, how crap is that?

Did he look relieved?

"Yes, we can – your friendship is really important to me. I wouldn't want to ruin that."

"No, of course not. Look, I'm really tired." I need to bang my head of the wall for several hours in despair.

"Yes, yes, sorry, you'll want me to get off the sofa so that you can get to bed."

No, you moron, I want you to get off the sofa so that you can get to bed.

I nodded mutely.

"Right, I'll ring a taxi. Should be here soon – they're quiet at this time of the night." He looked at his watch. "Bloody hell, Ellie, we've talked half the night away!"

He rang the taxi on his mobile and they assured him one would be arriving in under ten minutes. "Right, I'll help you get your bed sorted before I go."

I smiled weakly. Could we not even have had a meaningless sexual encounter that he could have regretted and I could use for fantasy material for the next five years?

He had only got as far as helping me pull the bed out of the sofa when the door bell rang.

"That's my taxi – listen, I'll ring you in the morning. Maybe we could have lunch or dinner tomorrow?"

"Yeah, sure, I'm not sure what we're up to."

"Well, you have my mobile number so ring me if you get a chance, OK?"

"OK."

He gave me a hug , kissed me on the forehead and pulled on his overcoat. When I heard the door shut I let the tears slide down my cheeks, and reached for my packet of cigarettes. I sat in the dark in Rachel and Brian's front room, smoking, looking out onto the deserted street and I just couldn't stop crying.

In the morning I woke up puffy-eyed, looking like I had just done a couple of rounds with Prince Naseem – no amount of eye cream was going to help but I didn't care.

When Chloe came down she immediately realised that I was not going to be the most inspiring shopping companion. I guess she thought I had a hangover.

She gave me a hug. "Why don't you just stay at home if you feel awful."

"No thanks – to be honest, Chlo, I think getting out would do me good – perhaps a little retail therapy would help."

"Hey, what's up?" She looked at me more keenly. "You look like you've been crying all night!"

"Something like that – I'll tell you later when we are out."

She still looked concerned but left it at that.

Rachel came thudding down the stairs looking like the cat that got the cream – well, judging by the state of her hair and the size of her grin it was more like the girl who got the bonk. And no trace of a hangover.

"Morning, girls!"

"Morning Rach, what have you been up to?" I asked. Wow! What a development!

"You look like you've been doing something other than sleeping." Chloe's eyebrows were almost on top of her head.

"Well, Brian and I may have slept in the same bed last night for body heat. It was very cold last night." She grinned her way into the kitchen and put the kettle on. Chloe and I toddled after her, dead keen to hear the details.

Yes, life was stirring again in my veins – curiosity was overriding my heartbreak. It always does.

"Now, before you ask, it was my idea – well, all good

ones are. He was sleeping on the floor last night and I woke up about four this morning to find him still staring at the ceiling, so I asked him if he wouldn't be more comfortable sleeping in his own bed. He said he would and well one thing led to another – it was nice."

I didn't have the heart to tell her he had only been in bed for about fifteen minutes at that stage.

"Nice?" asked Chloe.

"Yes, it was nice." She was grinning again, like a bloody great Cheshire cat.

"Can you have *nice* sex?" Chloe questioned.

"OK, it was bloody amazing. I just wish he was crap in bed, then I wouldn't be tempted to sleep with him."

"You are tempted to sleep with him?" Again Chloe's eyebrows soared into her hairline.

"Of course I bloody am! I have hormones too you know and we practically live together! It's hard to always say no!"

Oh this was one for the gossip columns! "God, Rach, I had no idea you felt that way about him." I was thinking how agreeable it would be to live with a tasty bloke who was constantly trying to seduce me.

"I love Brian to pieces but the reason nothing happens is that I am scared of what might happen."

"What do you mean, what might happen? It would be great – we all want it to happen."

"Yes, but what if it went wrong, and we fell out? I'd have lost my best friend and flatmate in one go, what would I do?"

"Och, I'm sure you and Brian could work it out," I said helpfully

"Have you discussed this with him?" Chloe asked.

"No, he has no idea – I half-think that trying to get me back into bed with him was just all bravado – you know, something to tell his mates?"

"Sure, Rachel, that's why he takes you out for expensive dinners, buys you drinks in the pub, gets you great birthday and Christmas pressies and stays here living with you in this tiny place, when he could have moved in with George to an enormous chick-pulling pad – just for a shag! No man goes to those lengths for sex – surely it would be a lot cheaper just to bonk the nympho in Accounts?" Again another helpful outburst from me.

"Don't you ever think that he does these things because he loves you?" Chloe putting it beautifully.

I should really have taken a moment and drunk some tea or eaten some toast, but I was so pissed off with Jake and my head that hurt both from crying and a rotten hangover, I was going to force my opinion on Rachel whether she wanted to hear it or not. Without giving her a chance to reply I launched into my tirade.

"Look, Rachel, if you continue occasionally sleeping with Brian you will break his heart, if you haven't already! Pretending you don't feel anything will only work for so long, until you can't take it anymore. By which time he will hate you because of your blasé behaviour towards him, he will move out, you can't afford the rent so you'll have to get another flatmate and then you'll spend your time boring your new flatmate to death with stories about Brian and how you fucked up because you were stupid and your best friend died when you were seventeen and Brian is the only person you have truly loved since Lizzie. What would she think if she could see you now? 'What a bloody arse!' in all probability. Rachel, we are your friends and we love you – it makes me want to kick you in the shins when I see you throwing something brilliant away – what do you have to lose? Brian is the best thing that has ever almost happened to you! Don't mess this up – why can't you let yourself be happy?"

Rachel had big tears rolling down her cheeks. I realised I had just been shouting at her, dredging up the past and accusing her of not seeing the wood for the trees – just what you want on a Saturday morning from a friend who is too stingy to stay in a hotel.

I threw my arms around her. "I'm sorry! That was too harsh, you didn't deserve it."

Rachel's chest was heaving, she was sobbing her heart out. Chloe put her arms 'round Rachel too and the three of us stood with our arms round each other in our nighties in the tiny kitchen.

"What's wrong? Have I interrupted an interesting tryst?"

We all looked up. Brian was standing in his dressing-gown in the kitchen doorway laughing. He promptly stopped laughing when confronted with three tear-stained faces. Rachel immediately went over to him and buried her head in his chest and flung her arms round him. Clearly somewhat confused by this less than normal reaction he hugged her close and looked at us in bewilderment.

He was mouthing "What's happened?" to us. I was about to do my Lionel Blair impression, three words, second word two syllables –

"We had better go and get showers – we don't want

to be late for our first appointment." Chloe grabbed my arm, pulled me up the stairs after her and locked us both in the bathroom.

"Nice one, Dr Ruth!" Chloe had her hands on her hips, never a good sign.

"What? What! Oh, come on, Chlo, like you weren't thinking exactly the same thing?"

"OK, so I might have been – doesn't mean I bollock the poor girl in her own house, when I could be accused of the same thing!"

OK – so Chloe may score a little higher on the sensitivity front.

"What do you mean you could be accused of the same thing?"

"Not me, you prat. You! Oh stop gaping! I mean Jake, Ellie, and you acting like a chaste lunatic. Why don't you just stop arsing around and snog the guy? Everyone knows how you feel about him. God, sometimes, Ellie, I could thump you!"

Now it was my turn to burst into tears.

"What now? Why are you crying? Oh God, I'm sorry! I shouldn't have shouted. What's happened?"

"He knows how I feel about him!" I wailed. "And he's leaving to go to America for two years and he's trying to be nice to me and let me down gently, telling me he thinks it's stupid to start something now as he is leaving in two months and he knows long distance relationships never work and he's been there before and he doesn't want it to happen again!"

"Oh God, I had no idea, oh Ellie!" Chloe put her arms around me.

"I just sat there like a stewed prune while he said all this and then I said fine, we'd just be friends. And then he said goodnight, told me to ring him today and got a taxi home."

"Will you?"

"Will I what?"

"Ring him."

"No, what's the point? He can't really care for me – I think he was relieved I left him off the hook. He went off quite cheerfully for his bloody taxi! Anyway, he only said he was fond of me – not that he loved me or anything." I dried my eyes and wiped my nose on the back of my hand. "If you ask me, he's just being nice for Ben's sake. And anyway, whatever he feels, he's going to America."

"The point is, my dear, that you should talk to him! Tell him that you don't care if he's away for two years – you'll be happy to wait. If you don't tell him he'll never know! After the lecture you have just given Rachel I think it is the least you could do. And it sounds like you've nothing to lose. "

"And nothing to gain. He's going anyway."

"*Oh shut up.* Nothing beats an ask."

"God, you sound like my bloody mother."

"Well, it's better than sounding like mine!"

We both smiled and Chloe gave me a big hug.

"Right, do you want to go first in the shower or will I? I feel like I'm sweating pure alcohol!"

"Me too. You can go first. I think I will sit on the loo and put my head against the window." I rested my head against the cool glass and shut my eyes while the bathroom filled up with the smell of lemons from Chloe's shower gel. Forty minutes later I felt like a new woman. I had hidden my stinky clothes from last night at the bottom of my bag, had a long shower and put on make-up to hide the dark circles round my eyes.

"Ready?" Chloe asked.

"Ready," I replied.

"Right, first stop Selfridges."

We grabbed our handbags and went down the stairs. Rachel and Brian were still in an emotional embrace in much the same position we had left them in an hour ago. They were oblivious to us. I left a note on the back of the front door to say we would be back around sixish and would see them then.

"God, I hope they get everything sorted," I said as I pulled the front door behind me.

"Looks like they already have!" Chlo replied. We headed for the nearest tube station.

The rest of the day passed in a kind of bridal blur, the large department stores (I won't name names as I don't want to put you off) were generally unhelpful, well maybe just very busy but Chloe didn't see anything that was nicer than we had already seen and the dresses were twice the price of ones she had seen in Scotland. One shop in particular was hilarious – we found lots of dresses that looked exactly like ones you have nightmares about, Bo Peep styles, giant meringues, ones with twenty-foot trains, truly appalling displays of bad taste. To top it all they had been handled by grubby shoppers so much that they looked a bit tatty, hardly inspiring you to spend four thousand pounds. One of the sales assistants wouldn't leave Chloe alone and tried to sell her a revolting tiara for three hundred. When I asked her if they were real diamonds she just looked at me as if she had discovered me on the sole of her shoe. I generally am a fan of tiaras, some are really funky and unusual, others are beautiful and intricate; this one was neither – it screamed 'over-priced rubbish' to us both.

When we finally managed to back out of the bridal department without a fight from the clinging assistant we gave up on the department stores as they were too much hard work. We found a beautiful shop on Sloane Street. The women who worked there were remarkably nice but we reckoned, short of Chloe selling her soul to Satan, there was no way her father would fork out twenty thousand for the dress alone. Completely knackered we retired to an expresso bar in Joseph's for some refreshment and a sneaky look at their autumn collection. A couple of pairs of new trousers later we actually managed to make it downstairs for coffee. I insisted on a large sticky Danish for each of us.

"God, Ellie, why does this all have to be so difficult? Maybe I should just get one made?" Chloe was leaning on the table her head in her hands.

"Not a bad idea – there was that stunning one in the magazine you bought last week."

"Yeah, there was. I'll take the picture to Yvonne's on Monday and ask what she thinks."

I had half a Danish wedged in my mouth so I could only nod. Yvonne was the dressmaker who had made our graduation dresses. She was really good and not horrifically expensive.

That decided, we spent the last hour before the shops shut browsing round the King's Road – bliss. I spent sixty quid in an exclusive cosmetics shop one can only find in London – I had visions of my mum having a hairy fit if she could see me. After the assistant assured me the make-up could withstand a big night out, Chloe had to prise the Visa card out of my hand and drag me away. It was starting to get dark so we headed for home. I had managed not to think about Jake more than thirty times and I was quite proud of myself. We were passing a phone box on the way back to the tube station when Chloe handed me twenty pence.

"Phone him."

"No."

"Do it or I will get really cross."

I made huffing sounds and screwed up my face. Chloe's expression didn't change – she just calmly looked at me.

"Do it."

"OK, OK, bloody hell, so pushy!" I looked heavenward in an attempt to look frustrated, but was secretly pleased she was making me phone him. I don't think I could have done it on my own. I took the money from her and pulled open the door of the kiosk. It promptly shut as I was halfway in, trapping me between the fresh air from outside and the smell of cat's piss from inside. Once I had managed to fit my whole self inside, with the help of Chloe shoving me in from behind, I had to take several deep breaths (which was no mean feat) before I could dial his number.

Jake picked up on the second ring.

"Hello, Jake Croft here?"

"Hi, it's me." Um . . . Jake Croft, dreamy name.

"Ellie?"

"Yes, hi there." I was blushing even in a phone box.

"I'm glad you called – I thought you maybe wouldn't."

My heart lifted at the thought of him thinking about me.

"Yes, of course I called. Chloe and I wanted to know what you're up to tonight? We're fed up with shopping and our feet hurt."

"Great. I've been on the phone to Brian – incidentally there seem to have been some interesting developments between him and Rachel since last night."

I gave the thumbs up to Chloe, who hadn't the faintest notion what I meant.

"Good."

"Anyway they wanted to know if you fancied a quiet night in, or a big night out?"

"Hang on a mo, I'll ask Chloe."

I shoved my head out the gap in the door. "Jake wants to know what we want to do this evening – do you have any more money?"

She beamed and handed me fifty pence. "Something quiet preferably, I'm totally buggered from shopping."

I ducked back into the phone box, "Chloe says something quiet."

"Fine, how about a Chinese and a video?"

"Sounds good, what time?"

"Say seven thirty or eight at my place?"

"We'll see you there – I take it Brian knows where you live?"

"Yeah, he does."

"OK, see you then, bye."

"Bye, sweetheart." And he hung up.

Sweetheart! From anyone else that would have sounded vaguely patronising and naf but from Jake it sounded like magic! God, I thought, maybe I'm even more sad than I initially reckoned!

When Chloe and I got back to the house there was no sign of Rachel or Brian, the lights were all off and the answer machine was flashing. I went into the kitchen to boil the kettle for tea, turning lights on as I went and Chloe listened to Rachel's messages in case David had called.

"You have one new message." The answer machine's electronic voice told her.

"Ellie, look I know you're in London – I saw you and Chloe get on the train and I just want to say how rude I think you're being towards me – there is no need to ignore me. I'll call you when you get back which I presume will be Sunday sometime."

The answer machine clicked off and stopped flashing. The hair was standing up on the back of my neck. I walked into the living-room with the two cups of tea in my hands.

"Did you hear that?" Chloe asked.

"Yeah." I sat down on the sofa and Chloe reached into my bag and pulled out my cigarettes. She passed me one; I took it, my hands shaking.

"You could probably phone the police about this, you know."

"And they would tell me what? Sorry, we can't do anything until he actually quits scaring the shit out of you and actually threatens your life? I don't think they're interested in telephone harassment." I inhaled deeply on my cigarette and blew the smoke out, up towards the ceiling.

"Actually I think there is something you can do. The telephone company can change your number and monitor your calls for a start." Chloe blew on her tea to cool it down before tentatively taking a sip.

"Well, how exactly did he get Rachel's number?" My cigarette was disappearing fast.

"He met Rachel, didn't he, when you went out with him?" She slurped more tea. "Shit . . . that's hot!" as she burnt her tongue.

"Yes . . . but how did he know I was here? We could have been staying at Linda and Maureen's – he met them too."

"Maybe he tried there first? Why don't you ring them to see if he did."

"No, it's OK, they'll only get cross that we didn't tell them we were coming down.."

"Um . . . true."

We heard an enormous thud upstairs.

"Oh God, he's coming to get me!" I grabbed hold of Chloe's arm.

The thud was followed by laughter, Rachel's laugher.

"They must both be upstairs," Chloe said smiling. "God, bloody Mark has us both climbing the walls!"

"Sorry, I'm sorry."

"Why the hell are you sorry? You didn't ask Mark to be Mr Freaky Stalker, did you?"

"No, of course not, but well . . ."

"But nothing – when we get home you're calling the police. You have to start keeping a record of all the calls he makes to you. Take that tape out of the machine, it's evidence."

"But then they can't use their answer machine!"

"Oh, they'll be fine without it for one day, Brian can replace it on Monday or we'll get one tomorrow if the shops are open."

I took the 'evidence' out of the answer machine and put it into my bag, in the little zipper compartment where I always mean to keep a couple of quid for emergencies, but seem to spend it on chocolate, so there is often little more than sixpence knocking around in there – well, that and some Galaxy wrappers.

The landing light came on, we heard voices at the top of the stairs and the thud-thud-thudding of Rachel and Brian descending the staircase. Neither of them had got dressed. Rach was still in her nightie, only now it was on back to front. Brian was wearing his dressing-gown – underneath it he had on a pair of pyjamas though judging by the Marks & Spencer label sticking out of the leg, they were inside out.

"Hi guys, any joy today?" Rachel looked at our bags which were sadly devoid of anything bridal.

"Well, not unless you include buying enough make-up to do up the cast of *Cats* for a couple of weeks," I said, staring at the Marks & Sparks label, "and some lovely but non-essential trousers."

"Not even a tiara? Didn't you say you were keen on one?"

"Don't even go there! We did get some good ideas though."

164

"One being that we couldn't cope with all the shops in London."

"Well, when you live here you don't have to visit them all in the same day – it takes the pressure off," said Rachel chattily filling up the kettle, as if it was a perfectly normal day and perfectly normal for her and Brian to be gambolling about in bed all day.

"I think I've decided to get my dress made in Edinburgh," said Chloe, also trying to pretend everything was normal. I know a really nice girl who is very good and I think she'd be able to make it for me in time."

"When is it again?"

"June the 25th."

"Are we free on the 25th?" Rachel asked Brian, smiling as Brian pretended to consult the calendar.

"Yup, looks like we can make it."

Chloe and I looked up at them from the sofa.

"Aren't you going to sit down?" said Chloe.

They both sat. Which was surprising as it was perfectly evident that, if a troop of killer penguins had stormed the living-room and taken Chloe and myself hostage, neither of them would have noticed, let alone cared.

"So," I began, "how was your day? Anything interesting happen?"

"You could say something did." Rachel's smile was almost behind her ears it was so big.

"We've decided to make a go of it, just see what happens," Brian told us but he looking at Rachel, who appeared to have dissolved from our sorted, savvy friend into a gooey mass of adoration. They kept touching each other as if to make sure they were really there and this was really happening.

"Bloody well done, lads!" I said loudly, trying to get their attention.

"Thanks," Rachel said and kissed Brian on the cheek.

"Aw, you guys are so good together," said Chloe and they both laughed.

"A bit of a turn around from this morning, eh Rachel?" I added.

"Yeah, what you said really made sense, Ellie. Sorry for being so dramatic, I suppose sometimes you need your friends to point out the obvious. Thank you!"

"So you aren't cross with me?" Ha, ha, so sometimes I could make sense – Louisa first and now Rachel, perhaps I should open a counselling service.

"God no, of course not! If you hadn't said everything then I would still be pricking about instead of having spent the most glorious day in bed with my live-in lover!"

Brian actually went a bit pink and giggled. Brian giggled! When was the last time you heard a man giggle? We all laughed at him.

"Jake was talking about getting a Chinese takeaway and going round to his house for a video – are you two still up for it? Or have you tired each other out?" Chloe asked.

"No, we're definitely going to come out tonight – Jake has got cable and the football is on."

"Not a bloody chance, mate!" Rachel punched Brian on the arm in a revoltingly I'm in love with you way.

"Stop with all this love stuff," I grumbled, only half joking. "You're making me seriously jealous – I'll have to go out and accost some poor bloke in the street!"

Rachel looked at Brian and then at me. "So there's no one closer to home that you'd like to tell us about?"

"No. Why?"

"Oh, I thought you had leanings towards a certain friend of mine," Brian probed.

"Funny how men often get it wrong!" I forced a smile. The last thing I wanted was Brian to announce to Jake how much I liked him. Public humiliation was not really my thing.

"Who was on the answer phone? Was that Jake?" Rachel cut in.

"God, sorry, it was Mark – I meant to tell you. I'll replace the tape tomorrow."

"The tape?" Rachel looked baffled.

"I have to keep all his phone calls as evidence."

"What? Your ex?"

"Mark has started to virtually stalk Ellie," said Chloe. "He watches her flat and rings her in the middle of the night, very creepy. He even saw us get on the train to come down here – so when he rang I told Ellie to take the tape out so we would gather evidence to take to the police."

"You gave him this number?" Rachel asked in surprise.

"No!"

"Then how did he know you were here?"

"That's what we were just talking about. He could have made a lucky guess or else he rang round everyone else," said Chloe.

"Jeez, is it that serious?" Brian asked.

"It's getting pretty freaky," I nodded.

"He phoned her up to ask who was the bloke who dropped her home in a taxi the night Jake told her about Ben going away. Then he rang again to tell her he had bought tickets to take her to a concert in Glasgow and when she didn't turn up he got really angry. So Ellie spent a few days at my place."

"After that, he seemed to have calmed down and forgotten about me," I added. "I hadn't heard from him in two weeks until tonight."

"God, you poor thing! That is so scary. Have you changed your number?"

"No, I suppose I'd been trying not to take it too seriously but now I'm finding it hard to laugh it off. He really is getting to me."

"Have you been to the police yet?" said Brian.

"No but I will when I get home. I don't know how much they can do."

"Well, it's worth telling them anyway – to alert them. Does Jake know about this?"

"No, why?"

"I think you should tell him."

I looked at Chloe who nodded in agreement and then Rachel who did the same.

"Why should I tell Jake? What's he going to do? Beat Mark up?"

"That would be good of him," said Chloe.

"Well, maybe he should know for his own protection," said Brian. "If Mark has identified him as your new boyfriend."

I flushed. I hadn't thought of that. "Look, it's quarter past seven. I told Jake we'd be round at eight. Brian, will you drive or do we need to order a taxi?" I wanted to change the subject as I was too embarrassed to tell them that Jake was so interested in me he was moving to another continent.

"No, I'll drive – does anyone need to change?" Brian said.

"Call me old-fashioned," I said, "but can't you get arrested for driving round London in your jammies?"

Brian laughed and he and Rachel went upstairs to put some clothes on.

"And we're timing you too!" Chloe called up after them.

"God, I'm starving," I said. "That wee roll at lunch wasn't nearly enough. I'll have another fag to stave off the hunger. Who said that smokers are thin? Bloody liars!"

"Listen," said Chloe, putting a hand on my shoulder. "Are you really OK? About Mark?"

"Yeah, I'm fine, he can only phone me. right? He's in Edinburgh and I'm in London. It's not like he's going to turn up on the doorstep – I don't really think dark alleyways and binoculars are Mark's scene."

"Which begs the question: how did he know to be at Waverley on Friday morning?"

"Leave it, Chlo, please, I'm not in the mood to discuss that wanker right now. I promise to go and see the police and get my number changed when we get home, OK?"

"OK. Thank you."

Sitting in the back of Brian's lovely BMW the streets whisked silently past us on the way round to Jake's flat.

I was looking out the car window at the busy streets full of people going out for Saturday night. London must be one of the few places in the world were anything goes and no one bats an eyelid. We passed two men sitting in nothing but their underwear at a bus stop – Chloe was in fits of giggles – Brian reckoned they'd probably lost the rest of the stag party. Rachel was oblivious to what was going on outside the car; she had her hand on Brian's knee while he drove. She was looking out the windows like me but she had a dreamy faraway expression on her face which was reflected by the window.

It took around twenty minutes to get to Jake's flat in Battersea. He buzzed us in and was waiting, waving a Chinese menu, to greet us at the door when we got to the top of the stairs. We ordered rapidly as everyone was famished, then Chloe and I had a nose round his flat under the guise of going to the loo – together of course. It was less masculine than I had expected, though a definite relief to find the bedroom was devoid of all black ash veneer units and black and white posters of half-naked women pouting over the bed. In fact I was very impressed to see that Jake appeared to come from the 'less is more' school of taste: a large brass double bed with plain navy sheets, wooden floorboards and white walls, very tasteful and very effective. There were some interesting prints on the walls, mainly abstract shapes in deep colours and a few photos on his chest of drawers. On closer inspection they were photos of his parents, his brother and himself on holiday in Thailand and a very old one of a Golden Retriever and a tiny boy, presumably Jake or his brother. The only drawback I could immediately see was that Jake was incredibly tidy and therefore if he spent any longer than three minutes in a room with me he would want to wring my neck, as I am at the other end of the tidiness spectrum. Cast your mind back to the description of my flat and its glorious grottiness.

Chloe had made her way back into the living-room where everyone was, but I continued on my fact-finding mission to the bathroom, passing on my way the spare room – nothing much in there, just a few boxes of books and a very old TV. In the bathroom I discovered an old enamel bath which seemed about seven feet long, with big brass taps and an exciting array of bath foams and gels on one side. The bathroom was completely white, tiles, loo, sink, bath, everything – the only splash of colour was a massive mosaic mirror above the sink – bloody hell, Jake had serious taste. This only served to piss me off even more. He even bought decent loo-rolls instead of the bum-grater stuff favoured by most single males.

I sat on the edge of the bath and looked at myself in the mirror: my skin was blotchy, hair needed washing or at the very least a good brush, I hadn't even bothered to put on any of that expensive make-up on before I came out – I didn't fit in that bathroom. How could I expect to tempt Jake to pack in his job in the States, with its massive salary and chance at the big-time to come to live in a shit-hole in Edinburgh with a girl who can't iron, a dog who moults and a nutty ex-boyfriend thrown in for good measure?

Maybe I shouldn't tell him about Mark after all.

As I was contemplating Feng Shui lessons, something

caught my eye beside the sink, just sticking out from behind a box of tissues. On closer inspection it turned out to be a little old-fashioned picture frame with a photo of a glamorous-looking blonde, hair blowing across her face. I stared. Who? What? The possibilities were sickening. Why in the bathroom? He took his baths with it propped up in front of him?

A knock on the door made me jump, I dropped the photo onto the floor and shattered the glass.

"Bugger!" I got down on my hands and knees and started to pick up the glass.

"Ellie, are you in there?" Jake's voice was on the other side of the door.

'Um . . . yeah, sorry, I won't be much longer!" I was getting flustered – what was I going to do with all the broken glass? I looked round for a bin and in the process managed to stab myself in the wrist with a piece of the broken glass.

"Ouch! Shit!!"

"What's wrong? Are you OK?" Bloody Jake was still on the other side of door.

"Yeah, I'm grand, has the Chinese arrived yet?" Actually I'm bleeding into your very smart grouting, sorry about that, I'm sure it will bleach off. No, no, I'm not trying to do away with myself, I was just being nosy and dropping breakable glass items in your bathroom . . .

"No, it hasn't – look, are you sure you're OK?"

Now I'm sorry to sound like a total wimp but I had started to feel faint. I don't think it was the blood loss which I'm sure was minimal, as I don't think I could hit an artery if my life depended on it. I think it was the sight of the blood, I'm a tad squeamish and have trouble coping with Animal Hospital – and of course it might have had something to do with that photo.

"I'm – oh – I'm feeling a little bit weird." I managed to unlock the door and dramatically fell into Jake's arms, getting blood all over his shirt.

"Jesus, Ellie, what have you done?"

"I broke your picture, sorry." Then I very pathetically passed out cold.

I came to and, finding Jake's arms around me, decided not to come to too quickly. I could hear the others talking and a lot of agitation as they buzzed round. I lolled back in Jake's arms and – oh, the thrill – felt him lift me and carry me out of the bathroom. Next, I was being laid on a bed and they were fussing about with my wrist with lots of "Are you OK, Ellie?" and concerned faces. When they eventually covered me with a blanket, telling me to rest, I closed my eyes. Someone kissed me on the forehead but it wasn't him. They turned out the light and left. I fell asleep.

I woke up starving in a dark room and couldn't remember where I was for a moment. I could hear the television and people chatting in the next room.

I sat up. *"Ouch!"* I had a sharp pain in my wrist. *"Shit, that's sore."* I lay back down. I could feel a bandage on my wrist. Oh, yes. Slowly my eyes grew accustomed to the darkness. I must be in Jake's room – the prints on the walls looked familiar.

"Well, it was nice of him to let me bleed all over his bed, rather than the spare room," I muttered to myself.

I got up and turned on the light. I was indeed in Jake's

room, but I had not bled all over his bed. I opened the door and went out into the hallway and into the bathroom. I could smell food and I could hear them talking about what they were watching on the television. I turned on the bathroom light to see if there was still blood on the floor – it had all been cleaned up apart from a stain on the grouting, which as I had predicted pre-faint, could probably be lifted via the wonders of bleach. I turned the light off again and went into the living-room. Everyone stood up when I walked in and Rachel and Chloe came straight over to have a look at my wrist.

"Are you OK, love?" asked Chloe.

"Yeah, yeah, sorry about that."

"God, you just passed out right in Jake's arms," Rachel said.

"Well, you know me and my natural sense of drama."

"Yeah but that was a big gash – we were debating whether or not to take you to hospital," said Brian. "How in God's name did you manage to do it?"

"Oh, leave it to me!"

"Do you want to go and lie back down again?" Jake asked.

"No, I feel fine – just a little sore. Is there any Chinese left?"

"Sure, I'll get you some." He went into the kitchen.

"Are you sure you're fine?" Chloe whispered.

I nodded.

"Jake was really worried about you," she whispered. "Well, we all were, but him in particular."

"God, did I make a mess of his bathroom?" I will ignore that last comment, thank you, Chloe.

"A bit, but it didn't take long to clear up – what did you drop? We couldn't work it out – it looked like glass from a picture frame, but where was the picture?' Chloe wanted to know.

"God, I don't know." I realised that Jake must have hidden the photograph before the others arrived. Why? But I was glad the others hadn't seen it – or seen that I'd seen it – well, been looking with it.

Jake arrived back with a plate piled high with sweet and sour pork, crispy shredded chicken and beef in black bean sauce, a generous helping of fried rice and a handful of prawn crackers, all of which I devoured in about two minutes.

The video was just finishing. Brian said it was not the best choice they had ever made and I hadn't missed anything. We sat on for another hour chatting and then Rachel said she was tired and wanted to go home. I would loved to have been able to stay longer but since I had no excuse, other than a repeat of the bathroom drama, I had to leave with everyone else.

"Take care of that wrist, Ellie," said Jake. "You should probably have it looked at when you get home."

Always the nice guy. Big brother.

"Yeah, I will, thanks. Sorry about the mess." Who the hell is she?

I got another kiss on the forehead and he made me promise to ring him when I got back up to Edinburgh. I got into the back of Brian's car, waved and we were off back to Rachel and Brian's with Rachel chatting like someone had wound her up.

I sat wondering how long ago it was that I met Jake

in our kitchen – it couldn't have been any longer than about nine months. Interesting about that photo, if not plain devastating. The plot thickens.

Chloe and I planned to be on the eleven o'clock train back up to Edinburgh the next morning. Sunday service always takes twice as long as the train stops in every hole in the hedge and Chloe couldn't bear the thought of arriving home late at night, as she hadn't seen David all weekend and she would have to ring her mum before she got suspicious as to her whereabouts. When we got back to the house Brian said his goodnights and headed straight up the stairs. Rachel made us all coffee and sat and chatted for a while about how much she loved Brian, how it was all totally wonderful and how much she owed us for coming down and sorting her head out. She headed off to bed still smiling and telling us how much she loved us and that we had to visit her more often.

"Are you in love with Jake?" Chloe asked me when Rachel had disappeared up the stairs. "I mean really in love?"

I glared at her. "Yeah, I am. That is probably why I spent the wee small hours of the morning crying into my Silk Cut packet, you dunce! Help me with this frigging bed, would you?" I was trying to get the sofa to release the bed it was hiding inside it.

"No – I know you are but do you think that it really is the real thing?" She tugged on a leg and the whole thing came out on top of her.

"You OK?"

"Yes, fine."

"I think it is, but not having a vast experience in this area I am not entirely sure. When he told me he was moving to America I felt sick – does that count?"

"Yeah, I think it probably does. You know, I think everything will work itself out."

"You do? But what about America?"

"I do. Forget about America – trust me, I'm an expert in these things."

"Oh, right."

I lay down beside her in possibly the most uncomfortable sofabed in the world, one on an angle, that made all the blood run to our heads.

Why hadn't I told her about the photo? She might even know who the girl was. Did she know? Did they all know and were they covering it up on me? Poor Ellie, we really mustn't let her know about Jemima or Patricia or Sophie or Elaine – she'd be so hurt . . .

No. Chloe didn't know. And I didn't want her to. It would be the last degree in humiliation.

My last thought before I slept was that neither had I told Jake about Mark.

Chapter Eleven

We sat unspeaking on the train as it chuntered in apparently no great rush back to Edinburgh. The carriage was warm, the gentle rocking of the train sent me to sleep. When Chloe woke me, we were just outside Newcastle.

"Why did you wake me so soon? We've got ages yet."

"You were drooling all over the window, that man over there was staring at you."

"Oh right, thanks."

I took a tissue out of my bag and wiped down the damp patch on the window, and stared back at the man who had been watching me dribble on myself for four hours, sicko!

"Not too much longer now – God, I am bloody starving, what time is it?"

"Two thirty – you slept through the delicious BR cuisine."

"Yeah, I'm sure, is there a trolley service?"

"Don't get excited but there's even a restaurant carriage – well, that's maybe a bit grand but the pizza didn't look bad."

"Um, pizza – yes, I think I could definitely go for a piece of that, as long as it's less than a tenner of course?"

"Yes, I think it was only two seventy five."

"Any anchovies?

"Don't be ridiculous – British Rail put anchovies on a pizza? You'd be lucky to get tuna."

"Good, I hate anchovies. Now, do they sell wine?"

"Didn't notice, you'll have to check."

Chloe went back to her book and I wobbled my way up the carriage, past the obligatory screaming children (one reason I may never have one of my own) and of course everybody's favourite, drunken footie supporters who got on at Darlington. The train bumped over the Tyne, and through the heavily built up industrial city that is Newcastle – saying that though, you can't beat it for a decent night out.

Very few cities can hold a candle to it for its amazing night life – the only city I know where girls wear crop-tops and micro-minis, no coats and big hair, while it rains, snows and hails. The girls travel in under-dressed packs, teetering along the wet streets in toe-crunchingly high shoes, laughing and smoking, death-staring anyone who looks at them for too long. Crowds of blokes follow behind with neatly ironed Ted Baker shirts, D & G jeans, gelled hair and earrings. They drink horrific amounts of Newcastle Brown ale and invariably throw it back up after a kebab on the way home. All that said, Geordies are some of the nicest people in the world, I even have some as close personal friends.

But I digress, I was on my way to the restaurant carriage. Thankfully the footie supporters were more interested in the pyramid they were building out of empty cans of larger rather than harassing me as I passed. I arrived at the restaurant carriage unscathed and totally starving to find the restaurant was closed and all was left was a serving-hatch. The guy serving looked like he had a serious hangover and hadn't changed from the night before; he also appeared to be fighting a losing battle with acne not to mention a dose of body odour.

"Could I have a pizza, please?"

"None left."

He didn't apologise or offer a substitute. He just stared back at me in a rather uninterested fashion. Rather like a father who has been forced to take his kids to the zoo and couldn't give a monkeys about the monkeys.

"Well, could I have a hot dog then?"

"None of them either."

"Um . . . " I scanned down the menu that was stuck to the side of the carriage with blu-tack.

"Quiche?"

"Nope."

"Steak sandwich?"

"Nah."

"What do you have then?"

"I've got a cheese and pickle sandwich, ham and pickle sandwich or a tuna and pickle sandwich."

Tuna and pickle! "Cheese and pickle, please."

It was clearly a bad idea to wait until Newcastle to have something to eat when travelling from King's Cross on a Sunday afternoon.

He picked up one of the three sad-looking *sarnies* off the shelf behind him and set it in front of me.

"Anything else?"

"Um . . . a packet of cheese and onion crisps and a Diet Coke, please."

"That it?"

"Yes, thanks."

"Five pounds exactly."

I looked at him to see if he was taking the piss, but he just stared at me like a dead fish and held his hand out.

"How much for the crisps?"

"A pound."

"And the Diet Coke?"

"A pound."

"So you're charging three pounds for a shitty dried-up cheese and pickle *sarnie?* Do you or do you not provide a service?"

No reply.

"Ripping off people who can't afford to fly isn't nice – I shall write to my local MP when I get home and I shall write to your superior."

He just looked bored like he heard threats and complaints every day, which he probably did. I also suspected he didn't know what an MP was, or quite possibly who his superior was. Mind you, if he had eaten too much of his own food, it was probably rotting his brain.

"Don't you want the sandwich then?" he said at last.

"No thanks," I said. "My sense of value will not allow me to pay three quid for a crappy sandwich."

"Well, the tuna and pickle is only two pounds."

"Why?"

"They aren't very popular."

"Oh." Give me strength.

"So just the coke and the crisps then?"

"No – just give me the sandwich, the tuna one."

Chris, as his badge told me, looked non-plussed. He put the crisps and the coke back and handed me my bargain sandwich. I paid him the two pounds, wondering why I didn't just ask for a coffee and go and have cigarette to stave off the hunger for another couple of hours. Sometimes I could be so stupid. Often, in fact.

When I got back to my seat Chloe had dozed off, but she woke up as I sat down.

"What did you get?"

"Don't ask . . . tuna and pickle sandwich."

"Gross!"

Chloe pulled a face, so did I once I bit into it. One bite was enough, the rest went into the bin.

Was everything in life going to go wrong for me now? It seemed hardly fair – a broken heart was bad enough but a tuna and pickle sandwich on top of it was the last straw.

I made Chloe go and get me a coffee as I was too embarrassed to go back and tell Chris where he could stick his sandwiches. I stood between carriages and had a cigarette out the window.

An hour and a half later we pulled into Edinburgh Waverley. We heaved our bags off the train, thankful that it was not raining.

David was waiting to pick us up. He gave Chloe a big hug and a kiss and lifted our bags into the boot of his car.

"Are either of you hungry?"

I loved this man – I knew he was about to marry my best friend but if he was going to take us out to dinner then I loved him too.

"I have a casserole in the oven for you both."

I take that back, I thought, I only marginally like him now – what men make casseroles?

"Oh, David, that's wonderful! You're so thoughtful! Did you miss me?"

I stared at Chloe in shock and wonder. Being in love must weaken your sense of normality so you think your beloved should have spent all day chopping carrots and bits of stewing steak in preparation for your return.

"I also got a video – it's – um, *Moonstruck*, I think. Do you like that one, Ellie?"

I love you again, David – *Moonstruck* is only my favourite all-time film. Cher is brilliant and it has Nicholas Cage, swoon. I haven't mentioned my Nicholas Cage fetish before now but now I'm ready to spill my guts so to speak. OK, so I regularly rent his films – even Hector groans when I put *The Rock* in the video recorder one more time – and recently I managed to pick up a copy of *Moonstruck* for a few quid and have had many a happy evening watching that fabulous film. Nicholas Cage fetish or not, anyone is the better for seeing it.

Anyway, now that I had something to look forward to I felt better able to deal with David's casserole.

I sat in the back seat of David's glamorous leather-seated BMW and tried not to notice that Chloe kept leaning over to kiss David as he was driving, firstly because it isn't very safe to snog and drive, and secondly because I was extremely jealous. Jake was going to America soon so I had better get used to it and stop being pathetic. I found myself repeating this mantra later when it was just Hector and me at home.

'Oh Hect, why is my life so complicated?'

We were both lying on the floor in the living-room as the sofa and chair were full of my ever-increasing ironing pile. My answer phone was flashing, I was torn between listening to it or not – it could be Jake or it could be Mark, and I really was in no mood to deal with Mark's witterings. No doubt this time he would want to take me to Germany to the Munich Beer Fest or to something equally inappropriate.

But I couldn't just let the light flash; it could be Jake regretting not snogging the face off me in London and wanting to profess undying love to me. I pressed play.

It was Mark.

"Hi Sorrell, Mark here, wanting to know if you are free on Thursday night. I've been invited to the premiere of *The Gaelic Thistle,* the new film they made in the Highlands. Well, I get to bring a partner so I thought I'd ask you! Lots of big names will be there so dress up! I'll call round for you about 6.45 just to make sure we get a good seat. My number is 01431 8954 21488. Love you."

My initial reaction was to throw the answer phone out of the window but then I thought – a premiere? Why not? Surely he couldn't do anything too terrible if we were going to a premiere in public, and really any chance to see some famous faces shouldn't be passed up merely because you could be putting your life in jeopardy. I rang Chloe to see what she thought of the idea.

She didn't like it much.

"Are you completely bonkers? Sorrel Clarke, I cannot believe that you would even consider this for even one minute! I mean, one minute you're collecting evidence to take to the police, the next you're going to black-tie events with this mad man! Anyway, how the hell did he get invited to the premiere? He has nothing to do with film-making, does he?"

"Not as far as I know – I don't know what he does these days. He could be an aerobics teacher."

"Now what would an aerobics teacher be doing at a film premiere?"

"OK, OK, you're right, I won't go, I just thought for a moment – God, Chloe, how often do we get the chance to meet any famous folk?"

"Not often I grant you, but seriously, Ellie, come on. I don't think you should go. Jake would go mad if he thought you were going to go out with that guy."

"Jake wouldn't give a damn!" "You know he would, stop being such a pain in the arse."

"Look, it's got nothing to do with Jake. It was a stupid idea, I won't go, end of discussion."

"Fine."

"Fine."

I hung up on Chloe, angry that she was quite possibly right, and I had been on the verge of making a total arse out of myself. I was also remembering a bit guiltily that I hadn't got round to telling (warning?) Jake about Mark. But probably Brian would have told him by now.

"It's not such a bad idea!" I shouted at a rather surprised Hector who was busy making yet another nest in my various ironing piles. He cocked his head to one side. The effect was almost as if he had said, "Oh, come on, who are you trying to kid? It's the worst idea you ever came up with in your whole life!"

Only he didn't have to say it. I already knew. I called Chloe back to apologise.

"I'm sorry."

"It's OK."

"No, really you were right, it was a totally terrible idea. I'll ring him back and put him off."

"What will you say?"

"I'm not actually sure, to be honest, he isn't that easy to bluff. A lot of the time he seems to know what I'm doing and where I'm going."

"Well, use me and David for an excuse if you need to, or else just give it to him straight."

"What do you mean?"

"Tell him enough is enough, you don't appreciate the phone calls or the invitations and it's about time that he got on with his life and left you to yours."

"That sounds good. I think I'll try that."

"Now, just remember what he's like. He'll try and talk you round."

"Right."

"Don't let him talk about the good times – God, don't let him talk about the great sex you used to have – tell him it wasn't that great."

"OK, I will not let him talk me round. Do you think I should get my number changed?"

"Wait and see what he says. If he doesn't play ball, then contact BT and ask them what you should do, but hopefully it won't come to that."

"Right, will I do it now?"

"Do you think he would be in?"

"Now seems like as good a time as any – I'll ring you back as soon as I've done it, OK?"

"OK, good luck."

"Bye."

I got out my cigarettes and lit one – a couple of strong inhalations and a cup of black coffee set me up to ring Mark back.

"Well, here goes," I said to Hector.

I picked up the phone and dialled the number he had left on the machine.

The phone rang twice before someone picked it up. It was a woman's voice.

"Good evening, Kitson's Productions, may I help you?"

Who the hell were Kitson's Productions? I had never heard of them. Why had he left that number on my machine? Did I have a wrong number?

"Um, I'm looking for Mark McKay, does he work with you?"

"One moment, please, I'll check for you."

I sat staring at the phone number I had written down – maybe I got it wrong. The hold button was playing 'Greensleeves'.

"Hello?"

"Yes, I'm still here."

"We did have a Mark McKay working here until last week – he has now left, I'm afraid."

"Oh, do you have a home address for him?"

"I'm afraid I cannot give that out."

"Cheers, thanks for your help – oh, one more question, what did he do at your company?"

A pause while she wondered about the bluntness of my question. But then she answered. "Checking for you . . . he was a freelance make-up artist."

"I beg your pardon, he was what?"

"He was one of our make-up artists."

"Thanks."

"You're welcome."

The phone line went dead.

Mark a make-up artist? God, how weird – could it be a different Mark?

I rang Chloe back to tell her what had happened. She told me she'd be straight round.

"Well, I don't know how I'm going to get in contact with him now."

"God, I didn't know he knew the difference between a pan-stick and a lipstick, but there you are!"

"I know, I thought I'd maybe got the wrong person. It appears that Macho Mark is actually Maybelline Mark!"

We were howling with laughter, sitting on the floor, a bottle of wine between us, and a family pack of cheese and onion.

"But how I am going to put him off for Thursday night?"

"Come round to my flat with Hector and we'll hide under the sofa."

We burst out laughing again.

"Maybe it wasn't me he was interested in after all –

maybe he had his eye on my Estee Lauder eyeshadows!"

"God, do you think he wears make-up? Or just puts in on other people?"

"I don't know. He didn't use to wear it that's for sure, but then he didn't use to stalk me either so who the hell knows!"

"Very, very strange."

"What is David doing tonight?"

"Not sure exactly – he may be going out on a boy's night out, why?"

"Do you want to go out for dinner or something?"

"Love to."

"Which reminds me – I'm going to have to get on the ball about your hen night! Not long now!"

"God, don't remind me, I still have to phone Yvonne. Mum is going to do her nut."

"How come?"

"I told her I got a dress in London."

"Oh God, Chloe, why?"

"She was hassling me about the dress and in a moment of weakness I lied and told her I had bought one and she would love it. Only problem is that now she wants to see it."

"Bloody marvellous, Chloe. Ring Yvonne now if you value your life."

"Can I use your phone?"

"Yeah, sure, but do you think she is going to give you an appointment tomorrow?"

"I hope so!"

"When are you next seeing your mum?"

"In four weeks!"

"Excellent, at least Yvonne won't be under any pressure."

"Well, I know what I want."

"You have a pattern?"

"No, I have it in my head."

"Ring Yvonne!"

After Chloe had managed to persuade Yvonne to see her the following morning I dragged her out for a drink. We went round to my local, Carnaby's, for a couple of glasses of wine. It was fairly quiet for a Friday night, and we got a table without too much bother.

"So you have to get your wedding dress designed and made in four weeks. Great. Did Yvonne sound at all hopeful?'

"Actually once I had calmed her down she thought she might be able to make it in time, if all the fabrics that I want are in stock."

I once again reminded Chloe how she was dicing with death lying to Margo about anything so central to the wedding as the actual dress. Chloe for once didn't seem scared of her mum. This really appeared to be progress.

"So, enough boring wedding chat," said Chloe wanting to get off the subject of her mother. "How are you?"

"I'm grand, slightly perturbed about Mark but then I suppose it keeps my mind off Jake."

"I um . . ."

"You, what?"

"Nothing, no really, nothing at all. God, Ellie, stop staring at me in that way!"

"What do you know that you aren't telling me?"

"Jake is leaving in two weeks for Boston."

"How the hell do you know?"

"I was on the phone to Rachel before I came round to see you. Jake had been round for dinner or something and told Brian when Rachel was making the coffee."

Oh, so that's why she had come flying around. "It sounds like he doesn't want anyone to know . . . He's going about a month early though, I wonder why? God, I am now driving men out of Britain. Now I know how Ally McBeal feels when every time she falls for someone they apply for a passport." I felt a bit lightheaded.

"That's a TV programme, not real life. Anyway, you knew he was going so what does it matter if he goes a little early?"

"It doesn't I suppose." Though to be perfectly honest I felt like I had been punched in the stomach by the Fairy of Crap Relationships.

"I know I told you I had a good feeling about you and Jake – well, it's just going to take a little longer than was originally expected. I'm sure he'll be home at Christmas – you could go to London and see him then, that's only a couple of months."

She still didn't know about the photo in the bathroom. Must tell her. She was my best friend, after all.

"Nope, I am sick of hanging around waiting for stuff to happen to me," I said. "It never does. I'm going to become a self-starter."

"A what?"

"A self-starter, I am going to make things happen for me. Firstly I am going to forget about Jake – his career is more important to him than I am and frankly I don't blame him. Who'd want to end up with a flake like me?"

"You're not a flake, Ellie – loads of men would love to end up with you. But I thought you were against marriage?"

"I may be changing my mind!"

"So what are you saying? You're looking for a husband now?"

"Exactly!"

"But, Ellie, you go off men after ten minutes! And anyway you already love someone."

"That's where you're wrong, my dear. I did love someone else, it didn't work out, so I am moving on. I am also going to start applying for new jobs. The world, dear Chloe, is my oyster! I'm going to find the man of my dreams and simultaneously earn pots of cash."

Chloe stared at me, wondering if I was taking the piss or being entirely serious.

"I am being entirely serious, Chloe, no messing." I was beginning to believe myself. "This girl is going to find herself a husband."

I suppose to Chloe that's a bit like me saying: "I think I'll go see if I can catch the black death."

"OK, so you want a husband – stranger things have happened – but how are you going to earn pots of cash?"

"I am going to resign from my job and invest my savings on the stock market. I know a bloke in London – in fact, we know quite a few blokes who would be more than qualified to double our money."

"It's not the safest way to make profit."

"But it's the quickest! I'm going to make a few grand,

then I'm going to go to Cannes or St Tropez and find myself a gorgeous man." Yes, why not?

"Um . . . now? In the middle of winter?"

"Yes – Nicole lives in Cannes. I'll ring her and see if there is any talent around at the moment – then, my dear, I am off for a month, on the pull for rich older men!"

I was convinced. It suddenly seemed like a great idea.

"Oh God, Ellie." Chloe put her head in her hands as I pulled out my address book to look up Nicole's address.

After about two hours arguing with Chloe I insisted on ringing Nicole. I mean what harm could ringing her do?

"For God's sake, Ellie – what a mad notion! Wait a couple of days – I'm sure Jake will ring you and tell you about going to America early – "

"Who says this has anything to do with Jake?"

"Ok, but please don't do anything stupid!"

"Oh, so now I'm being stupid? Right. Well, I know who my friends are now!"

Chloe was totally raging with me, I was being a total prat but have you ever argued yourself into a corner and felt, in order to save face, you have to go through with whatever you were arguing about?

In the end we had a massive falling out, the first one in ages. She left in tears, telling me if I wanted to fuck up my life well that was my prerogative. At that stage I should have admitted defeat, told her I was sorry and picked up the recruitment section in The Scotsman.

But what did I do instead?

I rang Nicole, who was slightly confused but said she would be delighted to see me.

First thing Saturday morning I went down to the travel agents and booked an open-ended return to Nice, leaving in one week's time, on my Mastercard. Then I went home and wrote my letter of resignation to Mr McBain, who probably wouldn't know who I was anyway, let alone be sorry to see me go. That was the only part I didn't mind, leaving my job. I would miss Fiona like mad but I was buggered if I was going to let loss of salary and missing friends get in the way of the argument with Chloe.

"Hi Fiona, it's Ellie. I need to talk to you."

"Oh aye, what are you up to, dearie?"

"Well, I'm about to hand in my notice at work."

"Oh, I see."

"I'm going to France to find a husband."

"Right, to find a husband. Wouldn't it be easier to get one in Scotland?"

"Not really. I've booked my ticket, I'm leaving next Saturday."

"And the job?"

"I'm handing in my notice."

"Right. Have you enough money to be going abroad?"

"Not really but I'll get a job once I'm there."

"So, you have really thought this through?"

"Oh, stop taking the piss, Fee! I really am going. OK?"

"OK, fine, whatever you want. It's a bit sudden, all this leaving the country stuff. How long are you going for?"

"I don't know, probably a month – I'm not really sure how long these things take."

"And Hector?"

"Oh God, I hadn't thought about that – Chloe can look after him."

"Well, that's all settled then. Where are you off to?"

"Cannes – I've got a friend there who I can stay with."

"Ellie, if it's not a stupid question, why a husband? I thought you were a career girl."

"Yeah, well, the career doesn't seem to be going too far at the moment, so I thought a change would be good. I need security, a man with money, so I reckon the south of France has to be a good bet."

"Sure – spend the rest of your life with a man who can't pronounce your name properly and needs two walking-sticks to get into bed. Good move, my dear."

"It won't be like that."

"Och, silly me, how will it be?"

"He will be young and romantic and fall madly in love with me. We will sail around the Cote d'Azur in his yacht, drinking champagne and eating violet creams. He will want to buy me amazing diamonds and apartments in Monte Carlo and New York."

"I'm cancelling your subscription to *Hello*. Are you selling your flat?"

"I hadn't thought."

"I suppose now would not be the time to tell you that you and I are up for a pay rise, and possibly a promotion."

"What? Money? You didn't mention this at work yesterday."

"If you remember – you were too busy being a

miserable cow to notice, but Avril came round to discuss the chance of two researchers being moved to more roving-reporter positions for the *Eyes and Ears* programme. She thought we might have been good candidates, but I suppose they can select another researcher without too much bother."

"You mean we would get to be on TV?"

"Yup."

"How come? I mean, I hadn't heard of any jobs for *Eyes and Ears*. Why didn't Avril tell me?"

"She couldn't find you. She was checking through CVs and noticed that you used to be a reporter . . ."

"In the loosest sense of the word – I mean, I used to cover church fetes."

"No matter, in your CV you said you were an experienced journalist and that your move out of newspapers and into television had been to give you a rounded view of media."

"I wrote that?"

"Apparently so. The point is, with your journalistic experience no matter how banal, and my near perfect knowledge of Scotland – "

"What you do you mean your knowledge of Scotland?"

"Well, my knowledge of Scotland is virtually encyclopaedic – I was a contender for Mastermind."

"I never knew that! *Bloody hell, Fiona, that's brilliant!* How come you never went on?"

"I had an argument with Magnus Magnusson just before my heat started."

"An argument about what?"

"The correct cooking method for haggis. I mean, the man was obviously a moron – I mean, he is Scandinavian, isn't he?"

"Yeah, I think he's Norwegian or something, but why were you arguing about the correct ingredients for a bloody haggis and why was he obviously a moron?"

"He said you can only boil it. But anyone could tell you that it is delicious baked, or indeed sliced and shallow-fried as well. Well, Magnus wasn't having any of it, so I called him a fool and was promptly escorted off the set."

The vision of Fiona and Magnus Magnusson arguing over the best way to cook haggis was a wonderful one.

"God, Fiona, only you. I'll bet you didn't go quietly either."

"I certainly did not. I am a leading expert on Scottish cuisine whether that little twerp acknowledges the fact or not."

"So – because you can cook haggis to perfection and I can give the nitty-gritty on the egg and spoon race, this means we are up for a possible promotion?"

"In a nutshell, yes. I may have embellished slightly on the old qualifications and experience front, but I mean it's nothing we couldn't cope with. I left Avril's office with her thinking you and I would make great candidates – so she is putting us forward."

"Bloody hell, Fi, I guess I better tear up that resignation letter."

"You haven't written one yet. What about your Euro-hubby?"

"I suppose he will have to wait."

"How much was your ticket?"

"Two hundred and forty quid."

"Maybe Avril will be able to convince Mr McBain that you need a holiday at short notice and you could still go for a week?"

"I'll ask her, but I don't care if we get this promotion. God, this is exciting. A pay rise – do we know how much yet?"

"No, but just imagine: you and I touring Scotland reporting on any lies and untruths in the world of consumerism."

"We'll be the next Anne Robinson and Alice Beer – bags be Alice, I quite fancy being a sleek chick rather than a lumpy frump. Oh Fiona, we'll get our own make-up artists!"

"Now don't get too excited, we don't have the jobs yet, but I reckon if they employ internally we stand a really good chance."

"When do we find out who gets the jobs?"

"Two weeks, but I think we're in with a really good chance."

"Oh Lordy, I'm so excited! I want to tell Chloe – except we aren't speaking to each other at the minute, she's really hacked off with me."

"Over your husband excursion to France?"

"How did you guess? Yeah, something like that – God, I am such a prick sometimes."

"You don't need to tell me. But admit it, it was a completely crap idea. No offence, mate, but if I was a multi-millionaire I don't think I'd marry you."

"Why the hell not?"

"Well, all megarich blokes go out with pop stars and models. You know, girls who wouldn't know what the inside of a Miss Selfridge looked like let alone wear anything they sell. Believe me it's for the best – the French eat horses you know."

"Oh, piss off, you cheeky cow! I can't believe you don't think millionaires would want to marry me!"

"Oh shut up – like you wanted to get married anyway. Now go and ring bloody Avril and see if you can wangle some leave."

I laughed – relieved I had a watertight excuse not to move to France. Now all I had to do was to tell Chloe I was only going for a week and the whole thing could be forgotten about.

The next day I went to see our Director's PA and she was incredibly nice for about the first time ever, she didn't think Mr McBain would mind at all if I took a week's holiday, in fact she told me to go ahead, she would deal with him. I don't know what Fiona had said to her but it certainly seemed to have worked. All I had to do was pack, ring Nicole and tell her not to panic, I would not be a permanent fixture in her life.

Oh yes, and ring my Bank Manager and tell him not to panic either.

Chapter Twelve

Chloe and David took me to the airport, which was really nice considering my flight was 8 am on a Saturday morning.

"Now promise you will come home, preferably without a fifty-year-old Sugar Daddy!" said Chloe.

"OK, OK, sorry for being such an arse, will you ever let this lie?"

"Never."

"Ellie, you are our constant source of entertainment," David added helpfully.

"Cheers, mate. Now, Chloe, you have Nicole's number in case Fee rings about the job?"

"Yes, I have the number, it's in my filofax. I also have the vet's number, Hector's favourite food list, a dog bed, a lead and various other canine accoutrements. God, Ellie, you'd think we'd never had the little bugger to stay before."

"Sorry, sorry, thank you both so much."

I got out of the car and David helped me lift my bag

onto one of the airport trolleys – you know, the ones that are automatically attracted to the kerb, and you have to fight with them all the way to the check-in desk.

"Have a great time and we'll be here to pick you up next week."

They waved me off until I was inside the terminal building.

Trying to keep my swearing to a minimum, I battled with the trolley over to the Sabena check-in and handed over my ticket. I had a brief moment of panic when I couldn't locate my passport, but it was just hiding with my French francs under my make-up bag in the furthest corner of my handbag. I only had twenty pounds worth of francs in cash – the bank had assured me that I could use my bank card in France to take money out of the autotellers over there. The lady at the check-in was very nice and told me that the flight was boarding in half an hour through gate number two.

All set, I headed to the shop to get a magazine to read on the flight. Standing in front of the huge magazine rack I started to feel a little inadequate: 'Satisfy Your Man', '20 Ways to Achieve Better Oral Sex', 'Are You Getting IT Right?', 'What Men Really Think About Your Body', 'He Says He Loves You But He is Sleeping With Your Best Friend'. These cover stories were accompanied by the obligatory, stunningly flawless model – it was enough to make anyone run for the shortbread section (only to be found in Scottish airports).

I stood staring at the display, wondering would men stop thinking about my body if I was achieving and administering better oral sex? And exactly how would I know if I was getting IT right? Would someone tell me? Choosing a magazine was starting to give me a headache so I headed over to the paperback section. I was still standing trying to work out if the body part on the front of the new Julie Burchill was a knee or an odd-shaped boob when my flight was called. I made an impulse purchase of a book by an author I had never heard of because I liked the look of the front cover, and a packet of chewing gum.

I made my way to gate two and stood in the queue waiting for hand-luggage to go through the x-ray machine. When it got to my turn I put my bag onto the conveyor belt and walked through the archway thingy they have, to stop you taking your guns and fireworks on board. As I passed through, the machine bleeped.

An enormous bottle-blonde woman stepped forward in a security uniform and asked me to spread my arms so she could give me a body search. While she was checking my ankles to see if I had grenades strapped to them I noticed that her roots were awful and she had a touch of dandruff – bad luck, love. I am well used to these searches after years of travelling to and from Belfast, but this woman must have known the brand of my underpants by the time she was finished.

When I went to pick up my bag there was another security guard standing behind it.

"Is this your bag, madam?"

"Eh . . . yes."

"May I take a look inside?"

I nodded, trying to look nonchalant, but praying he wouldn't unpack everything. Other travellers were looking at me suspiciously, a body check and a bag search!

The guard carefully took everything out of my bag, looked through my make-up, opened pens and lipsticks and then asked me to press play on my personal stereo. I did this, and he was almost deafened by The Best of Duran Duran. He seemed satisfied and after spreading my personal possessions all over the counter he left me to put everything back.

Hand-luggage is something I have never really got to grips with. I always bring far too much thus giving the air-stewardesses of the world nervous breakdowns as I try and shove it into inadequate overhead lockers. And by the time I have carted it round various airports I have crippled my shoulder. So it took me the best part of ten minutes to re-pack my bag without dropping tampons, tapes and make-up all over the floor. Why is it that even when you don't need them, tampons appear out of nowhere to embarrass you?

I ended up having to sprint to the boarding-gate. Thankfully, when I got there, there was still a queue of people waiting to board, so I managed to get to the Duty Free shop. Two hundred Silk Cut, one large bottle of gin and a tin of shortbread better off, I boarded my flight to Brussels. Behind me in the queque at the gate was a very earnest-looking Japanese man, armed with a trolley-suitcase-type thing that made my hand-luggage look positively acceptable. He was so keen to get on the plane that he wheeled his bloody suitcase over my ankles. I could feel his breath on the back of my neck and I didn't think he had any shares in Colgate.

As I could have predicted he was sitting beside me on the flight. He kept looking over at me as if he wanted to talk to me, but I was still huffing from the ankle incident so I focused on looking out the window at the wet tarmac. This of course only served to indictate to him that there was something interesting outside. He too wanted to look. I got quite annoyed when he almost landed in my lap.

"Excuse me, perhaps you should ask the stewardess for a window-seat?"

"So sorry, I want to see the castle."

"Well, you won't see it from here – it's too far away."

"OK, I wait till we take off, yes?"

"Yes, why don't you?"

He nodded, and sat back in his seat.

I shot him the smile that I usually reserve for children who eat their own boogies, but he didn't seem to notice my disdain.

As the plane took off down the runway I started to get excited, I hadn't been abroad for over a year and I was really looking forward to getting away! I watched as Edinburgh fast disappeared and my Japanese friend craned his neck in a vain attempt to see the castle.

When we landed I managed to lose the earnest Japanese man, or rather he lost me. He practically climbed over the other passengers to get off the plane first, and we were sitting in row twenty.

I like Brussels airport. For one thing, I can't work out the exchange rate between Sterling and Belgian francs (and now they also give you the amount in Euros which just confuses me even more), so I always think I'm getting a bargain. Secondly and most importantly, the Duty Free shops in Brussels airport sell every perfume and aftershave practically ever made – heaven! I love Jil Sander perfumes, which are notoriously hard to get hold of, and Brussels has the whole range – bliss. Anyway, I can wile away hours wandering contentedly round the perfume shelves, spraying myself with hunderds of scents till I quite frankly stink! Oh and I almost forgot, they have an awe-inspiring array of chocolate, seriously fantastic. So, safe in the knowledge that I had credit on my Mastercard I spent a happy half hour purchasing to my heart's content.

What I don't like about Brussels airport is the fact that even though you are in an international departure terminal, you still need to go through a passport control. There was a huge queue and I grew steadily frantic as my flight was leaving in twenty minutes. Then they called my flight. The queue was moving forward slowly but there were still around forty people in front of me. And it seemed all forty were dodgy customers as passport control was taking forever to let them through. There were still twenty when they announced the final call on *Sabena 986* to Nice. Shoving people out of my way, shouting *"Final Call, Final Call!"* I pushed my way to the front of the queue and thrust my passport into the guard's face. He studied me, then my photo, then looked at my bag of chocolate as if trying to decide if I was going to eat it all myself. He waved me through, in that lovely friendly fashion all passport control people seem to adopt.

I started to sprint towards my gate, and almost immediately I started to feel sick. "I will join a gym," I panted to myself as I cleared a pram and kept on running. I managed to make my flight with moments to spare and had to sit sweating on the plane for half an hour before my heart-rate returned to normal.

The wonderful thing about flying with Sabena – the Belgian airline – like that's a boast – has to be the food. After I had finished sweating, an airhostess came round and offered me a roll: I could have plastic ham or cheese and apple – I went for cheese and apple. Unfortunately potato had been substituted for the apple and was unpalatable to say the least.

"Excuse me, this roll has potato in it."

"Yes?" The airhostess smiled at me expectantly.

"Well, it's supposed to be *apple.*"

"Yes?" No noticable change in her facial expression.

"But it is potato, not apple, and it doesn't taste nice."

"Have a ham roll." Still smiling, she handed me a plastic ham roll, which I dumbly accepted.

The rest of the flight was uneventful. Thankfully there were no strange-smelling aggressive people sitting beside me. In fact, no one was sitting beside me, so I was able to doze in complete peace (and drool on the headrest).

An hour and a half later we landed in Nice Airport. The runway is right beside the Med and as you land, on one side there's brilliant blue water and on the other palm trees and restaurants – very chic.

You know you are in France when the authorities are standing about in their uniforms, smoking and not paying you the least bit of attention.

Heaving my bag onto a trolley, I pushed my way through the automatic doors. As they slid open I looked about for Nicole.

As I searched for her familiar face I realised I was standing beside this rather attractive business man. He looked late twenties/early thirties and I had had about four gin and tonics on the flight so I was all set to chat him up. But just as I was in the middle of thinking of something cool and interesting to say he started talking to me.

"I take it you're not here on business?" he asked. His accent was faintly Scottish, I thought.

Well, I was wearing a pair of snake-print bellbottoms and a T-shirt that said "I love Frenchies", so who could blame him?

He was wearing a dark suit with a white shirt and was fairly well built with sandy blonde hair – not really the sort of bloke I would usually go for, but at least he could dress himself. Anyway, who was I trying to kid? He had a pulse and that was definitely an advantage.

"Um no, I'm on holiday." Crimson flush creeping up my neck and over my cheeks in a most unbecoming fashion.

"Someone late?" Yes, definitely Scottish.

"Oh, I'm sure she'll be here in a minute," I said, trying to sound casual.

He nodded. "My driver hasn't shown up either, perhaps the traffic is bad. You know Nice."

Driver? Oh yes, a pulse and money too. Definitely worth a shot.

"Whereabouts are you staying?" he said, as he took off his jacket and slung it on his shoulder.

This guy was very slick.

"Cannes." Another one of my thrilling responses. For God's sake, Ellie, say something interesting. "I've come to find a husband . . ." I trailed off – was I insane?

"Pardon?" He was smiling at me in a very puzzled way.

"I mean, well of course not really . . . I'm here to see a friend not find a husband."

If I had a gun I would have shot myself in the head right then, where the hell was Nicole while I was humiliating myself?

"Right – do you normally go looking for husbands in the south of France?"

I was amazed he didn't grab his bags and make a run for it. "No – sorry, just a silly joke. I'm going to stay in La Bocca for a week with my friend Nicole."

He smiled again – this time I was sure it was in a slightly suggestive way.

"I'm Tom, by the way." He extended his hand to me.

"Hi, I'm Sorrel," I replied, shaking it.

"Pleased to meet you, Sorrel. I hope you enjoy Cannes."

"Thanks – are you here on business?"

"Yes, I have a conference. Sadly not a holiday. I always think there is nothing nicer than sitting on the Croisette in the early evening watching the world go by. Listening to the people on the street while the sea crashes onto the beach behind you."

"You've obviously been before."

"Yeah, normally for the film festival – it's such a drag, I much prefer late summer, early autumn."

Half of me was thinking "What a wanker!" but the other half was thinking "Definitely loaded".

We continued our conversation or rather he continued his monologue. I'm ashamed to admit it, but I was so flattered at the attention he was paying me I just hung on his every word. It turned out he was actually from Edinburgh – another big plus. Being in the same country – let alone the same city – was a qualification currently at the very top of my list of courtship requirements.

"So do I get your phone number?" he asked as a man came rushing forward towards us with a very apologetic look on his face. "One moment, Eric."

The man nodded and loaded his bags onto a trolley.

A tiny figure in green caught my eye – turning, I saw Nicole jumping up and down waving her arms in the air.

"Oh, my lift has arrived too." I was relieved that the attention was momentarily taken away from my crimson cheeks.

"Well?"

"My number? Oh yes, sure." I gabbled Nicole's number to him and he scribbled it down in a very expensive-looking filofax.

"I'll call you – we could meet for a drink."

Wow, a pick-up and I hadn't even left the airport yet!

"Great!" I replied as Nicole arrived. She came galloping towards me and threw herself at me, hugging me and kissing me on both cheeks at the same time, and exclaiming about my short hair. She had a small fox terrier on a lead and it was wagging its tail in a most enthusiastic way – considering Nicole had just dragged it halfway across the arrivals hall.

"Ellie – I am so sorry I am late." She looked from me to Tom and back to me again.

"I thought I'd missed you, I was in traffic on the Autoroute."

"Nic, this is Tom – Tom, this is Nic."

"Nice to meet you."

"And you."

"Hey, thank you for coming all this way to pick me up – I could have caught a bus," I jumped in to fill the awkward silence.

"A *boos?*" Her hands went up to her face in mock horror. *"Mais non,* you would still be waiting to get to Cannes tonight, the *boos* it is so slow. Anyway I must take you out for lunch, a new restaurant has opened on the Croisette. We go today as *zere* will be a lot of nice men, *non?"*

"Sure, Nicole, whatever you want." I laughed, delighted to see her in action again – she was all hand-gestures, shoulder-lifting and eyebrow-raising – I have never met anyone else with such an expressive face.

"I'll be going – nice to meet you both." Tom moved away, Eric following with the trolley.

"Yes, indeed – bye!" I waved.

He headed out of the arrivals hall without so much as a backward glance.

"Is this your dog?" I looked down at the fox terrier who was now wagging its tail so ferociously it was in danger of knocking itself over.

"Oui, do you like her? She is called 'Bambette'. And who was that? You are talking to strange men in the airport?"

"Bambette? What does that mean?" I asked, ignoring her question.

"Nothing I don't think." Then she frowned as if concentrating on something.

"Ah, merde. ma voiture!" She took off down the terminal, dragging Bambette after her.

"I am outside, *Ellieeee!"* she shouted back at me, not slowing down.

When I caught up with her she was arguing with a traffic warden. Apparently she had just parked her mini outside on the kerb and this was highly illegal. I put my stuff into the back seat, and climbed in on the passenger side, while she continued to argue with the poor man who appeared to be on the verge of tears. Two minutes later she got into the driver's seat.

"Bon, stupeed man, he says I cannot leave my car here. I tell him I did not know, and now I want to leave. He says first he must fine me – we argue – I win."

We headed out towards Cannes. Bambette was sitting in the back seat – we had the radio on and the windows open. It was a beautiful day, warm and balmy.

"So, you Irish tart, who was the man?"

"Oh, just someone I got talking to while I was waiting for you."

"Bah! You blame me – I do not like the look of him."

"Nic, you didn't say more than two words to him – how would you know?"

"I know!"

We took the long way round to Cannes instead of going on the Autoroute. We had the sea on our left; it sparkled in the afternoon sun and made me glad to be away from Edinburgh and the shitty rain. Boats bobbed in the little bays as we passed, even the breeze from the open window was warm and comforting.

"There is too much traffic today, I cannot be bothered to sit in this hot little car. I must get a car with air-conditioning."

"OK, whatever you want – you're driving." I laughed. Nicole has always had a thing for minis, ever since she could drive she has been driving them. Having said that, this one was particularly glamorous: black – with cream leather interior, chrome everywhere and still completely tiny. Entirely suitable for parking in places other cars couldn't.

We drove through the little towns along the Cote d' Azur. We passed through Cagnes sur Mer, Villeneuve-Lobet, Antibes, round the Cap d'Antibes – where the wealthy people who just want to be left alone live – through Juan Les Pins, Golfe Juan and into Cannes. The sun was shining and I was delighted to be here – it was more like a spring morning than early autumn. Jake – and Tom – were temporarily forgotten.

I first met Nicole when we were both thirteen. Mum and Dad had sent me to a summer school in Cannes, in a vain attempt to improve my French. My French remained positively abysmal, but I met Nic and had one of the greatest summers ever on record.

I was staying with a strange family quite far out of town. They were nice people but their idea of a good time was changing the television channel – not exactly wild people. I was considering asking Mum and Dad if I could come home after two weeks – I had decided I hated France and the even more horrible French people.

On my first Sunday the family and I were sitting round the table having lunch. Now I am pretty good about eating most things, but Madame Louvey served up a strange grey dish of which I was automatically suspicious. The rest of the family tucked in and I pushed it round on my plate. After about ten minutes I had finally constructed the sentence I wanted to say (the family spoke no English).

"Excuse me, what is this we are eating? I don't think I have had it before?"

"Eat, it is good for you," was the reply I got, not exactly very satisfactory.

I had a couple of mouthfuls, but it was tasteless and a horrible mushy texture.

"It is sheep's brains, very good for study," Madame Louvey told me once we were clearing the table. I spent the rest of the afternoon with my head down the toilet.

After that, I was determined to meet someone nice and make the best of this holiday. Mum and Dad told me there was no chance I could come home early, barring serious illness or civil war breaking out – neither of these looked likely to happen. Thankfully halfway through my second week I met Nic and I ended up spending most of my time with her. After three weeks I moved out completely from the Louveys' house and into the DeLaval's.

The DeLavals were a prominent family in Cannes. They had a fabulous apartment on the Croisette – the main street along the seafront. They also had a farmhouse in the mountains near Grasse with a lovely cherry orchard and a pool. Grasse is famous for perfume – you can even smell it in the air so walking through the woods with Nicole I thought I had died and gone to heaven. We spent weekends in the mountains and the rest of the week in the apartment in the centre of town. Summer school suddenly didn't seem so bad.

The Croisette, where they lived, sees most of the action when it comes to the film festival – visiting dignitaries, film stars and anyone who wants to be seen like to pose on the Croisette. The wealth is incredible; I don't think I will ever get used to the amount of money that gets flaunted so shamelessly down in the south of France. There are two harbours on Croisette, both filled to bursting with huge yachts, cruisers and speedboats, with large crews for each yacht. We were once watching a couple so dripping in gold that we thought maybe they couldn't get up when the husband rang one of the five-star hotels that line the front and had lunch delivered by a waiter to his boat moored only a hundred yards away. No matter how often I go back I am always amazed.

Nic and I would wander along the front at night, eating crêpes and giggling. Thankfully her English was superior to my French so communication was never a problem. Throughout the whole summer I was treated by Nicole's parents, Henri and Celine, like their second daughter. Philippe, Nicole's brother, was away in America so I was spoiled rotten.

They took us all over the Côte D' Azur – to places like Vallauris, world famous for pottery and olive wood with an amazing waxy texture (Picasso had a studio there), and Vence, built into the hillside, with honey-coloured brick and tiles. When we visited Vence they always took us to a pizzeria which had over five hundred different types of pizza – Le Pecheur du Soleil.

It was all so beautiful. In the mountains behind Cannes there are hundreds of tiny villages, all in the same honey-coloured stone, looking like they are straight out of a film set, and the roadsides are a mass of different greens – mimosa, eucalyptus, plantanes, olive trees and pine trees. The French have a lovely habit of manicuring their pine trees into long thin shapes that look like fingers pointing up towards the sky.

Other times we took the coastal routes past Nice towards Monte Carlo: to St Jean Cap Ferrat, which is where the European jet-set gather, to Eze which is a stunning old monastic town built into the cliff-face overlooking Cap Ferrat, and to Monte Carlo to see the Grimaldi Palace and the famous Casino.

I always kept half an eye open for James Bond but never managed to see him. Unfortunately always managed to miss the *Hello* team too, as I quite fancied appearing in one of their issues with Stephanie and Caroline.

Monaco is not far from the Italian border and we went to Italy a few times, normally to buy things that Madame DeLaval claimed tasted better when bought in Italy. She was a fabulous cook so we quite often went over to buy various different types of olive oil, sundried tomatoes and other things I had never heard of, but which tasted wonderful.

But best of all was the DeLavals' boat – well, it was

more of a yacht. It was moored in one of the harbours I
mentioned though it was nothing like some of the boats
that stayed there. We went on weekend trips to two
islands out in the bay off Cannes – Ile St-Honorat and Ile
Ste-Maguerite. The water between the islands was crystal
clear and very safe, with no strong currents or sea
monsters. Sometimes we had the whole place to
ourselves. We would go snorkelling, water-skiing and
windsurfing – the water was so clear you could see to
the bottom and watch the schools of tiny fish as they
darted away among the beds of seaweed that looked
like large bushes blowing in the wind.

Meeting Nicole turned my potentially dull summer
into every thirteen-year-old's dream holiday. Needless to
say, we remained good friends and I never had to eat
sheep's brains again.

The following summer Nicole came over to stay with
me in Belfast, and Mum and Dad took us away round
Ireland for a holiday. Not as glamorous as the DeLavals'
way of life but nevertheless Nicole claimed she had the
time of her life catching crabs in Donegal, walking along
the Carrick-a-reed rope bridge, pony-trekking in
Tullymore Forest and eating fresh scampi at Portaferry.
When I went to Edinburgh she came over a few times
and we would go to London at the end of her trip and
spend the weekend shopping before she flew back to
Nice.

We sped on towards Cannes.

"So, *cherie,* 'ave you any plans this week? Or are you
going to see this Tom again?"

"Well, I gave him your number but I don't think he'll ring – I'd just met him there in the arrivals hall. Other than that I am a free agent. What about you? Do you have to work?"

Nicole is an architect and had recently become a partner in her father's practice.

"I have to work on Monday but after that I am free. Papa has made allowances – you are still a favourite with him."

"Thank you, Henri!" I said with a laugh.

"OK, so now for lunch – I have to park the car."

Nicole parked in the underground carpark at the Gray D'Albion centre, a lovely shopping centre in the centre of town. Once outside the car we were back in the heat again – such a delicious feeling when you have been subjected to grim windy sleet for two months. We had a glance in the shop windows on the way to the restaurant. Everything was so glamorous and expensive: Stephane Kelian for amazing shoes, La Pearla for fabulous underwear, Hermes, Celine, Cartier . . . I could practically feel my credit card burrowing deeper into my purse in the hope that it wouldn't be found.

We walked down the Croisette which has the beach on one side and all the hotels, shops and restaurants on the other. The main street has palm trees on the beach side and also in the islands between the roads. As usual the beautiful people were out and about in shades and designer outfits. No matter how dressed-up I ever get, I feel like a bag-lady after spending twenty minutes on the Croisette. We passed the Carlton and the Martinez, fabulous hotels which have been in lots of films over the years. A little further on Nic led me down some steps to a restaurant on the beach. We sat under a large sun umbrella and as we scanned the menu the waiter brought bread, olives and a jug of water.

"God, I love it here."

I sat back in my chair, enjoying the feeling of sitting in a strappy top in the middle of October.

Nic smiled at me as she took a piece of bread, tore it apart and popped a piece into her mouth. "What do you want?" she asked.

"I think I'll have the tuna salad."

"Sounds good, I'll join you."

"Deux salades de thon, s'il vous plaît," Nic ordered when the waiter returned. "So, Ellie, why are you here? What has made you decide to visit me at this time of year? You sounded so strange on the phone."

I skewered a couple of olives on my cocktail-stick and, waiting for the oil to drip off, started into recounting the saga about almost handing in my notice at work, being generally fed up, my argument with Chloe, panicking about Jake and the sudden unexpected possibility of a promotion.

"Nic, I just didn't really know what to do. I thought if I came down here to stay with you maybe I would meet someone, fall in love and then I wouldn't be left behind anymore. But then Fiona at work told me about the promotion and I decided to come anyway and just have a holiday without having to find a husband."

"Oh Ellie – do you think if there were eligible men around I would be single? Ha, I don't think so! Forget about being left behind – enjoy yourself. Just because

Chloe is getting married doesn't mean that you have to. If I were you, I would concentrate on my promotion – everything else will fall into place – at least you will have money while you wait."

I nodded – sometimes my friend could be as wise as Yoda. Our salads arrived at the table.

"Bon, now eat and forget about *stupeed* men."

We sat in the early afternoon sunshine, eating fresh salad on the beach. Edinburgh seemed like a million miles away.

After lunch we went for another wander and bought ice cream. I made a mental note to go back and look at some shoes that caught my eye.

Then we went back to Nic's apartment in La Bocca – just outside the centre of town. Though her parents still lived on the Croisette, Nic favoured the hills just behind Cannes – they were peaceful and the view was stunning. Her building was cleverly designed on a slope – the effect was like a large white ribbon against the green of the surrounding trees. It was set in its own beautiful gardens with its own pool and tennis courts. Nicole's apartment was on the sixth floor; on balmy evenings she could eat out on the balcony, with a spectacular view over Cannes and the Med spread out below her, distant sounds of the city floating up to her apartment.

She threw open the door to the apartment and we heaved my bag in.

"I think we deserve a drink after all that – don't you?"

"Oh, yes, please."

She disappeared into the kitchen to get wine.

I took my bag into the spare room, which she had

made up for me. The room smelt of the lavender that grew in the gardens below – Nicole had put a little vase of it by my bed. Bliss. I left the shortbread and gin I had brought on Nicole's bed. I opened my duty free carton of cigarettes, grabbed a packet and went out to the balcony. I could hear all the city noises, but also the sound of birds and a tennis ball being thwacked in one of the nearby courts.

"So, do you want to go for a swim?" Nicole asked as she handed me a glass of cold white wine.

"Um . . . yeah, that sounds good."

After the wine we spent the rest of the afternoon by the pool, relaxing and catching up. Nicole was intrigued to hear about Jake and wanted to know more. I felt a bit ridiculous talking about something that had never really happened. But Nicole was such an old friend – she wouldn't judge me for acting like a woman possessed.

Here, relaxed and browning myself, I even had the courage to tell her about the photo in the bathroom.

"Pouf!" she said with a huge shrug. "An old girlfriend! Who cares!"

It was a very French response and therefore not that much of a comfort really.

Still . . .

"Ellie, do you know what I am thinking?"

"No, what are you thinking?"

"I am thinking that this man, he loves you, but I am thinking he is also a bit afraid."

"Of what exactly? Are you saying that I scare men?"

"*Mais non, cherie,* but for him, you are his best friend's *leetle* sister. He has got more to lose than you."

220

Aha! The big-brother syndrome! "Pardon?"

Nic continued in her Dr Ruth role. "He could lose his best friend as well as you. I am sure he is in America thinking about you right now – unless he is asleep of course – then he would be dreaming about you."

I thumped her. I couldn't help smiling – Nicole was such an optimist. "Whatever – you mad old cow!"

"Enough of your misery – we are going out for dinner tonight and then we go dancing. Tomorrow Mama and Papa want to see you, so we go to them for lunch, OK?"

"OK."

"Now let's get ready – I am getting cold now."

Walking back through the gardens to the apartment I couldn't help thinking how lucky I was to have such a good friend – this holiday might be just what I needed.

That night, after much glamorising, Nicole and I hit the town. We ate and then went dancing to a little club that Nicole knew. The music was salsa and after a few drinks you couldn't help but feel as sexy as the music. What an ego boost! We were surrounded by men all night – unfortunately I have never found over-Brylcreamed hair a huge turn-on and most of these men seemed to be working on the premise that this was the way to ensure female devotion. I don't claim to speak for all women here, but greasy locks are not on my top ten list of desirable male attributes – or waking up beside someone whose pillow you could fry eggs on. Still, it was flattering to be made such a fuss of – even if I could only understand about half of what they were saying to me.

Then just as we were leaving someone tapped my arm.

"Sorrel?"

"Tom! God – what are you doing here?" What are the chances?

"Same as you, I imagine." He pushed his hair back off his face.

He looked fairly pissed. Nic hadn't noticed him, she was trying to retrieve her jacket from under a snogging couple. He was attractive though and I had consumed just the right amount of booze to find him irresistible.

Even more so when he said, slurring slightly, "Tell you something – you look better than any other woman in here."

Drunk but what a charmer!

"Are you going home already?" He even managed to look disappointed, bless him.

"Me? No – why?"

"Great!"

He threw his arm round me and hugged me. Nic, who was also a bit the worse for wear, eventually got her jacket back and joined us.

"Ah – Tom! We meet again." She looked at me looking up at him with my special drunken doe-eyed expression. "Ellie, you remember my address?"

"Yes – why?"

"I'm going home – I will see you in the morning – don't forget lunch." She disappeared into the crowd and was gone, leaving me with the half-pissed Tom.

Chapter Thirteen

Sunday morning arrived at the same time as my bloody hangover. I pulled the duvet over my head and tried to go back to sleep, but it was no good – I felt like alcohol was seeping out of my pores.

Then I was suddenly aware that I was not in the single bed in Nic's flat. Moving my arm I felt someone else beside me. Shit! Last night was a bit blurry.

"Morning, sleepyhead . . ."

Omigod, I'm bed with Tom!

Bits of the night before started coming back to me. Tom and I had walked back to his hotel – the Carlton. Well, I had always wanted to stay there but I hadn't imagined it would be like this. We had drunk pretty much everything in his mini-bar and then fallen into bed. After that things really were a blur. What had I done?

"Morning." Oh, the shame of being an easy woman. "What time is it?"

"Oh, it's still early – go back to sleep."

A hairy arm snaked round my waist – I was now fully

awake and completely naked – and so was he. I lay quietly so as not to disturb him – trying to locate my clothes, which I had clearly removed with gay abandon some hours earlier.

When Tom started to snore gently I thought it was safe enough to get up. I crept round the darkened hotel room, gathering up my garments, and padded into the bathroom.

I looked revolting, but now was not the time to be worrying about that. I needed to get out of there immediately and get back to Nic's. I pulled last night's little black dress over my head and padded back out of the bathroom, shoes in hand and as quietly as I could, towards the door. Tom didn't stir – I was hardly breathing as I opened the door and stepped into the corridor. The door clicked shut behind me and I hurried to the lift. The hotel was quiet – it was seven thirty – so it was only the reception staff and a couple of elderly guests who saw me leave, head bowed. I jumped into the nearest taxi at the rank outside.

"Nic, are you awake?"

I peered into her darkened room and was nearly knocked backwards with the smell of alcohol.

"Aie! Ellie, I think I am going to be sick, please do not turn on the light. Would you open my curtains slowly, please?"

I shuffled over to her balcony and gently pulled back the curtain. Light flooded the room and Nicole hid under her duvet. I also took the precaution of opening her balcony doors a little, to let some fresh air in.

"It is no good, I am definitely going to be sick," her muffled voice came from under the covers.

She got up and rushed into the bathroom, thankfully closing the door behind her. I went into the kitchen and took a glass from the cupboard, filled it with bottled water from the fridge and downed it in one go. After searching through the kitchen cupboards I managed to locate some Paracetamol and washed two down with some more water.

"Nic, do you want some water and Paracetamol?" I offered through the bathroom door.

"Oui, very much." She opened the door, her face white as a sheet. She sat on the edge of the bath while I administered the drug.

"What time did you get home?" she asked in a whisper.

"About five minutes ago."

She tried to raise a smile. *"Oh mon Dieu,* I feel like I am dying, Mama will not be pleased if we are late. Ellie, we must get ready for lunch."

"OK, do you want to shower first or will I?"

"You, I can't stand up – I will have a bath after you." She headed back to her room.

"Now don't fall asleep again! You'll feel worse."

"I know, I know," was the grumpy reply.

Bambette was lying in the middle of the hall watching our goings on with some amusement – I stepped over her on my way to the shower.

Standing under the hot jet of water I began to feel slightly less revolting. Covering myself liberally in lemon shower gel, I soon smelt less like a brewery and more like an air freshener. I even managed to get the remains of last night's make-up off my face without a heavy-duty scrub.

Twenty minutes later I was dressed and standing on the balcony squinting at the beautiful day. Nicole was in the bath claiming that she would never drink again. After gentle cajoling I managed to make her get dressed and dry her hair.

"OK, so we will have lunch, but I don't want to stay all afternoon – I'd like to go to the beach if I'm feeling any better – oh, and we need to go food shopping."

"Fine, the beach sounds good health permitting. I could always go shopping tomorrow while you're at work."

"But you would have to carry all the bags up the hill, the bus does not come here – *non*, we will do it this afternoon."

The DeLavals had an underground garage which you accessed off the street. Descending into the darkness I felt my stomach flip.

"Slowly, Nicole – I don't want to be sick in here!"

"Shut up, tart!"

"Oh God – don't I feel bad enough?"

She laughed and slowed down. Her parents' Mercedes were parked side by side and Nicole tucked her mini in at the back. We took the lift up into the apartment building. The lift doors opened and I was suddenly reminded of being thirteen again.

The huge marble staircase curved up to the front door. Nicole used her key to get in rather than ringing the door bell, but her parents must have heard us as they were waiting on the other side.

"Sorrel, so lovely to see you, how good you look!" Henri DeLaval beamed at me.

There was much hugging and kissing of cheeks, as is their customary style.

"I am glad to see you back in Cannes – has our Nicole been good to you?" Celine wanted to know. Then, "Come, come – lunch is ready. I hope you don't mind but we will eat just in the kitchen today."

She ushered us all into the kitchen – delicious smells assaulted my nostrils and I decided that ill though I felt I would have to have a crack at the garlic lamb that was being removed from the oven. We sat round the table and Celine served lunch. Even though this was supposed to be a casual Sunday lunch with the family, there was a linen tablecloth, silver cutlery, crystal wine glasses and Celine and Henri looked like they were ready for a photo shoot in *Hello*.

"So, Ellie, you have cut your hair. I like the style very much, it is very *chic, non?*"

"Thanks, yeah, it was definitely time for a change." It had grown out a bit, thankfully. "Anyway how are you both?" I took a bite of lamb – melt in the mouth job – divine. And I didn't throw up.

"Ah, you know, we are both well. Henri is just as busy as ever and now he has Nicole to work with as you know. I still teach three days – we seem to get more and more children all the time."

Celine teaches riding for the disabled, mainly children, at the local riding school above Nicole's apartment in the hills. She taught me to ride when I first stayed with them and usually takes me out on a trek through the forests when I come to stay. She used to ride competitively but a damaged knee – plus having Philip and Nicole – made her retire early.

"You're still enjoying the teaching?" I asked.

"Ah, there is nothing I enjoy more. Do you ride at home any more?"

"Not recently, but I do still try when I get the time."

"I will take you out on Wednesday if you like. We could take the horses down to the beach. The beaches are quiet at the moment with the sunbathers gone back to Paris."

"I'd love that!"

"Have you any other plans while you are here?" Henri asked.

"No, just a rest – but I would like to take you out to dinner if you would allow me."

"Oh, *cherie,* I think we should be taking you out to dinner!" Henri protested. "Celine – what nights are we free this week?"

"No, I really mean – "

"Nonsense! We must make an effort for you," said Celine. "We are free Tuesday, Wednesday and Thursday. Remember we have dinner with the Renos on Friday night."

"Oh I had forgotten completely! Where are we eating?"

"Elise is cooking."

"Oh non, she cannot even boil eggs, *oh mon Dieu* – why did you agree?"

"I could not say no, she thought she was being kind."

Nicole laughed. "Papa, you can eat something before you go out, and tell Madame Reno you are not hungry."

"Nicole, do not encourage him."

The banter round the table continued – it felt like being in a home from home. Nicole was a bit subdued and only picked at her food – well, by Irish standards – but her parents didn't seem to notice anything amiss. The food was so delicious that no hangover on earth could have prevented me from eating it and I even managed to drink the glass of red wine that had been set in front of me. For dessert Celine had made wild plum cake, which she knows I adore. Every year she goes to the same plum tree and picks as many plums as she can – then she makes jam, cakes and compôte from them.

After lunch was over Nicole made our excuses, telling her parents that we had things to do, and invited them round for dinner the following evening. We also arranged that we would all go out for dinner on Wednesday night.

I tried again to insist on treating them. "Henri, Celine, you must let me take you out for dinner. Please!"

"Absolument non!" was Henri's response to my feeble attempt at returning their generosity – he still thinks of Nic and me as thirteen-year-olds.

"I think we should go to Le Suquet," said Nicole.

"Oh yes! I love Le Suquet!" I said, delighted.

Le Suquet is the old town in the hills behind Cannes – it looks down over the harbour and the rest of Cannes has sort of grown round it. It has lovely little restaurants on its cobbled streets and they tend to be less touristy and expensive than those on the Croisette.

After thanking Nic's parents we left and headed back to her apartment where we agreed we could cope with the beach. We packed a bag full of magazines, sun screen and many bottles of water and headed off. The mini is a perfect car for parking when the beach is busy – Nic can usually fit it under the foot bridges that run over the railway line – but today there were few cars and parking was no problem.

We lay in the sunshine, our hangovers fading away. I could hear the cars on the road above the beach.

"You know, when I make my first million I think I'll buy a villa here," I said. "Yes, that would be a great idea."

"One with a pool."

"When you make your second million, where will you live?"

"Oh, I think I'll buy a flat in London so that we can spend long weekends with our personal shopper in Harvey Nick's and then have my driver take us home – Chelsea, I think."

"Very nice."

"Where do you think I should buy in Cannes?"

"La Californie is very nice."

"Yes, a good choice I think."

"Ellie, how are you going to make your millions?"

"Not sure yet, any good ideas?"

She shook her head and closed her eyes.

I began to doze, my magazine unopened. When I woke the sun had gone in and I was starting to feel cold. I realised I had been dreaming of Tom or at least of a hairy arm thrown around me in bed. That disturbed me – as if it was disloyal to Jake. Which was ridiculous as I had actually slept with Tom – and I didn't owe Jake anything anyway. I shook the dream off and sat up.

"Nic?"

"Uh . . ."

"Are you awake?"

"Uh . . ."

"It's getting cold."

"Uh . . ."

Nicole was face down in her beach towel.

"Nic, wake up, it's after five."

"I'm awake."

She sat up and looked at me.

"You are right, I'm cold now too. Shall we go?"

I nodded. We packed up our beach things. We were the only people left on the beach.

"Oh merde!" Nicole stopped to shake sand out of her shoes. "I love the beach, but I hate the sand!"

When we got back to her apartment we threw on our sweaters – in October when the sun goes in, it can be very cold. We sat on the sofa in the living- room with large bowls of pasta in front of us, and even larger glasses of water.

"I really do not want to have to work tomorrow," Nicole groaned. "You'll be on your own!"

"That's cool, I'll shop. I've seen a pair of shoes that I quite fancy."

"You never change!"

"Nope!" I said with a laugh.

The next morning I heard Nicole leave the apartment around eight. I stayed in bed, dozing and dreaming of

Jake – or was it Tom? I woke at ten, so hot from the sun coming in the curtains that I thought I was going to boil to death. After a leisurely breakfast on the balcony, watching an elderly couple walk their little poodle round the garden below, I got dressed and made my way to town. Nicole must have taken Bambette to work with her – only the French! The buses are fairly straightforward, so applying what little French I had I managed to get myself to the town centre.

Rue D'Antibes is the main shopping street – just behind the Croisette – it's a much narrower road, full of traffic and shoppers. I looked in Joseph – they always have such lovely things, fab little boutiques and fashionable French labels. I bought a necklace in an amazing shop which was like an Aladdin's cave – everything I saw I wanted: rings, bracelets, earrings. The shop assistant smiled at me as I picked up one thing after another. Leaving twenty minutes later I was very pleased with my purchase.

As I dandered along looking in shoe shops and cafes something caught my eye. It was a chocolatier called Bruno. I remember being taken in there when I was much younger by Madame DeLaval for a treat. I pushed open the door and went inside. The first thing to hit me was the smell – the smell of chocolate was incredible – like you could taste the air. The chocolates were displayed on silver trays and they looked absolutely delicious.

"Bonjour, Mademoiselle."

I looked up and a shop assistant was smiling at me.

"Bonjour."

"If you need any help with anything please let me know," she said in English.

"Thank you." God, was my French accent so bad that you could tell from a simple hello?

As I walked round the shop I decided to have a box made up of Nic's favourites, as a thank-you. The assistant lifted the chocolates I picked with little silver tongs and placed them into a box for me. Then I came to the fruit confits which both Nic and I loved – they reminded me of being thirteen again. Fruit confits can be any kind of fruit slow-boiled in sugar syrup. My favourites are the clementines which you must pop whole into your mouth, peel and all, bite into it and feel the syrupy juice burst on your tongue. I asked for four of the clementines. The shop assistant tied up the box with silver ribbon. I asked her to put a clementine in a separate bag for me.

Back out on the street again I took the fruit out of its bag. It was sticky and my mouth watered as the smell hit my nose. I popped the whole thing in my mouth and smiled as the juice oozed out over my tongue.

"Fantastic," I said to myself.

I stopped to look in interesting windows: Emir where they have the most fabulous Persian rugs and the strangest glass sculptures (odd mix), a shop that only sold razors, one that sold ball-dresses for children and one that only sold pens made out of different types of wood. Catering for very eclectic tastes, I thought to myself. When I reached the Gray D'Albion centre I went in, in search of my shoes. It was getting close to lunchtime – when the shop assistants stop being quite so helpful as they want to get rid of you as quickly as possible so they can go for their break. I decided perhaps I would come back after lunch when I wouldn't be treated like a leper.

Back out in the sunshine I decided to have a drink opposite the building where Nic worked and wait for her there. Sitting in the sunshine listening to the whine of the mopeds and the bustle of shoppers I shut my eyes and enjoyed the heat. I nearly jumped out of my skin when something wet and rough touched my hand. Opening my eyes I saw Nicole laughing at me and Bambette snuffling round my shopping bags – she could smell the chocolate.

"What do you have in those bags?"

"A surprise for you and a necklace for me."

"Ah ha, un cadeau for me?"

"But you only get it if you take me to an nice restaurant for lunch."

"Come on, I have booked a table."

We walked down onto the Croisette and into the Blue Bar, a well-known haunt of the famous, where it is *de rigeur* to wear one's sunglasses while having lunch on the sun terrace. I searched my bag for my sunglasses – they were fake Guccis with a wobbly leg – but chances were nobody would notice. I slipped them onto my nose and promptly walked into a table, to Nicole's immense amusement. Thankfully no one was sitting at it. There was sun-cream all over the lenses. Pushing them down my nose – so I could see over the top of them – I followed the waiter to our table. Once we were seated I surreptitiously cleaned my glasses on the tablecloth.

"Did you hurt yourself?" asked Nicole, still giggling.

"No."

"OK, so where is my present?"

"God! So pushy!" I sighed in mock resignation.

I handed over the Bruno bag to her.

"Oh, Bruno! My favourite! Ellie, you are spoiling me!"

"Well, you are letting me stay and embarrass you in public places!"

She tore into the wrapping and looked inside the box.

"My God, there is everything in here! Ah, even *les clementines!* Oh thank you so much, I have not bought good chocolate for a long time – we will have some for our dessert."

She stood up, leant across the table and gave me a kiss on the cheek. Unfortunately, in the process she almost strangled Bambette whose lead she had wrapped round the legs of the chair. A small choking noise could be heard from under the table.

We ordered our lunch and sat back to watch the world go by. The Blue Bar is right on the street and is the perfect place to people-watch.

"Tomorrow I thought we could maybe take a trip to Grasse or to Biot?" Nicole suggested with her mouth full of bread.

"I'd love to go to both places. I might be able to get Chloe and David a wedding present in Biot."

"OK, we can do that. I must get them something too."

Grasse, as I mentioned before, is famous for its perfume. Biot has a glass factory where they make the most amazing things – you can even have a go at blowing your own bottle. I tried this before but my attempt ended up looking like a giant glass raisin, and anyway I don't think Chloe would particularly appreciate a homemade wedding present.

Lunch arrived and the conversation came to a brief halt as we began to eat.

"So what will you do for the rest of the afternoon?" asked Nicole after a while.

"Shop, sit in the sun, you know, nice stuff," I said, brandishing an enormous forkful of Salade Nicoise.

"Tonight we will go out for dinner with some friends of mine – I don't think you have met them before, they are good fun and they speak good English!"

"Fine, where are we eating?"

"La Moule qui Rit."

"The laughing mussel?"

"*Oui,* it is really good fun."

After lunch Nicole returned to work and I set out to continue on my shopping extravaganza. The shops were still closed for lunch so I found a seat on the boardwalk above the beach and sat with my face up to the sun for half an hour. The sun reflecting off the sea was very strong and even though it was October I could feel my nose start to burn.

I went back to the shoe shop I had my eye on. The sales assistants were much more agreeable after having had their lunch so I was able to try on a selection of shoes without pissing them off too much.

I have a split personality, one half is a normal rational female, the other is a half-crazed impulse shopper. Instead of buying the shoes I originally had my eye on I settled for a pair of strappy heels that would give even Naomi Campbell cause for concern. Well, when I stay strappy I should say 'strap'. The shoes had one single thin diamante strap across the toes, after that they were just all heel, but they were the sexiest shoes I had ever seen and well, they had to be mine. I stood with my fingers crossed when the sales assistant swiped my card through the till.

"Please let me have credit, please let me have credit," I whispered quietly.

The till bleeped into life and spewed out my receipt; the great god of shopping was smiling down on me today. I said a quiet prayer of thanks and signed the credit slip.

"OK, no more shopping," I told myself sternly as I walked out of the shop, with a spring in my step. "Well . . . Chloe is different, you have to buy something for her."

I had already informed Chloe that I wouldn't be buying her something off her wedding list.

"Well, anything is great," she had said in reply, trying to sound enthusiastic. "But nothing edible – OK?"

"Right, nothing edible. Why?" I asked.

"Oh Ellie!"

"Only joking, I'll get you something nice I promise. Where is your list anyway?"

"Habitat."

"Oh, that's quite cool."

"Yeah, well, they don't have a John Lewis in Belfast and Mum didn't want Debenhams."

"Why not?"

"Don't ask."

"I just did."

"I'm ignoring you, it's too embarrassing."

"Chlo, you just know that I'll harass you till you tell me."

"Promise not to breathe a word?"

"Promise."

"OK. Well, we were walking past the one in Castle Court at home and they had this A-board outside offering battered fish, chips, beans and a soft drink for four pounds fifty or something. Anyway Mum refused to let me have a list anywhere that served battered fish. She said Habitat is more chic."

"I'm sure it was breaded haddock, you know."

"Stop taking the piss."

"I am not even in the same league as your mum. Do you think she was abducted by aliens and they stole her brain?"

"Ellie!"

"Oh, come on, Chloe, Habitat doesn't even have a cafe."

"I know, but she has been quite good about everything so far so I thought I'd let this one slide – keep her happy, you know?"

"She is bonkers. But your secret is safe with me."

I laughed as I recalled the conversation and thanked the stars that Chloe was nothing like her clearly nutty mother.

When I got back to Nicole's apartment her answer phone was beeping. I stood staring at it – wondering if I should listen to the messages. Tom may have phoned but I wasn't so sure I ever wanted to see him again. The beeping was very irritating so I thought what the hell, if they are French I won't understand them anyway. I pressed the button and the machine rewound itself to play her messages. The first was from one of her friends who we were meeting later.

"Hello, Nicole, it is Paul here. Sorry but tonight I will be a little late. If you don't mind would you order for me? Anything – I don't mind as long as it isn't mussels!" Paul then laughed at his own joke. "Only joking, I'll see you tonight."

"God, what an asshole – can't wait to meet him," I said to myself.

"Beeeeeep!" The second message played.

"Hello, Nicole, it is Ellie's mum here. Just ringing to make sure she arrived safely and to let her know that Ben phoned. He and Sonia are fine, apparently recovering from a horrible bout of food poisoning but nothing too serious. He sends his love. He said he thought you would find the idea of Sonia with the squits amusing – I'm sure I don't know what he is talking about. Anyway, hope you are both well, give me a ring if you get the chance. Oh and Nicole, if you could tell Ellie that Lucy has a new boyfriend – a doctor she tells me. Anyway I must go, lots of love, *byeeeee.*"

A new man? Interesting – I wondered how long he would last.

"Beeeep!" Another message.

I listened. Nothing. A long silence and then whoever was on the other end hung up.

"Beeeep!" Again a long silence, a little heavy breathing and the sound of the phone being hung up.

A dull heavy feeling swept through me.

I knew it was him. I just knew it. Mark.

"Beeeep!"

I waited.

"This is a message for Sorrel from Tom. Sorry – hope you don't mind me ringing. You're probably busy but I was wondering if you'd like to meet up later? I had a great time last night – bit annoyed that you didn't wake me before you left. The number of the hotel is six, seven, four, three, double five. Please call – bye."

While I was still trying to digest that, the phone rang.

I stared at it – debating with myself whether to answer it or not. The answer machine hadn't come on as I was listening to the messages. My feeling that it was Mark who had rung was probably paranoia and it could be Tom or even Nicole trying to reach me.

"Bollocks!" I took my chances and picked the receiver up.

"Allo, oui?" I tried to sound authentic just in case it could be Mark.

"Oh – sorry. I was looking for Sorrel. It's Tom here."

"Hi Tom!" I was greatly relieved to here his voice. " I got your message – I've just got in."

"Sorry to hassle you – just wondering what you were up to this evening?"

"Going out with friends of Nic's actually. What about you?"

"No plans actually." He sounded a bit let down. "I was going to ask you out to dinner."

"Well, why don't you join us then?" The words were out before I had time to think.

"Wouldn't your friends mind?" Now he sounded delighted.

"No – not at all." They probably would – but oh well, fuck it – why not? I had been to bed with him after all!

"That would be great! Where are you eating?"

"La Moule qui Rit – do you know it?"

"The little bistro in Le Suquet? Yes, I do."

"Great. We're eating at eight thirty – meet you there?"

"Yeah, that would be great – if you're sure it will be OK?"

"Course it will, see you then."

"Sure – see you then."

I hung up the phone and tried to think about Tom, Jake – anyone except Mark.

I told Nic a little nervously I had invited Tom out for dinner but she didn't seem to mind at all – she seemed more concerned about the strange non-messsages on her machine. She tried to be ultra chirpy to keep my mind off the phone calls, but I couldn't shake off the feeling that it had been Mark. It was really starting to get to me. I had read magazine articles before about people who had been harassed by phone calls and now they were afraid to leave their houses – I had laughed in the past, but now I was beginning to see their point of view. Nicole had dialled the last number retrieval service, and it had told her that it could not record an international number. So at least he wasn't here in France.

The evening turned out to be excellent. Tom was waiting for us at our table. Nic seemed to warm to him more this time. Anna and Paul, Nic's friends, were really nice and the restaurant as Nic had promised was good fun. I nearly fainted at one point when Tom tried to hold my hand under the table. He got on well with the others and even paid for the whole thing – which went down really well with everyone else.

As I started to get a red wine glow Tom increased in desirability, but I displayed tremendous restraint and went home with Nic – turning down his invitation for a nightcap back at the Carlton and leaving him really crestfallen.

My restraint had nothing whatsoever to do with Jake, of course.

Chapter Fourteen

Nicole had taken the rest of the week off, so the following day just before lunch we headed off towards Grasse. The hour's drive through the hills is really beautiful and soon I had virtually forgotten Mark Norris even existed. I didn't even think much about Tom (a bit tough I hadn't gone back with him when he had paid for the dinner!) though I did have one brief daydream about him while I looked out the window, but somehow his face kept turning into Jake's and that was just weird.

We wandered round the old perfume factory, which is now a museum. They make the perfume elsewhere now, but they still sell perfume in the old factory, right in the centre of the town. We looked at the old copper drums that used to store the different essences before they were added together to make the hundreds of different fragrances. We covered ourselves in about twenty different scents – then couldn't differentiate between any of them. We then drove on to Vence, another pretty town on a hillside, for some lunch in a sunny courtyard, and watched two little boys entertain themselves for an hour and a half with two sticks, having a sword fight.

After our late lunch we decided against driving on to Biot, deciding we could do that the next day. We took a leisurely drive back towards Cannes, getting back to the apartment late afternoon.

We spent a quiet evening in, taking Bambette for an evening walk round the gardens before we had dinner. The phone didn't ring which was a relief. We lay on Nicole's bed and watched videos of us when we were young – Henri always had a video camera handy.

"God I can't believe we wore those clothes."

"I think yours are worse than mine."

"Oh thanks a lot, I have to say I notice no difference, we both look as bad as each other."

We spent the rest of the evening laughing at our dreadful 80's fashion, and wondering how we could have thought we were so cool back then.

Wednesday morning was hot, and I got straight into a bikini after my shower and lay on one of the loungers on the balcony. Private sunbathing – you couldn't beat it with a big stick.

"What time is Maman calling to take you horse riding?" Nicole came out onto the balcony and sat beside me

"I think she said lunch-time."

"OK, the route that she will take you normally takes a couple of hours. What do you want to do when you get back?"

"Not really sure."

"OK, I am going to stay here while you are away and

decide what to do. I think tomorrow we will go to Valbonne for lunch and Biot to buy the glass for Chloe. Then on Friday we should go to Monte Carlo for the day. Are you seeing Tom before you go back?"

"Don't really know, he hasn't called and I don't really want to ring him. I'm not sure how much I like him."

"What about Jake?"

"What about him?"

"Come, Ellie, stop pretending you don't care. Are you trying to tell me you haven't thought about him once?"

"OK, I may have thought about him a bit – but what is the point?"

Nic raised her eyes heavenward. "You are impossible. Self-denial that is what you suffer from."

"Oh, pass the sun-cream and shut up!" I lay back on the sun-lounger and rubbed cream into my arms. Wondering, not for the first time, what Jake was up to. "Hey, did you know you're invited to Chloe's hen night?" To change the subject.

"Really? What do we do with these hens?"

"No, no it is when the bride's closest friends go out for night, or go away for a weekend – just girls."

"Ah, we have the same here. What are we going to do?"

"I'm not entirely sure yet, it's up to me to organise, so I'll let you know as soon as I've thought of something good."

"When will it be?"

"Well, the wedding is in May, so I suppose it will be in April. Give everyone time to get organised."

"OK, I like that. You will let me know and I will come to Scotland."

"It may not be in Scotland."

"Oh, in Ireland then?"

"I'd like to do something different.'

"Well, go to Wales then."

"Thank you, Nicole," I said to her retreating back as she got up and went back into the apartment.

I closed my eyes and enjoyed the heat. I must have dozed off as when I woke up Nicole was standing over me with her arms crossed and she was blocking out my sun.

"I have been talking to you for ten minutes, and all the time you are lying here snoring away. It is only eleven in the morning, how can you be tired already?"

"Sorry, it's just the heat, mustn't be used to it." I motioned for her to move.

"Maman just rang – she is leaving to come over here now, so she will be about twenty minutes. Have you got something to wear for riding?" She shifted to the left and nearly blinded me as I was left looking directly into the sun.

"Yeah, I have some stretchy trousers that will do the job."

"Coffee?"

"Lovely."

Celine arrived and had coffee with us. Then she and I went to her riding school up in the hills behind Nic's apartment.

"I haven't been horse-riding for a while."

"That's OK. I will get you a quiet horse so that you will soon feel confident."

One of the nice things about Celine is that she is so calm and never makes you do anything you are not comfortable with – you don't have to prove anything to her. That may be why she is so good working with disabled children.

The riding school is set in a secluded site surrounded by olive trees, very peaceful and quiet with the horses grazing in the surrounding fields.

After several unsuccessful attempt to get my arse into the saddle I led my trusty steed over to the mounting-block and got on from there.

Celine took me on a trek through the woods. Looking down the hillside I could see flashes of the sea between the trees. The air was fresh and with the gentle pace that the horses set I soon found myself relaxing back into it and starting to enjoy myself. It was hot but the trees provided shade.

We rode side by side and started to chat.

"I should make more time to do this sort of thing at home."

"I discovered, when I got a bit older than you, that it was time to start making myself happy. For me when I was working as a translator it was always so stressful and a good way for me to unwind was with the horses. The school let me take a horse out on my own for treks a couple of times a week. I don't think I would have lasted so long in my business if I had not had the chance to get a way from it occasionally. I would come up here on Tuesday and Thursday late afternoon and just ride for an hour in no particular direction, but as long as there were no phones or faxes I was happy."

"Sounds like you had the right idea." I pushed images of Jake hugging me out of my mind.

"When you feel that life is getting too much, it is good to have something or somewhere to go to unwind or you lose sight of what is important. You will end up wandering round your whole life full of tense knots."

I nodded. I was beginning to understand what she was talking about – though I wasn't sure where I could go to get away from Mark. Enrolling in the NASA space program could be the only answer.

I had loved the ride, especially the canter back to the riding-school, but I did feel slightly stiff and muscle-sore so I was glad when Nicole decided it was too hot to go anywhere in the car and we just went back to the beach. I was looking forward to annoying Fiona back at work with my tan.

There was a suprising amount of talent on the beach that afternoon and Nic and I seemed to spend most of our time lying on our beach towels looking over the tops of our glasses at the men as they walked past us.

"Why are there no men like this at home?" I pushed my glasses further down my nose to get a better look. "European men definitely have the edge on style and good looks."

I had begun to think about work, now that my holiday was drawing to a close. They were not welcome thoughts. Spending your afternoon sunbathing and bobbing around in the Med is definitely preferable to sitting in a centrally heated office in sleety Edinburgh trying to find interesting local people to interview for the next week's programme.

"I hope Fiona and I get this promotion I was telling you about."

"Will they pay you lots more money?"

"God, I hope so! Imagine, I could pay off my debt, and maybe even do a job that I liked."

"I can't think of doing a job that I didn't like. But, you know, you could afford to go to America if you wanted every so often."

"Well, you're lucky," I said, ignoring her last comment. "Most of the people I know have to do it. Work to live, not live to work."

"That is very sad."

"Tell me about it. Oh my God, look at that girl over there – she is gorgeous."

"Yes and she knows it too. See how the men flock around her – it is sad."

"Oh, you're jealous! But you're right – she's more in love with herself than anyone else. Nice figure though – lucky cow."

The woman we were looking at was the sort that you never hope turns up on your beach: slim, drop-dead gorgeous, with at least four guys trying to chat her up. The last (and only) time I had four guys round me on a beach was when they pulled me out of the tide: in attempting to look cool with the surfy types, I had virtually drowned myself by getting dumped by a wave.

The girl in question was heading our way. As she walked past us on her way back to her towel, I heard Nicole take a sharp intake of breath. I looked up – to see a Tampax string hanging out the side of her bikini bottoms. How we laughed at her expense, nice to know that even wildly attractive people are flawed too.

Nicole and I went to Biot on the Thursday and got the most fabulous wine glasses and tumbers for Chloe and David. They arranged to have the glassware sent directly to them, thus stopping me from breaking them all on the way back home.

Friday we went to Monte Carlo, which is so glam. The most exciting way to come into the city is on the Grand Corniche – I think that was the road where Princess Grace had her car accident with Stephanie years ago. Anyway it is really winding and difficult to get down – limos notoriously get stuck on the turns – but it is undoubtedly the most fantastic view over the Cote D'Azur. Monaco, which is the tiny principality of which Monte Carlo is the capital, is independent and is also a tax haven. Thus it is full to bursting with models, formula one drivers, actors and other members of the seriously rich jet-set.

Nicole and I positioned ourselves at an outside table of a fairly exclusive cafe, ordered coffee and watched.

The thing about Monte Carlo is that everyone is loaded, even the locals. No one leaves home without their full designer wardrobe, accessories and small dog. Louis Vuitton, Gucci, Prada, Versace, Dior, Mugler, Chanel all paraded past us. Sunglasses must be worn at all times to at least give the tourists the impression that you may be famous. God, even the waiters are snooty, but it is one of my all-time favourite ultimate people-watching places. We did manage to see Karen Mulder and Helena Christensen who both have aparmtents there – surprisingly they were the least flashy of the lot. But then they are supermodels – women who make wearing bin-liners look cool.

"Nic, is that a famous racing driver?"

"How would I know? I don't know any famous racing drivers."

"God, you are useless. If we had my dad here he would be able to spot one at a hundred paces."

"Very exciting."

"Do you have your camera here?"

"Yes, why?"

"I'm going to take a picture of him."

"Ellie! He is just some stupid man wearing sunglasses! When he gets closer, he probably is your dad."

Nicole is not such an avid famous-folk-spotter as I am.

"OK. I won't take a picture then."

A group of four older ladies sat down at the table beside us. They must have been in their late fifties or early sixties but every single one of them was not dressed a day over twenty. Plunging necklines, bandage-tight dresses, huge black Versace sunglasses and heels that would rival the pair that I bought in Cannes. Though they did look faintly ridiculous, they still looked pretty good. Where else in the world could you get away with that? They ordered expressos and began to chat. Cartier cigarettes came out and ruby-red nails on the ends of diamond encrusted fingers flashed as they smoked.

"What are they saying?" I whispered to Nic.

"One of them is getting a divorce, the others seem to be giving her advice."

"What else?"

"Shhhhh! One of them is telling her not to give up her villa on Lake Como."

"Where is Lake Como?"

"Near Milan. She apparently lives near Giorgio Armani."

"Bloody hell. I wouldn't give it up either."

More expressos were brought to their table and their chatter continued at a furious pace. Nic was leaning back in her seat to try and catch all they were saying. She burst out laughing and quickly leant forward as if I had said something funny.

"What?"

"Just laugh and I will tell you in a minute."

The ladies glanced over at our table, but seeing us deep in conversation, quickly went back to theirs.

"Her husband apparently has a mistress in her twenties."

"Oh, how sad."

"Not really – she just told her friends he has been impotent for years, so the mistress is apparently after his bank balance and not his manhood!"

I laughed.

"No wonder she wants to take him to the cleaners."

"Ah, it is the same everywhere! Older men like to feel younger by dating much younger women but they end up looking stupid and their ex-wives end up extremely wealthy in the process."

The ladies were now all laughing. A third round of expressos were brought to their table.

"Jesus, they must be getting high on all that caffeine."

Nicole ordered two more cappuccinos from a passing waiter and listened some more. It took her a while this time before she thought fit to fill me in.

"One of the other women's husband left her for a younger woman. He had the same problem. It seems that the mistress came to see her in the middle of a busy restaurant and told her at the top of her voice that her husband couldn't perform. She says that she told the girl that he never had a problem making love to her, perhaps he didn't find the mistress attractive. Then the mistress left him and he tried to get back with his wife. She told him to piss off and kept the house, the cars and their chef!"

"Well, good for her! Isn't it amazing how the other half live?"

"It happens to a lot of people, Ellie."

"I suppose so, just on a much smaller scale, with not many private chefs involved."

"Perhaps not."

Our coffees arrived at the same time a very camp couple sat down at the table on the other side of us. Both incredibly good-looking men, they couldn't keep their hands off each other. We couldn't hear what they were saying as they whispered to each other, before bursting into fits of giggles. They were both wearing matching linen suits, one in olive green and one in purple. The waiter seemed to know them and for the first time since we sat down, he actually smiled and became quite animated.

So there we sat surrounded by the rich ladies, the passionately in-love gay couple and just when I thought it couldn't get any more entertaining it did. The French version of Barbara Cartland arrived, with poodle and a much younger man. Pink frou-frou dress, white tights, pink pumps, pink fluffy hair, pink cheeks and lots of pale blue eye shadow on her wrinkled eyelids. The young man with her helped her into a seat and then tied the poodle to the arm of her chair – it immediately tried to eat Bambette who was lying quietly under Nicole's chair.

The old lady giggled as her poodle snarled and growled under the table. The young man, smiling and keeping eye contact with her, gave the dog a swift kick under the table – it immediately stopped growling and sat in its little pink coat under her chair.

"Un cafe et une tasse de the, Earl Grey, s'il vous plait," the young man ordered from the waiter.

Now that I understood: coffee and tea.

"What a strange couple," I whispered to Nicole. "Do you think he is her grandson?"

Nicole shrugged but I could see that see that she was trying to hear what they were saying. The surrounding tables were only mildly interested in them, until the waiter came back with their order and then the old lady had histrionics. Everyone stopped what they were doing and listened.

"The waiter did not bring any hot milk for her tea. She also wants a saucer for her dog, apparently she can't drink her tea if he doesn't have any."

My jaw dropped. Earl Grey for dogs? Poor Hector, he has been deprived all these years. Jake would love this.

Nic raised her eyebrows but said nothing.

When the slightly harassed waiter returned with hot milk the woman shouted at him again.

"What's wrong now?"

"Apparently the milk is too hot, she is accusing him of trying to scald her."

"Oh. She is not very fluffy under all that pink, is she?"

Nicole laughed. The old woman turned round scowling to see what we were laughing at. We both smiled at her sweetly.

The young man poured some tea into the saucer the waiter had brought, and put it down near the poodle who ignored it and carried on biting at the pink coat it was wearing.

The old woman started to wail again. The waiter rushed over to the table.

"Apparently if the dog does not want to drink the tea there must be something wrong with it."

"Mad old bitch."

The glamorous divorcees were now listening intently to Barbara C's conversation; the camp couple had stopped canoodling and were engrossed too.

"She wants the waiter to bring her lightly boiled water and a slice of lemon, she won't drink the tea," Nicole whispered.

The young man raised his eyes heavenward, but kept smiling at her and patting her knee.

"How do you lightly boil water?" I asked.

"Who knows?"

We continued to be entertained by her antics for a further half an hour and after that my bum started to get numb. We paid for our coffees and continued on our jaunt round the port.

"I was totally dying to hear if he was her lover or her grandson."

"Probably her lover."

"Gross! How do you know?"

"Oh there are many rich old women that young men

are only too happy to be attached to. She probably gives him a large allowance."

"Poor guy."

"Poor guy nothing, he probably makes twice as much money as we do."

"Yeah, but look what he has to put up with! I'm surprised that she doesn't have him kitted out in a pink outfit."

Down at the port, there were more enormous boats but after staying in Cannes you get used to the flashy way wealth is exposed. The Grimaldi's Palace is on the far side of the harbour and it looks like it is made of fairy cakes and icing sugar, sadly not a *Hello* photographer in sight, so it seemed unlikely that Stephanie, Caroline or Albert were in residence.

Friday night we were back in Cannes sitting with Celine and Henri in Le Pacific Express eating duck and wishing I never had to go home. In fact the week had passed so quickly I started to get suspicious that someone was speeding the days up. Have you ever noticed that when you are at home, in the cold, working away, the days seem to take forever to get to five o'clock? But as soon as you go on holiday you wake up and it is virtually five already? *Bizzare*.

Before I knew it, I was waving goodbye to Nic and queuing up to check in back to Edinburgh. Standing leaning against my trolley as I waited to get to the check-in desk, I recognised a familiar figure who was talking to the girl at the desk – Tom.

"Hello, stranger," I said to him as he pushed his empty trolley past me.

"Oh, Sorrel, I didn't see you there." He looked pleased but wary.

"I didn't know we were on the same flight back," I said awkwardly.

"Me neither. Listen, I'll meet you for a coffee over there when you've checked in." He pointed to an expresso bar across the departure hall.

"Sure."

He didn't hug me or tell me that he was sorry he hadn't seen me for the rest of the week after dinner on Wednesday night. Well, I suppose my refusing to go for the nightcap might have something to do with that.

He really was attractive.

Thankfully, I was wearing something a bit more glamorous than when we had first met: dark blue jeans and a tightish shortsleeved black polo neck – a definite improvement on my snakeprint bellbottoms.

"So did you enjoy your conference?" I asked as I sat down beside him. He had ordered coffees for us both.

"Pretty dull actually. How about you? Milk?" He held the jug out.

"No, thank you. The rest of the week was great," I continued chattily. "Nic was in great form and we toured all over the countryside, seeing places we hadn't been in ages. I really had a great time."

We kept to the small talk until it was time to go through to the departure gate. Then, walking through the departure gate, he put his arm round my shoulder.

"Sorry I didn't ring you, by the way," he said. "Bit of

a crisis at the conference – one of the main speakers that my company had organised didn't turn up, so I had to try and find someone at short notice."

"Did you find someone?" I asked as I handed my boarding-card to the airhostess.

"Yeah, eventually. Though it very nearly all went wrong."

We walked down the gangway to the plane. It turned out Tom was sitting near the front in business class. I was well down the back with the screaming children and no leg-room.

"See you when we land," I said as I headed down the aisle.

"See ya," he said, putting his briefcase up in the overhead locker.

I squeezed myself into my seat at the window, past a woman in tears who didn't get up when I indicated where my seat was.

"Excuse me. Would you like a seat in business class?" I looked up to see Tom speaking to the tearful mess beside me. She stared at him, startled, then nodded and he handed her his boarding-card. "Row five, beside the window." She nodded again, thanked him profusely, then made a quick exit before he changed his mind. She left her snotty tissues in the seat pocket in front of her.

"What did you do that for?"

"The flight was too long to be separated from you." He grinned, leant over and gave me a peck on the cheek.

I smiled and looked out the window, trying to disguise the fact that I was smiling too.

When we landed in Edinburgh he helped me with my hand luggage and got me a trolley in the arrivals hall. He waited till my bags had come off the carousel, then he lifted them onto my trolley.

"So do I get your phone number for Edinburgh?" he asked, grinning, no doubt remembering our first conversation. He pulled on what appeared to be a very expensive overcoat – ooh, I do love men in suits.

"Oh, um . . . of course." I got a bit flustered and dropped my duty free bag on the floor.

"Hey, Sorrell, calm down, I don't want to marry you!" he said, laughing at his own joke.

Somehow this reminded me of Mark and I hesitated about giving my number.

Oh, enough of the paranoia! "Yeah, sorry, do you have a pen?"

He pulled a gold fountain-pen out of his inside pocket.

"It's nine nine four seven double eight – I have an answer machine if I'm not in."

"Excellent. Well, I shall ring you this week and take you out to dinner. Do you need a lift home? My car is in the carpark."

"No, it's fine, my friend is coming to meet me." I couldn't decide if I was sorry that Louisa had said she would pick me up or not. Was he or wasn't he a bit of a berk?

"OK, well, you take care. It was a pleasure making your acquaintance – you definitely were the best part of my visit to Cannes."

He leant over my trolley and gave me a kiss on the cheek. It wasn't a peck nor was it a slobbery gross one.

I was definitely annoyed I was getting an alternative lift home.

We walked through the airport together, him pushing my trolley, an arm slung round me again. He was tall and handsome and I was shorter and less well dressed. I saw Louisa leaning against a pillar having a fag beside the No Smoking sign – her mouth fell open when she saw Tom walking beside me. I waved, she dropped the fag and squished it out with her foot. A cleaner behind her tutted loudly.

"Hi honey! Louisa, this is Tom. Tom, this is Louisa." I hugged her.

"Hi there, delighted to meet you. This lovely lady has been keeping me entertained for most of last week."

"Oh." Louisa laughed and looked at me. "Well, delighted to meet you too."

I love to discover my friends are no better when faced with an attractive man than I am.

"Well, I must be off." He took his bags off the trolley, gave one last smile and strode away.

"Byeee!" we chorused.

"Who the fuck was that?" Louisa stared after him

"That is my potential new boyfriend." I tried not to look smug.

"No, seriously, who is he? What about Jake ?"

"He is Tom – God, I never even found out his surname. I met him on the plane on the way to Nice – he spoke to me while I was waiting for Nic."

"He is totally gorgeous. Bet you have slept with him?"

"Not really sure, memory is a bit fuzzy on that one. He is this odd mix of wildly attractive and arsehole. The jury is still out on this one. Mind you, he's taking me to dinner this week."

"You are so lucky – I never meet men like that."

"Oh and I do?"

"You just *did*."

"I know but it's not like it happens every day. Actually this is my very first time. Do you think it's a sign?"

"That you are over Jake?"

I looked at her. I hadn't thought about Jake quite as obbessively since I had met Tom. "Possibly – He was in Cannes all week."

"Who, Jake?"

"No! Tom! He was at some conference or other."

"What for?"

"I forgot to ask. But I will – if he ever phones me."

"Oh, he *will.*"

"You reckon?"

"Nobody pushes your trolley with one arm round you unless they really like you."

Chapter Fifteen

At the beginning of November I started to worry about my Christmas shopping. Would I remember everyone? Would my friendly Bank Manager lend me enough money to buy all the pressies I wanted? You might think I was jumping the gun a little worrying about Christmas shopping in November but bitter experience has shown that my family do not appreciate being given pots of my experimental home-made jam. Two years ago in the middle of a financial crisis I decided to make everyone's Christmas pressies. Jam seemed like a winner: a dozen empty jars – dead cheap – some gingham fabric, elastic bands and blackberries I could find on the hedgerows, left over from September. The end of October is not the best time to find tasty blackberries and most of them had begun to disintegrate. Undeterred, I mixed the shrivelled blackberries with a packet of frozen raspberries from Marks and Spencer and set about making my wonderful Christmas jam. Couple of hours later, the air in the kitchen was blue and my jam was more like toffee. Ever the optimist I figured that toffee makes good presents too, failing to recognise rule number one: only if made by a professional. None of the family would speak to me until well into February. They all tried the berry toffee – truly a taste sensation – trying not to retch in front of me. Dad had to get two fillings replaced and Lucy practically glued her teeth shut for the whole of Christmas day. Ben and Mum quietly dropped their gingham gifts into the nearest bin. Eventually they made me promise never to make anything for them ever again, to avoid any unnecessary dental work in the future and unnecessary cruelty to fruit.

Hence the fact that I dragged Chloe to Glasgow for a day in November. This year I was going to impress the family by buying gifts for them. I had read that a new London cosmetics shop had opened in Glasgow and Lucy was a fan of very expensive make-up, especially when she didn't have to pay for it herself. I myself was now indoctrinated into the fellowship of expensive make-up lovers, wanting nothing more but to peruse the glossy packages of interesting make-up, no matter what ludicrous price was slapped on them, possibly buying her a small gift in the process.

As we wandered in and out of shops which already had their Christmas decorations up I thought about Jake – unofficially of course, as strictly speaking I no longer fancied him and was busy expecting Tom to call. I wondered how Jake was getting on in Boston. He had been gone two months and so far had sent me a few postcards and one message on my machine – unfortunately the tape had wiped off half the message, but as long as I knew it was him I didn't really mind what it said. It looked like he was surviving without me in his life – though I am sure, only just. It was nice that he still stayed in touch, most men I know have a keen aversion for any forms of communication. If I was completely honest I missed him like hell; I kept thinking about our last conversation and wondering if he regretted anything or was just glad to get shot of me.

We had arrived in Glasgow's Queen Street Station and made our way straight to Prince's Square. I like shopping with Chloe. It's like a sport that we are both really good at. Unfortunately it hasn't been given Olympic status yet, but we would be strong contenders for the Irish or British teams. Anyway, so there we were in the new wildly glamorous cosmetics shop trying not to look complety overexcited because we had both taken the day off work to come shopping.

First impressions however were not good. The shop assistants were all wearing black which gave them a kind of sinister cult-member look. Also they had their fringes cut at odd angles, starting high up above their left eyebrow and finishing below the right, hum . . . clearly a key look I was unaware of. One of the many things in the whole world I cannot stand is a sales assistant with an over-inflated sense of importance, even one with a key-look fringes. I was one for a while after graduating, before I convinced the newspaper to give me a job but I was always nice with it. I never openly sneered at customers, I went into the stockroom to do that. As we walked round the shop I was looked up and down by one of these asymmetric fringes. She had intentionally given herself two black eyes, blood-red lips and a pale face. She looked more like a member of the undead than a make-up expert. The shop was completely white – even the stuff on the shelves was white. The floor was white too. They were playing weird Chinese or Japanese music, a kind of soft disconcerting wailing. I found myself yearning for the 'No7' counter at Boots; at least the ladies there had the decency to have an orange tide-mark round their necklines and wore lip-liner outside their lips to remove any chance of being intimidating to a customer.

The shop assistant approached me. I was tempted to run for the door before she got near me, though she only wanted to know if I needed any help, and not of the spirtual kind. Twenty minutes later I left with a large impressive bag with four tiny purchases rattling round in it. Chloe and I went to a nearby cafe to have lunch and more importantly a large glass of red wine. As we sat down a waitress shuffled up to us, looking like she was already wearing the 'specials' splashed up her shirt. We ordered a couple of large glasses of wine and she shuffled off again – I willed her to pick up her feet.

"I cannot believe you spent ninety five pounds on that crap," Chloe said as she picked up a menu.

"I know, am I mad?"

"Quite possibly. Anyway, I thought you said you were skint?"

"I am," I said, miserably staring into the bag. "God, why did I buy them? I was so embarrassed when the girl rang up the total. Did I look shocked?"

"Well, a bit. I think when your face turned whiter than the decor and it took three shop assistants to help you sign your name, it was a give-away. Personally, I think you dealt with it really well. At least they gave you a paper bag you can use later to hyperventilate in when you read your bank statement!"

"Cheers. One of those pressies is for you."

"You are very kind but I really think twenty quid is too much for a nail varnish no matter how groovy the colour is. Anyway, Lucy isn't going to notice if her mascara isn't Stila – what is Stila, anyway?"

"I'm not entirely sure."

"Surely Lancôme would do?"

"Probably."

I gracefully thumped my forehead off the table. Yet again I had overspent on silly things I didn't need so the shop assistant wouldn't think I was a total moron. I lifted my head off the table and Chloe kindly removed a stray slice mushroom off my forehead.

"Glad to see this place takes its health and hygiene so seriously," she commented as she flicked the offending vegetable into the ashtray.

I lit a cigarette, blowing the smoke upwards to the glass ceiling.

Chloe grimaced. "God, must you, before lunch?"

"Oh shut up, I need it."

"Why don't you take a couple of things back? Tell them you bought the wrong things?"

I looked at her, a shinning beacon of hope in my overdraft nightmare.

"Do you think they would let me?"

"Of course. Tell them you bought the wrong brand and they don't sell the one you want. Take my nail varnish back and Lucy's mascara."

"Right. Will I go now?"

"Yes, I'll order for you, what do you want?"

"Surprise me."

I walked purposefully back to the shop to return the two most expensive items. The slanty-fringed, black-eyed assistant smiled generously at me as I walked up to the cash desk. I set my bag of purchases on the counter.

"Hi, I was in here about half an hour ago."

She nodded as if to say, "I'd remember that outfit anywhere."

"Well, I bought I few things and I have realised they are not the ones I thought they were. They're not the right brand."

"Oh I see."

I lifted the twenty pound nail varnish and twenty pound mascara out of the bag. Then in a moment of supreme courage I lifted the face moisturiser and toner out too.

"These ones." I handed them all to her.

"Which brand were you looking for?"

Oh shit, think posh, think your godmother's bathroom cabinets (she is very posh and I love her).

"Avon!" Oh God, that was so wrong, I meant to say Aveda.

"Right. Avon. An easy mistake to make." She looked at me like I was carrying the bubonic plague.

I smiled at her, resisting the urge to walk round to her side of the cash desk and kick her in the shins.

She credited my account with ninety five pounds and I bounced back to the cafe a much happier girl, ready to spend my money on something else.

When I got back to the cafe Chloe was looking

through her filofax with a worried expression on her face.

"What's up?"

"Oh, just that the wedding isn't long away as you keep reminding me and you need to get your dress made. When can you make an appointment for a fitting?"

"I am available for fittings whenever you want me." I had visions of me wearing a revolting lilac floral concoction dancing in the arms of Alex – the ginger best man. People always say that the bridesmaid traditionally pulls the best man. Forgive me if I break tradition, I thought, I'd rather snog Robin Cook. Nowhere does tradition say I shall end up with Mr Result of Cruel Medical Experiment. I could pull someone attractive and employed, though chance would be a fine thing.

"How about Tuesday night?"

"Grand, what time?"

"I'll have to check with Yvonne but probably around seven thirty."

"No problem. What did you order for me?"

"Greek salad."

I wrinkled up my nose. Always a bad idea to let Chloe order food. I remain convinced she was born a rabbit in an earlier life.

"It's good for you. Stop making faces."

"I wanted a BLT with chips."

"Well, you never said, anyway you like Greek salads."

The waitress arrived as I was about to argue about never having had strong feelings towards salads of any kind let alone a Greek one.

"Did you take everything back?" asked Chloe.

I nodded, she laughed.

"Where are we going next?" I asked between delicious mouthfuls of feta cheese and green peppers. OK, so the Greeks really know how to make salads.

"I want to nip into Frasers to look at their shoe department."

"I think I'd like a Gucci key-ring. I saw a nice one in Cosmo – it was only thirty pounds."

"Hold it right there, Ellie. You have just returned ninety-five quid of unwanted skin-care products because you couldn't afford them and now you want a thirty pound key-ring?"

"Ah, but it would last a lifetime."

"Or until you went off it and wanted something else."

"Well, I am not getting married. I'm single with only a small dog to think of, few responsibilities, so why not? What else would I do?"

"If you managed your finances your dad wouldn't have to phone your Bank Manager and pay off the excess on your overdraft. You could save up and book a flight to Boston and go and see Jake like you really want to but won't admit to. You could get that really good promotion Fiona was talking about if you would just push yourself more. Screen tests can't be that difficult, anyway you are practically a dead cert. You could employ a cleaner to do your ironing, tidy your flat and do your dishes."

I stared at her, black olive on the end of my fork, just inches from my mouth.

"You sanctimonious oul' bitch!"

"Don't get huffy just because you can't handle the truth."

"Well!" I said with huge amounts of indignation.

"Well, what? Shout at me, go on then!" She didn't even ruffle a feather.

"There is nothing wrong with my ironing pile." It was the first and weakest argument that came into my head.

"For God's sake, Ellie, I can't remember if you even have a sofa or remember what colour your carpet is in the living-room."

What a bitch! We sat in silence eating our salads. I wanted to hurl the greasy little olives at her, but I knew she was without a doubt entirely right, which made the whole thing so annoying. We finished our lunch and I followed her into Frazers shoe department, hoping if I looked stroppy enough she would apologise for being mean. She didn't. Instead she just ignored me. God, I hate that!

I was starting to mellow as we headed back in the direction of Queen Street Station some time later. It was getting dark and Christmas lights were twinkling in shop windows; it was also bloody freezing. We ducked into shops along Buchanan Street, then dandered through the Argyle Arcade, which is just packed full of jewellers. We had to stop and look at the rings – lots of shops sell secondhand and antique jewellery which I love. Since Chloe got engaged my favourite pastime while looking in shop windows is: 'If I was getting engaged what ring would I pick?' Keeps me entertained for hours. Anyway, I saw about six potentials. Unfortunately my favourite was eight thousand pounds, a beautiful square-cut solitaire set in a platinum band, big enough to be impressive but small enough not to cause anyone serious injury while hailing taxis – you couldn't catch a bus with that ring.

Chloe dragged me out of the arcade into Argyle Street. Street vendors were selling stinking Christmas wrapping paper, twenty sheets for a pound, flashing Santa hats and white sports socks, interesting combination. Only bus drivers wear white socks when not in a sporting environment. Have you ever noticed that? They always seem to wear those hideous white socks with trousers too short and black soft-soled shoes. It must be something they teach all bus drivers – black socks bad, white socks good. Well, anyway, it keeps the street sellers in business. I bought a pair of kitten-heel mules that I had seen in a shop window. I thought they were magic but Chloe assured me they would be out next season and I'd moan that I had spent too much on a pair of un-trendy shoes. Personally I thought I looked dead sexy and wished I could show them off to someone, possibly Tom. Chloe and I pottered for a little while longer and then made our way to the train station.

"This will be your last Christmas as a single woman," I said to Chloe as the train got under way.

"Thank Christ, I don't think I could stand another at home."

"I don't know, I always enjoy a family Christmas. I've taken two weeks off this year, I am going to drink as much as my body will let me and catch up with what's been going on at home."

"Well, for starters your mother doesn't get the caterers in, invite twenty people you have never even met and then have a nervous breakdown because she can't cope with all the people."

"That's very true."

"If I took a fortnight at home, I'd be on Valium before the end of the first week."

"That's also very true."

"Next year David and I are going to go either up north to some remote cottage or to Barbados, so I can come home and piss you off with a tan in January."

"Now that sounds heavenly. How much would you like to wake up to a beautiful sunny day?"

"People waiting on me hand and foot."

"Ah stop now, you're making me jealous."

"Well, you never know. It could be that Tom will take you there next year."

"Unlikely, he would really need to phone me first."

A month after I got back from France it had started to snow, well, sleet really – you know, the grey and very wet kind.

"Ah, a British winter! How I love it!"

I was sitting with Hector on my knee contemplating moving my ironing into the spare bedroom, so Chloe would think I was tidy – I had invited her round for something to eat – when the phone rang.

"Hello, could I speak to Sorrel please?

"Speaking."

"It's Tom."

"Tom who?" Hurrah! Tom from the plane! A bit late but he phoned, someone I like actually phoned! I had just about given up hope of ever hearing from him again.

"Yes, this is Ellie speaking." Nonchalant reply, disguising underlying feeling of jubilation.

"Hi, Sorrel – Ellie, I thought I'd give you a ring to see

if you were free any night this week. I thought we could go out for dinner if you feel like it."

"Oh, dinner? That would be nice." Play it cool, don't sound like you are drooling into the receiver.

Hector, realising he was no longer the centre of attention, jumped off my knee and went into the kitchen, no doubt to snuffle around to see if there were any Bonio biscuits that he had missed, hiding in corners. In the process he managed to pluck my tights with his little claws – I did the fingers to his retreating back – those cost me five pounds fifty!

"So, have you been to Calamare? I love it – we could eat about eight or thereabouts and then – "

Tom, bringing me back from my hosiery catastrophe.

"Actually, would you mind if we went somewhere else?"

A small pause.

"Oh, right – well, it's an excellent restaurant and I thought you'd like it – "

Was it my imagination or did he sound pissed off? Think quick – I couldn't very well tell him I nearly demolished the place the last and only time I'd been there.

"I don't really mind – it's just I got food poisoning the last time I was there, and well . . . it's kind of put me off." Was that lame or what?

"Are you sure it just wasn't the drink?"

I could hear Tom chuckling to himself – smarmy git.

"No, actually I was on antibiotics, I couldn't drink." Lies, lies, lies.

"Sorry, that wasn't very sympathetic. Of course we can go wherever you want. Name a restaurant."

"Mama Roma's is nice, how about there?"

"What's that? Italian?"

Nil points for deductive reasoning. What does he think it is – Indian?

"Yes, it is. What do you think?"

Another pause. "Not very glamorous, Ellie."

"Oh, right, well you pick somewhere then."

I was now sitting with a scowl on my face, "I love Chez Maurice, how about that?"

"Fine, sounds good." Sounds pretentious but then I am not paying the bill – at least I hope not.

"I'll pick you up at eight then tomorrow night, OK?"

"OK."

"See you tomorrow, bye,"

He hung up before I had a chance to say goodbye.

I sat looking at the phone wondering if he was sophisticated dream-man or poncy show-off man which was not nearly so attractive?

Hector wandered back into the room, finally satisfied that he had missed no doggie treats.

"It would appear that I am going on a date tomorrow night with a flash git," I informed him.

So anyway to cut a long and painful clothes crisis short, Tom arrived to pick me up the next evening. I was my usual charming self, determined not to drink myself under the table, break anything, leave without my coat etc.

Tom looked really great: he was wearing a black polo neck (which not all men can get away with) and black trousers, very sexy. He didn't come up to the flat which I was very glad about, even though I had hidden all the

274

ironing behind the sofa. When I opened the front door to my building he was standing beside his car holding the door. It was a big silver shiny Mercedes and I was impressed. The only time my Fiat was clean was when it had rained.

It suddenly occurred to me I hadn't ever asked him what he did for a living, come to think of it he hadn't asked me either. Actually other than the fact that I knew he liked to bum about the Cannes film festival I knew bugger all about him. Oh, what the hell, how often do I get asked out for dinner?

"You look nice." The words were out before I could stop them.

"Thank you, so do you."

He shut the door behind me as I climbed into the front seat – leather seats, very plush.

"So, how are you? I haven't seen you since the airport. I see you have changed."

"No, I'm exactly the same person I was a month ago." Hum, maybe a bit sad that I knew how long ago it was since we had seen each other – stay aloof, Ellie.

"No, no, I meant your clothes – you look more glamorous."

"Oh?" That wouldn't be too difficult.

"I hadn't expected leather trousers. I had you down as more of a jeans girl."

I smiled, my what-I-hoped-was-my-mysterious-woman smile. But probably looked more like a my-pants-are-up-my-bum kind of a smile.

Tom climbed into the driver's seat beside me. "I thought I'd take you out of the city if that's all right."

"I thought we were going to Chez Maurice?"

"Well, I changed my mind – OK with you?"

"Absolutely."

I was swithering – was I wise to go careering off into the night with a virtual stranger I still wasn't sure I even liked even if I had slept with him? Or should I just say "fuck it" and go and have a good time with a nice man who fancied me? "Fuck it" won.

Tom started the car. I was impressed. It started first time. It had been a long time since my car started first time. In fact to be honest, I couldn't have told you the last time it did. The car roared over the cobbles without a bone-shaking, boob-jiggling effect. It was a revelation to be in a car whose shock absorbers actually worked. We sped out of the city and towards the Forth Road Bridge.

"Where exactly are we going?" I asked, trying not to sound at all nervous.

"To a lovely restaurant I know in St Andrews."

"St Andrews!"

"Yes – why, is there something wrong?"

"God, that will take us ages to get to."

"About forty-five minutes – is that too long? We can turn back and go into town if you prefer?"

"No, no, it's fine. I've never done it that quickly, that's all."

Normally I would have to take a packed lunch and the AA direct phone number when embarking on such a gargantuan trip.

Tom smiled, and I sat back into the leather seat and watched the houses at Barnton whiz by.

True to his word we arrived in St Andrews fifty minutes later (there had been some road works). He found a parking space right outside the restaurant, lucky git.

It was a lovely restaurant, not at all pretentious like I thought he might have picked. The staff all seemed to know him and it was a warm friendly atmosphere.

"How did you find this place?" I asked him as we were shown to our seats.

"I used to go out with a girl who lived in Dundee. We used to come here quite a lot – I'm glad you like it."

I handed my coat to the waitress who was standing by our table. She took our drinks order and appeared back very quickly with two gin and tonics.

"Oh, right – well, I hope no unhappy memories." I was a bit surprised that he had brought me to an old haunt of his and his ex-girlfriend's.

"She was my fiancée for two years."

Tom looked down into his gin and swirled his lemon around the glass – I nearly swallowed the stone in the olive I was eating. Oh God, please don't let them have broken up last week, I think that would be more than I can bear. What do you say to that? I had a feeling the conversation was about to take a bit of an odd turn.

"Ah," I said as if I came across spurned lovers on a regular basis. "Do you miss her?" I tried to appear unfazed.

"Now and then, but I have to move on. She got married two years ago."

I didn't say a word; at least it wasn't last week and he hadn't brought me here to bend my ear for two hours on his lost love.

Perhaps I spoke too soon: Tom looked like he was about to embark on a heart-rending monologue. I popped another olive into my mouth and tried to look interested.

"She went on a skiing holiday with her girlfriends and when she came back she broke off the engagement. Apparently I didn't set her on fire anymore. I mean what the hell was I supposed to do? I didn't even know she was unhappy. I could have gone to counselling with her, for Christ's sake – but Judy had to do everything her own way. She buggered off with some bloke she met on her holiday – he was her sodding ski instructor."

Tom was going speedily from self-pity to anger and I was running out of olives.

"So was that the guy she married?"

"No, she got bored with him, apparently she was only using him for sex. He only lasted a couple of months – he was from somewhere down south and went back to finish the ski season. She then had an affair with her boss – he wanted to leave his wife, so Judy left him before he got a chance. She married a pilot she met at Japanese evening classes – he can fly her to Paris for a tenner and he speaks four different languages. She had only known him for five months but according to her – she just knew."

"When did you split up?"

"Four years ago."

A man with serious baggage – good choice, Ellie.

"Do you still keep in touch?"

"She won't return my calls."

Eeeeeeeek!

We ordered some food from the obliging smiley waitress. I was tempted to leave the table under the guise of going to the loo and ring a taxi and get the hell out of there, but:

a) I didn't have enough money to get back to Edinburgh

b) He knew where I lived, and the last thing I needed was another stalker thank you very much

c) I was totally starving and I had just ordered roast lamb.

I decided to stay put and just try and enjoy the rest of the evening as best I could.

Surprisingly, after his shock revelation Tom seemed to relax and enjoy the rest of the evening. He was attentive, funny and good company. OK, so he was a little intense, but then I was used to men I found attractive to either become mentally unhinged or leave the country, so a little intense was a piece of cake in comparison.

We were among the last diners to leave the restaurant. It was around midnight when we finally left St Andrews. We drove back towards Edinburgh. Tom was quiet, so for once instead of making inane comments, I sat in silence and looked out at the dark hills as we passed, busily wondering when he would get around to the 'my place or yours' bit. And what I would say when he did.

He finally broke the silence. "I'd really like to see you again, Ellie, if that's all right with you?"

"Yes, I'd like that." And I found that I actually would.

"Maybe I could take you out for dinner again next week?"

"Maybe I could take you out?"

"Sure!" He laughed.

We sat in companionable silence after that.

He must really like me, I thought. Despite our night of passion (none of which I had ever remembered, of course) he had decided to take it slow. No 'your place or mine' then. I was surprised to find I was actually sorry.

I could see the orange glow of Edinburgh in the distance; in the foreground the Forth Road Bridge came into view. One of the lanes was closed for resurfacing and the contractors had it blocked off using hundreds of traffic cones. Tom slowed down as we got onto the bridge – there were strong crosswinds and a flashing sign indicated we should go no faster than thirty miles per hour. I looked across to the rail bridge and watched a freight train chugging over the bridge towards Edinburgh. We must have been about half-way across when headlights half-blinded us and my attention snapped back to the road.

"What the fuck!" Tom shouted with surprise.

"That car is on our side of the road!" I screamed.

Tom sounded his horn but the oncoming vehicle didn't slow – he swerved to avoid the oncoming car and sent us crashing through the traffic cones – the front wheels of the car went into a large hole dug by the workmen, we were both thrown forward, then sharply backwards. I remember our seat belts locking and the airbag exploding into my face – then I blacked out.

Coming round minutes later, the horn from the car was going and I couldn't see past the airbag.

"Ellie, Ellie!" Tom was calling.

"Yes, I'm here."

"Are you OK?"

"I think so, I can't move though."

"Don't try to, I don't know how deep this hole in the road is. I think I hear sirens – the bridge control must have seen the accident."

"OK, I'll stay still." Tears were streaming down my face. It must have been the shock as I couldn't feel any pain.

"I can't believe that someone just put us off the road and drove on like that!"

"Sir, are you able to move your head?"

A third voice – the paramedics had arrived very quickly.

"Yes, I think I am fine but my girlfriend could be in some pain."

Just as Tom said 'girlfriend could be in some pain', I felt a searing pain in my legs – I cried out.

"It's OK, love, we're here now – just relax and let me take a look at you. What's your name?"

"Sorrel, my name is Sorrel."

"That's a beautiful name."

Now I know the paramedic was only trying to take my mind off the pain but I think I told him to "fuck off" – I can't really remember as I seemed to come in and out of consciousness.

The fire engine had turned up.

They were going to have to cut me out of the car.

My side of the car had hit the barrier at the side of the bridge, which had stopped us going into the Firth of Forth, but it meant that I was trapped inside. The paramedics helped Tom out of the car. They thought he had broken his left arm – it had been squashed between him and the steering wheel when we hit the hole and the airbags had exploded.

"Oh, Ellie, I am so sorry!"

I could hear Tom in the background. I had my face buried in the airbag – it hurt too much to try and move my head to either side.

"It wasn't his fault," I sobbed. "There was a car on the wrong side of the road."

"We know, love, now relax and try and stay with us."

I panicked. I wasn't going to die.

"I'm not going to die, am I?"

"No, love, don't be silly, just try and stay conscious."

I had this irrational desire to tell the men who were trying to get me out of the car that Tom wasn't really my boyfriend – this was our first date and it had just taken a turn for the worse. Before I got the chance, a loud dull hum filled my ears and drowned out the words. It was the sound of the hydraulic cutters – they were taking the door and part of the front wing off the car.

I fought the urge to pass out and forced myself to be aware of what they were doing.

Once they had the door off the car someone put a collar round my neck and I was gently removed from the passenger seat and onto a stretcher. Since they didn't know if I had any back or neck injuries they had a special board for me. The pain in my legs was making me dizzy and I couldn't stop crying. One of the paramedics gave me an injection to ease my agony. As my muscles relaxed I couldn't help myself – I totally slipped out of consciousness and into a black nothingness.

Chapter Sixteen

As I started to come round I dreamt that Jake was beside me, telling me that he would love me even though I would never walk again. It was like the closing scene in *An Affair to Remember,* when Cary Grant realises that Deborah Kerr is paralysed. I woke up with a start. There was a nurse beside me. When she saw me come round she smiled and went to get the doctor. I looked round. Jake was definitely not with me, unless of course he was hiding under the bed.

I lay looking at the ceiling wondering what time it was – the glass had smashed in my watch and it now said 02.35 am.

"Ellie! Thank God!"

It was Tom. He was standing beside me with his left arm in plaster.

"It's broken then?" I said stupidly.

He nodded, looking totally wretched. I felt sorry for him. He took my hand and held it to him and I fought the urge to cry again.

"I need to speak to Chloe," I said. "Hector is home alone."

"Hector?" Tom looked confused.

"My dog."

"Right, I'll get to a phone – I think I left my mobile at the car."

He returned seconds later.

"What's her number?"

I told him, he scribbled it down on a scrap of paper and went off in search of a phone.

"Well, young lady, how are you doing?"

I opened my eyes to see a gruff-looking man in a white coat looking at a metal clipboard at the end of my bed. His badge said Doctor Brook.

"OK, I think."

"Good, good. A bit of bad news for you, I'm afraid."

I looked immediately at my legs expecting to see stumps wrapped up in bandages, but they seemed to still be attached.

"What?"

"You have some nasty injuries to both your legs. Nothing that won't heal but your left leg has sustained a fracture of the femur, that's your thigh bone. You also have some severe soft-tissue damage to your right leg. It isn't pretty but I assure you it will heal with virtually no scarring. You also have some severe bruising to your chest and ribs from the airbag, nothing broken but it will hurt like hell for a few days. Oh and you have some abrasions to your face, where the airbag impacted, but like I said, nothing that won't heal."

"Can I see?"

"I think it's better if you don't look at anything just yet.

We'll need to operate as soon as possible and then you'll be spending some time in traction, I'm afraid, just to make sure the bones set correctly. We can't operate tonight – I believe you were out for dinner?"

I nodded, dumbstruck.

"Well, you need to be fasting. We'll get to work tomorrow morning."

"I don't think anyone knows I'm here – could I have a phone?"

"I'll see what I can do for you."

Dr Brook smiled at me, patted my shoulder and told me not to worry. As he moved away from the bed I saw two policemen standing behind him. They asked a passing nurse if it would be OK to talk to me and she nodded assent – as long as they weren't too long – as I had to rest.

"Miss Clarke, I am Sergeant McLeod and this is PC Lewis. Would you mind if we asked you some questions?"

Actually there was nothing I'd have liked less. My head was spinning, my legs were agony, I was lying in a horrible gown on plasticised sheets. Oh God, where was Tom? Had he got hold of Chloe?

"Oh, OK," I said.

"We've found the driver that forced you and Mr Quinn off the road earlier tonight."

Funny I didn't know that Tom's surname was Quinn.

"Well, that's good." My voice sounded so weak.

"Can you tell us what speed Mr Quinn was driving at?"

"He was going quite slow, with one of the lanes on the bridge being closed off. I think it was about thirty miles an hour or less."

"Thank you, Miss Clarke, we'll let you rest now."

"Why are you asking about Tom? It was that other driver who was on the wrong side of the road, you know."

"Just some routine questions, thank you for your help."

"No, really, I would appreciate it if you would tell me what is going on." I involuntarily winced in pain. I could only imagine what it was going to be like when the painkillers wore off.

The policemen were very nice, realising my discomfort.

"Well, if you think you're up to it?"

"I'm up to it."

"We realise that Mr Quinn was not speeding tonight, but since there were no eye-witnesses on the bridge we needed you to confirm that for us."

I nodded, not really sure what they were leading up to. I tried to relax against the pillows in an futile attempt to make myself more comfortable.

"Miss Clarke, I really don't think this is appropriate just now." Sergeant McLeod had noticed my discomfort and looked very concerned.

"Please, I don't understand why you're here asking questions about Tom if you know he wasn't doing anything wrong."

"Do you know Mr Mark Norris?" the Sergeant asked gently.

Gentle though it was, the unexpectedness of the question shocked me.

"Yes, I do, he is an ex-boyfriend of mine, why?" I could hear my voice shake.

"Have you seen Mr Norris recently?"

Why were they asking about Mark? Weren't they here

to talk about our accident? I made a big effort to stay calm. "I haven't seen him for a while – he was acting really weird so I stopped returning his calls, but I do think I saw him in town shopping recently – but I don't think he saw me. Why are you asking me about him?"

"Has Mr Norris ever been violent towards you, or your family?"

"Violent? Why are you asking me this?"

"Could you just try to answer, if you're strong enough? Then we'll explain."

Oh God, what was going on? What had happened?

"My family live in Ireland – and no, he has never been violent towards me. He had sort of been harassing me by phone. Chloe, my friend, told me I should keep the answer-phone tapes as evidence. I think I have one in the living-room in my flat. I jokingly referred to him as my stalker but he was never violent, no way."

The policemen looked at each other. Sergeant McLeod continued.

"Miss Clarke, Mr Norris broke into your flat this evening while you were out with Mr Quinn – your neighbour reported a disturbance."

"Mrs Arnold?"

"Yes, we believe that she called in the burglary."

I had a vision of Mrs Arnold, an unfeasibly nosy eighty-year-old in a pink housecoat who never tired of telling me that I should have twenty children at my age. I usually pretended to be out whenever she rang my door bell. She had a habit of calling in unannounced with a batch of her home-made shortbread for me which would have been lovely if she had been able to cook.

Unfortunately the shortbread tasted like it had been deep-fried along with last night's battered haddock. She also had a Yorkshire terrier, imaginatively called Yorkie, who Hector detested and always tried to eat whenever they met in the stairwell. Mrs Arnold was convinced they were in love and Yorkie wanted to give Hector his babies. She seemed oblivious that Hector not only had a boy's name but was a boy dog and the chances of puppies were slim. But if she hadn't got to grips with the birds and bees, I was not about to fill in the gaps – I didn't want to be responsible for bringing on a cardiac arrest.

"She heard Mr Norris breaking into your flat and immediately contacted the police but unfortunately by the time they arrived on the scene Mr Norris had left."

Who did I annoy in a previous life? A broken leg and various other delightful injuries, a night in Accident and Emergency while some mad bastard is breaking into my flat. This was not a night to forget quickly.

"What did he take?" I think I must have been in shock, I was so calm – like it was happening to someone else.

"He stole your car."

"My car! He stole my frigging car!" I was astounded. "If he was stealing my car why did he break into my flat?"

"We believe he broke in to get your car keys, as the car door was not forced and the keys are not in the flat."

I laughed out loud. "You have to be bloody joking – Mark must have been more nuts than I thought! The car door wasn't forced – you must have got it back then? Did you catch him?"

"Yes, we did . . . but he had crashed the car. And there's one more thing, Miss Clarke."

"What?"

"It was Mr Norris who forced you off the road tonight."

I think it was about this time that I came out of shock as I was no longer calm. In fact, I did a repeat performance of what I'd done to the poor doctor – swore my bloody head off at them. After I had finished screaming profanities at them, the nurse came back in with some sedatives. She shot the police a dirty look for getting me worked up.

"Can we contact anyone for you, Miss Clarke?" asked the Sergeant, still kindly despite my violent verbal assault.

"Yes, could you please ring Chloe Williams? She'll contact my mum and dad in Ireland." I gave them her number.

They got to their feet. "We're very sorry, Miss Clarke, to have disturbed you. We'll leave you now to rest. Your flat has been secured and your car has been impounded.

The police left and Tom came back into the room. He said nothing about Mark so I guessed he didn't know but I didn't feel up to telling him it was inadvertently my fault that his beautiful car had been written off. I told him to go home and rest and he eventually left unwillingly.

I lay in my hospital bed running through the events of the past few hours.

It all seemed so unbelievable. I meet a man I like and who to all intents and purposes appears to be interested in me. He takes me out for a beautiful meal. Then psycho ex-boyfriend breaks into my flat to get my car keys, steals my car and then drives me and aforementioned dinner date off the road and practically into the Firth of Forth via a two-hundred-foot drop.

Thankfully the sedatives kicked in and I drifted off into a black hole of sleep.

When I woke up, Chloe was sitting beside me, holding my hand.

"Is that not a wee bit dramatic?"

"Oh, Ellie, I didn't realise you were awake, sorry!"

She withdrew her hand – I took it back.

"Thanks for coming, I thought I was going to be stranded here with an emotional wreck I hardly know!"

"Shhhh – Tom is still outside in the passage way. God, Ellie, Tom rang in a state and David took the call and could hardly make out what he was saying. Then the police rang and told us you were OK."

"What time is it?"

"Four fifty in the morning."

"You should be in your bed."

"And leave you in here on your own? Not bloody likely. Anyway I spoke to the doctor and they're going to operate on you first thing. Apparently you'll be on morphine and I won't be able to get much sense out of you then. So I thought I'd call in before to see how you were. I spoke to your mum and dad by the way."

"Oh God, how are they?"

"They were very shocked and shaken but I told them you'd live. They'll be over on the first flight in the morning."

"Chloe, the doctor says I'm going to be in traction for a couple of weeks."

"Traction? You mean like flat on your back type of a thing?"

I nodded and started to cry.

"Oh Ellie!" Chloe threw her arms round me, well as best she could considering I was well wrapped up in the hospital bed.

"What else did the doctor say?"

"Nothing – well, I can't really remember," I sobbed.

"Listen, don't worry about anything," she said, trying to calm me. "I'm sure it won't be too bad. Now, tell me, do you want your mum and dad to stay in your flat?"

I nodded. "Oh, Chloe, could you hide any tampons or any stuff like that – Dad gets really embarrassed."

"Yeah, sure, all dads are the same, eh?"

She doled me out some tissues and I wiped my eyes and nose. "Chloe? Did you hear about Mark?"

"Yes but don't worry about him now – he's safe in a police cell and I hardly think he'll be able to bother you from there."

"Does he know I'm in here?"

"I don't know, I'll find out from Sergeant McLeod. Now do you think you can sleep?"

"I think so. Jeez, this leg is so sore. The doctor even told me not to look at it!"

"Um . . . I'd follow his advice if I were you. Now, they're operating on you first thing, so your mum and dad will probably be here when you wake up. Ellie?"

"What?"

"You had your eyes closed. OK, I'm going now, but I'll be in again tomorrow."

"OK, thanks, Chloe."

"I love you, you great mug." She kissed me. "I'll see you tomorrow."

I nodded again, swinging between an overwhelming urge to sleep and crying at the short bursts of pain when I breathed.

After Chloe left, I drifted in and out of a drug-induced sleep. I imagined Mark was in the hospital still driving my car, trying to run me over while I was in bed. Then I was running away from him – we were on a motorway and he was shouting at me.

I woke up with a painful jolt. A nurse was standing beside me with her hand on my arm.

"Now, Miss Clarke, we're going to take you down to theatre."

I just stared at her. I must have looked like I had just seen a ghost, as she patted my hand and told me everything would be fine. When my expression didn't change she just smiled.

She and a porter accompanied me and my wheely-bed down towards the operating part. I prayed for bravery and surprised myself by not crying. I was really hoping they were going to wheel me into the stalls at the Festival Theatre, but it was the operating theatre, there could be no mistaking it, unless of course the Festival Theatre had seriously changed its interior decor.

The nice doctor from last night was downstairs and he smiled as I was wheeled into the room.

"Sorrel, I realise this is not a pleasant experience for you, but we shall try to make it as painless as possible. Now just relax, this won't hurt a bit."

I had "Liar, liar, pants on fire" running round my head. I had everything clenched. I was trying desperately to relax but if I had been able to get up I would have run for my life – unfortunately I was a sitting duck for the anaesthetist. The needle went into my arm – it didn't hurt as much as I had thought. Nothing happened.

"It's not working!" I screamed, only I couldn't get my mouth to open. The doctors and nurses were starting to wobble like jelly and getting further away.

When I woke up I was beside a window and the light was very bright. The clouds seemed to have come right into the room, above my bed. I reached up to try and touch them but my arms were too heavy and I couldn't lift them out of the bed.

"Ellie? You're awake."

I recognised the voice. I looked down the bed and saw Mum and Dad and they were floating too. Strange that my leg didn't hurt anymore, nothing hurt.

"Hi," I said to my parents.

They both moved towards me, smiling.

"Why are you floating? Just like the clouds, they're in the room."

A flash of concern across my father's face made me think he hadn't understood what I was saying.

"The clouds, Daddy, you're floating like the clouds."

"Yes, pet, of course, silly me." Dad put a hand up and stroked my hair as I drifted away from them on my morphine dream.

I was aware that the doctor had come into the room and was talking to my parents, but I didn't want to open my eyes in case I lost the wonderful floating sensation. I felt more lucid than before though and could hear their conversation quite clearly.

"She's talking about floating on the clouds, Doctor." That was Mum.

"Yes, that's quite normal, just a reaction to the morphine – she's hallucinating slightly. Because of the severity of the break and the subsequent work we had to do on the leg, her dosage of morphine is quite high initially . . . she won't make much sense for a couple of days. Once we have moved her onto Codeine she'll be much better though she'll be very sore."

There was a long pause and then I heard: "I'll pop in later when she has come round fully."

Mum and Dad returned to my bedside. I knew they had as they were each holding one of my hands.

"Ellie, sweetheart?"

I opened my eyes – yes, I still seemed to be floating, lovely.

"Ellie, your father and I are going to your flat to get some lunch – we'll come back later, OK? You go back to sleep, love, and we'll see you later."

I nodded and closed my eyes.

I came to again some time later. The doctor had returned. The floating feeling had lessened and my head was clear but I still felt pain-free. I kept my eyes closed, just lay and listened.

"How long will she have those pins in her legs?" I heard Dad asking.

"It will probably be at least two weeks before she can come off traction. After that she'll need a full leg cast for at least another four to six weeks."

"Oh, my goodness! Two weeks with those things in her leg!" That was Mum.

"The weights on the pins work on a pulley system, so

if her leg moves, so do they. This way we ensure that the femur sets correctly and she will have no reccurring pain in the leg after it has healed."

"Will her face be scarred?" Still Mum.

"No, I shouldn't think so, the grazes are superficial – caused when the airbag inflated and it caught her right cheek. It really just looks worse than it is. She also has severe bruising to her chest from the airbag, though the morphine will have temporarily taken away the pain from that – the airbag will have prevented the seat belt from breaking any of her ribs. She'll be immobile for roughly six weeks but by that time everything should have healed. The flesh wounds to her other leg should also heal without scarring."

"Oh God, poor Ellie!" Dad said quietly.

Next time I woke up Chloe, David and Mum and Dad were all round the bed. I didn't feel like floating anymore, I wanted to be sick. I tried to sit up, but could only manage a little way.

"Sick," I whispered to Chloe who was nearest.

"She said 'sick'. What does that mean?"

Everyone stared at me in a very concerned way.

"No, love, you are not sick, you have had an operation." Dad was exaggerating his words as if I was a child who didn't understand.

"No, I want to be sick!" I managed to croak back.

"Oh right – should we leave?"

I nodded. Chloe grabbed a little basin in my beside cabinet and thrust it at me. Dad and David left the room hastily.

My stomach churning, I threw up into the little basin and all over the sheets. Oh God, what was wrong? I felt like I had a mother of a hangover about to descend on me. Mum ran into the corridor to fetch a nurse, returning moments later with a lady in a dark blue uniform who looked important.

"She threw up – she got the sheets, I'm sorry."

"Don't be sorry, that's what laundries are for," the uniformed lady said cheerfully. "Looks like you have taken a reaction to the morphine, let's see if we can't get you more comfortable. I'll get a nurse to help us change your sheets.

The Ward Sister, as she turned out to be, went out and returned with another nurse.

"Now, ladies, this will not be pretty. Ellie has had some major surgery – do you want to leave?"

Chloe asked me would I mind – she had gone quite green. I shook my head. I would have quite liked to leave at this point. Mum held my hand and the nurses busied themselves with the vomit-covered sheet. They gently lifted it away and both Mum and I gasped in horror at what lay underneath. I had a bed-cage over them but my legs looked like they had been attacked by Freddie Kruger and all his pals. One leg was lacerated, bloody and swollen. But the leg with the break was black, with a long line of stitches running up the inside of my thigh. There was also a large metal pin sticking out of my leg; it appeared to run right through my leg to the other side of the traction bed-thingy. OK, so perhaps enough detail. Mum and I looked at each other, speechless. The nurses replaced the sheet with a clean sheet and had the legs covered before I got the chance to feel queasy again.

"Now, I'll go and find Dr Brook and see if we can't get you off the morphine and onto something that agrees with you, OK?"

I nodded, too shocked to speak. I started to cry again. Mum put her arm round my shoulders and hugged me.

"Oh, honey, it looks worse because of the bruising. You'll be fine, hardly any scarring the doctor said. No bikini competitions for a while but I think you can cope with that."

Dr Brook announced the next day that I probably would be in traction for only ten days. After that I would have to get a full leg cast but at least I would be mobile and I could go home.

"I expect most of the bruising to be gone by the time you get the cast. Since you took a reaction to the morphine we've had to move you to codeine. You may be in a little discomfort but at least you won't be nauseous."

I'll not fill you in on any more disgusting and vivid details of my stay in hospital but suffice it to say that the next couple of days were anything but pleasant. Bed baths, hospital food and vaguely patronising doctors coming to look at my 'interesting break'. There is nothing worse than being stared at, like a culture growing on a petri dish, by a group of large disposable incomes in white coats.

Thank God for the nurses, who I have to say were nothing short of saints. If it wasn't for their kindness and caring I would have gone mad. Just when I thought I couldn't take the boredom of staring at the magnolia gloss ceiling for one more day, one of them would come in and read me stories from *Hello* or *OK* and make me feel a lot better.

Chloe, Fiona, Clare and Lousia popped in a few times to see me, usually with some tale of drunken debauchery which just served to make me jealous. Mum and Dad were always in, though when I heard Mum tell me what she had tidied/bleached/ironed that day I always felt tearful. There is something about being told that your flat is now 'shipshape' that breeds concern. Dad had taken to bathing Hector once a day 'because he smells'; even my pointing out that Hector was in fact a dog and had every right to smell didn't stop Dad from his canine ablutions. I hadn't seen Hector for a week, as I am sure you know dogs are not allowed into fracture wards, or indeed any areas of hospitals, but I was sure that wherever he was he was huffing. Hector enjoys a bath as much as I enjoy walking him on dark rainy nights – not much.

So with my parents daily visits to "cheer me up" and visits from a guilt-ridden Tom, I could not wait to get out of the hospital. Tom had managed to partially assuage his feelings of guilt when I explained to him about mad Mark, though he still felt responsible for everything, even Third World Debt as far as I could see.

It became apparent while I was lying on my back with my leg screwed into the bed that Tom and I would never be an item. It's hard to respect someone who constantly has tears in his eyes every time he looks at you, nor may

I add is it particularly flattering. I planned to tell Tom that when I got out of hospital I would need some time on my own to settle back into life.

Fiona was covering my position at work, but she couldn't do it for ever and I was keen to get back to work. I know that sounds mad, but spend ten days in any infirmary round the country, watching daytime TV and reading *Woman's Own,* and you will soon be clamouring to get back to full-time employment. I was also kind of wishing that I could see Jake. I would have loved it if he had been there to visit me in hospital – but then I was looking anything but attractive, so perhaps it was best if he didn't see that.

"Ellie, I'll visit every day. Make sure you don't need anything," Tom informed me the day before I was to be released – sorry, discharged.

"No, really, I'll be fine. Mum and Dad will be here for another week and I need a bit of time to myself."

Tom looked heartbroken.

"I'll ring you and let you know how I'm getting on, OK?"

He nodded miserably.

I had to relent. "How about you come round on Thursday night? Mum could make us all dinner."

"Yeah, that would be great."

He beamed a smile at me; I stared at the magnolia gloss ceiling feeling decidedly glum.

Later that night while I sat watching *The Bill* there was a knock on the door. It was well past visiting hours, so I reckoned it must be one of the nurses with some painkiller I had forgotten to take.

"Ellie?"

Oh God, it was a man's voice. Not Tom – I couldn't bear him again. Shit, could it be Mark? Would he have been released on bail or whatever happens to criminal nutters? I was considering an escape route (none), when the voice spoke again.

"Sorry it's so late, but I wanted to see you. May I come in?"

I recognised the voice and my plans of escape vanished in an instant.

"Come in." I tried to sound calm and nonchalant.

Jake stuck his head round the door and smiled when he saw me.

"Ellie, you poor old thing. God, you look like an advert for private health care!"

I laughed, I was so pleased to see him.

He came over to me and threw his arms round me in a big after-shavey hug.

"Oh Jake, I'm glad it's you. But are you not supposed to be in Boston?"

"Yeah, but a guy has to take holidays, you know. Anyway, I heard this girl I really like was in hospital so I thought I had to visit. I mean, I wouldn't want her to think I was rude!"

"As if!"

"Anyway, I know you won't be in the mood for this stuff now but I brought you some pressies." And he produced a carton of Silk Cut, an enormous bottle of Dolce and Gabbana and litre of vodka. "I thought we could have a party whenever you get out. Which I believe is tomorrow."

"Thanks a million – you didn't need to buy me all this stuff!"

"Well, you know they're getting rid of Duty Free, so I thought I should buy before it's too late."

"They're only getting rid of it in Europe, you buffoon!"

"Oh well, I admit it – I'm trying to buy my way back into your affections."

"You are?"

"Well, I haven't phoned for over a month, and I know some girls who would unleash the death penalty on me for that."

"Well, I hate to disappoint you but I didn't spend November sitting by the phone waiting for you to ring."

"You didn't?" Jake burst out laughing. "Well, give it all back then! Maybe I can return it on the way back."

"No chance! There's enough perfume here to make even Hector smell nice."

"He looked fairly sparkly when I saw him."

"You saw Hector?"

"Yup, I went round to your flat to surprise you with a visit, but I surprised your mum and dad instead. They told me you were here, so I had to come and see you straight away."

"How did you get past the nurses? They're really strict about visiting times."

"To be honest, there was a big box of chocolates in that bag too, until about ten minutes ago."

"Ah, I see, bribing the nurses!"

"Well, I didn't think my male charms were going to work on them. They like you a lot it would appear and not just anyone is allowed in to see you."

"I'm just so popular, what can I say?"

"I'm glad to see you're in good form. Your Mum told me all the details. Sounds really nasty."

"Well, not something I would rush back to repeat. But thankfully I was unconscious for the really horrid bits, like being cut out of the car and the operation."

"What are you going to do about this Mark? I don't know anything about this guy but Chloe tells me he's been harassing you for ages."

"You saw Chloe?"

"Yeah, she was round at your flat having dinner with your mum and dad. David is away at some dental conference in Bristol, so your mum asked her round."

"Bloody hell, Mum and Dad are now entertaining my friends in my flat – very social!"

"I'm going back for a drink with them, after I've seen you."

"Well, the cheek!" I laughed.

"So anyway, about Mark, where is he now?"

"I believe he's in a psychiatric hospital for observation. The police haven't been back to see me since the accident. What do you think will happen to him?"

"I really don't know – we'd need to ask George, he's a defence lawyer."

"I never want to see Mark again. Did Mum and Dad tell you he wrote off my car?"

"Yes, they did – your Dad is dealing with all the insurance stuff for you. Hopefully it won't take too long to get some money through, so that you can get another car."

"I'll probably only be able to afford a hairdryer once they value the Fiat. How long are you up in Scotland for?"

"Well, I took a fortnight's leave and I got back five days ago, so my plan was to spend a long weekend up in Edinburgh before going back to London."

"God, is it Friday night already?"

"Nope, it's Thursday, but I wanted a really long weekend. I have missed you, you know."

On cue I turned crimson and a ridiculous grin broke out on my face.

"You have?"

"Yes, of course. It hasn't been that easy, Ellie. Trying to deal with leaving everyone behind, fitting into a totally new lifestyle – Americans are so different you know."

Oh, so he hadn't actually missed me in particular. "Where are you staying?" I asked.

"In your flat if you don't mind. Your mum offered me your spare room. I've been in your flat before, but I don't remember it being so tidy or so big."

My chin dropped. "My flat is not big, by any stretch of the imagination. The tidiness is due to my mother, without whom no one would ever know what colour my carpet was."

"You don't mind me staying?"

"No, of course, not at all." It was a glorious idea.

"Listen, I had better go but I'll be back tomorrow to take you away from all of this."

"You're picking me up?"

"Is that OK? It was actually your mum's idea, she and

your dad are going to Perth tomorrow to look at pottery or something. Apparently they don't see enough of Scotland when they come over to visit," he said quite innocently.

I laughed out loud. My mother could win prizes for her diplomacy. She seemed to be able to pick out a man I fancied in a line-up, even if she had never previously met him before. Mind you, that weekend in Belfast I was not exactly subtle.

"Well, I'll be here – just be sure you don't leave me lying here for too long. The doctor is going to put the cast on my leg around ten in the morning, so once they've got the pins out, me out of bed and the cast on, it should be around lunch-time."

"I think I can manage that, try and enjoy your last night in hospital!"

"Oh, thank you very much."

"See you tomorrow." A kiss on the forehead – again – and then he was gone.

Well, I could hardly expect more: I was lying pinned to a hospital bed, with greasy hair and with my luck probably the onset of gangrene. How desirable can you get?

The whole time I had been in hospital I had given as little thought as possible to Mark. But after talking to Jake, he seeped back into my thoughts. Initially I couldn't believe that he had done what he had done. I think I was in a bit of shock. Then I didn't care where he was – I just wanted to make sure I never had to see him again after what he did to Tom and me, not to mention my car. Struggling to come to terms with the last couple of weeks, thinking about Mark just made me very emotional – not scared, but very angry. I thought if I ever saw that (please excuse the expletive) fucker again, I would do something I would later probably not regret.

So, lying in bed thinking about Jake – naked (that was completely imagined) – a major lottery win and a small deserted Caribbean island my mind began to wander. I began to think about my recent near-death experience. I was a bit disappointed that my life hadn't flashed before my eyes. Perhaps my inner-self knew that I was going to be OK and therefore didn't bother – I was wittering again, that was the painkillers.

So lying in bed having happy thoughts about naked men and a huge disposable income, my mind wandered and I got to thinking about Mark. Then I had this horrible feeling come over me – like someone was watching me. I was suddenly acutely aware of my surroundings. I was in a little room off a side ward and I hadn't seen a nurse since before Jake had called in. I'd had this kind of feeling before – when Mark was near me, watching me, but I couldn't see him.

I knew he had been removed for observation to a psychiatric hospital. My imagination must be running riot, I thought. It's spending all this time on my own having conversations with water glasses, the wall and really anyone who will listen to me. I must get a grip, the nurses are only at the station down the corridor and one should be along in a minute. I took a deep breath and laughed out loud at my own sudden edginess.

"Hello Sorrel, somebody say something funny?"

Had I not been pinned to the bed I would have jumped

ten feet into the air. Mark was standing at the side of my bed, his clothes muddy and torn.

"Mark, what are you doing here?" My voice sounded all funny and high, I could hardly breathe.

"Just wanted to see how the patient was getting on. Have they been treating you all right in here?"

I couldn't form the thoughts in my head fast enough – what was he doing here, why wasn't he locked up?

I could only nod in reply.

"Well, you realise you were never meant to be in here."

I stared at him, struck dumb with fear. So much for giving him a piece of my mind, though this confrontation was to have happened with Mark in prison and me safely behind some six-inch plate glass, not bolted to a hospital bed with the EC Codeine mountain inside me.

"You were supposed to be in the morgue." He laughed at me. I suppose I must have had a look of complete horror on my face.

My blood ran cold. *"Why?"* was all I could say.

"Because that's what I had planned – only you didn't die, did you? God, you just broke a few bones, like that silly boyfriend of yours, I see he didn't hang around long. You shouldn't really waste your time on people like him, they're only after you for one thing."

"Oh." Please let a nurse come soon! All this talk of morgues was unsettling to say the least. His eyes had a manic gleam to them I had never seen before, like something had snapped.

"Oh Sorrel, you are so naive sometimes, I wonder how you manage to get by at all. When we were together you never even noticed when someone tried to take advantage of you." He pulled up a chair beside me and leant his face almost into mine. "You used to stand in Boots or wherever and let those sales women bully you into buying things you didn't really want or need. You stood there like a dumb animal – that's when I realised."

"What? That I was an impulse shopper?" I could hardly keep the contempt out of my voice.

"I hated you, for being weak, for being like everyone else. You are just a sheep, someone who gets pushed around."

Suddenly I didn't care that I was alone with him, I forgot that I was to all intents and purposes completely helpless and I got angry – though in hindsight I blame the Codeine.

"Mark, you are an asshole! Did I ever tell you that when we were together? I'm sure I meant to."

"Sorrel, I am superior to you, I always was . . ."

"No, Mark, like I said, you are and were an asshole. Now I also think you are a freak who needs help. If you want to get rid of people just because they are suckers for clever marketing, you're going to have a busy time."

He looked surprised for a moment and pulled back, but then his face darkened and he leant forward in his chair again, close to my face.

"Like I said, you were not supposed to be here – you were supposed to be downstairs."

My heart nearly stopped as he pulled a syringe out of his pocket and began to take the cover off the needle.

"This shouldn't really hurt much, it won't take long."

Self-preservation kicked in and I screamed blue

murder. Before he could cover my mouth I had half the hospital running to my aid. Mark quickly replaced the cover over the needle and slipped it back into his pocket.

"Don't think I won't be back," he whispered and ran out of my room.

The nurses arrived moments later, security guards seconds after them.

"He's here, he's in the hospital, he tried to kill me!"

"Who, Ellie? Who tried to kill you?"

"Mark!"

"The guy from the car crash?"

I nodded.

"But I thought he had been moved to Royal Ed?"

"Well, he was in this room two minutes ago."

Security went to see if he was still in the building, but of course they couldn't find him. The nurse called the police who arrived very quickly.

I remembered Sergeant McLeod very well – he had interviewed me after the crash. He told me that, earlier that day, Mark had disappeared from High Ed where he was being assessed while he awaited trail, for the attempted murder of both me and Tom. I told them about Mark's muddy torn clothing and his manic attitude and the syringe.

The policemen looked very worried when I mentioned this last item.

"Mr Norris appears to have stolen a certain amount of Vecuronium used to anaesthetise patients in the hospital. A high dosage is lethal within two minutes. He lifted a loaded syringe from a tray being used for an operation.

He had already injured an orderly while escaping from his secure ward and we know he has a history of violence."

"I never thought Mark was violent."

"Well, he attacked a former girlfriend while he was at school."

"I never knew that."

"She never reported it. But her mother did – to us, eight years ago. He has been quiet since then. But it appears that his mental state has continued to deteriorate. According to the psychologist who counselled him in the last couple of weeks he began to fixate on you after your relationship with him broke down."

"But he left, he went to a kibbutz in Israel."

"It appears he was asked to leave the kibbutz after a month as he made the others there uncomfortable – they found his behaviour threatening. Unfortunately we don't know where he was during the six months he was not in Britain."

"He had a job working as a make-up artist for some production company at some stage," I recalled.

"That was more recent. He lost that job a couple of months ago, again due to threatening behaviour. We spoke to the personnel director of Kitson's Productions – Mr Norris falsified his CV and wrote some fake references for himself."

"And no one thought to check?"

"Apparently not."

"It just all seems a little bizarre."

"Well, before that he was a supply teacher at a primary school."

"A primary school?"

"Again he falsified his qualifications and experience."

"Shit, I cannot believe he got away with all of that."

"He was only employed briefly at the school before they realised he was not a qualified teacher – when confronted he became violent and the police were called."

"God!"

"I would say you have had a lucky escape. We think he had been planning the attack on you for some time."

"So you mean trying to get me to go out with him was just a ploy?"

"We believe so."

"Sorry, I don't seem to be dealing with this very well. It just all seems so unreal."

"On the contrary, Miss Clarke, you have dealt with this whole situation remarkably well. We're sorry you had to deal with Mr Norris alone. We'll have a policeman outside your ward tonight."

"Thank you. Why didn't you tell me sooner that he had escaped?"

"We had only just been informed – we suspect the psychiatric hospital were just a little bit tardy in admitting they had lost one of their patients and a dangerous drug. Don't worry – we'll catch him, he won't be able to threaten you again. He did verbally threaten you, didn't he?"

"Yes, he said I was supposed to be in the morgue."

"I'm terribly sorry, Miss Clarke. I'll let your parents know what has happened."

"No, don't. I don't want to get them worried. There isn't anything they can do tonight anyway apart from panic."

"Well, if you are sure?"

"I'm sure."

"OK, but as I say there will be an officer outside your room, just call out if you need him."

"Thank you."

The nurses fussed round me for ages, making sure I was comfortable. I refused a sleeping pill – too nervous at the idea of being helpless and drugged-up – and lay awake for a long long time.

Chapter Seventeen

I was woken at seven in the morning and Dr Brook came in to see me at eight.

"Right, we will give a local anaesthetic while we remove the pins. Sister Morrison will clean your leg with antiseptic before we put the cast on."

"OK."

"You are feeling up to it?"

"Can't wait to get out of this bed! I feel as if my bum is about to put down roots!"

"Well, I hope not," he smiled at me.

An hour later I was in the operating theatre looking at two smallish holes in my thigh.

"Don't worry – these will close over very quickly," the doctor assured me.

"Your leg is still swollen so you may have to come in again to have the cast replaced if it becomes too loose as the swelling goes down."

First my leg was wrapped in a bandage, then another and finally Dr Brook got his hands into the plaster of Paris and with a little help from one of the nurses they set about giving me a full leg cast – right up to my hip.

"OK, now this is a large cast and it will get heavy for you, so try not to go on any long shopping trips."

"I promise!" I laughed.

"It's an improvement on the pins – at least you can move around, though I would like you to come back in a week so we can check that no infection has got into the wounds and the swelling has started to go down."

"How long will I have to wear the cast?"

"Six weeks at the maximum, and four at the minimum. It was a severe break and we want it to heal completely before you put any real weight on the leg. Now we'll wait until the cast has completely dried and then you can try walking with these crutches."

Once the doctor was satisfied that the plaster was dry, the nurse produced a set of crutches and handed them to me. I positioned myself at the edge of the bed and using my good leg I pushed myself off. I managed to get to one end of the corridor with the nurse's support and on my way back I saw Jake grinning at me. Then he noticed the police officer who was sitting on a seat outside the theatre, stopped grinning but didn't say anything.

"Now your toes will swell up, so try and keep your leg up when you are not moving around," advised the nurse.

"Will she live?" Jake asked.

"Oh I think so," she replied.

"Now make an appointment with out-patients for early next week, and good luck. Before you go I'll just get you some painkillers as you'll need them once the anaesthetic wears off completely."

"Thanks."

She handed me the little brown bottle. "So see you next week."

With Jake making sure my exit was clear, opening doors and supporting me, I made my way out of the hospital.

"You have no idea how glad I am to be getting out of here."

"You were early. I thought you wouldn't be ready till lunch-time. How come the Doc decided to unpin you early?"

"Well, there was a bit of a commotion last night so the Doc didn't want to keep me hanging around unnecessarily."

"What sort of commotion?" Jake held the last door open for me and we were outside.

"Ah . . . fresh air!"

"Ellie, what sort of commotion?"

"Um – the Mark kind."

"What! What the hell do you mean?"

"God, stop shouting, you don't want me to fall over, do you?"

"Shit, sorry, no of course not. Sit down here." He motioned to a bench.

"Do you mind getting the car – I'll explain on the way home."

"Yes, of course, I'll be right back."

I sat trying to think of a way to explain last night

without my whole family going ballistic. I just didn't feel up to dealing with a scene right away. I fancied a decent lunch, a cigarette and an afternoon watching telly.

Five minutes later Jake appeared round the corner in his hired car. I hobbled over to the car and tried to get into the passenger seat as elegantly as I could. Jake had moved the seat back as far as it could go, and I could just about get my cast in.

"OK, so what the hell happened last night?"

"Mark appeared in my room not long after you left."

Jake looked absolutely horrified but he didn't say anything.

"He told me I was supposed to have died in the crash and he threatened me with a syringe."

"Oh Christ, Ellie, why didn't you phone us?"

"The police came really quickly, he had run off and well, there wasn't anything you could have done. It would only have worried Mum and Dad."

"We could have come and stayed with you last night!"

"Oh, and listen to Dad snoring, no thanks," I joked.

"This is definitely not funny. What did the police say?"

"They said he had escaped from his secure ward, beaten up an orderly, had a history of violence and had lied his way into his previous jobs."

Jake appeared momentarily lost for words.

"They say he has fixated on me, and they think he had been planning the attack for a while."

"Where is he now?"

"They're looking for him."

"Shit! You mean he is running round Edinburgh with a lethal syringe in his pocket waiting to get you?"

"That's about the height of it."

"When did you go out with this guy?"

"Over a year ago. I finished it with him and he left to work on a kibbutz. But Sergeant McLeod told me last night he was asked to leave as he made the other people there uncomfortable."

"So then what?"

"Well, they're not sure, he seemed to vanish for six months – they think he probably worked in Europe."

"But he came back to get you?"

"The police think so."

"This is utterly incredible – you wouldn't believe it if you read about it."

"I know, sorry."

"What are you sorry for?"

"Well, it's my fault."

"Oh, come on, Ellie, I hardly think you asked nut-boy to stalk you!"

"No."

"Well then, it's his agenda and nothing to do with you. We'll just have to make sure he is caught and can't harm you or anyone else again. There was me thinking I was just going to visit a friend in hospital, but right now I think you need a bodyguard."

"Ha, very funny." Oh God, he said friend, not love of his life, reason for living.

"I'll have to get my leave extended," Jake broke into my reverie.

"What?"

"Well, I can hardly go back to the States knowing that your life is at risk, now can I?"

"Will they let you?"

"They'll just have to."

"Mum and Dad can look after me, don't feel you have to."

"I don't feel I have to – I want to."

"Oh." Well, that has to count for something. "My knight in a shining Honda."

"Ha, something like that. I cannot get my head round the fact that Mark actually managed to get into your room last night. I promise you this, he won't get within a mile of you ever again."

"The police are going to watch my building. They think if he is mad enough to come back to the hospital, he might try to get me at home."

"Let's hope they catch him pretty quick. Now how is your leg?"

"OK, but I think the anaesthetic is starting to wear off. I might take a bunch of painkillers when we get home."

"Do you mind me staying? I could go and stay at Chloe and David's if you prefer?"

"God and subject you to the wedding of the year? I hardly think that would be fair."

"Is she getting excited?"

"Well, it is only three months away – June 14th."

"I know, I've been invited."

"I'm supposed to be going for dress fittings this week – how am I going to look in a cast?"

"Well, it's not like you're going to have to drag the cast up the aisle. Anyway I'm sure the dressmaker can make an allowance for that."

"I suppose, but I'm worried it will give Margo the

opportunity to get rid of me as chief bridesmaid: 'Chloe, if she can't even attend the fittings then how is she going to look on the day in a half-finished dress?' God, I can just hear her whinging at Chlo right now!"

"I'm sure Chloe has the measure of her mum, I don't think she is that easily bullied. Now stop panicking about a dress. I think you have more important things to worry about. Actually, now that I think about it, if you are Chloe's best friend does this mean you are supposed to organise the hen night?"

"Yes," I nodded miserably. "But Chloe hasn't decided what she wants to do – one big night out, or a weekend away with a smaller group."

"A weekend sounds good, makes more of an occasion out of it. Lots of stag and hen parties go to Dublin or Edinburgh."

"Well, we live in Edinburgh so that's no good, and we go to Dublin shopping every time we are home. No, I think if we do the weekend thing it should be somewhere more exciting."

"You mean like abroad?"

"Well, I don't mean Blackpool."

"Point taken. How about America? I mean – you could do a weekend shopping in New York."

"Oh, that sounds good."

"Or what about the south of France? You've got friends there right? Doesn't Chloe know Nicole?"

"Yes, she does, that's a great idea. I wonder how much all that would cost?"

"There are travel agents who specialise in that sort of thing. How many people where you thinking of? Some agents can get discounts depending on how many people are travelling."

"Well, there's Chloe of course and me, Rachel, Louisa, Clare and a couple of girls from home – so that's six."

"Then you can ring round some travel agents when you get home, then let the girls know when you have found a decent price."

"That's a great idea, thanks."

"No problem, that's what I'm going to do whenever Ben gets round to popping the question."

"God don't – sorry, I know you really like Sonia but I am just getting used to the idea that she may not be a completely humourless cow."

Jake shot me a look.

"Don't say it, OK, I may have been a bit harsh but, come on, she treated Mum like her maid whenever she visited at home."

"That's just Sonia – she was probably just asserting herself."

"Whatever." I looked out of the window trying to hint that I did not want to talk about Sonia and the fact that she might indeed one day want to marry my brother.

"Sorrel Clarke."

"What!"

"How many girls do you know would have jacked in a good career and up sticks to a poverty-stricken country to build hospitals and be with your brother? Not many, I can tell you."

"OK, she's a saint, can we leave it at that?" I snapped.

"For the meantime, but I think you would be surprised if you knew what she had sacrificed to be with Ben."

"Oh what? Like swapping tips on this year's hottest designers, which restaurants one really must be seen in?" I was getting really narked with this conversation and the growing discomfort in my leg didn't help.

"Have you any idea how much Sonia was earning when she left London?"

"Oh, for God's sake, Jake, she was a PA!"

"Yes and a bloody good one, working for the most powerful man in advertising in London. Sonia was earning over thirty five thousand when she resigned."

I gulped.

"Pounds?"

"Yes."

"Shit!"

"So it wasn't like she was using Ben for his credit card, she was doing very well in her own right and she dropped it all for him."

Suddenly I felt very mean and hateful.

"Sorry, I didn't realise."

"Well, now you do."

"She must really love him."

"Yes, she must."

We arrived in front of my building. Jake got out of the car and lifted my crutches out of the back seat and then helped me out of the passenger side. There is a lift in my building, but it hadn't worked in so long, people kind of forgot that it was there. Mum and Dad had arranged to have it fixed, so that I wouldn't have any trouble getting around. This made me feel even shittier.

"Ellie."

"Yes?"

We were in the lift waiting to arrive at my floor.

"Sorry, I shouldn't have had a go at you like that."

"No, I'm sorry, I shouldn't be such a hateful little gobshite."

"You are not a gobshite, whatever the hell that is," said Jake laughing.

"When they come home, I'll be really nice to her."

"I didn't mean to bully you."

"You didn't, You just highlighted a few facts for me."

The lift doors opened on my floor and Jake helped me to my door. Mum and Dad were waiting and flung the door open.

"Welcome home," they chorused.

"Thanks." I hobbled into the living-room.

"Bloody hell, did someone sell my flat and buy a new one when I was incapacitated?"

"Do you mind? I just had a little tidy." Mum looked a bit doubtful. "I hope I have put everything where you like it."

"Mum, it's fab, I didn't put anything anywhere so I don't give a monkeys. Where is the ironing pile?" My living-room looked about twice the size it had done two weeks ago.

"Ironed and put away."

"The plate mountain?"

"Washed and put away."

"My stinky mutt?"

"Also washed but very excited to see you."

Hector came out of my room like a tornado and nearly knocked me over. I tried to bend down to stroke him, but I couldn't reach.

"Hector, I don't think you have ever been so clean in your entire life! Mum, have you had him Scotchguarded?"

"Well, he has actually started to enjoy his baths."

"I think I should go into hospital a bit more often. Guys, this is really amazing. The place is immaculate, thank you so much."

"Sweetheart, it was the least we could do. Now come and sit down, your mother has made your favourite lunch."

"Cheese and baked bean toasties?"

"Yes."

"Excellent!"

Jake looked seriously dubious.

"No, you really have to try these, a taste sensation!"

"Well, if you insist."

"I do."

After our lunch-time feast of toasties I settled myself in front of the telly and Dad even temporarily gave up sole command of the remote control. Mum and Jake went into the kitchen to make coffee and I suspected to give Jake a chance to tell Mum about Mark's late-night visit to me.

My suspicions were confirmed as Mum came rushing into the living-room just as I was getting involved in *Murder She Wrote* and Jessica's nephew had wrongly (of course) been accused of murdering his boss.

"*Sorrel! Why didn't you tell us?*"

Dad looked up from his vantage-point on the sofa. "Tell us what?"

"*That psychotic maniac is on the loose trying to kill my daughter!*"

Dad sat forward in his seat. "What have you not been telling us?"

"Mark has escaped from Royal Ed!"

"What's Royal Ed?"

"The psychiatric hospital were he was being held until his trial."

"Jesus Christ, why didn't the police let us know?"

"Because I asked them not to," I said.

"You did what!"

"It was late last night. I didn't want to worry you. I had an officer outside my door the whole night and security in the grounds – he couldn't have got back in if he had tried."

"If he had just escaped from the hospital why would he want to get back in?"

"No, Dad. To my ward, he got into my ward last night, and threatened me there."

Dad looked as if he was about to have a seizure and Mum began to cry.

"Well, that's it, we're taking you home."

"No!"

"Yes, and I won't argue. I will not let my daughter stay here while this crazy man is running about, especially when you are on crutches."

"I'll go and pack a bag for you, love. You can stay at home till the police find him and lock him up." Mum patted me on the shoulder. "At least until after Christmas."

Suddenly the idea of being looked after for a while by my parents didn't seem such a bad idea. At least at home I wouldn't have to look over my shoulder every time I left the house. Christmas was always good fun at home anyway.

"You can organise the hen weekend from home," Jake suggested.

"Give your leg time to heal. Oh and you can help me wrap pressies," Mum continued.

"OK, OK, I'll go home for a couple of weeks, maximum, all right?"

"It would give your mother and me peace of mind, to know you are safe."

Dad rang the airport and got us booked on a morning flight back to Belfast and Mum packed a bag for me to take home. Jake then rang the police to tell them that my parents were taking me home and Sergeant McLeod thought that was a good idea but cautioned us to mention it to as few people as possible, for my own safety.

I rang Chloe first.

"Are you going to be OK? I'm so sorry this has happened to you. I never liked him, but I never thought anything like this would happen."

"What do you mean you never liked him?"

"Sorry, that's a horrible thing to say, but I always thought he was a bit shifty, sort of on edge."

"You could have pointed it out at the time!"

"Sorrel, you told me he was the bonk of the century. You missed a whole week of lectures – the only reason you came in was because he thought eating crisps in bed was disgusting. That was one thing we did agree on."

"What?"

"Eating crisps in bed is disgusting."

"Och, piss off!"

"Sorry, not very helpful. Listen, if anyone asks, I'll tell them you've gone abroad for a while."

"That would be great. Listen, I'm sorry about missing the dress fitting. Have I mucked up your plans?"

"Mark has mucked up our plans – this was not your fault. I asked Yvonne how quickly she could make a dress and she said if she got the initial fitting done then she could finish in about a week, so no worries. You can go for a fitting once you have that cast off and you are feeling more like it."

"Thanks – oh, one last thing."

"Yup?"

"Your hen weekend."

"Oh yes, I was going to leave it up to you."

"I know you were. How does going abroad sound?"

"Fabulous. Can we go to Italy?"

"Italy?"

"Yeah, I've never been, though I've wanted to go to Venice since I was little."

"I know you have. Venice, sounds good. I'll see what I can come up with. It's going to be my project while I am at home being tormented by Mum and Dad."

"Take care, Ellie, I'll ring you every day to find out how you're getting on."

"Cheers, Chloe."

After that I rang Fiona. Apparently at work Avril was full of concern for me and she told Fiona that as far as the station was concerned, they just wanted me to recover and come back whenever I was fit. Though since the accident had been in the news everyone knew what had happened and, according to Fiona, I had become a minor celebrity. During my stay in hospital we had also got the promotions for our roving reportage, which was completely brilliant. We would start when I came back – in the meantime I was to take care.

"Oh, before I forget," said Fiona. "You may get a phone call from those people at *OK!*"

"The magazine?"

"Yes, that weekly one with all the photos of Posh Spice."

"Why are they phoning me?" I asked, amazed.

"Well, apparently they haven't featured a woman who is the victim of a violent stalker."

"I didn't think that was really their style!"

"Well, no one worth noting is getting married so they have a slot to fill is the only answer I can give you, but they did mention a fee."

"They did?

"Aye."

"Did they mention how much?"

"Aye."

"Fiona! How much?" I shrieked.

"Oh, five grand for exclusive rights to your story, with photos of course."

They will supply the fashion."

"The fashion?"

"Ellie, is there an echo on this phone?"

"Fiona, if it's not a stupid question, why have they told you all this and not me?"

"Well, I was acting as your agent while you were in hospital."

"My agent?"

"Yes, dearie, you have suddenly become interesting to the rest of the nation. Even Mr McBain is convinced that you would raise the profile of the show with your sudden media fame."

"Pardon? Fi, I ring you up to tell you I am going into hiding due to an unwarranted attack on my life from manic ex-lover. And you tell me that you are now my agent, *OK!* want me in their magazine and McBain thinks I will raise the profile of a television programme, forgive me for being just a tad confused."

"Sorry, was I going a bit fast for you?"

"A bit." I reached down to pick up my chin which had fallen on the floor somewhere.

"Well, what has happened since your accident is this: Britain has never had a serious stalking incident, not one that had such a dramatic conclusion anyway. The papers are now asking what women can do to protect themselves from such unwanted attention. You are a figurehead for anyone who has suffered from this kind of harassment – i.e. hot media property. Of course, I haven't said yes to *OK!* I wanted to speak to you first."

"Fi, I'll have to call you back, I need time to let this all sink in."

"Don't leave it too long, I hear Fergie is strapped for cash again and I don't want her stealing your limelight by selling a kidney or something."

"Gross! Bye, Fiona!" I hung up. "Mum, Dad, Jake, you are never going to believe this!"

"What, pet?"

"*OK!* want me to be in their magazine. For five GRAND!"

"We know, Fiona rang us a couple of days ago. *The*

News of the World have also rung her to see if you want to set up The Sorrel Clarke Trust for Stalked Women. They want to start a petition for changing the law before *The Sun* does."

"They want to do what? What did you tell them? This is crazy!"

"I know, I said I didn't think so."

"Oh my God. I think I need to lie down."

"Are you all right, Ellie?" Jake asked.

"Yeah, this is all just too weird."

"I know, but it will all blow over. I just want Mark to be found and then you can get on with your life."

"Maybe going home is the best thing to do."

"I think so. Listen, if you don't mind, I'll go back to London., I think I would just be in the way if I went back to Belfast with you all! Fiona would sell a story about us and then my career would be over!"

"Of course, thank you for staying as long as you did. Will you stay tonight?"

"Yes, I'll go with you to the airport tomorrow morning and get the first available flight."

Next morning at the airport Jake managed to get on a flight leaving before ours so he first said goodbye to Mum and Dad and then, as Mum pulled Dad discreetly away, we hurriedly said goodbye.

"Have a great Christmas!" I said and really meant it.

"I'll ring you to see how you're getting on. I'll be staying with Mum. I'm going back to Boston on the second of January. The Americans don't seem to believe in long holidays."

"Thank you so much for visiting me." I had a lump in my throat and felt very awkward.

"It was my pleasure. When you're speaking to Ben – "

"If I'm speaking to Ben."

"He'll ring, it's Christmas, more than his life is worth not to ring home."

"Good point."

"Tell him I was asking after him."

"Sure, not a problem."

I wished to God I wasn't anchored to a chair by a heavy cast, I wished I wasn't looking like shit, I wished Mum wasn't peering at us pretending not to, I wished we had more time.

Jake was looking at me a bit uncertainly, I thought. Then he bent down swiftly and gave me a brief hug, planting a light kiss on my lips.

Could mean anything or nothing, I thought with a sigh as I waved after him.

After saying goodbye to Jake I felt strangely calm, even with a completely inept British Airways wheelchair-pusher. After we narrowly avoided a large group of Japanese tourists closely followed by a couple romantically kissing goodbye to each other, Dad asked the guy if it wouldn't be easier if he pushed me instead. Mr British Airways didn't seem to have any objections so he left us to it after painstakingly giving us directions to gate two. I think there are only two gates in Edinburgh airport, which cuts down on your chances of getting lost. But still I suppose it was nice of him.

Chapter Eighteen

On arrival back at Belfast airport, Hector seemed none the worse for his brief flight across the Irish Sea. Dad went to get the car.

"Lucy should be at home when we get there."

"She has come up early," I said.

"Well, you *are* her sister, and she wants to make sure you're OK."

"Is she staying for Christmas?"

"Of course."

"Good. What about Ben?"

"Well, he won't be home, but he promised he'd ring on Christmas day. We've sent him and Sonia a Christmas package, I hope they get it, apparently the authorities have a tendency to open anything that looks interesting and quite often help themselves, so I tried to make it look like I was just sending books, something they wouldn't be particularly interested in."

"How are they getting on?"

"Oh, they seem to be getting on fabulously. Actually I have been surprised at how well Sonia has adjusted to life over there – I mean compared to how she was at home."

"I know – Jake was telling me too. How is Ben?"

"Your brother is fine, he is loving every minute of it. I think he would like to stay if they can."

"What about Sonia?"

"Oh, I think she wouldn't be entirely adverse to it either."

"Really?" I was feeling sceptical again.

Mum nodded.

At that moment Dad pulled up in the car. I let Hector out of his travelling cage and into the back seat.

"I don't want dog-hair all over the back seat now, Ellie."

"OK, Dad, he's sitting on his blanket."

Actually, Hector was busy trying to get up onto the back shelf, his most favourite place in the whole world.

I find that being at home is comforting for the first couple of days, then I start to go quietly mad. This time though Mum and Dad were really good with me, and I have no doubt that I was a right little awkward bitch. Having what felt like half my body in a plaster cast meant that I was unable to go anywhere without the aid of one or both parents. I spent the first few days round the house, watching television until I felt my brain was atrophying. It was too cold to sit outside and I couldn't walk very far as I had already given myself blisters on the palms of my hands from using the crutches.

Lucy would walk into the living-room and say, "Still here?"

"Where do you expect me to go?"

"God, don't you get bored?"

"Lucy, I have spent the afternoon watching the racing on Channel four. I'm surprised I'm still conscious.

After I had been home for about a week, I was starting to despair. Mum came into my room early one morning, woke me up and informed me that we were going shopping.

"No offence, Mum, but what good would I be if I can't even make it out of the carpark. It's no use, you go on without me."

"Ah, shut up and get washed. I have phoned ahead and booked you a mobility scooter."

"You have phoned where? And booked me what?"

"I have phoned Castle Court and booked you a mobility scooter. They're great, your grandfather uses one when I take him shopping."

"Oh fabulous, I get to look like a total moron, only this time I get to do it in public."

"We're leaving in half and hour, get ready."

Mum left me to it. It took me five minutes to orchestrate my getting out of bed. I got my crutches and hobbled into the bathroom. I couldn't get the cast wet which meant no shower or bath, but I had devised a cunning method (which I won't go into) for getting myself as clean as I could manage. Mum and Dad still sat with me at the dinner table so it must have been working. Lucy hadn't said anything smart either.

Once I had dressed in my extra wide, wide-leg trousers, my one shoe and my one extra thick and warm woolly sock and a polo neck, I didn't look too bad, save for the fact that I looked like I was suffering from elephantiasis in one leg.

I began my descent of the stair. This involved me using a crutch in my left hand and clinging on to the hand-rail of the banister with my right.

On arrival in the kitchen Mum and Lucy were sitting at the kitchen table drinking coffee.

"You have time for a quick cup and a piece of toast if you like?" said Mum.

"Yes, please."

"OK, put a bit in for yourself and I'll get the coffee."

I looked at her as if she was joking.

"Come on, love, you have to get used to doing things even with a broken leg," Mum said.

"OK, toast coming up, anyone else want a bit?"

"No thanks, already had some," said Lucy.

"You're up early by the way," I said.

"Well, when Mum told me that you were going shopping on a scooter I thought it was too good a chance to miss."

"Oh, very funny."

"No, seriously, it's good that you're getting out. If I have to witness you cry your way through one more crappy episode of *Montel Williams* I will be forced to shoot you."

After my cup of tea we left for Castle Court.

"So how come I have never heard of these things before?" I asked.

"Well, why would you?" said Mum. "You never needed one before."

"How do you know about them?"

"Well, I'd seen them in some of the bigger shopping

centres round town and I made a few enquiries. They're free to hire for a couple of hours and it gives so many people a freedom that they wouldn't have had before. I take your grandfather food-shopping in Sprucefield and he just zooms along beside me, though he has a tendency to try and run people over."

When we had got parked in the shopping centre Mum and Lucy helped me into the lift. "The scooters are just in front of you as you go in."

There was a little row of four electric scooters facing us as we entered Castle Court and the man in charge came forward to help me.

"Sorrel Clarke?"

"Yes."

"This red one is yours. How's that leg?"

"Oh, not so bad, thanks."

"I'm not too busy today so you can probably have the scooter for the whole morning."

"Thanks a lot."

"Now just squeeze this handle forward to go forward and squeeze back to go back."

"OK."

He helped me into the scooter – surprisingly there was room for my leg to stick out in front of me. I did as he said and the scooter moved forward and back.

"Piece of cake."

"Good, now just take care."

"I will, thanks."

"My pleasure, have a nice time shopping."

I moved off.

"You look so funny." Lucy, of course.

"Shut up, Luce, this is fun. Now where will we go first?"

Mum and Lucy looked at each other and burst out laughing.

"Oh, I wish I had a camera," Mum sighed.

I squeezed the forward handle and zoomed off. *"Come on!"* I shouted back at them.

We spent a great day in the shopping centre, and discovered that you could take the scooter out round Belfast into all the other shops. I was very surprised just how nice people in shops were towards me. Shoppers got out of my way, sales assistants couldn't have been more charming, I got entire changing rooms to myself, and best of all I didn't get sore feet.

"Can we stop for a coffee?"

"Tired, Lucy? But we have only just started." I laughed – my basket at the front was full of shopping bags.

We made a beeline for Bewleys and all had frothy cappuccinos and sticky buns.

"Mum, thank you so much for finding out about this scooter thing, I haven't had so much fun in ages."

"It's a pleasure, sweetheart – it's nice to be able to get out and about without having to rely on your crutches."

"I'm just a bit disappointed that we didn't run into anyone we knew," Lucy complained. "Next time, Mum, you'll have to give me more notice so that I can organise a few well-chosen spectators."

"So kind, Lucy. Anyway, I forgot to ask, are you still going out with that doctor?"

"Nope, he was always showing off, trying to impress me."

"In what way?"

"Well, he couldn't just say 'I've got a sore knee' he had to say 'I believe I have pulled my intertarsal tendon across the scapula' or whatever."

"You mean you didn't understand a word he said?"

"Of course I could understand him – do you think I'm stupid?"

"No, but I never have a clue about medical jargon. I had to have everyone in hospital translate what they were saying to me the whole time."

"Well, it wasn't that I couldn't understand him, OK?"

"Fine, whatever you say."

She looked across at Mum.

"Mum, isn't that Marjorie Evans?"

"Where?" said Mum craning her neck around.

"Oh, bummer!" I exclaimed.

"I don't see Marjorie anywhere, dear."

"Sorry, Mum, that woman just looked like her from the back." Lucy smirked at me. "What about you then?"

"What about me? Men in my life are about as scarce as footballers with degrees."

"Ha, what about Jake? Mum tells me that he flew up for a couple of days to see you when he heard you were in hospital! Something has got to be going on there!"

"Sadly I have nothing to report, though I do really like him. I have resigned myself to a life of spinsterhood, or at least meaningless one-night stands once this bloody cast comes off."

"Ellie!"

"Sorry Mum, only joking."

"I hate to hear my girls talk like that."

"Och, shut up, old woman, and finish your cappuccino," Lucy said winking at Mum.

The run-up to Christmas was relatively painless. Mum took me out shopping with her whenever she could. We spent lots of money and quality time together. My mother tends to food-shop in preparation for Christmas, like she is preparing for a siege. The cupboards, fridge and freezer groan under the weight of the food being forced into them. She buys enough alcohol to give an entire battalion of heavy drinkers a serious hangover. And hides presents all over the house. Unfortunately she never remembers where she hid everything and inevitably a family member finds a jar of cherries in kirsch and gift-wrapped socks under their bed.

I had the presents that I had bought in Glasgow and some more I had picked up in Boots on a double-points evening. Lucy and I sat on Christmas Eve and wrapped our pressies together.

"Who are you giving pipe tobacco to?" I asked.

"Dad."

"But he doesn't smoke a pipe!"

"I know, but I thought it would be pretty cool if he did. They smell so nice and it would give him that kind of Captain Birdseye look."

"I don't think you should encourage Dad to take up smoking. Mum may shorten your life by say – fifty years."

Lucy made a face, but continued to wrap and label the tobacco.

"What did you really get him?"

"I really got him tobacco."

"Sad."

"What?"

"Dementia in one so young."

"Piss off."

"Lucy, please tell me you are not giving Dealing with your Menopause to Mum."

"I thought it might be useful."

"Are you trying to incite a riot on Christmas morning? Jesus, I don't want to know what you've bought for me."

"OK, if you're so brilliant what did you get them?"

"I bought Mum some Escada perfume, as she told me she was running out and some Velcro rollers that she had been after."

"Oh."

"For Dad I bought tickets for an evening with Hank Marvin – I checked with Mum that they were free on that evening. And a shirt from Marks and Sparks – Mum says they're great 'because they don't need ironing'."

"Oh. Those are pretty good presents."

"Thank you."

"Ellie?"

"Are you busy for the rest of the afternoon?"

"No, just going to finish off this wrapping – why?"

"Would you come shopping with me?"

"Lucy, it's Christmas Eve, the shops will be mobbed, I'll never get a scooter or a wheelchair."

"Well, what if you just sat in the car and I could bring things out to you?"

"Don't be silly, I'll come. I can probably walk OK on the crutches."

"Thanks a million, you're a star."

"Lucy, you unnerve me when you are so nice to me."

"Sorry, get your coat on, cripple!"

"That's better."

As I predicted the shops were a total nightmare. Thankfully Lucy didn't hang about and ended up getting Mum body lotion to match the perfume I had bought her. Dad got a gift voucher for HMV, so he could buy whatever hideous country CD he wanted, and a bottle of Polo for Men. We were heading back to the car, when that horrible creepy feeling of being watched came over me. Mark. I stared about.

"What's wrong, Ellie?"

"Oh nothing, just thought I saw someone."

"Oh, right."

She didn't say any more. She didn't need to. I knew what we were both thinking.

The police had phoned the day before to say that they had not yet found any trace of Mark. I uneasily thought I might know why: he wasn't in Edinburgh any more – he was here, near me.

"Let's get home before Mum does some serious damage to that poor turkey," said Lucy.

"God knows why she has to buy the biggest one she can find, we'll be asking people in off the street to try and get this year's all used up!"

I tried to shake off the horrible feeling.

Christmas day passed in a blur of food and wrapping paper, I got some more wide-leg trousers to fit over my cast and some other lovely clothes, a couple of CDs that I had wanted and a pair of boots that I had had my beady eyes on for ages. Mum never missed a trick. They would have to wait until the cast came off.

"Not long to go now, Ellie," I was told by every single member of my extended family over the next few days.

This, of course, was true but I hated being told that by cousins who could cartwheel round the kitchen if they felt like it.

I had had the cast on for two weeks. Because I had gone home I changed my hospital appointment in Edinburgh for one in the hospital in Dundonald near me. I had gone in the week before Christmas and the doctors seemed really pleased with my progress. Dr Brook had sent over my initial x-rays and apparently I was doing better than expected. I had to get a new cast since the swelling in my leg was starting to go down and the movement of my leg inside the cast would cause more damage.

"I'd say another fortnight and we could send you home with an elasticated bandage," the doctor told me. "Come in again after New Year and we'll take another x-ray."

I had a fairly subdued New Year with some friends. We went out for a meal and then they went on to a party. I was too scared to drink too much with my leg in a cast in case I fell over and had to start all over again. I got home at eleven thirty to an empty house, the rest of the family being out living it up.

Feeling more confident back in the house I got

myself a mug of wine (easier to carry than a glass) and watched the telly as I wasn't too tired.

Around five to midnight the phone rang – someone phoning to wish me Happy New year, I thought.

I could hear Mum's voice on the answering machine.

"Sorry no one is available to take your call at the moment, leave your message and number and we will call you back as soon as we can."

The machine waited for its message while I sat stock still waiting to hear a drunken voice on the other end witter 'Happy New Year's', but nothing.

The person on the other end hadn't hung up and the machine continued to record silence.

I quietly burst into tears, sitting alone on the sofa with my mug of wine at two minutes to midnight. I realised that if he wanted to Mark could get me whenever he liked and there was probably nothing that anyone could do about it. I saw fireworks across Belfast Lough, it must be midnight. The answer machine whirred back to the start of the message.

Mark must have hung up.

I wanted to crawl into my bed and pull the covers over my head, but instead I struggled to my feet, went over to the phone and dialled 1471.

"The caller withheld their number," the familiar mechanical voice told me.

I ejected the tape out of the machine and labelled it phone call number 54. I had a growing pile of answer phone tapes in a box under my bed. Then I rang the police in Edinburgh and asked to speak to Sergeant McLeod.

"I'm afraid Sergeant McLeod is not on duty tonight. Can I get him to call you back?"

"Yes, please. Could you tell him that Sorrel Clarke rang and that I have started receiving phone calls again."

"Yes, of course, the sergeant will call you first thing tomorrow morning."

"Thank you."

"Happy Hogmany!"

"Oh yes, same to you," I told the cheery police woman at the other end. Then I went to bed.

When I woke up the next morning I felt less defeated than I had done the previous night. I decided that I was going to go back to Edinburgh as soon as I had my second appointment at the hospital.

"I think going back to work would be good for me," I told my parents later over the breakfast table where they were nursing sore heads and glasses of Alka Seltzer.

"Oh darling, I don't know. I mean, what if Mark is still around."

"Mum, I told you that he rang here last night. It doesn't matter where I go, he will follow me, so I may as well get on with the rest of my life. When will the travel agents be open?"

"They won't be open till the third. Why?"

"I'm going to organise Chloe's hen weekend. She wants to go to Venice and I'm going the find out the cheapest way for six of us to do just that and have fun doing so. If Mark is going to insist that he follows me, at least I have the pleasure of bankrupting him in the process!"

"You go, girl!" Lucy walked in the back door, still in last night's dress. Now if I had done that Mum and Dad would have taken a hairy fit.

"Cheers, Lucy. I take it you scored last night?"

"A total dream called Declan, I think I'm in love." She made straight for the kettle.

"What is he this time? An actor? Musician? Or a coalman?"

"None of the above, he is a double glazing salesman from Wicklow."

"Double glazing? I didn't think that was your style."

"Oh shut up, he didn't always want to sell glass – his first love is horses."

"I'll bet it is."

"No, I mean he wants to run an animal sanctuary." She plonked herself down on a chair with a mug of tea in her hand.

"Lucy, tell me you didn't believe him?"

"Why would he lie?"

"Because that's his job, you eejit, he's a bloody salesman."

"I'm afraid your sister may have a point," Dad butted in.

"God, I go out, meet a nice man and my family turn on me."

"What was he doing up here on New Year's Eve? Trying to sell glass to the guests at the Europa?"

"He was enjoying our great northern hospitality."

"Now she sounds like an advert at the airport," I sneered.

"Well, bullshitter or not, he was a great kisser."

"That's not all by the sound of things."

343

"Girls, this is too much information," Dad groaned, getting up from the table.

"I think I'm going back to bed."

The conversation that ensued just highlighted to me how ridiculously gullible my sister could be when she was trying to pull a man.

The next couple of days went by very very slowly while I waited for the travel agent to re-open. I desperately wanted to be busy and I wanted to organise something to help me feel more in control. Sergeant McLeod had been on the phone and was very concerned when I told him I had been receiving calls again. I was actually starting to get paranoid that the police thought I was losing it, but they still seemed to be quite sympathetic. I think the fact that Mark was somewhere with a syringe full of a lethal drug was scaring the shit out of them. It was certainly scaring me shitless. I was glad I hadn't known what was in the syringe when he paid his visit to me in hospital.

"Miss Clarke," said the sergeant in his kindly but pompous way. "We are very sorry that we have been unable to apprehend Mr Norris. I assure you that I will be alerting the RUC today of the possible situation."

"I'm coming back to Edinburgh in a few days. If he can follow me here I may as well go back to my flat and my job. That way he may be easier to find."

It wasn't until I said it that I realised that the idea had been in the back of my mind all the time.

Chloe came round to visit me. She had come home for New Year, after spending Christmas with David's parents.

We pulled armchairs right in front of the fire in the living-room – it was freezing. Lucy had mercifully pissed off back to Dublin, no doubt to take up with her double-glazing salesman, and Mum and Dad had gone out to a drinks party though they swore they were only fit to drink mineral water.

"Do you think you will be able to make the dress fittings at the end of February?"

"Of course I will, the cast will be long gone by then, I hope."

"Great, Mum was starting to panic me, even though Yvonne said it really would be no problem to leave yours till the last minute. Now I want to talk to you about headresses."

Oh God, 'Invasion of the Body Snatchers' again.

"Help, someone has stolen my friend's brain!"

"Oh, shut up, Ellie, I know you think I've taken leave of my senses but this important to me."

"OK, sorry, I will endeavour to take this more seriously."

"You are such a pain in the arse sometimes, do you know that?"

"Yes, I am completely aware, I get told every day."

"Ellie!"

"Sorry. You were saying headresses?"

"Yes, well more like mini tiaras."

"That sounds more like it, I like the sound of that."

"Yes, good, now I need to ask you a favour."

"Oh yes?"

"There is a bridal fair in the SECC in Glasgow at the end of January, and I haven't seen anything I really like and everyone has told me that this one is really good and I really want to go."

"And you would like me to go with you?"

"Yes."

"OK."

"OK, you'll go?"

"OK, I'll go."

"Oh thanks so much!" Chloe gave me such a massive hug you'd think I just offered to donate a major organ rather than agree to go to a bridal fair. What are they all about anyway?

"Chloe, what do we do at a bridal fair?"

"Oh, I'm just going for ideas but all the businesses involved in weddings are there to sell themselves, so there will be a catwalk for the dresses."

"The bridal dresses?"

"Yes and the bridesmaids' too."

"Oh God, what have I agreed to?"

"I also want to get ideas for my menu. Mum has her ideas but I have some of my own."

"Great – you're even arguing about the sodding menu!"

"We are not arguing."

"It's early days. So when is this thing?"

"The last Saturday in January."

"You mean I have to give up one of my exciting Saturdays?"

Chloe stuck her tongue out at me.

"Oh, before I forget," I added. "How much do you want to spend on this hen weekend?"

"I don't know. Have you got flight prices yet?"

"No, the travel agents don't open till tomorrow, but I'll let you know."

"OK, I'm back to Edinburgh tomorrow – I think David has had just about enough of Mum. You know, I think she's getting worse."

"She can't get any worse."

Chloe laughed. "OK, so ring me whenever you know more about Venice."

"No problem."

"I'd better go home before David decides he doesn't love me enough to put up with my mother for the rest of his life."

"Well, there's always emigration."

"Always so helpful."

When the travel agents re-opened I rang round them like a woman possessed. Mission: bargain Venice two nights, return flights and accommodation. The first place I tried told me they could do it for six hundred pounds. Perhaps this wasn't such a good idea after all. I kept going and was a bit more optimistic when the next place told me they had could do it for three hundred and since there were six of us travelling they would do it for two hundred and fifty. I told them I would ring them straight back. There were still seven more agents on my list so I was determined to ring all of them.

Eventually, after repeating my request nine times to nine different agents with varying degrees of helpfulness, I finally got a great deal for two hundred pounds.

"Now it is flying to Venice. We're not getting a coach or flying to an airport a hundred miles away?"

"No, that's six people travelling on Friday 18th of April from Edinburgh to Venice, via London, at eighteen hundred hours, arriving at twenty-one hundred hours. Two nights accommodation at the Pensione A'Gamaggia, in central Venice. Returning on Sunday the 20th of April at sixteen hundred hours arriving Edinburgh nineteen hundred hours."

"God, that's brilliant – who would we be flying with?"

"That would be British Midland."

"What's their in-flight service like?"

"I'm sorry?"

"What is the food like?"

"I believe it is very nice."

"Great, could you hold those flights for me and I'll ring you straight back?"

"I can only hold them at this price if you book today."

"Yes, I know, I'll phone you straight back."

I phoned Chloe who thought it sounded reasonable, Rachel who agreed, Louisa and Clare were fine with that price. I got all their credit-card details except for one of Chloe's old friends from home, Melissa, who thought it too dear and said she would make her own arrangements.

"OK but remember we're going on the 18th of April and we're coming home on the 20th."

"Fine, I'm sure I can get something more reasonable."

"OK whatever. We are staying in Pensione A'Gamaggia – your travel agent should be able to book that for you."

"Can you spell that?"

"No."

"Ellie, that isn't terribly helpful."

"Sorry, I don't speak Italian either."

Silly bitch, I could understand if she didn't have much dough, but she was married to a plastic surgeon, she didn't even work. Melissa probably spent that much money on a pair of pants. But I was quite happy not to have to travel with her. She and Margo would have made great travelling companions; they could have sat and bitched to each other. Thankfully Evil Margo wasn't coming.

Finally I rang Nicole to tell her the dates; since she would fly from Nice it was easier if she booked her own flights. I would book her accommodation.

"No problem, cherie, now that is the . . . hang on while I find my diary. OK, so it is the 18th of April till the 20th of April. I am free. I will book my flight."

"OK great, I must get back to this woman before she sells the seats to someone else."

I called the agent back and booked the flights. Great! That was that organised; now I could pack for going back to Edinburgh.

Just as I was getting ready to leave the house the next day I got a phone call from Melissa. She was absolutely raging. She hadn't bothered to ring any travel agents the day before after speaking to me. Then when she rang round that morning the price had changed, the cheapest she could get was three hundred pounds and she was threatening not to go.

"Melissa, I told you yesterday that they were the cheapest flights I could get and you didn't believe me. Now this weekend is for Chloe, so stop being such a tight-arsed bitch and book your bloody flight! It serves you right that you have to pay more than everyone else after all the fuss you made!"

"Well, I am not going to be spoken to like that!"

"Good, piss off then and book your flight." I hung up on her and had a good laugh to myself at her expense.

Chapter Nineteen

Once I was back in Edinburgh, things were a little more awkward. Without Mum running after me I didn't have anyone to help me. I was met off the plane with a wheelchair, but they deposited me beside the baggage carousel as they needed the chair back. I struggled to get my bags and Hector onto a trolley. Once I had managed to bounce the trolley off a few walls I got outside where a kindly taxi driver lifted everything into the back of his cab. The media frenzy that Fiona had told me about seemed to have abated. There were no photographers hiding in bushes waiting to take a picture of my battered body. I managed to get the driver to help me into the lift in my building with my bags. There weren't any messages from anyone on the answer machine, which was a bit odd, as I thought someone would have phoned while I was away, considering that I had only told two people that I was actually going away. Perhaps I had less friends than I thought. God, how depressing.

Chloe and David came round to the flat that evening and Chloe cooked dinner while David took Hector for a walk.

"How do you feel to be back?"

"Good actually. David survived New Year at your house then?"

"Just. Dad kindly took him off to the golf course every day. I think they just sat in the bar."

"Ah, Margo driving people to drink again."

"Any more comments like that and I will double the amount of chilli powder in here – I'd like to see you run to the loo with that cast on."

"What a horrible girl you are! Just be glad David has no idea of your nastiness."

"Did you organise those flights?"

"God, sorry yes, I was supposed to ring you. wasn't I"

"You were, but I knew you would forget."

"I have something to tell you – now listen, this wasn't my fault but it was really funny."

"What? What have you not done?"

"It's Melissa."

"OK, Ellie, I know she isn't your favourite person but we are old friends and I have to ask her."

"No, no, I asked her all right, but she was a bit difficult."

"Oh?"

"She thought the flights were too expensive."

"You have to be joking me!"

"No, I am entirely serious. You know when I rang you to check that the price was OK and you gave me your credit card details?"

"Yes? You rang everyone and everyone said yes."

"Everyone except Melissa, who said she was sure she could get a better deal."

"Than two hundred pounds for return flights and accommodation? What sort of holidays must Basil take her on?"

"Butlins in Skegness by the sounds of it. Anyway she phoned before I left for the airport this morning. The silly cow couldn't get a cheaper flight and now she can't even get one as cheap as ours, so she threatened me with not coming."

"What did you say?"

"I told her to get her finger out and book a flight."

"Oh." Chloe looked a bit disappointed.

"I was quite rude if that makes you feel any better?"

"It's a horrible thing to say, but I was hoping she was going to be busy that weekend – tennis in Spain or golfing in Portugal."

"Or taking a coach trip to the Giant's Causeway with her discount coach card."

We both burst out laughing.

"Don't worry! I am in charge. I will not let her sabotage the weekend. You're going to have the time of your life!"

We went through the details of the weekend over dinner. Alex wasn't telling David what he was doing for his weekend.

"David thinks it is going to be a golfing weekend in Gleneagles or Donegal. But I reckon knowing Alex it is bound to be tacky and involve the police."

The following morning Fiona picked me up for work, as she promised to do every day until my cast came off.

"You're looking nae bad."

"Thanks, did you have a nice Christmas?"

"Hum . . . "

"That's very non-committal. Was it awful?"

"No, not awful, but Tavy's ex-boyfriend tried to burn our flat down."

"Oh my God, are you both OK?"

"Oh we were plastered at the time and threw the contents of our compost bin out the window and over his head."

"Your compost bin?"

"Aye. Tavy decided that things like potato peelings, ends of veg and any old fruit we should keep in a bin and use for the back garden."

"Nice. And you keep this in the house?"

"By the back door, discourages burglars."

"Is this Ricardo the Spanish boyfriend?"

"It is, or it was."

"I didn't know they'd split up."

"Well, she was fed up with his infidelity."

"Ricardo two timed her?"

"Six-timed her as it happens."

"God, poor Tavy, is she OK?"

"Aye, she burnt all of his stuff in our back garden. Dipped two tampons in a tin of tuna and hid them under his mattress. We have had his flatmates on the phone begging her to tell them what is making that awful smell – apparently it is making them all sick."

"Good for her, though that is completely disgusting."

"No less than he deserved." Fiona swerved to avoid a parked car and flicked the fingers at a bus driver attempting to pull out.

"So did she tell them what was making the smell?"

"No."

We both had a laugh at this.

"So do *OK!* still want me?"

"Do you want to do it?"

"I don't know – five grand is a lot of money and if it was going to be tasteful, I think I probably would."

"Great. I'll ring them when we get into work."

"Fiona, do you get a cut of this money as my manager?"

"Nah, of course not, I was just protecting your interests in your absence."

"Oh, because you're welcome to ten percent or whatever managers get. You know, buy yourself a new kilt or something."

"That's very kind of you, Ellie, but my parents got me one for Christmas."

"So you didn't tell me what Christmas was like in Inverness."

"It was cold."

"Yes."

"I went out a couple of times, met a few nice people."

I looked across at her and there was just the slighted hint of colour in her cheeks.

"Fiona!"

"What!" She jumped in her seat, nearly knocking over a cyclist in her surprise.

"Sorry, I didn't mean to startle you. You met a man, didn't you?"

"No, I didn't."

"Yes, you did, look at the colour in your face!"

"What was he called?"

"Duncan."

"Ah ha! I knew it. Is it love? Are you seeing him again? What happened?"

I spent the rest of the drive to work getting the low-down on Fiona's sex-fest of a Christmas, with Duncan who co-owned a salmon fishery outside Inverness. He was coming down to stay with her the coming weekend and Fiona was actually nervous.

In fact, I spent the next few weeks listening to Fiona tell me about her growing love affair, with just the slightest hint of jealously. Work was fine, our boss was now a much changed man, apparently the threat of his wife leaving him had shaken him really badly and he was now spending much more time with his family. Fiona and I worked on the plans for our new slot on the consumer programme which was due to start in the summer. Fiona wanted to concentrate on things happening up North, surprise, surprise. But this suited me fine.

As promised on the last Saturday in January I went to the bridal fair in Glasgow with Chloe. I don't know what I was expecting, but this was serious wedding fever. It was in the main exhibition hall, which is huge and rather than a few giggly girls and their mothers the place was crammed with women, some with their mothers, some with their wedding co-ordinators, friends or alone. There was a catwalk show of bridal dresses which were stunning and the whole thing was completely professional. There was everything there from napkin holders, florists to marquee hire, wedding bands and some travel agents giving advice on honeymoon locations. This was a seriously big industry, a slick well-oiled money-making machine – and they say that romance is dead.

Chloe concentrated on the stands selling tiaras and headresses, they even had hairpieces which you could buy attached to the head-bands, made to tone in with your own hair. I was actually surprised at just how lovely the stuff they were selling was. Most of it was hand-made by the people there. There were huge displays and some vendors even had models wandering around with the tiaras on. Everything that we saw was for sale or could be ordered and delivered within six weeks.

Chloe eventually found a small stand selling handmade tiaras of a slightly less gaudy variety and began looking through what was available. I wanted to go and wander in among the stands, but my hands were aching from the crutches, so I was happy to sit and watch. The girl selling them said that they could be made in any colour if Chloe didn't see ones that suited her. They were made out of fine gold and silver wire with tiny crystals and metallic rose buds with gold leaves. Chloe tried several until she put one on that was just perfect. It was made up of hundreds of tiny crystals and tiny seed pearls all held together with a gold wire. After Chloe was satisfied that she had found the perfect tiara for herself she then concentrated on getting ones for the bridesmaids.

"These are much nicer than the ones we saw in Butler and Wilson," I said helpfully under half a ton of gold beads.

"I know, aren't they?" Chloe was in her element here.

So I sat back and relaxed, well as much as you can

in a full leg cast with your hair getting stuck in the wire of these fiddly wee things.

"That's the one!" she cried, pointing at the one I had put on my head.

"It is?"

"Yes, that's the one, here look!"

Chloe handed me a mirror. I looked, right enough I didn't look half bad.

I moved my head around, viewing it from the side and over my left shoulder, in the reflection, I saw Mark.

He was leaning up against one of the stands behind us.

My heart gave a great sickening jolt.

"Chloe, it's great, order them, I have to go."

"What's wrong? Are you sure you're happy with this one?"

"Yes, now can we please go?"

"OK, OK, give me a minute!"

I got up and started moving clumsily towards the exit, terrified. Chloe came running after me, grabbing caterer's menus on the way past.

"Jesus, Ellie, I wanted to spend a bit longer here! Aren't you enjoying it?"

"I was until I saw Mark behind us."

Chloe paled. "Shit, come on, let's get out of here. Is he following us?"

"Probably."

We hurried back to the car as fast as my cast would allow making sure we passed close to lots of security guards along the way.

"Do you want to ring the police?"

"I guess I should but let's get away from here first."

"Ellie, this is scary."

"I know, I'm sorry. Do you want to stay?"

"No, don't be stupid! How could I stay with that maniac around! Besides, I got what I came for – let's go home."

For a while after the fair I couldn't go out of my flat unless I knew Chloe or Fiona was waiting for me in the car downstairs. I threw myself into work as it took my mind off Mark. Jake rang once a week to find out how I was getting on; I didn't tell him about Mark.

The Edinburgh police were now on the alert but of course Mark had disappeared.

Dr Brook took my cast off finally in the middle of February. It had taken just a little longer than he had originally thought, but he was very pleased with the way it had healed. The leg was a bit weak to begin with, but that was apparently normal as the muscles had wasted while they had been in the cast. So I had to slowly start building them back up.

With the cast off I started to feel a little more confident. I was still a little jumpy about Mark but I wasn't having constant panic attacks. Work was going better, I was getting paid more, and since I had become a social recluse I hadn't been shopping for over a month, so I had saved a fair bit of cash and this made me feel great too. For the first time in my adult life I was paying off my student loan, had almost paid off my overdraft and hadn't had a personal letter from my Bank Manager since I came back from France – a new personal best.

Then on a bright sunny Saturday morning a knock came on my front door.

"It must be the lovely Mrs Arnold with some more of her delicious home cooking for us," I said to Hector as I got up to open the front door.

I knew it had to be someone from the building because of our intercom system – no one can just walk in if they feel like it.

Mrs Arnold, my next door neighbour and shortbread-maker supreme, had taken to making things for me to save me cooking while I was still in plaster. Bless her, you may recall I mentioned her earlier as she was possibly the world's worst cook. The week before she had brought me Black Pudding and Smash pie, so I had to get the pizza delivery man to be extra quiet when he was delivering my Extra Large Olive Deep Pan, as I didn't want to hurt her feelings.

But instead of the diminutive Mrs Arnold on my doorstep it was a huge man in a black overcoat.

"Miss Clarke?"

"Yes?"

"I have come from MacAndrew's Hi-fi and Video to remind you that you are now one month late on your first payment for the thirty-inch, flat-screen digital television that you purchased last month."

"Television?"

"Yes, that's right."

"But I didn't buy a television, flat-screen or whatever it was. Who are you again?"

"I'm from MacAndrew's."

"I don't even know where that is!"

"I'm sorry, miss, I'm here to collect the first instalment."

"Come here and look."

I brought him (perhaps unwisely) into my living-room and pointed out my twelve-inch Matsui TV, which I bought secondhand five years before.

"Does that look like whatever you were talking about?"

"No."

"There, well you see, I don't own such a thing, I never bought it and I have absolutely no idea what you are talking about."

The bailiff looked in a notebook.

"Do you know a Mr Norris?"

"Why?"

"Does he live here with you?"

"No, he bloody does not!"

"This was bought by Mr Norris on your behalf. Mr Norris informed my company that you were cohabiting and you would pay the instalments of sixty seven pounds fifty over a period of twelve months."

"He did what!"

"Like I say, you are to pay the instalments."

"I'm sorry but I will not pay anything for anyone! I haven't signed anything."

"I have your signature here."

"That's not my signature, you stupid man!"

"That is what we have on our form, it is legally binding and I would remind you that further late payment could result in you being put on a credit black list."

"Have you gone mad? That is not my signature."

"Miss, this is not my problem. My company requires payment and that is why I am here."

"I'm calling the police, this is crazy."

"Fine."

I went into my bedroom and, hands trembling, rang Sergeant McLeod, who was not on duty. But I got PC Lewis who had interviewed me with McLeod straight after the car crash and he said he and another officer be with me right away.

When I came back in the living-room I found the bailiff had unplugged my stereo and was about to make off with it.

"Where the fuck do you think you are going with that?" I went quickly over to bar him at the door.

"If I am unable to get cash payment I am authorised to take something to the value of the instalment."

"That stereo is worth a lot more than sixty seven bloody pounds, now put it down, the police are on their way. You didn't show me any identification, can I please see some?" I held out a hand, trying not to show that I was scared to death.

"Miss, please get out of my way, I have no wish to cause you bodily harm."

He took a step towards me.

"No!" I shouted at him. "You are not going anywhere with my bloody stereo, that fucking psycho is not getting away with any more, do you hear me?!"

Mr Bailiff looked a bit uncertain for the first time since his arrival.

Suddenly we could hear sirens in the road outside as the police arrived. The bailiff dropped my stereo on the sofa, pushed me out of the way and ran out of my front door.

"Oi, come back here! What's your name?" I ran out after him. I heard his footsteps running down the stairs, then a bit of scuffle.

Five minutes later a very pink PC Lewis arrived at my front door. "We've apprehended the man and we're taking him in for questioning. You were right to call us. I'll come back later so you can give me the details of what happened."

"Oh right, thanks. Excuse me, PC Lewis?"

"Yes?"

"Was he really from a Hi-fi shop?"

"I wouldn't have thought so, Miss Clarke."

"Thanks."

I shut the door behind me, and leant on it for a few minutes. This whole thing just got weirder and weirder.

Later on that afternoon I got a call from Sergeant McLeod, who had been called in on his day off to question the man from my flat.

"His name is John Turner. He is a local thug, who was paid by Mark to scare you into thinking he would rough you up if you didn't pay up for the television."

"So there is no television?"

"No."

"Thank God! I had visions of hundreds of debt collectors knocking down my door asking for money for toasters and microwaves that Mark had bought in my name."

"We think he was just doing it to scare you. Credit agencies cannot do that. If Mr Norris has bought anything and forged your signature, as soon as you proved that it is a fake they cannot ask you to pay for anything that he purchased. The fact that you are not married to him also helps."

"Don't even tell me!"

"Anyway, Miss Clarke, he will not bother you again. Unfortunately he was unable to tell us where Mr Norris lives as they always met in John Turner's local pub."

I spent the rest of the weekend at Chloe and David's. They were most sympathetic but could not believe that Mark still had not been found.

"How can that bastard get away with all that he has done to you?"

"I don't know. But I hope to God they catch him."

I went back to my own flat on Sunday night. Again there were no messages on my machine, just like when I got back from Christmas. I would at least have thought Jake would have phoned as he normally rang on Sunday afternoons.

I went into my kitchen and put the kettle on. Something was different. I looked around but couldn't put my finger on what it was. I stared at the work surfaces, they hadn't changed. I looked in my cupboards, they were the same.

I walked out and then walked back in again. Again I got the feeling that something had moved. The toaster and kettle were in the same place.

Then my eye fell on the cork-board on one of the walls. It was full of Chinese takeaway menus, vet surgery times, telephone numbers and a few funny photographs: Chloe and me, when we were fifteen, dressed up like Hare Krishnas for a fancy dress party; Ben, Lucy and me when we were all really little – eating Easter eggs; one from the weekend when I first met Jake at home; Fiona and me when we went to visit the Deep Sea aquarium and she nearly fainted when she came face to face with a Moray eel. They were all kind of stuck up in no particular order, just there to make me laugh. I looked again; one was missing. I couldn't think which one it was. I made a cup of tea while I racked my brains trying to remember.

Then I saw there were a pair of scissors on the floor, why were they there? Did I leave them there after Saturday morning? I picked them up, frowning.

"Jake! The picture of Jake that Rachel took that night we all went out for dinner in London!" I shouted aloud.

Hector came running in from the living-room to see what all the commotion was about.

"What the hell did I do with that photo? I'm sure I didn't move it. I wonder if Chloe pinched it to do something silly for the hen weekend. But why would she? It's my job to get silly pictures of her and David."

Hector cocked his head to one side and looked at me in a questioning type canine way.

I looked closer at the board and then suddenly recoiled in horror at what I saw.

"Oh my God!" My hands went up to my mouth in shock. I took a sharp intake of breath and sat down suddenly on the floor of the kitchen. Hector started to growl, as he sometimes does when he knows something is wrong.

Right at the back of the photos, so that you would hardly notice, unless you really looked, was a pair of eyes. The other photos had been positioned so that they hid the rest of the photograph.

They were Mark's eyes. The effect was chilling.

I crawled on my hands and knees into my bedroom and rang Chloe.

"That is so freaky." David was staring at the way the photos showed only Mark's eyes. "And it's not your photo?"

"I don't have any pictures of Mark."

"And the one Rachel sent you of Jake is gone?" said Chloe.

I nodded.

"Do you mean that Mark got in here when you were staying with us?"

I nodded again.

'Shit!'

"When I came back after Christmas there weren't any messages on my machine, even though you guys and Fiona were the only people who knew I wasn't here. I thought it was a bit weird and that maybe the machine had broken again, but it's been working since."

"Do you think he is listening to your messages as well?"

"Yes."

"Girls, I think you should come and see this."

We went over to see what David had found. I hadn't touched or been near the photos since I had first seen Mark's eyes but David had now moved the rest of the photos out of the way to reveal the one Mark had put there. It was a picture of him holding up another picture torn in half. He was smiling and he was holding one piece of the photo in each hand.

"Bizarre," said Chloe looking at the photo.

David unpinned it, held it up and looked at it closely.

"Shit Ellie, that's you!" he exclaimed.

"What!"

"The picture he has torn in half, it's a picture of you!"

"No way!" Chloe said. "This guy is totally sick!"

"Ellie, ring the police, they need to see this."

The CID arrived at my front door about an hour later. They wanted to know if Mark had touched or moved anything else. I didn't think so but I did mention the answer machine and my missing messages. They wanted to know if he had phoned recently. No, I told them but he did turn up at the Bridal fair in Glasgow and sent the heavy round to scare me.

The police admitted that this was quite an unusual case. Normally stalkers are not quite so creative. Then they admitted that most do not threaten to kill their victims. Sergeant McLeod had obviously filled them in on my case so far. They left suggesting that I change my locks immediately and have someone to stay for couple of nights, so that Mark would know that I was not alone in the flat, nor would I be forced to go and stay somewhere else.

Chloe and David offered to stay, but they had done enough – I was not about to have the pair of them sleep over into the bargain. Louisa and Clare came instead. They thought the whole thing was rather exciting and, since their flatmate had recently come back from travelling and claimed that soap, shampoo or any other products relating to personal hygiene were interfering with her energy meridians so she no longer believed in using any of them, they were only to delighted to sleep in a body-odour free area.

Having the girls to stay was fun; they were easy company and I was glad that they decided to stay for a full week. I got the locks changed the day after the CID had been round. There was no sign of Mark, no phone calls or anything. I got lots of stuff organised for the hen weekend, which was now only a month away. My leg was almost back to its old self – on the doctor's advice I had gone out walking every day to build it up and I had started to really enjoy the walks. Hector and I were both looking better for the exercise and the fresh air.

Chapter Twenty

The Friday we were set to leave for Venice we all met in the airport. Melissa, who had eventually booked her flight, was flying from Belfast, so we were meeting up with her in Heathrow. The flight down to London wasn't delayed so there were no mad panics trying to make our connection. We were all really excited and were looking forward to a fun weekend.

We met Melissa without a hitch and the flight to Venice was trouble free. We waited for one of the ATVO water buses which took us to the centre of town in twenty minutes. No cars or coaches are allowed in the centre – also not having any roads is a great deterrent. I had been instructed by the travel agent that the fastest way round the centre of Venice is on foot. This was convenient as I discovered that Venice is one of the most expensive cities in Italy.

Venice is amazing. Hundreds of little boats zoom up and down the waterways and the beautiful old buildings positively reek of history and look straight out of a film set. Four hundred bridges join the streets of Venice together and you just can't help thinking that you would be passionately in love if you lived there. The water bus dropped us off along the Grand Canal, the main waterway in Venice, near our pensione. A two-minute walk through the narrow streets and we found where we were staying. I was surprised it was so nice, I had half expected a grotty back-street establishment for the money we were paying, but the hotel was lovely – old-fashioned with a little restaurant underneath. Chloe and I were sharing a room with Nicole who was already there. The smell of garlic wafted through the window, reminding us we were all starving.

"Shall we just go downstairs to eat?" I asked Chloe.

"Why not? It's too late to go exploring anyhow."

We got the rest of the girls from their rooms and went downstairs.

We had a great meal, with lots of flirting from the waiters. After copious amounts of red wine we wobbled back up to our rooms and passed out.

The next morning was bright and sunny. We went in search of a cafe for breakfast. We found one a little way down the street and sat and ate croissants and drank milky coffee. An interesting fact about Venice is the amount of cats there are there. Venetians are huge cat lovers and think nothing of having one jump onto their laps in the middle of a cafe, which happened this morning. Unfortunately for the poor cat it chose to jump onto Melissa's lap, who leaped ten feet into the air screaming that she had got rabies. The rest of us laughed which made her even crosser. The cat, it turned out, belonged to the owner of the cafe, who assured Melissa that his cat was rabies free. He seemed bewildered by her reaction.

"Bloody foreigners!" she muttered when he was out of earshot. *"How unhygienic is that!"*

"I don't think he lets the cat wander over the croissants," Nicole said, patting her on the shoulder. Melissa paled and clutched her throat.

We split up into groups and went sightseeing while Melissa went back to the hotel to ring her doctor in case she should need to rush to a nearby hospital for a shot. We walked for ages, jumping on and off the water buses as we felt like it.

Chloe and I bought a map and walked to the Piazza San Marco, which is where the first rulers of Venice built their citadel. It is vast and truly awe-inspiring. We wandered through the Doge's Palace, one of the most ornate Gothic buildings in Venice, down over the Bridge of Sighs (so named because of the sighs of the prisoners as they passed on their way to prison). We felt very virtuous with all our historical sightseeing so stopped for a caffeine break. The Piazza is also the most expensive area in Venice, its cafes, restaurants and cafes the plushest and most famous. We stopped and had a coffee in one of the grand cafes under the arches, and tried to look nonchalant when the bill arrived. The shops around were all top Italian designers – Trussardi, Gucci, Dolce Gabbana, Prada, Krizia. We decided against any shopping. After the Piazza we wandered along the Grand Canal and stood and looked over the Rialto bridge, marvelling at the little sleek water taxis ferrying their passengers up and down. They actually have the gondolas with the singing boatmen;

a surprising amount were actually singing, though to be honest, not terribly well – it was just like a Cornetto advert. Then we looked through the Rialto market, one of the liveliest areas of the city, where hundreds of tourists and Venetians alike wandered round the food market. Venice is coming down with palaces – and coming down in general, apparently: it's sinking into the water which is a tragedy. Chloe and I then jumped on a *vaporetto,* one of the larger, slower water buses and just watched the splendour as we passed by.

We met up with the others for lunch. Melissa made a guest appearance after having been assured by her GP that she did not in fact have rabies. We sat in a shady courtyard and had pizzas. Louisa couldn't get over the amount of couples who just stopped what they were doing and snogged the faces off each other.

That night, however, was the main event.

The shower room in our room was full with me in the shower, Nicole plucking her eyebrows at the mirror and Chloe trying to get her nail varnish to set by running it under the cold tap. After much preening and primping we were ready. We looked more like we were going to the Oscars than out for dinner, but who the hell cared?

I had organised cocktails at the Gritti Place before dinner. The Gritti Place is a fabulous five-star hotel on the main waterway, one of the grandest locations in Venice. It has a floating veranda for dinner and drinks. I didn't think we could stretch to dinner, but a few cocktails we could just about afford.

We sat on the veranda drinking our Belinis and being treated like royalty. I was having the time of my life and

I certainly hoped Chloe was. A light drizzle started so we moved into the bar which was lit by chandeliers that had candles rather than electric light, giving the room a very romantic atmosphere. The bar was quite busy; it was a Saturday night. After an hour of delicious cocktails made with the pulp of fresh fruit we made a move to the restaurant I had booked. We giggled off down the street and found the restaurant without too much difficulty.

We were all kissed on both cheeks by the proprietor we entered. The family that ran the restaurant were delighted to meet Irish and Scottish girls and the flirting that started up with the two sons who were waiters was outrageous but very funny. The husband called his wife out of the kitchen to meet us. She told us not to look at the menus as she would bring a selection of the finest dishes and we would love them all. Everyone thought that this was a fantastic idea, well all except Melissa who thought they were going to try and fob us off with horse-meat.

"We don't even know these people. What if they try and give us squid?" She scrunched up her face in disgust.

"Squid is my favourite," said Nicole trying not to slip off her chair onto the floor.

"God, the French!" Melissa said under her breath, then she winced suddenly and looked at Chloe accusingly so I can only imagine that Chloe gave her a dig in the shin.

We started off with champagne and toasts and went on to four bottles of red wine. Soon the sons set two enormous plates piled high with our antipasti on the circular table and we set to. We feasted on roasted aubergine and red peppers, swordfish sliced very thinly and covered in lemon juice, olive tapanade with sun-dried tomato ciabatta and other delicious concoctions that I got a bit too drunk to remember. For main course they set out three different pasta and risotto dishes: risotto di mare with smoked salmon, prawns, cream and brandy, tortellini stuffed with olives and capers, in a light chilli tomato sauce, and handmade ravioli with diced seafood and mushrooms with ricotta in a pesto, pine nut and vodka sauce. They were all fabulous. For dessert we all insisted on having tiramisu. These were served with little glasses of Sambuca with coffee beans floating on the surface. After eating and drinking an obscene amount we almost needed an industrial crane to lift us out of our chairs.

When we finally left the restaurant it was well after midnight. We kissed the whole family goodbye on both cheeks, thanking them for our fabulous meal, and left. Outside it was still raining and the pavements were slippy. I should have been more careful, what with my inebriation and my weak leg. Suddenly my ankle twisted with a searing pain and I fell. The others burst out laughing. I tried to get up but my ankle wouldn't let me – it was twisted under me and despite all the alcohol I had consumed I was feeling the pain. It took the others a few moments to register that I had really hurt myself.

"Ellie, are you OK?" Melissa was the first to notice.

Chloe was swirling round in a circle, yelling *"I'm sing-ing in the rain, just sing-ing in the rain!"* She burled round, tripped over her own feet and fell, right on top of me. Right on top of the ankle, naturally.

I screamed in agony. Clare and Louisa pulled Chloe off me.

"Oh God, Ellie, I'm so sorry!" Chloe looked absolutely horrified. I think she thought she had knocked me over to begin with.

The family from the restaurant had come running out. I started to feel faint and I blacked out. When I came round I found myself on a bench in the restaurant covered with rugs, a cushion under my head with the proprietor trying to get something very alcoholic between my lips.

Ten minutes later I was in the back of an ambulance with Melissa and Nicole – an ambulance that was rocking – a boat, naturally.

"Are you OK?" Nicole asked me anxiously.

"I'm OK. What did the paramedic say?"

"Well, he doesn't speak much English but he seems to think you have broken your ankle."

"Oh God, I can't believe this." I was sick at the thought. More hospitals.

The rest of the journey I stared at the roof of the ambulance and tried not to cry. How could I have been so stupid? Now I really would have to go up the aisle behind Chloe on crutches, that was if Margo would let me anywhere near the church.

On arrival, the hospital wanted my medical insurance details.

"They're back in the hotel," I said in dismay.

"I'll go and get them," Melissa volunteered.

I forgave her for being a pain in the arse and she rose in my estimation.

"Thank you, Melissa.

"I will go with her," Nicole told me. "It is very late for her to be alone – you will be OK on your own for a while?"

"Yes."

So I was left lying on a gurney in the middle of a hallway until they returned with proof of my insurance. A couple of doctors came to have a look at my ankle. They both made faces which is never very reassuring, muttering away in Italian to each other.

"Excuse me."

"*Si?*"

"Could I have something for the pain?"

They looked at each other blankly, then one shrugged at the other.

"Pain!" I shouted at them, pointing at my leg, grimacing.

A small light of recognition went on in one of the doctor's minds and he disappeared off returning with what looked like a couple of Paracetamol.

"Thank you." I swallowed the pills. "Jesus, if I had a headache – " But the doctors lost interest at that point and wandered away.

I must have looked a picture – wet hair, make-up running all over my face, sexy cocktail dress and blue, swollen ankle lying on a trolley mouthing off to passing doctors.

At last, after what seemed like an eternity, Melissa and Nicole returned with my travel and medical insurance and I was moved to a private room, with lots of smiling and chatting to me in Italian, of which I can unfortunately speak not one word.

The girls were asked to leave by a nurse. "You go now, come back tomorrow for her. In the morning."

"But she is flying home tomorrow.'

"Yes, yes, but now go home."

"Ellie, we'll be back first thing in the morning," said Melissa, trying not to look alarmed. "I think they will let you out."

"Fuck!" I moaned as I turned over in the bed catching my ankle.

"Look now, don't be worrying, I'll get something sorted out. At least get you a translator for pity's sake – this is ridiculous. Now will you be OK? We are going to have to leave."

She appeared to be quite level-headed in a crisis – a translator was a very good idea.

"I'll be OK, thanks for everything."

"Try and sleep, we'll be in to see you tomorrow."

A nurse came in and took a blood sample – I can only assume to measure my blood-alcohol level, which I am sure was embarrassingly high. She gave me two more of the pills and left me to sleep. I couldn't sleep, I couldn't move, and I didn't know how to ask for a phone in Italian.

I was taken for an x-ray first thing in the morning. Melissa, true to her word, arrived at nine with a translator in tow. She was waiting for me when I was wheeled back into my room.

"Morning, how are you feeling?"

"Pretty shite."

"God, I'm sure. My hangover is pounding, I can't

imagine what you are going through. This is Elena, she can translate for you."

"Hi."

"Hello." She smiled at me gently. A kind Italian-speaking person – I'm saved!

She went off to make enquiries and came back to say that I hadn't broken my ankle after all – it was just a very severe sprain and I would be able to travel.

The relief was enormous.

"You've been brilliant," I said to Melissa.

"No problem. I just thought I should just come on my own this morning to get things sorted and I thought it would be less hassle. The girls are still absolutely steaming! I've organised a taxi to take us back to the hotel – so we can get going any time you feel ready."

"I'm ready now." I struggled out of bed.

"OK, I'll go and get a nurse to help you get dressed." Melissa vanished. Minutes later a nurse appeared with some crutches. Crutches agin. Oh God. She led me out to a bathroom across the hall.

"No, I need to get dressed, my clothes are back there." I pointed to my room. Where had Mel gone?

The nurse gestured to a gurney in the bathroom.

"You want me to sit on that?"

She nodded.

I sat.

Then she gestured for me to lie down, facing the other way. I should have been immediately suspicious, but when you haven't a clue what is going on you just do what you're told. I lay down facing the other way. The nurse left the room.

"What the fuck is going on?" I asked the empty bathroom.

Five minutes later she returned with a long plastic tube and a strange-looking machine that was humming. I really wish I could forget what happened next – suffice it to say Princess Di used to pay a lot of money to have it done and she was a braver woman than I. When the nurse had finished filling my bowel with warm water she left, indicating the toilet. I felt the strangest sensation, grabbed my crutches and dashed for the nearest stall, a difficult operation. I got myself on the toilet with seconds to spare.

"Ellie?" Melissa appeared.

"Yes, Melissa?" I replied miserably.

"Oh my God, are you OK?"

"No."

"I think there must have been some mistake."

"You're telling me! I don't think I'll ever be able to get off this loo seat again."

"Oh my God, I'm so sorry. I was talking to the translator about the best way to move you."

"Much good a translator has done us. Oh shit, Melissa, could you leave me for a few minutes?"

"Of course. I'll be right outside – call me if you need me."

Eventually I was able to get off the loo. I felt very wobbly and weak. Melissa was waiting in the hallway for me. I hobbled out on my crutches, white as a sheet and about seven pounds lighter.

"Are you OK?"

"I think so. You were telling me there had been a mistake?"

"Apparently the nurse thought you were going to have a general anaesthetic so you needed to empty your bowel – it's normal."

"And I just wanted to get dressed." I collapsed against her, and she helped me back to my room. "Oh for Christ's sake, get me out of this place Melissa."

"Taxi is outside. Here, let me help you with your clothes."

I felt so humiliated I could just cry. Alone in a foreign hospital receiving unnecessary colonic irrigation was not my idea of a great hen weekend. I got dressed slowly with Mel's help and a more well-informed nurse arrived to strap my ankle up.

"Please, Mel, make them promise not to do anything else to me!"

"They won't!" she laughed.

The girls were waiting in the lobby of the hotel when we arrived back an hour later. They had my bags and some magazines for me to read.

"Ellie, will you ever forgive me?" Chloe asked, apparently still convinced she had caused all the damage.

"Yes, as long as I'm still allowed to limp down the aisle after you."

"God, of course – shit, I am so sorry."

"Listen, I had already done something to it by the time you landed on me."

"Yes but I doubt you would be in such abject agony if I hadn't fallen on you!"

"It's all character-building."

"Are we ready to leave? Everyone got everything?"

Melissa had taken charge and rounded everyone up like an efficient sheepdog.

"Ellie, borrow my personal stereo, it might take your mind off your ankle."

"Thanks, Louisa, that's really kind."

Our progress to the airport was very slow. I was close to tears with the pain in my ankle every time I moved it. Dragging a bad sprain round the Venetian public transport route is not the best idea. In any case, I was strung out and exhausted. At the airport I rang Mum to tell her what had happened.

"Oh sweetheart, you poor old thing. You'll be fine, the girls will take care of you. Oh and Jake phoned this evening for you. He had been trying your flat for a couple of days and he thought you had perhaps come home again. He sends you all his love."

All? "That was sweet."

"He really seemed concerned that he hadn't been able to get hold of you."

I listened to her telling me how much she thought Jake was concerned until my money ran out. The flight was delayed by an hour, so we sat in the hot airport trying not to mind. My ankle really started to ache so I shut my eyes and turned Clare's personal stereo up full blast. Clare's and my music tastes are poles apart, I discovered too late, as my ears were assaulted with Iron Maiden. I spent the next hour planning my perfect imaginary life with Jake, well, it was something that kept me going while listening to "Take Your Daughter to the Slaughter". Maybe I should start worrying about Clare? Blocking out Bruce Dickenson's less than dulcet tones I went back to Jake. I was concentrating on a particular fantasy that involved me moving to Boston and spending my weekends in the outlet stores stocking up on essential Donna Karan and Ralph Lauren outfits. We would fly home from America first class and have several homes, a country mansion in Ireland, a penthouse in London, a villa in the south of France and an apartment in New York – overlooking Central Park I think. Oh yes and a large lottery win too. Jake would say to me on one of our transatlantic flights, "You know darling, I never knew what living was until I met you." No, that's a bit too cheesy, how about something like, "Ellie, I'm sorry I took so long to admit to myself that I was deeply in love with you. Sorry for putting you through the agony. Oh and by the way Mark is going to be used for cruel medical experiments." Yes, I definitely liked that better. Too evil with the cruel medical experiments? OK, how about a course of electric shock therapy?

I laughed out loud. The girls all looked at me.

"Ok?" Chloe asked with a concerned look on her face.

"Sorry. I'm fine, just thinking about something stupid." I grinned. The sheer ludicrous nature of the situation had just hit me. There I was sitting in a sweating airport with a crowd of badly hungover friends mentally caressing the buttocks of my brother's best friend – Jesus, you couldn't write a better script!

Thankfully, about the time that I couldn't take any more Iron Maiden they announced that our flight would be boarding in five minutes. I turned the stereo off and could hear Italian mumbling over the tannoy.

On board I got a seat right at the front and I was

looked after like a VIP all the way to London. When we landed we were met by a British Airways rep in Heathrow who let us go to the Executive lounge "to minimise my discomfort". We were waited on hand and foot until our connection to Edinburgh.

"There is something to be said for travelling with a cripple," Lousia remarked as she swigged her third complimentary Bloody Mary from the bar.

"How are you feeling now?" asked Melissa as she trundled our trolley out to the arrivals hall in Edinburgh.

"My arse is still recovering."

"I'm so sorry, can you forgive me?" She totally blamed herself for leaving me on my own.

"Don't be ridiculous, of course I forgive you. I'm supposed to be a grown-up."

I stopped short. Fiona was standing there waiting for us.

"Good Lord, what have you done to yourself this time?" she asked, staring at the crutches.

"Don't ask, long and ridiculous story. Nice of you to come! I didn't expect you."

"Oh, there was something I needed to tell you."

That didn't sound good. Now that I noticed, she looked very strained and pale-faced.

"What? To tell me I've been promoted to the board? Jake has moved to Edinburgh because life is too much for him without me? Mark burnt down my flat?"

At the mention of Mark Fiona looked down at her feet.

"What! He burnt down my flat!" I shrieked.

"No, no. But, Ellie, I don't quite know how to tell you this."

"What, for Christ's sake?"

"Yes, it's Mark."

The girls gathered round the empty trolleys.

"Oh my God, what's happened?" I wobbled on my crutches.

"While you were away I'm afraid he got into your flat again."

"But I had the locks changed!"

"I'm afraid it wasn't locked . . . "She looked at me, shamefaced. "I had been in the flat and had just gone in to see Mrs Arnold for a few minutes . . ."

"Shit!"

"I can't tell you how sorry I am, Ellie." She really did look dreadful.

"So tell me the worst – what did he do or take this time?"

"That's the thing . . . he took . . ."

"What? What did the bastard take this time?"

"I'm so sorry, Ellie."

"What?"

"He took Hector."

I slumped into Chloe and started to cry.

"I'm so sorry," said Fiona.

I just sobbed.

"Why was Hector in the flat anyway? I thought you were supposed to be looking after him?"

"He just happened to be there. I had brought him around to check if he had a coat – the weather has been so wet. I was through with Mrs Arnold – she thought she had a spare coat that would fit and we were chatting when Mark got in."

"Jesus, he came in the middle of the day?"

"Yeah, the police think he knew you were away and meant to break in to nose around. But instead he had Hector doing his vicious dog impersonation. So he grabbed him and ran off. Or else he was actually after Hector and saw me go in with him." She paused. "And there's something else."

"What?" I looked up at her in dread.

"He left a note."

"A note?"

She nodded.

"What did it say?"

"Are you sure you want to know right now?"

"Of course I bloody want to know right now! He's taken my dog hostage!"

"OK. It said, *'The bitch will have to come to me now'*."

"That's it?"

"That's it."

"Cryptic bastard isn't he? One can only presume it has something do with me, a loaded lethal syringe and a deserted warehouse."

A horrible thought struck me.

"Do they think Hector is still alive?"

"Yes, they do – judging from the note they think he'll really use him as a hostage."

"Well, I want to go and see them today."

"Your parents are here – I rang them as soon as I could. They got the first available flight."

"They knew and they didn't tell me?"

"They didn't want to worry you by contacting you earlier.

"Oh,"

"Will you be all right for a minute? I'll take your bag and go get the car."

"Yes, I'll be fine."

The girls all started to disperse. Chloe and I would get a lift back to Chloe's with Fiona. My head was buzzing with the information that Fiona had just given me. Mark had taken my Hector. It seemed that nothing short of topping me was going to stop him. I couldn't believe that police still hadn't caught up with him. He seemed to be more elusive than the bloody Scarlet Pimpernel! Chloe hugged me while we waited for Fiona.

She arrived back in five minutes, helped me into the car, and we headed back to Chloe's flat.

"The police don't want you to go back to your flat just yet."

"So where are Mum and Dad?"

"They're in Chloe's flat at the minute, though they're staying in a guest house just down the road. Not really enough room for everyone. David let them in – hope that is OK, Chloe."

"God, of course," Chloe nodded emphatically.

"Are they not allowed to stay at mine either?" I asked.

"No, just to be on the safe side."

"Oh, poor Hector. Please, please let him be OK!"

"I'm sure he is fine. I am so fucking sorry."

"Oh, God, it's not like it's your fault. I'm glad you're OK. It could have been nasty for you if you had been in the flat when Mark arrived."

"Duncan has come to stay with me for the past few

days. I was quite shaken after it all. I tried to run after Mark but Mrs Arnold wouldn't let me – double-locked the door and called the police."

When we arrived, David, Mum and Dad were all there. Everyone was being so nice to me. Fiona didn't stay. Mum had made an appointment with Dr Brook for the following morning and Sergeant McLeod wanted to call in at a time that suited me. Mum and Chloe thought it might take my mind off things if I went for my first dress fitting – the wedding was only three and half weeks away. Poor Chloe, she had her mind full of all sorts of things – she was going home in a week to spend the fortnight before her wedding at home making sure everything had been arranged. I secretly thought this was a terrible idea – Margo would be a nightmare of gargantuan proportions. I agreed to go for the fitting, otherwise I would be following her up the aisle in my bra and pants.

The next morning in the hospital Dr Brook looked at my ankle and declared I would live, but it would be fairly painful for a few weeks, considering the severity of the damage to tendons and ligaments. He recommended physiotherapy.

After the doctor Mum drove me to the police station. Sergeant McLeod was glad to see me all in one piece.

"Seems like you're not enjoying the luck of the Irish at the moment, Ellie."

"No, I don't think so."

"Now we don't want you to worry about your dog. We think he will be fine. Mark wasn't expecting him – he knew you were on holiday. He probably intended to break in to take some personal item of yours. Once your dog started barking, it panicked him and he just grabbed the dog and ran. Also the police were on the scene very quickly. Your parents are fairly sure he didn't take anything else. Of course you will need to verify that with us."

I was only half convinced by all this. What of the other theory – that he had intended to get hold of Hector as hostage?

"Well, I can go back to my flat later on this afternoon," I said. "We have a couple of things we have to do first."

"At your own convenience. I also wanted to let you know that a criminal psychologist has been involved in the case over the past couple of weeks, trying to understand why Mark has been fixating on you for so long, and why he has turned violent."

"I gave up trying to answer that question after the car crash. Nothing that happened between us could have been that bad. I mean we broke up, but so do hundreds of couples – it doesn't mean everyone goes round trying to wreak revenge for a broken heart or an injured ego."

"I quite agree, but Mr Norris is an unusual case. As we know, he has a bit of form in this area. And the longer he is roaming round Edinburgh the greater risk he is to himself and to everyone else."

"Don't you think it would be a good idea to try to trap him?" An idea had popped full-grown into my head.

"Well, that is a possibility we are considering."

"Well, how about using me as a bait?"

Mum looked horrified but didn't say anything.

"Ellie, I have to thank you," said the sergeant with a smile."But using civilians is not an option."

"So you think it's better to have a nutter running

round stealing dogs and threatening people?" I said rather agressively.

"Your safety is our concern."

I would not back down – the idea had gripped me. I was suddenly convinced that this was the way, the only way, to put an end to this nightmare.

"Ellie, it's out of the question!" said Mum.

"Well, it's not like I would be doing it alone, the police would be there too. Sergeant, if you're convinced he's watching the building, then have plainclothes officers go in as if they live in the building and they can hide in my bedroom or something. If he thinks I'm going to be in there alone, I think he'll try to come in and get me. You read the note." First snag: the note had said that I would come to him.

"Ellie, the risk to you is too great," said the sergeant.

"Think about it: you catch him, I get my dog and my life back. You can bug the place, train tele-photo lenses on the place, have officers dotted about the building and in my flat, what could possibly go wrong?"

"There is always a large margin of error, believe me. And you're forgetting the syringe. He could lunge at you with it at any point."

"Then I wear protective clothing!"

My earnestness was obviously making some impression on Sergeant McLeod. He leant back in his chair and considered. Finally he spoke. "I'll need to consult my seniors on this. Are you sure you are want to do it?"

"Of course. I'm deadly serious. I have had about enough as I can take. Hector was the last straw."

Sergeant McLeod looked at Mum.

She looked deeply unhappy. She looked at me. I glared at her.

"If she wants to do it . . ." Her eyes filled up with tears. "I can't say I'm happy about it but, if your father agrees, I won't stop you."

"Cheers, Mum." I gave her a hug.

"You've gone a bit commando haven't you?" Mum said as we drove over to Chloe's to take her to Yvonne's for the fitting.

"If it happened to you, you would want to put an end to it too, Mum. I don't think he is going to stop. I've been lucky so far, so why not try to catch him in a controlled environment?"

"Your father will have kittens."

"I'm sure he'll agree."

Mum gave me a sideways glance and I laughed. "He doesn't have a choice," I said. "Anyway, it is affecting us all. Now not a word to anyone else, not even Chloe. The fewer people know about this the better the chances of it being a success."

"You don't even know if the police will agree."

"Of course they will, it's their best chance of catching him. Their efforts have been abysmal so far. What other options do they have? Wait till he actually does get me?"

"Ellie, don't talk like that!"

"Well, it's true."

Chloe was waiting for us outside her flat. She climbed into the back seat.

"Jake rang. I told him what happened to you. He couldn't believe it and he sent his love – again.

"Oh, that's kind of him!" said Mum.

"Did he say anything else?" I asked.

"Yup, he's coming home in a couple of weeks for some leave. He wanted to let us know that he will definitely be at the wedding."

"I think we should ask him if he wants to stay with us," Mum suggested.

"That's a great idea." Chloe said, not catching my eye.

"We can ring him later then, I have his number back in the flat."

Chapter Twenty-one

Yvonne, it turned out, was a lovely girl who was a full-time seamstress and had everything under control. Chloe's dress was virtually finished and she had finally decided to have me as her only bridesmaid. They had decided to make my dress long enough to hide my bandages and injuries but not too long that I tripped over it and did myself any more damage! At least Margo couldn't accuse me of ruining the wedding photos.

Chloe had taken the unusual decision to have my dress made in a deep petrol-blue chiffon, which was absolutely fab and I loved it. Mum and Chloe helped me stand up while Yvonne took some quick measurements. Shoes were going to be a bit of a problem, as I might be requiring only one, as my other foot was the size of a balloon. Yvonne told us about a little shop on Broughton Street that would dye fabric shoes any colour you wanted, so something plain while could be dyed petrol-blue to match my dress. Once Yvonne had the measurement she needed I could sit down again. She brought out Chloe's dress for Mum and me to have a look.

"Well, it's superb. Yvonne, you've done a great job."
Mum looked at the tiny neat stitches. She was clearly
impressed, coming from a generation of women who
used make themselves a dress for Saturday night at the
drop of a hat.

We persuaded Chloe to try the dress on, as so far only
she and Yvonne had seen it on her.

Mum and I were both speechless. It was a hundred
times nicer than the ones she had tried on in Philomena
Lambley's in Fulham and minus the price tag.

"God Chloe, you are going to look utterly stunning."

She blushed. "Do you think so?"

"Without doubt. Oh Chloe, you will look divine!"
Mum exclaimed. "Has your mum seen it yet?"

"Er, no, that's a bit of sore point at the moment. I
really wanted to do this without her, and it hasn't gone
down too well."

"No surprises there then," I said.

Mum gave me a dig in the ribs. "Well, I think she'll
be delighted with your choice."

"Oh thanks, Hazel." Chloe was genuinely relieved
her dress was such a success.

"Can you come back next week for another fitting?"
Yvonne asked me.

"Yes, that shouldn't be a problem."

We arranged that Chloe would bring me back for my
second fitting and this time I would have something to
try on, albeit with pins in.

When we got back to Chloe's there was a message for
me from Sergeant McLeod. I rang him back in Chloe and
David's bedroom, so no one else could hear the call.

"It would appear that your idea has been approved," he told me minutes later. He sounded somewhat amazed that it had.

"Really?" I immediately started to have second thoughts.

"If you're still interested we'd like a few days to get everything organised. We will want to set you up with a wire-tap. We don't want too many strangers coming and going from your flat to make him suspicious."

"No, of course not."

"So with your neighbours permission we will set up surveillance in the flat opposite yours and possibly have an officer in your bathroom or bedroom. It's really a question of being prepared for any eventuality. Though you can never be completely prepared, especially with someone so unpredictable. I hope you realise that?"

"Oh yes, I do, of course." Oh God, what had I let myself in for? "But how are we sure he will turn up? He knows I'm hardly going to buzz him in."

"Once he realises you have gone back to your flat we think he will contact you. It all depends on that. He knows the net is closing round him. Armed with a lethal syringe, he has put himself under pressure. He wants to get you and he has to do it soon."

"Thanks a lot."

"Sorry, you know what I mean – he realises time is running out."

"Do you think he will bring Hector with him?"

"We're counting on that. We believe he will use the dog as a bargaining tool to gain access from you into the building."

We decided I should move back into the flat the

following week. Sergeant McLeod thought Tuesday would be a good day. He also wanted me to call into the station so that I could be briefed and get my protective gear.

Sunday seemed to drag by. Mum and Dad both knew about the plan, but I didn't want Chloe or Fiona to know. I had rung Fiona in Inverness and spoken to her. I told her not to worry and that the police thought that Hector would be fine. She calmed down considerably when I told her this and she promised to stay up in Inverness with Duncan for the rest of the following week.

Margo kept ringing on Sunday evening to speak to Chloe and ask her questions about the wedding. First of all she didn't think that the Salsa band that Chloe had booked was entirely appropriate, she didn't think her friends would like that sort of music. She seemed most put out when Chloe pointed out that she didn't really care what Margo's friends thought, it was her wedding and she and David both wanted the Salsa band. Then she wanted to know why Chloe hadn't used the caterer that Rose Bendall had recommended, and why hadn't she ordered her wine from Bertie McNeill – didn't she know that Bertie was the husband of a Isabel McNeill, a great friend of hers? Would Margo ever be able to live this down? Chloe's Dad hadn't said a peep about anything – bless him. Chloe pointed out to her mum that she had used a caterer who went to school with us, and was apparently extremely good, and that the wine had been ordered through a contact of Melissa's husband, and she and David had got a great deal on it. Chloe's

Dad had been delighted, as unbeknown to Margo he had been helping pay for everything. Margo had ordered the biggest marquee that the hire firm was able to provide. She had also been allowed to ask thirty of her own friends and had been outraged that Chloe and David were limiting her guest list so tightly.

"She'll just have to lump it as we're not going to change our minds. I think our friends are the most important."

"I'm sorry, come again, did I just see Miss Williams display some backbone?"

I looked at Chloe who raised her hands up in a mock fighting gesture.

"No, I'm afraid violence doesn't solve anything, Chloe."

Jake phoned and I chatted to him for over half an hour. I was tempted to tell him about the Mark-trap, but I concluded that Jake would probably go ballistic and it would be best if I said nothing. Funny but even though I had spent relatively little time in Jake's company I knew him so well. Our telephone non-relationship was going really well and we spent happy hours chatting to each other, thousands of miles away. I believed I had managed to convince everyone including myself that I was perfectly happy with this arrangement. Tonight though, Jake kept asking me if something was wrong and seemed dissatisfied when I told him everything was totally great.

"Why don't you take Hector out for a walk to clear your head if you have a headache?"

I bit my lip at the mention of Hector's name. I hoped he was OK.

"I don't have a headache – now, what were you telling me about baseball?"

"Basketball, Ellie."

"That's what I said, basketball."

I attempted to concentrate on what he was saying, but all I could visualise was Mark standing in my living-room threatening me and/or Hector with his loaded syringe of lethal anaesthetic. Virtually instant death, no antidote, aware of what was happening to me while I died. I shuddered at the thought and went back to baseball or basketball or whatever it was Jake was trying to explain to me.

I woke early on the Monday morning wondering what I was going to do to take my mind off things. Thankfully David was at work and Chloe was so busy fighting her mum off via BT that she didn't notice me acting in a strange way, i.e. not talking incessantly. Mum and Dad called round to take me to the police station for our briefing. They had insisted that they be included in everything even if they weren't going to be there.

We sat surrounded by officers in plainclothes who were going to be involved in the operation. PC Colin Waverly and WPC Suzy Albert were going to be posing as other residents in the building – they were the ones who would be hiding in my bedroom. The rest would be dotted around the surrounding area to prevent Mark from doing a runner, if he sussed the situation before the police had time to take him down. It was all quite scary but I was excited at the thought of never being tormented by him again. We talked things through for about an hour until everyone was happy with what was happening. The officers would be in the building from seven the next morning. I would arrive at nine with lots of bags to make it look like I was moving back in.

We had no way of predicting how long it would take Mark to show but the police thought he wouldn't wait long after he realised I was back.

The rest of Monday passed as slowly as Sunday. Mum and Dad took me out for dinner – Chloe and David were going to a reception for the Edinburgh Dental association and I didn't fancy sitting in all night. They took me to Fishers on the Shore not far from my flat. We ate seafood and drank wine that none of us really wanted. But we forced ourselves to make conversation though it inevitably came back to what was going to happen the next morning.

"There's no point in you sitting outside my flat, Dad! Mark would recognise you! And it could take days!"

Mum kept coming up with more practical suggestions. "I hope he doesn't see the protective vest under your clothes – wear one of your old baggy jumpers."

"That's a good idea, the ones I used to think were wildly fashionable but in fact made me look like I was about eighteen stone."

Back at Chloe's I packed some bags with my clothes and put them in the back of Chloe's car. She was letting me use it while the insurance company decided what to do about my old one that Mark had managed to destroy. Every time I thought I was doing something stupid I thought of Hector and how I would probably never see him again. I hoped Mark brought him to the flat.

I ran through all the ways the next few days could go. First of all Mark might not show up – this was unlikely, so determined was he to get me. Secondly, he could turn up, but without Hector, who he had already done away with or hidden somewhere we would never find him and he would starve to death and . . . oh, God! Thirdly, he turns up with Hect, and gets me with the syringe before the police have a chance to get him. Lastly . . .

I decided to fuck it, what did I have to lose? My life was getting smaller and smaller as I began to live in increasing fear. It was just unfortunate that I would have to do the whole thing with my stupid ankle. But I could hop pretty fast.

I got into bed and thought about Chloe's wedding. I wanted to see my best friend – me – walk up the aisle and marry the man that she loved more than I suspected. When this was all over I was going to go out and find the man of my dreams and I was going to make myself happy, wherever that happened to be. I had a feeling that I would not stay in Edinburgh forever. London perhaps? Or possibly Dublin? Why not Belfast? I feel asleep mentally decorating my country mansion.

I woke up. It was still dark. I looked over at the clock. 5.15 am, the red glow told me. I had thrown my duvet on the floor and I got out of bed to retrieve it. I looked out at the orange glow of the street outside. There was no noise, no cars passed and everything was very still. Then something moved down below in the street outside. A dog, I thought.

Then I saw him. He moved out of the shadows and stood on the pavement looking up at the flat. I jumped back, away from the window, almost falling over my crutches in the process. My first reaction was to wake Chloe and David and ring the police, but he would be long gone by then. I took a small step towards the window. He was still there, standing brazen as you like, right outside. I wasn't sure if he had seen me, he was standing with his hands in his pockets not moving. Slowly he took one of his hands out his pocket and waved up my window.

"Shit," I whispered, and stepped back from the window. I sat on the edge of the bed and took a deep breath. I opened my bedroom door and hobbled into the hall.

Now don't panic, I told myself, and don't do anything stupid like in those films where half-dressed women go down to the basement in the dark armed with only a nightie and a kirby-grip to fight off the madman with a hook for a right arm. I checked to see if the front door had been double-locked and all the windows were shut. Everything was locked up tight. I went back into my bedroom. I took a quick glance out the window to make sure Mark was still out there.

He was still there but this time he was standing with Hector beside him on a lead. I put my hands up to the glass on the window, tears streaming down my face. Mark put his index finger up to his lips, as if to tell me to be quiet. He smiled and turned away, walking down the street taking Hector with him. My first reaction was to run after them – half-dressed women disappeared from my mind as I limped back into the hall, fumbling with the lock as I tried to get out. I hopped down the two flights of stairs and out the main door into the street.

The street was deserted, no sign of Mark or Hector. An early morning milk float passed by, the elderly milkman giving my pyjamas a strange look. I looked up and down the street again, no sign. My leg ached with the sudden exercise I had just given it. I turned and went back inside and up to the flat. Chloe and David didn't seem to have heard me.

I couldn't get back to sleep. I tossed and turned, getting my wretched ankle twisted up the sheets.

It occurred to me that Mark's visit was a very good omen. It now looked that the police predictions were accurate. He was there, he had Hector, he was watching me and he was ready to take risks to make contact. He probably would turn up at the flat as soon as I got back there.

I finally fell asleep ten minutes before my alarm went off. Light flooded my room. 07.30 am, the red figures announced. The radio came on and a newsreader told listeners that Tuesday was going to be a bright sunny April day. My eyes were puffy and I was sweaty from tossing and turning. I felt like shit and fur had somehow managed to grow quite successfully in my mouth.

"Ellie?" Chloe peered round my door.

"I'm awake." I dragged myself up into sitting position

"Well, I've certainly seen you look better." She sat on the side of my bed

"Cheers," I said as she handed me the cup of Earl Grey in her hand.

"Didn't you sleep very well?"

"Mark was here last night."

"What!"

"Outside the window, he was here."

"How do you know?"

"I woke up, I had thrown the duvet off, so I got up to get it and looked out of the window. There he was."

"Oh my God!"

"I know – the worst part was that he had Hector with him."

"Oh Ellie, why didn't you wake us up?"

"You know as well as I do that he would have disappeared before David got down the stairs."

"They'll catch him soon, Ellie, I know they will."

"I know they will too."

Chloe looked at me sideways, but I didn't offer an explanation.

"It is OK, isn't it, if I borrow your car?"

"Of course. I'm being picked up for work today, but you would have been welcome to it anyway.

"Thanks."

"Do you want to go back to sleep?"

"Nah, I've got a couple of things to do today."

"Right, I'm leaving in five minutes, will you be OK? You can manage the bath and everything?"

"Got it down to a fine art."

"You don't think he will be out there this morning, do you?" Chloe looked decidedly uncomfortable.

"Oh no, of course not, Chloe. I'm so sorry that I've brought him here."

"He brought himself, and we don't mind at all." She leant forward and gave me a quick hug.

A car peeped its horn outside.

"Oh that will be Carol. I'd better go, sure you'll be OK?"

I nodded.

"The keys are on the hall table."

"See you tonight."

"Yeah, see you later."

She left, locking the front door behind her.

I sat in bed and finished off the tea Chloe had brought me. I hadn't told her I was leaving. She would never have let me go. I'd have to phone her later – when the horse had bolted.

I listened to a couple of songs on the radio, and then I got up and went and ran a bath. I had to be outside my flat in just over an hour. I bathed and dressed slowly, my ankle sore from last night's attempt to catch up with Mark.

Then I made a certain very important phone call.

Chloe's car was automatic so it was easy for me to drive, even with my bad foot. I drove over to my flat. Everything looked normal, no sign of Mark or the police. I knew they were there somewhere nearby. I slung a smallish rucksack onto my shoulders, took just one of my crutches and slowly made my way over to my building.

I heard a dog bark behind me. I started but didn't look round. Could it be Hector? Could Mark have followed me straight from Chloe's? If so, everything could happen more rapidly than we had hoped.

I pushed the front door open with my shoulder and hobbled in. I took the lift up to my floor. Mrs Arnold was nowhere to be seen. I could only imagine the police had told her to stay well hidden. I opened the door to my flat and went inside. It looked as if I had never been away. The answer machine was flashing. I ignored it and took my rucksack into the bedroom. PC Waverly and WPC Albert were standing just behind the door. Even though I knew they were supposed to be there I jumped when I saw them.

"Sorry, Miss Clarke."

"No, no, my fault, I'm just a bit jumpy. I heard a dog bark downstairs."

They nodded. "It could be him. He could have followed you."

"What should I do?"

"Make yourself a cup of coffee or something. If he's there he may be able to see you move around the flat, so just do something like that, or watch television."

"Would either of you like a cup?"

"That would be lovely. Both just with milk."

"Right."

I went into the kitchen and put the kettle on. I looked out the window as casually as I could, but I couldn't see anyone in the street outside. I made the coffees and brought them into the officers one at a time.

"Right, I'm off to sit in the living-room and look natural."

I turned on the telly and tried to watch an early-morning discussion show about stepmothers dealing with stepchildren. I listened to a few horror stories and then turned over to see what Trisha had to say for herself: a half-hour chat show about football being responsible for breaking up marriages. God, no wonder they call daytime telly 'dole TV' – this sort of stuff sucks your will to live, or at least think rationally. I channel-flicked for a couple of minutes and watched my coffee go cold. I lit a cigarette and went back to the step-mothers, who were just terribly misunderstood. Kilroy-Silk was smiling at them in a most patronising fashion; it was so ridiculous it was funny.

My intercom buzzed and I jumped so high I almost hit the ceiling. I got up.

"Is it all right to answer it?" I hissed towards the bedroom.

"Absolutely." WPC Albert had appeared at my bedroom door.

"Don't worry – we're here."

I nodded and tried to smile. I picked up the handset.

"Hello?" I tried to sound calm. I put a hand up to my chest to make sure I had remembered to put my protective vest on. I felt its comforting bulk under my jumper.

"I have someone who would like to see you." Mark's voice filled my ears

"Hector?"

"I think he misses his mummy."

I felt sick to my stomach.

"If you don't hurt him, I'll let you in."

I could hear Mark laughing.

"If you don't let me in, I'll post you his paws one by one."

I retched at the thought, glad I had only had a cup of tea that morning. "Let me see him first. I'll go to the window."

"OK. Do that."

I stumbled to the window. Mark stood below, with

Hector in his arms. I signalled to him and he strode back into the building.

I buzzed him in, my hands trembling.

"He's coming!" I whispered towards the bedroom. I opened the front door and heard the lift whirring as it brought Mark – and hopefully Hector – up to my floor. The lift doors opened and Mark appeared. I couldn't see Hector.

I had the door on the safety chain.

"Where is he?" I hissed at Mark.

"Oh he's here, but he can't walk awfully well. I think he's as clumsy as his mistress."

Hector came out of the lift slowly; he was limping on three legs, his front right leg tucked up. He wagged his tail when he saw me standing in the door way and tried to come to me but Mark kicked him back.

"Hector!" I took the safety catch off the door and knelt down holding my arms out, for him to come to me.

Mark moved faster than I would have thought humanly possible. He kicked me back into the flat. I hit the floor hard, my knee twisting as I fell backwards. Hector stood outside the doorway, trembling. Clearly he was terrified of Mark. Just as Mark slammed my door shut behind him. I saw Mrs Arnold scuttle out of her flat and sweep Hector into her arms.

"Oh, thank you, God," I whispered.

"Get up, bitch!"

I struggled to my feet.

Not a squeak out of the police.

"Mark listen, I . . ."

"Shut up, I don't want to hear the sound of your whining little voice, OK?"

He was standing in front of the window his hands on his hips. He had army fatigues on, as if he was trying to playact some sort of soldier. The whole thing would have been funny if he hadn't just pulled out the syringe he threatened me with several months ago.

"First of all, I want to tell you what I am going to do to you, before I end your pathetic life."

He took a step towards me, talking all the time.

"I am going to stick this in your neck and then I am going to watch you die. Afterwards, I am going to set fire to this place, destroying the evidence and burning your precious dog with you."

I stared at him, meeting his eye. I kept my mouth clamped shut.

He came so close our noses were almost touching. I fought the urge to shut my eyes, making myself return his gaze without flinching. For a second I thought he was going to kiss me, but he pulled away. I breathed a sigh of relief, then the pain hit me and I found myself on the floor of my living-room again. Mark had kicked my ankle.

I writhed on the floor in agony; tears pricked my eyes and I was fighting for breath.

"You really should be more careful, Sorrel."

He walked away from me. I waited for the officers to come out and arrest him, but nothing, not a peep out of them. Mark picked up the syringe he had set on top of the television.

"I'm bored with you now, I think you were more fun when you were bolshy, now you just lie there like a broken doll. I'm fairly certain this will hurt a lot."

He took the plastic casing off the syringe and walked towards me. I shut my eyes, willing the police to come out of their hiding-place.

"Hold it right there, Mr Norris, we have the building surrounded – you'll not be killing Miss Clarke or anyone else today."

The two officers arrived in the living-room, guns pointing at Mark. The look of shock on Mark's face is something that will probably stay with me forever. He expression changed again in a split second back to the sneer he had been using earlier.

"I'm afraid not, Constable. You see, if I can't take Sorrel's life, then I will have to take my own."

The officers edged towards him.

"Come any closer and I will use this." Mark pointed the syringe at himself.

The officers lowered their guns.

"You don't want to do this," Waverly said.

Mark's expression had changed again; this time I saw fear in his face as he backed into the corner beside the television.

"Put the needle down," Albert said to him.

Mark looked at me. "You bitch," he whispered as he raised the needle and then plunged it into his chest, dispensing the lethal drug into his system. The police officers lunged forward and grabbed him but too late – the syringe was empty. Mark dropped it on the floor.

We watched as we waited for Mark to go into spasms and then die within two minutes, knowing there was nothing that could be done to save him.

Nothing happened.

Five minutes passed and Mark was still standing.

We all looked down at the empty syringe.

The door was forced open as the rest of the officers rushed in. Everyone stopped when they saw the empty syringe. Still nothing had happened. An ambulance arrived and the paramedics rushed up the stairs and into the flat.

"He's taken a lethal dose of Vecruonium," Waverley told them.

"He wouldn't be standing if he had!" said one of the paramedics, picking up the syringe. He pulled the plunger out and a revolting stink filled the air.

Both paramedics burst out laughing.

"What is so bloody funny?" Mark demanded.

"You didn't take a lethal drug – you just had a shot of Parenterovite."

"What the hell is that?" Sergeant McLeod asked.

"It's a very smelly but effective shot of pure vitamins the psychiatric hospitals use to treat alcoholics. You have just done yourself a power of good, mate." The paramedic shook his head. "I don't think you need us anymore. You can take him to the station."

"You mean I haven't killed myself?" Mark asked.

"'Fraid not, mate."

Mark even managed to look crestfallen.

"You should have a look at Ellie's ankle, he gave her a bit of a kicking," Waverley told the paramedics.

They helped me to my feet but I seemed fine. As Mark was being led out to a waiting police car, the phone rang.

"Miss Clarke?" said a strange male voice.

"Speaking."

"Nigel Moreland speaking. I'm from The Edinburgh

Property Centre. I'm returning your call. I believe you want to put your flat on the market."

"Yes, indeed I do."

Later on Mum and Dad took me back to Chloe's flat. She was sitting in her living-room watching the news.

"What the hell have you been up to today?" She asked from her position in front of the television.

"Mark has been caught."

"I can see that – you are all over the bloody news, woman!" She got up and came over to me. I thought I was going to get a lecture on being irresponsible but instead she flung her arms round me and gave me a massive hug.

"Well done, love, I'm so glad it's all over."

Dad took us all out for a huge meal to celebrate. I couldn't quite believe that it was all over and no one, not even Hector, had been seriously injured. After a visit to the vets it turned out that Hector's paw was just a bit bruised, nothing broken. Hector's natural sense of drama meant he insisted on limping everywhere, thus ensuring maximum attention and sympathy.

Chapter Twenty-two

It was now only two days before Chloe and David's wedding and we were all back in Belfast. Unfortunately my ankle had taken a turn for the worse again after Mark's tender treatment but I was a demon at getting round on my crutches.

Jake was due to land at the Belfast International Airport so Mum was running me up to the airport to go and collect him. I carefully applied some lipstick in the sun-visor mirror.

"I thought you and Jake were just good friends?"

"We are, the lipstick is for me, not him," I said indignantly.

Mum smiled and said nothing more, continuing to laugh at Terry Wogan as he chatted through Thursday breakfast.

"Do you think his plane will be on time?" I asked nervously.

"British Airways are normally fairly reliable."

"Do you think he will want to go to bed when he gets in?"

"You'll need to ask him that."

"He could have jet-lag."

"Unlikely." Mum smiled one of her really irritating and cryptic smiles and did not volunteer any further information.

I would have interrogated her but we were nearly there and I still had to do my eyes.

When we arrived at the airport my heart was in my mouth. I hadn't seen Jake for four months, though I was still sporting my crutch fashion accessories, so I hadn't changed that much. I wondered if he had. Perhaps he had finally got himself an American girlfriend, one who looks fabulous but thinks that sarcasm is the capital of California. At least then I could see the funny side. God please, don't let him have a girlfriend.

But what about the lady in the photo in the bathroom?

Mum parked the car outside the arrivals hall.

"Do you want to go in by yourself?"

"No, I think I would prefer if you came with me."

"I can't really leave the car."

"Oh, right." I climbed out of the car thinking that Mum was definitely acting in a marginally odd manner, perhaps it was the menopause, hot flushes or something. More likely rampant matchmaking.

I went into the terminal building, walking slowly up towards the arrivals hall. Northern Ireland companies, never ones to miss out on an advertising opportunity, had had a carpet especially woven with all their logos on, so one would walk off the plane and immediately start receiving subliminal messages for crystal and cheese and onion crisps – very clever eh?

Unfortunately the airport had been slightly remodelled since my last visit, and I got slightly lost. Arriving red-faced and puffing was not part of my plan but thank God Jake's plane was slightly delayed, giving my heartrate time to return to normal.

When Jake walked through the arrivals door I was the picture of composed calm and serenity. My first thoughts were that he didn't really travel light for a bloke – weren't they always the ones asking was it necessary to bring the kitchen sink? This particular bloke looked like he couldn't decide which colour to bring, so had brought several alternatives.

His face broke into a smile when he saw me. He abandoned his packed trolley in order to give me a big hug.

"It's good to see you, Ellie!"

"You too." I smiled a bit too brightly, trying to cover the fact that I blushing like a madwoman.

"How is the leg?"

"Oh, it's better. But now I have a shattered ankle instead. I'm not limping too badly – I think no one will notice."

Jake retrieved his trolley and we walked out of the airport together.

"How come you have so much stuff? I thought men always travelled light."

"Didn't your mum tell you?"

"Tell me what?" My brain buzzed with Mum's recent evasive behaviour.

"I've decided to stay in Belfast for a while."

I stopped walking – well, I stopped limping.

"You're doing what?"

"I'm staying in Belfast for a while. We have a client in

Dungannon so the boss has asked me to stay here for a couple of months to be able to work closely with him."

"Where are you going to live?" I was still digesting his last sentence.

"I'm renting a house here – well, your mum found it, actually I haven't seen it, but Chloe tells me it is lovely."

"Chloe!" I exploded. "Why have my mother and my best friend been helping you rent a sodding house in Belfast and I know nothing about it?" Had I been in a position to kick him, I would have.

"Well, I didn't want to upset you."

"Upset me!" Steam was starting to come out of my ears, I was raging. There was nothing I hated more than being the last person to know something. I just knew it, he really wasn't interested in me at all.

"Sorry, I just thought after all you've been through you wouldn't want any more shocks." Jake looked a little unsure.

I stopped walking. "Why would you renting a house need to be such a shock for me?"

"I was going to ask you to live in it with me."

Now I was shocked. *What? What? What?* Could he mean . . . ? I tried to cover up my reaction. "Well, that's just silly," I said, "because I live in Edinburgh."

"But you're selling your flat."

"I'm going to buy another one."

"But what about your job?"

"What about it?"

"Fiona told me you're leaving work."

I'd only just decided that! And I hadn't told anyone – only Fiona . . .

"Jesus, is nothing sacred? What I intend to do with the rest of my life is no one's business, except mine." I was warming to my subject now. "Anyway, why would I want to live with you?"

"Well, I have a spare room, and I thought you might be sick of living with your parents. So how about it?"

Spare room. Oh well, what did I expect? That he was asking me to share a bed? "Live together – like flatmates?"

"Yes, what do you think?"

"Well, I don't know." Daily torture living platonically with the man I love? Yeah, right after I finish my walking-on-hot-coals course.

"You don't need to make a decision now, just think about it. You might not like the house."

I opened my mouth to say something else, when I found I couldn't. My brain turned to glue, my knees went weak and I started to cry.

"Oh God, sorry I didn't mean to upset you."

"But you live in America!"

I was sobbing in a most unbecoming fashion, mascara making dark grey rivulets down my cheeks and people were starting to look at us. Jake put his arms round me, and I instantly covered him in mascara and lipstick, but he didn't seem to notice.

"Ellie, I'm sorry! I didn't think you would mind so much not knowing about the house. I should have told you earlier!"

"But . . ."

We were standing on the map of Northern Ireland, which some misguided interior decorator had thought would make a fantastic beginning to the great advertising carpet, which was fine until someone put their fag out in the middle of Lough Neagh.

"Listen, don't think about it anymore. You have Chloe's wedding to concentrate on. We can discuss this later. I can find another flatmate, no problem at all."

I wanted to throw large heavy objects at his head while screaming, *"I love you, you unobservant maniac! Marry me, marry me!"* But of course I didn't. I wiped the tears away with the sleeve of my jacket and nodded. "OK, we can talk about it in a couple of days."

I waited for him to burst out laughing and shout *"Sucker!"* at me. But he didn't – he just looked really upset and genuine. I couldn't really imagine Jake living in Belfast. Oh why does my life have to be so bloody complicated? What would I do if he wanted to bring girls back to the house? I would kill them.

Several people had stopped and were listening to us – they didn't really have a choice as we were blocking their exit.

"Ellie?"

"Yes?"

"We should move, we are in everyone's way."

I looked round. A small crowd was waiting in the Axminster Irish Sea to get past us.

Suddenly the crowd parted and people leapt back to avoid a trolley trundling at high speed with an enormous red-faced perspiring man at its helm. He saw us and instead of braking, let go. Jake and I stood frozen as the trolley careered towards us – towards me, actually. All I could think about was amputations – surely my leg would not survive another accident? I closed my eyes and waited for more pain to hit me. But in the tradition of all airport trolleys, it swerved at the last minute, hit Jake instead and fell over. He lay unmoving as an enormous red-faced man came to retrieve it and apologise for the accident.

"You could have killed my friend!" I shouted at him.

"I'm fine," came a voice from beneath the trolley.

"Jake! Are you OK?"

"I'm fine!"

The fat man righted his trolley and made a sharp exit.

"We could sue you!" I shouted to his disappearing back.

"Well, at least he was good enough to leave us his duty free!" Jake rolled over to reveal a litre of whiskey and one of vodka.

I began to grin. "Are you all right?"

"Ouch, I think so." Jake got to his feet slowly.

There was a lump forming on his forehead where the trolley had whacked him.

The pair of us limped slowly out of the terminal, Jake pushing his trolley very slowly in front of him.

Mum came bustling over, beaming, no doubt expecting the engagement announcement, then stopped short when she saw Jake's forehead and my tear-streaked face.

"Don't even ask," I said.

When we got back to the house, Dad was waiting and was equally nonplussed by the state of us. "What happened to you lot?"

"A run-in with an airport trolley," I answered shortly.

Dad looked none the wiser. He was staring at Jake's

forehead which was slowly turning an attractive shade of eggshell blue.

"I was the one who had the accident and was floored by the trolley," Jake said. "Not Ellie, this time."

"Bloody hell, are you sure you're all right?"

"Perfectly fine, Mr Clarke."

"Dad, why are you grinning?" I asked him.

"Well, with you limping and Jake looking like he just lost a fight, Margo is going to do her nut at this wedding!"

"Dad, you are not helping." I limped past him towards the house.

Having Jake in the house was going to be a little bit weird. I wasn't sure how I should be acting around him. I hadn't seen him since the hospital in Edinburgh, and so much had happened since then. Though my feelings hadn't changed at all – if anything they had got stronger. Jake just seemed the same, and I still really couldn't believe he wasn't going back to America. I had resigned myself to spending the rest of my life reading cheap flight deals on Ceefax and wondering would it be wise just to take a chance and catch a flight over to see him.

I know I had led the world to believe I was pretty much anti-marriage, though very much for casual sex, especially with unavailable men. But if the truth be told, I was more than a little bit jealous of Chloe, though that guest list was really nothing to be jealous about. I suppose I realised that when we were in London, watching her try on those beautiful dresses. You would have needed a heart of stone not let it affect you. I think I started out trying to convince myself that I was quite a cool character. But by now I had worked out my own cunning deception and realised that in truth I actually am a large pile of slush. And probably as far from cool as you can get. Nonetheless it was an image that I was trying to cultivate though somewhat unsuccessfully. How many times had I seen couples in restaurants, or the park, or just out shopping, so clearly in love with each other you could almost feel it (even if you were standing in the freezer compartment). So here I was, on the brink of eternal misery, being close – like next-room close – to the man of my dreams, and all he wanted from me was the rent.

Anyway, I digress. I was sitting quietly in the kitchen methodically working my way through a packet of Hob Nobs when Jake came down and sat beside me.

"Can I have one or are you doing the biscuit marathon?"

"No, help yourself." I pushed the packet towards him, I was starting to feel sick anyway.

"What's the matter?"

"Oh nothing, I think I just ate too many biscuits."

"Really?" Jake took my hand off the table and squeezed it.

I nodded, and squeezed his hand back. I tried not to think about sex while we were sitting at the kitchen table; there was something faintly gross about it. I wondered if he had any idea what I was thinking. The moment grew awkward. Say something, Ellie.

"So a long-distance relationship wouldn't have been a problem after all – you're back!" I suddenly blurted out to my horror.

"Eh . . . right," he said, letting go my hand. "I may have been over-cautious. As I told you, I had a bad experience before."

And suddenly it clicked: the blonde in the bathroom photo. I knew I was right. What I needed to do now was to confirm she was in the past tense in his life.

I opened my mouth to speak –

"So you've given up your job in Boston?" Dad asked, as he and Mum walked into the kitchen.

"Well, I'm still with the same company. I'm going to work in Belfast and Dungannon for a while and I'm not entirely sure where I'll go from there. It's a smaller outfit than the one in Boston obviously, but it should be a challenge, and it cuts down the transatlantic travel."

"Where were will your offices be?" Mum asked him.

"Somewhere near Queen's, I think." Jake replied.

"That's a lovely area to work, always a nice bustle round Queens and Stranmillis."

"I don't really know Belfast that well, but at least I'll be able to understand the menu over here – in the States everything was tall, skinny or double-mocha and that was just the coffee!"

"Oh fuck it!" I said jumping up from the table.

"Sorry?" Mum and Dad both said simultaneously.

"I don't want to sit here making small talk anymore. I'm going for a walk on the beach."

"Ellie, stop being a bitch!" Mum instructed me. "Anyway you should be resting that ankle not dragging it along the beach."

I picked up the phone and dialled Chloe's number. I would go round and see her instead. But then I would only drag her into the depths of depression along with me. I put the handset back down into the cradle.

It immediately rang back.

I picked it up, "Yes?"

"Why did you hang up?" Chloe inquired.

"Sorry, I thought it was the Pizza Hut."

"The Pizza Hut?"

"Yeah, sorry." I could see her face staring at the receiver incredulously at the other end of the telephone.

"At eleven thirty in the morning? Girl, you need help and I thought I was acting strange! Is Jake there yet?"

"Yeah, we picked him up from the airport an hour ago, but he was hungry, so I was phoning for pizza."

Mum, Dad and Jake were all shaking their heads.

"Anyway is there anything you need us to do for you today?" I asked.

"The dresses have arrived at the house, if you want to come over sometime today and try yours on. Mum seems convinced that everyone will have put weight on since the last fitting."

"You mean she thinks I will have."

"No. I didn't say . . ."

"You didn't need to, I know your mother too well. Tell her from me I have been averaging six vanilla slices a day – watch her turn puce. Sorry, sorry, only messing. I've been good as gold, if anything I think I may have lost some weight."

"You little swine, you have to be nice to my mother at the moment, she is driving herself and everyone else insane."

"Sorry, what time do you want me to come over?"

"Any time this afternoon."

"See you later. Chloe?"

"Yes?"

"Are you OK?"

"Fine, could do with seeing you though."

"I'll be over in a couple of hours."

"Bye."

I hung up the phone. "She wants me to go over as soon as possible. Margo is being a monster."

"What was that about the Pizza Hut?" Jake asked.

"Hey, you were hungry, what was I supposed to do?" Jake looked confused.

"You know, we could try ringing Ben and Sonia," Mum cut in. "I spoke to Ben a couple of weeks ago – they're getting a phone in their camp, so it should be easier to get in touch with them."

"Do you know the number?" asked Jake.

"I've it written down somewhere," said Mum, rummaging through the cork pin board which was covered in decades of Chinese menus, out of date calendars and old telephone numbers.

"Found it!" Mum waved a scrap of paper in the air proudly.

"Well, ring the number then." Dad handed her the phone

Mum kept misdialling.

"Oh give it here!" Dad took the phone off her and dialled the number. "It's ringing!" His expression changed after a few seconds and he handed the phone back to Mum.

"Don't have a bloody clue what the chap was saying."

"Ah, si si, Ben, por favor?" Mum asked in her most basic Spanish.

We had to wait for a few minutes.

"Ben? Hi darling! It's Mum here! We're all sitting round the kitchen table so we thought we would give you a quick ring." She handed me the phone.

"Hi Ben, it's Ellie."

"God, Ellie, haven't spoken to you in ages!"

The line was a bit crackly but it was definitely my brother at the other end. He could have just been on his crappy mobile in London, not thousands of miles away in Central America.

"How is Nicaragua?"

"Very, very hot with a lot of mozzies. Sonia is covered in bites from head to toe. But we're both fine. The camp is going really well – as you know, we now have our own phone line which is a total godsend to the staff here and we've got on really well building the hospital."

"God, it's so good to hear your voice, I can't believe you've been away for so long. When are you coming home?"

"We haven't decided yet, in around six months, I think."

"We all miss you loads. Jake is here by the way, for Chloe's wedding."

"You haven't managed to get off with him yet, I take it."

"Don't be such a bastard!" I hissed at him, terrified that Jake would somehow be able to hear.

"I was joking, by the way. Listen, can I tell you something that I didn't even tell Jake?"

"Yes but they are standing all round me listening too."

"Holy fuck! Well, they should really all know anyway."

"What?" I pressed the phone harder to my ear.

"Sonia and I got married last month in the church we built."

"You did what?"

"We got married. She even made her own dress – well, with a little help from the other girls."

"Are you telling me that Miss – sorry, Mrs Gucci actually made a dress, a wedding dress!"

Mum and Dad's jaws were so low by this time they would have to pick them up off the ground.

"Yes," said Ben.

"Bollocks! You have got to be kidding!."

"Well, are you not going to congratulate me then?"

"Congratulations. All I can say is that it must be very hot over there. I hope you took pictures, I want photographic evidence!"

I held my hand over the receiver, "Ben and Sonia got married last month. She made her own dress!"

The phone was wrenched from my hand as Mum and Dad fought about who would speak to Ben first.

"You don't look too surprised," I said to Jake.

"I thought they might have," Jake said smiling.

"God, it is so irritating when you look all smug and all knowing."

The next couple of days flew by. I should have been awarded the Victoria Cross for bravery. I didn't break down once, even when I knew he was sleeping in Ben's old room across the landing. Chloe, God love her, meanwhile was nearly demented by Margo who was becoming more histrionic the closer the wedding got.

"It will rain on the day, and Mum will commit suicide or something awful," Chloe told me as we lay on her bed watching telly. It was the night before her wedding and I got to spend her last night as a single person with her.

"Och shut up! What the hell does it matter if it rains?" Or if Margo tries to jump off the top of the marquee? But I didn't add that for fear of inflaming an already critical situation.

We spend the rest of the evening covered in face packs looking through old photos of us growing up, really tragic fashion moments captured forever on film.

"Ah yes, there was definitely something to be said for fingerless gloves, legwarmers and purple lurex leggings – we were the kids from Fame."

"God, do you remember the time we dressed up as tarts one Sunday morning and walked down the road to the paper shop?"

The never-to-be-forgotten image of us walking into the paper shop sprang into my mind and I giggled.

"I will never forget your Dad's face, thinking some hookers were walking up his driveway, only to discover it was us." Chloe fell over on her bed laughing at the memory.

"Yeah, he inhaled his orange juice."

"You don't think I will look back on tomorrow and think I must have been on drugs to have worn that dress?"

"Now if you were wearing a fishtail, white crimplene affair I think you might. I think you will look back on tomorrow and remember when you felt like the most beautiful woman in the world!"

Chloe reached over and gave me the biggest hug in the world. "You are the very best friend a person could have." Her eyes were all misty with tears.

"And you'll have the only bridesmaid with a limp – I can't wait to see what *Northern Woman* will make of that."

"Northern Woman?" Chloe's eyes demisted at the mention of one of Northern Ireland's most well-known magazines. Their cheesy wedding pics had given us hours of amusement in the past – to actually appear in one would be Chloe's biggest nightmare.

"Now even you must know that your mother is bound have organised some hideous photographers from one of the glossies to come and take a picture of the greatest day of her life."

Colour drained from Chloe's face at the thought of what Margo may have organised without her knowledge. "Oh fuck! You don't really think she would do something like that without telling me, do you?"

I shrugged my shoulders. I thought I should mention it, I had overheard the conversation with the *Ulster Tatler* on my way to the bathroom earlier on.

"Just don't be surprised, OK?"

"OK, oh my God, I am going to look ridiculous, oh, they will even make my foundation look orange!"

We have a theory about the Mac operators at these magazines – with their expertise they can alter anyone's face, clothes and make-up. God help you if they took a disliking to you – you could end up wearing purple and orange swirls with matching make-up.

"Anyway we should try and get to bed at a decent hour. I don't think I could bear it if I had to trail up the church behind you tomorrow with bags under my eyes. Your mum will blame me for making the wedding pictures look bad." I was cunningly trying to take Chloe's mind off Margo's media plotting.

Chloe looked down at her watch: she had a fair point, it was only eight in the evening.

"How is it going? Not too awkward, is it?"

"What?"

"Jake staying with you at home."

I nearly had to bite through my lip in the effort it took not to start moaning, but I had made myself promise to act like a grown-up.

"No, not at all, it's going really well as a matter of fact."

"Good, about bloody time too. I spoke to Rachel, she reckons you guys should get married – you're perfect for each other."

I had to coax my eyebrows back down onto my forehead as they had shot up towards the ceiling.

"Ha," was all I could manage.

"OK – we need to check our list to make sure we have done all our beauty treatments."

"Yes to face-packs – ugh, they've all cracked from us laughing." I was looking at my less than pleasing reflection in the mirror: pale green goo had dried and split on my face making me look like a convincingly good extra for *Star Trek*.

"OK. That leaves eyebrow-plucking, armpit-shaving, toe and fingernail-painting – oh, and you wanted to bleach your moustache, didn't you?"

"Yes, thanks for reminding me, where is the stuff for it?"

"In the Boots bag on the floor, over there behind the stereo. I'm going to run a bath and then do my nails."

While Chloe was in the bath, I decided to bleach my upper lip – there was no way I was going to look like Hercule Poirot in the photos tomorrow. I stirred up the bleach and the accelerator and applied it to my top lip.

Once I was happy that I hadn't missed a bit I put on one of Chloe's CDs.

Unfortunately she has a bit of a penchant for whale music and such like so I was hard pushed to find any thing worth listening to. I found one that looked quite interesting: Sounds of the Ocean or something. I lay back and listened while the strange noises filled the room with a gentle calming effect. This one wasn't too bad, very relaxing.

"Ellie!"

"What?"

I jumped up from the bed, immediately feeling a burning sensation in my upper-lip region.

"Oh fuck!" I ran into the bathroom.

"How long have you been asleep?" Chloe was wrapped in a bath towel, leaning against the door frame.

"Um . . . how long have you been in the bath?" I plunged my face into cold water in the sink. My lip felt like it was on fire.

"I was in for at least twenty minutes – have you been asleep the whole time?"

"It's your bloody music that did it, I was perfectly wide awake before."

I turned round and Chloe's hand went straight to cover her mouth.

"What?" I turned back round to look at the mirror and nearly died.

"Well, that's just great – I now look like this year's winner of the interesting rash competition!"

My skin had been burnt where the facial bleach had been left on too long and now I had a very noticable red rash on my upper lip.

Chloe burst out laughing. "I'm sorry, I know it's totally not funny, but I can't help it. *You moron!*"

"That is really great, thanks for your support," I snapped at her.

"Sorry." Chloe tried to keep a straight face, without much success. She was soon helpless with giggles.

"What is going on?"

Chloe immediately stopped laughing at the sound of her mother's voice. She turned round so she was blocking me from Margo's field of vision.

"Nothing, Mum, we were just messing around with some face-packs."

Margo was trying to peer over her daughter's shoulder but thankfully Chloe is two inches taller than her mum. I think Margo missed her vocation as a prison warder.

"Right, do you girls need anything?"

"No, we're grand thanks, Mum."

"Right."

Margo went downstairs to go and check the marquee for the millionth time.

"What the hell are we going to do with your face?"

I covered the red area on my face with Sudocrem in the hope that it would take some of the inflamation away.

"Hope that the make-up artist your mum has organised is shit hot!"

"Look, don't worry, it'll be grand in the morning. Let's paint our nails and forget about it."

"OK," I agreed, though I really felt like punching the manufacturers for not putting warning signs all over his packets of facial hair-lightener.

"I have something for you."

"Another cream?"

"No, a present to thank you for being my bridesmaid."

"Oh."

Chloe got a little bag out from a drawer in her beside table – she handed it to me. Inside the bag was a little box. I opened it and inside there was a pair of pearl earrings.

"They are gorgeous!" They really were.

"I'd really like it if you would wear them tomorrow. They're from David and me."

"Oh Chloe, of course I'll wear them tomorrow, they're beautiful. You didn't need to buy me anything."

"With the amount of crap you have had to put up with for this wedding, it was the least we could do. Anyway people will be so busy admiring your ears they won't notice your lip!"

"Cheeky bitch." But I hugged her anyway.

Chapter Twenty-Three

The next morning the sun was thankfully shining, and looking out the window the marquee was still standing. I woke up before Chloe.

I got up and went downstairs to watch some early morning television. It really was early. The clock in the kitchen said 06.30am; not even Margo was up at this time. I went into the living-room and turned on the television, settling down in one of the comfy armchairs to watch some rubbishy Pammy Anderson programme on Sky One. I took the earrings Chloe had given me out of my dressing-gown pocket – they really were lovely. I set them on the arm of the chair while I reached for the remote control to turn down the volume and when I sat back I noticed only one of the earrings was there.

"Bugger." I got up to look to see where it had gone to.

It had fallen under the seat of the chair. I lifted the cushion up and tried to retrieve the earring, but I only pushed it further away.

"Shit!" Everytime I reached for it, it rolled further

away. After five minutes I had managed to totally wedge the earring right at the back of the chair. I got down on my hands and knees, carefully setting the other earring out of the way so I wouldn't lose that too. I up-ended the armchair to see if I could reach it from the underneath, but the base was covered with a hessian material. I got up and went into the kitchen, checking there was still no sign of Margo. I got a pair of scissors out of one of the drawers and went back to investigate the chair further. I took the scissors and cut a small hole in the underneath of the chair. I put my finger in to see if I could feel the earring. The hole wasn't big enough, so I made it a bit bigger with the scissors and tried again.

After half an hour I still had not managed to find the earring and the hole was enormous. I could hear movement above me, someone was up and about. Not wanting to be caught vandalising the furniture, I turned the chair up again and returned it to its normal position, turned off the television and crept back upstairs to try and think of some other way to get the earring back.

"Ellie?" mumbled Chloe.

"Oh, sorry, did I wake you up?"

"Yes, but I'm sure I should be getting up, what time is it?"

"About seven, I think." I climbed back into my bed.

Moments later the door opened and Margo stuck her head round the door.

"Girls, it's time to get up and have some breakfast, come down in five minutes OK?"

"Yes, Mum."

"Ellie, are you awake?" Margo said sharply.

"Yes, Mrs Williams."

If Margo was up there was no way I could get the earring now. I lay in bed and contemplated my doom. What would Chloe say when she found out? Not to mention what would Margo do to me when she saw the chair. There really was only one thing to do – lie. Now people will tell you that lying doesn't get you anywhere. In general this is true, but today I would be an exception.

The make-up artist certainly earned her money that day. She did a tremendous job in covering my red face which was still beaming away even after the Sudocrem application. When I was dressed I looked remarkably OK – bar a strange tingingly sensation on my lip. The dress fitted, my hair had been done in a very tasteful style by the stylist Margo had employed – without telling Chloe. We had nearly come to blows as I insisted on not having a large headband of freesias stuck on my bonce. Margo had had them made especially for the day and they were so revolting Chloe and I both went on strike until she agreed that neither of us would have to wear them. We insisted on wearing the tiaras we had bought – sufficiently glamorous to take precedence over the freesia fiascos.

Chloe looked amazing – breath-taking in fact. I was so proud that I was going to limp up the aisle behind her. Margo's outfit for the day had cost more than Chloe's and my dresses together – thankfully she had not also chosen to wear cream. Margo had to leave before we did, so once she and the stylist had gone, I opened the fridge and took a bottle of champagne out that I had hidden earlier on. Chloe's dad joined in a toast to a great day and a great marriage.

"Here's to you and the lucky man!" Mr Williams raised his mug (all the glasses were in the marquee).

"Here's to a great day and to my best friend!" I raised my mug.

"Here's to not crying in the church and ruining my mascara!" Chloe raised her mug.

The three of us got quite pissed as we had all been too nervous to eat the continental breakfast that Margo had tried to force down our necks. I had a quick fag, taking extra special care not to get any ash on my dress.

Standing in the bathroom alone just before the car arrived to take us to the church I had still not worked out what to do about the missing earring.

Then I was struck with inspiration.

"OK, if I do this perhaps I will get away with it and Chloe will never know." I put the earring that I had managed not to lose on, and with some careful application I put a small blob of toothpaste on the other ear. Fingers crossed no one would notice that I smelt a bit pepperminty.

I should get away with it – bloody genius.

Chloe and her dad were waiting for me at the bottom of the stairs; the car had arrived and they were ready to go.

"All set, Ellie?"

"Sure thing, emergency bathroom trip." I hobbled out the door first so she wouldn't notice my left ear. I had made a last-minute decision not to take my crutches –

my ankle felt OK, so I thought I could manage well enough without them.

The caterers had arrived and were busy in the kitchen with last minute preparations, the band was also arriving. Thankfully Chloe and David had got their own way on that one and they had booked the Salsa jazz band, rather than Margo's choice, which would have involved most of the musicians in the western world. We left them all to get on with it. Margo had already read them the riot act.

"Does my dress look OK?" Chloe asked while we were driven to the church in the back of a gleaming navy Bentley.

"Darling, you look perfect, I only wish your mother had looked half that good when I married her."

"Dad!"

I laughed, but I had to keep looking out the window so Chloe wouldn't see my ear. So far so good.

"God, I hope David likes this dress."

"He would need to have had a taste transplant not to like it," I volunteered helpfully.

"Course he will, pet, you're wearing it." Her dad put his arm round her and hugged her. Tears welled up in her eyes.

"Ah, now, no tears, what did the make-up artist tell us about crying? You'll look like bride of Frankenstein rather than the bride of the year."

Her dad handed her a handkerchief from his morning coat.

"Thanks, Dad."

We stopped at some red traffic-lights and the children that were waiting to cross the road stared at the car. When they saw us in the back they waved like mad and we all waved back. Which thankfully seemed to lighten the mood in the car.

Minutes later the car pulled into the carpark of the church. Everyone seemed to be inside. Margo was inside too presumably, so there had obviously not been any hideous disasters. Otherwise, I suspected, she would be lying in the carpark kicking her heels in the air. We all got out of the car, and I made sure that Chloe's dress was hanging right at the back. Bouquets in hand I gave her a quick last hug before we went into the church.

She and her dad walked slowly so that I could keep up. Charlie and Tom, two of the ushers, were standing in the foyer waiting for us; they opened the doors into the main church as we appeared.

The organ started to play as we made our way up the aisle, a hush came over the congregation and people turned to sneak a peek at the bride as we passed. I tried not to make my limping look too obvious. I could see Jake sitting with Mum and Dad and I got a quick flutter of butterflies when he turned round and smiled, but I was too busy trying to hold everything together to do much. Bouquet, wedding ring and trying not to trip over Chloe's train, is a lot to concentrate the mind on. In an effort not to forget the wedding ring that Chloe would present to David I had taken the precaution of wearing it myself on the middle finger of my right hand, with a smaller ring on top so it wouldn't fall off and I would be sure to remember it.

When we got to the top of the church I was feeling quite pleased with myself; nothing awful had happened so far, and if it had, it hadn't been my fault. The church was hot and I was a bit flustered and I was teetering slightly trying not to put too much weight on my ankle but I wasn't about to fall over or anything.

Chloe's dad let go of her hand, raised the veil over her head and stepped back. David had a smile on his face that it was going to take days to wipe off – definitely the cat that got the cream – David's smile brought out a rash of smiling from Chloe, me and Alex the ginger best man.

The minister brought the guests to their feet and the first hymn started. I can't sing a note so I had to mime in a convincing fashion as every eye in the place was on Chloe and David and Jake was hopefully looking at me and not regretting our conversation of several days ago.

The service started and the minister started the weddingy bit. I thought I would get organised so I would have the ring ready when it was needed. "Who gives this woman to this man?"

"I do." Chloe's dad said and sat down beside Margo in the front pew.

We were off.

I tried to get the ring – the small one that was holding David's ring in place – off my finger, but my fingers had swollen in the heat and no way would it come off. Chloe saw me fidgeting and looked over at me. I stopped and smiled at her with what I hoped was a serene, calm type of expression. Once her focus had gone back to what the minister was saying I tried again – no luck. I surreptitiously put my finger in my mouth hoping that would help to slide the ring off. No go. Then I put my hands down at my side again so as not to draw attention to myself. Everyone was engrossed with the ceremony. I tugged at the ring – nothing. I attempted again; this time I pulled harder, the ring shot off my finger, the force overbalanced me and I wobbled. Chloe's arm shot out and steadied me, the ring flew across the church, bounced off the stone floor and rolled under the baptism font in the corner.

"Fuck!" I whispered under my breath.

I could hear two hundred heads as they turned to look at me. I couldn't raise my eyes from the floor I was so mortified. At least I still had David's ring, which I was now clutching in my right hand as if my life depended on it. The minister continued as if nothing had happened and Chloe took her arm away once she was sure I wasn't going to end up on the floor.

Chloe and David were now speaking and Chloe put her hand out for me to give her the ring, I opened my sweaty palm and she lifted the sticky wedding band. I looked at her and she winked at me. Thank God, she wasn't mad at me, though I could feel Margo's eyes burning a hole in my back. My leg was starting to ache. I was looking forward to going to sign the registry so I could sit down for a few minutes.

The minister moved off and Chloe and David who had just been pronounced man and wife followed. Alex took my arm and led me out into the vestry.

"Are you OK?" Chloe asked me as we followed the minister.

"Yes, sorry about that – the ring wouldn't come off."

David and Alex laughed. The bride and groom's parents followed behind us.

"Well, Miss Clarke, that was some performance!" Margo hissed at me while Chloe and David signed the register.

"Sorry."

"Mum, leave her alone, no one noticed."

"Everyone was looking, I was so embarrassed, but then I knew she would do something to let us all down."

"Margo, that's enough," Mr Williams intervened with a stern look on his face. "Your daughter has just got married – please try and look a little more delighted."

Amazingly, Margo's face broke into a smile and she hugged her daughter and then David.

"Well done, darling, you look marvellous. Congratulations David, I hope you are both very, very happy."

Chloe and David were holding hands and couldn't stop kissing each other.

"That could be us later," Alex whispered in my ear.

I looked at him with a horrified expression. "Not unless you're planning to drug me."

Alex ignored the comment. "I am irresistible towards women – your are helpless in my power," he grinned.

I slapped him on the arm in a jokey gesture but the thought of being helpless in Alex's power was disturbing to say the least!

After we had signed the register as witnesses we returned to the church where Margo had arranged for a soprano to entertain the guests while they waited. We made our way back out of the church to the flashes of a hundred cameras and smiles of well-wishers.

Outside the church I waited while Chloe and David shook the guests' hands.

"Well, I thought you were the most beautiful and interesting bridesmaid I have seen in a long time." Jake's voice.

I turned round to see Jake, Mum and Dad.

"Was it totally obvious?"

"Not at all, I only noticed whenever Robert had to restrain Margo. It was actually very entertaining, though if Chloe ever does this again, don't expect to be asked," Mum said giggling.

"My leg is killing me."

"Can you come back to the Williams' with us?" asked Jake.

"No, I think I have to wait to go back in one of the bridal cars – I don't want to piss Margo off anymore today. But thanks for the offer."

"Well, sit on the wall while you wait – we'll wait with you."

The crowd coming out of the church dispersed, heading back to the reception and Chloe and David appeared out of the church shortly afterward. Unfortunately I had to share a car to the house with the bride and groom's parents. I had only met David's mum and dad a few times and they were very nice, but not as posh as I fear Margo would have liked. Luckily, she couldn't give out to me in front of them and cause a scene.

"I thought you were very brave walking up the church without your crutches," David's mum said to me.

Margo sniffed and Robert shot her a warning glance – she looked out the window.

"Thank you, I thought the crutches would be a bit unsightly."

"Your dress is gorgeous too, did you pick it?" Mrs Campbell continued.

"Chloe picked the colour and we decided on the design between us."

"A very good choice," his dad added.

"We wish we had a daughter – weddings are a bit different for a daughter, aren't they? We have three sons though." Mrs Campbell looked at Margo when she said this.

Just at that moment, Margo caught sight of my ear. Her horrified expression spoke a thousand words and she almost turned purple. I tried to tease a ringlet over my left ear to hide my homemade pearl.

Margo managed to smile at Mrs Campbell but it looked like she was just seriously constipated. I almost laughed out loud.

When the car stopped Margo almost sprinted back to the house to get away from us and check her precious preparations, leaving Mr Williams and the Campbell's to watch her retreating Valentino rear.

Luckily the party was getting underway and the Campbell's were soon embraced into the champagne-swilling crowd, chatting to their friends and being introduced to the great and the good. I found a chair in the midst of the throng and lifted a couple of champagne flutes from a passing waiter.

"Oh my God! How gorgeous does Chloe look?" Rachel sat down beside me.

"I know, isn't she great?"

"Hi guys," Clare and Lousia joined us.

"What happened to your ear?" Melissa asked as she sat down.

"Why?"

"There's white goo all over it."

"Ah, I think my earring has begun to melt!"

Melissa and the others looked mystified – I didn't enlighten them.

We were soon surrounded by a crowd of friends, all under the influence of the great atmosphere and the plentiful champagne.

"Where are they?" Susie Taylor asked.

"They're getting their pictures taken – I'm getting my photo call when I'm required," I answered wiggling my toes at the relief of sitting down.

Next thing, there was an almighty crash behind and everyone jumped in shock.

"Fucking Hell!" a woman's voice screamed as if she was being murdered.

The others ran over to the corner of the marquee and I hobbled after them as fast as I could.

I could hardly believe my eyes when I finally managed to get a glimpse of what had happened. There was a communal intake of breath as people tried not to laugh. Margo was lying on her back on the floor on top of the wedding cake. Her skirt was up round her waist revealing a corset-type affair holding her gut into her skirt. She was also covered in icing and cutlery which had been on the table she had now flattened. Margo seemed to get over the initial shock of what had just happened; she struggled to her feet with the help of her husband. When she moved we were able to see that there was in fact a body underneath her – David's Great-uncle Alfred, whose false teeth were now lying three feet away from him in a pile of squashed cake.

"Get out of my house, you cretin!" Margo shrilled, looking distinctly as if she was on the verge of fibrillations.

Alfred did not reply, I was concerned that the force

of her landing had punctured one of his lungs, but he did appear to be breathing without too much difficulty. In fact on closer inspection he appeared to be laughing.

David's mother rushed in and pulled him to his feet. It emerged that Alfred was absolutely plastered and had made a pass at Margo when she was adding the finishing touches to the cake. In her effort to get away from him she had tripped over a loose bit of carpet and fallen, taking Alfred with her headlong into the cake, demolishing it and the table it had been sitting on.

Margo was now sobbing uncontrollably – Alfred was removed from the scene.

Jake and I looked at each other in amazement. I looked for Chloe to see her reaction. I was much relieved to see that both she and David were in hysterics – in fact she was doubled up, her dad giving her sidelong warning glances. The guests waited to see what would happen next, all thoughts of Beef Wellington forgotten in the face of this drama.

"Well, madam, I'm glad you find this all so amusing," spluttered Margo to Chloe.

"Sorry, Mum, it is kind of funny."

"Well, it's a warped kind of humour you must have to be laughing at a time like this!"

"It was only a cake, Mum, forget about it."

"Forget about it? I am wearing it – how can I forget about it?"

I could practically hear her brain working out the dry-cleaning bill.

The guests turned to Chloe to see what she was going to say next. It was like Wimbledon.

"Go and get changed, Mum, and we'll just get on with the rest of the reception."

Heads snapped back to Margo for her reaction.

"Get that horrible little man out of my house!"

"Mum! That is David's great-uncle."

"I don't care if he is the Prince of Persia – the leech is not welcome here – he has ruined everything, him and his ridiculous family."

Another sharp intake of breath as the guests waited for the Campbells to take up the gauntlet and defend their family honour. Alfred's sister Ethna was virtually bristling with anger and, if David's cousin Lewis had not restrained her, Margo could have found herself wearing the main course as well as dessert. He couldn't stop her talking however.

"I wasn't going to say anything, you now being family and all, but some things need to be said. *You are an uptight oul bitch!* Alfred wouldn't have meant you any harm, he's just a wee bit frisky!" Ethna stuck her chin out defiantly as if goading Margo to hit her.

Margo nearly swallowed her tongue with shock at being insulted in such a way.

"And while we are at it," Ethna continued, warming to her cause, "you are so busy trying to show off you have forgotten whose day this is supposed to be." She pointed towards Chloe, who was now leaning on David for support. The newly-weds had stopped laughing.

After that it got a bit confusing. Chloe's granny walloped David's grandfather over the head with her handbag – this wouldn't have been so bad except she had already stolen an ashtray off the table, so she virtually concussed the poor man, who being deaf had missed all the excitement anyway. A fight broke out, the rest of the guests moved in to try and break things up, and ended up joining in.

Chloe's beautiful reception degenerated into a scene more commonly found on Jerry Springer than in an overpriced marquee.

Next thing the guests were soaked as a jet of water covered them and the fighting stopped immediately. We turned to see Chloe standing in her wedding dress with a hose in her hand, laughing her head off.

"When you have all quite finished, this is my wedding and I am not remotely interested in any problems you have with each other. You may or may not have noticed the band have arrived!" She pointed up towards the top table which had been cleared and the band had set up. They were all standing looking bemused, staring at the soggy crowd in front of them.

"Now if you would all take your places, we are going to kick off the dancing with the 'Dashing White Sergeant'. It's a Scottish reel so we have a caller to shout out what you should all be doing. Follow the Scottish guests if you get lost! This is supposed to be good fun, *so no more fighting!*"

Unfortunately dancing was something I wasn't able to do, so I found my seat again, with a lonely bottle of champagne and one of David's auntie's cigarettes. Then, to my delight, Jake joined me and we got stuck into the champagne at a great rate. Around us the aggressive atmosphere was replaced with one of hilarity as most of the guests made a total bollocks of the Scottish dances.

Various young couples sloped off for illicit snogs away from the prying eyes of their parents; my younger sister in particular seemed a hit with the hormonally challenged young men. It could have just been the champagne but I was sure I saw her leave with one guy and come back into the marquee with another on more that one occasion. It appeared to the well-trained eye that she was giving them about ten minutes each, so at this rate she would be onto the forty-year-olds by about ten o'clock.

The Scottish dancing stopped soon after, as most of the women and some of the men had been thrown with gay abandon across the dancing floor, resulting in more than one severe limp and torn dress. Once the Kilmarnock Kilties had left the stage, Dan's Disco took over and our ears were assaulted with a barrage of Jive Bunny and Steps. There was a flurry of excitement as most of the couples old enough to have children at university age leapt to their feet in order to demonstrate how it was really done, shuffling round the floor to strains of 'Dancing Queen'. Roll on the Salsa band.

Giggling at the kids doing Fame impressions on the dance floor, I got to my feet to go to the loo. I left Jake chatting with Rachel and Brian – well, chatting to Rachel as Brian was too busy licking her neck to pay any attention to what anyone was saying.

I hobbled out of the marquee into the house. As the token cripple I had been given special dispensation on Chloe's request to be allowed to use the nice loo inside the house, rather than the portaloos Margo had organised. Inside the house it was very quiet, with just a few waitresses running about with the remains of the meal on huge platters. I stopped in the hall to look at some old photos of Chloe and myself.

A freezing draft slammed the kitchen door shut. I looked up to see who had come through the front door, but there was no one there. I shivered. The wooden floor upstairs creaked just above my head. I had one of those weird irrational moments when you panic, like trying to go to bed after a scary film. I rushed into the downstairs toilet and locked myself in. The panic subsided as I looked in the mirror and was horrified to discover that I looked a total shambles. My lipstick had been eaten off with the mini-quiches, my mascara had flaked under my eyes giving me that undesirable, 'Bride of Frankenstein' effect and my fake tan had vanished leaving my pale face looking like I needed a good night's sleep. On closer inspection I even discovered a few spots trying to make an appearance on my chin. Out of my mini fag-bag (fashion accessory big enough to carry only a credit card, mobile phone and packet of cigarettes) I produced flesh-coloured polyfilla – otherwise known as foundation you could lay bricks with. After I had filled in the cracks and hidden the emerging zits I slapped on some lippie, a bit more Illegal lengths from Maybelline and a good dose of Dolce and Gabbana for good measure. I left the toilet in a cloud of perfume looking marginally less grim than I had when I went in.

The hall was still quiet and totally deserted, the caterers having left shaking their heads. A shadow passed under the door in the dining-room. No one should be in there. I opened the door ready to laugh at the reddened faces of the two snogging fanatics I was sure I was going to see on the other side. But the light was switched off. I turned it on, there was nobody there, just a pile of wedding presents that hadn't yet been opened.

"Hello?"

Silence.

Something stopped me from going into the room any further. I retreated back into the hall closing the door quietly after me. The door handle started to turn before I had taken my hand off the handle. I stepped away from the door, taken by surprise, but the door didn't open. I rushed back out towards the marquee, with a horrible feeling in the pit of my stomach.

I was almost sure it was just a young couple having a laugh. But I had been traumatised by my recent experiences. I surrounded myself with as many people as I could, not looking back towards the house at all.

Jake and Rachel were still chatting – Brian was completely passed out on the ground beside them.

"Hi guys," I said.

"Where did you disappear to?"

"I went to the loo and then something funny happened." I told them about the dining-room, and how I had thought someone had been hiding there.

"Margo would have a hairy fit if she thought someone was having it off in her dining-room!" Rachel laughed.

"Come on and we'll have a look," Jake said getting to his feet unsteadily.

"No, I really don't want to go back inside. You go and have a look."

"OK, scaredy cat," Rachel joked.

Jake and Rachel left to investigate, while I reached for another of the many packets of cigarettes that had been left on the table, their owners still dancing rings round each other.

I lasted about two minutes and then I followed Jake and Rachel. I hate to miss out on anything interesting, even if it scares the bejesus out of me!

The light was on in the dining-room.

"Well, did you find anyone?" I asked as I walked through the door. I was aware my lip was stinging again, maybe it wasn't such a good idea to plaster foundation all over a raw upper lip.

"No, only this letter. It's addressed to you." Rachel had an envelope in her hand. She passed it to me.

"Strange." I opened the envelope, resisting the urge to scratch my lip. It was a single piece of paper.

"Follow your heart and the clues to find the one who is in love with you," I read out loud. "What the hell is this – what clues?"

Both Rachel and Jake looked mystified.

"Does it say anything else?" Jake asked.

"Um . . ." I scanned down the page. "Oh yeah: Look under the table."

We all got down on our hands and knees and looked under the dining-room table.

"There is something under there." Rachel pointed to a small object wrapped in newspaper.

I grabbed it and ripped off the paper. "A washing-up brush? What?" It had a tag attached which said, Put me back! "We have to go to the kitchen? Are you guys having a laugh on me?"

"No," they chorused in a most suspicious fashion.

"OK, OK, I'll play along, but I think this is highly immature."

Washing-up brush in hand, I went into the kitchen. They didn't follow me. I went to the kitchen sink and put the brush back in its pot. It wouldn't go in. I picked the pot off the shelf and looked inside. In the pot there was another envelope rolled up. I pulled it out and read it.

"Now take the watering-can and water the hothouse plants." I looked around. A little watering-can was on the work-surface to the left of the sink. "Hothouse plants? What – the conservatory?" I took the can and went into the conservatory – just off the kitchen. It was lit with candles and completely deserted. I had expected to find at least one teenage snogging session in here. A big cheese plant was right in front of me – it had a big ribbon tied round its top frond. I untied the ribbon, looking round to see if anyone was watching me. I couldn't see anyone. There was another message written on the inside of the ribbon.

"Upstairs where it is hot and steamy, take the rubber duck for luck." At the foot of the plant the aforementioned duck was half visible through the foliage. I lifted it up, shaking the soil off.

"OK, buddy, I guess we're going to the bathroom and I must say this whole thing is very bizarre," I told the duck. Up the stairs to the main bathroom. I set the duck down by the sink and looked around for my next clue. There was a pillow in the bath with a post-it stuck to it.

"Take one of these for sweet dreams." Bedroom? I popped my head round Chloe's bedroom door – all her pillows were present and correct. Next I went to her mum and dad's – nope, nothing missing there either. I opened one of the guest-room doors, one of the pillows was missing. I put the pillow back in its place and walked round the room. It was not immediately obvious, until I stubbed my toe on it.

"Fuck!" I shrieked in pain. Looking down I saw a car jack lying on a piece of newspaper. I rubbed my toe and then bent down to pick up the jack – immediately covering myself in oily grot. *"Bugger!"* Another clue was written in marker pen on the newspaper.

"We will need one of these to get us started." Garage maybe?

Wiping my dirty hands on the inside of the guest-room curtains I took the jack and beat a hasty retreat back downstairs. Outside the garage was in darkness. I put the jack down and struggled momentarily to get the garage door to open. When it swung up I walked forward to try and find the light switch, liberally covering myself in decades of spider-webs and dust.

"Very nice – now I think all that is missing is a generous helping of battery acid and I should be all set." I fiddled around for a moment and then found the light switch. I flipped it on.

In front of me was a shiny new VW Beetle.

"Oh wow!" I walked towards it, the driver's side of the window had "Open me, I'm yours!" taped to the inside of it. I opened the driver's door. There was a bark and Hector jumped out of the car, scaring me to death!

"Hector! What the hell are you doing in Chloe's garage in a strange car?" This was the most surprising turn of events yet. Hector did a quick tour of the garage and then came wagging back to me.

"Good boy." I bent down to stroke him and found he had something attached to his collar. "What have you got round yourself, pet?" I held him by his collar to see what it was, oblivious to the dirty marks I was inflicting on my dress.

There was a key-ring hanging off Hector's collar with a car key and a tag. On closer inspection the tag read: UBZ 3792, Owner Sorrel Clarke – for special instructions please check glove compartment. My jaw dropped, down with the rest of the cobwebs. This was definitely more significant than a rubber duck or a washing-up brush. My heart was thudding. I'd never owned a car with less than one hundred thousand miles on the clock, with windscreen wipers that worked, doors that locked. This was too much. I opened the glove compartment. My hands were shaking so much that I broke one of the nails I had been cultivating for a month.

Next to the driver's manual nestled a little cube, again wrapped in newspaper. I opened the newspaper carefully, not sure what I was going to find inside. A little burgundy box fell onto the floor. There was writing on the inside of the newspaper wrapping. I smoothed out the paper to get a better look – the light wasn't very good.

"Marry me, Sorrel, and make me the happiest man in the world." Quick double-take. *"Marry me, Sorrel, and make me the happiest man in the world?"*

A noise behind me made me swing around.

Jake was standing there, Hector staring adoringly up at him.

"What!" I hardly dared to believe what I had just read.

"Open it," he said, smiling.

I opened the little burgundy box – inside a magnificent solitaire diamond ring was sparkling. I gasped, wobbled on my bad leg and then collapsed in a heap on the garage floor, giving my head a smart bang against the concrete wall on the way down. Tiny VWs were spinning round before my eyes as a small bump rose on the back of my head. Jake sat down and pulled my head in his lap and Hector started licking my face.

"So will you?" Jake asked.

In my romantic daydreams I had often imagined being proposed to on bended knee, though I had never visualised lying on the floor of a dirty garage with my head on those knees.

What could a girl say?

THE END